Freeing Grace

Freeing Grace

CHARITY NORMAN

ALLEN&UNWIN

First published in Great Britain in 2011 by Allen & Unwin

First published in Australia in 2010 by Allen & Unwin

Allen & Unwin
c/o Atlantic Books
Ormond House
26–27 Boswell Street
London WC1N 3JZ
Phone: 020 7269 1610
Fax: 020 7430 0916
Email: UK@allenandunwin.com
Web: www.atlantic-books.co.uk

A CIP catalogue record for this book is available from the British Library.

ISBN 978 1 74237 534 2

Set in 12/15.5 pt Adobe Garamond Pro by Midland Typesetters, Australia
Printed and bound in Great Britain by the MPG Books Group

10 9 8 7 6 5 4 3 2 1

For Bill and Beryl Norman

Prologue

Grace Serenity had a mother, once. A real, flesh and blood mother, who gave birth to Grace in a great, grey hospital. Her name was Cherie King, and she was sixteen.

There was no proud father pacing in the delivery room. No anxious grandparents stood vigil, hankies and champagne at the ready, by their telephone. Not one cardigan or pair of bootees had been knitted. The only witness to Grace's arrival, save for the midwives who delivered her, was a social worker called Imogen Christie; and she was only there by accident.

Dropping in on Cherie's foster carer to discuss the unborn child, Imogen had found Cherie circling the kitchen table, dark eyes wide with fright, hands taut over her swollen middle.

'Isn't Ellen here?' Imogen's eyes flickered around the room, as though the foster mother might be hiding behind the door.

'London,' gasped Cherie, gripping the table with strong fingers. She was a graceful girl, with ebony skin and long legs. 'Had to go and see her grandson. Should be back any—' She stopped in her tracks, listening fearfully to something deep inside her body. 'Oh, fucking hell, here we go again.' And she convulsed, with a muffled shriek.

Imogen had no children; she was newly engaged, and believed in allowing these things to happen in the right order. Still, she knew where this was going. After all—she reached for her mobile phone—it wasn't rocket science, even if the baby wasn't due for a fortnight.

'Just my luck,' she grumbled, swiftly punching numbers. 'Ambulance, please. Hold on, Cherie.'

It was a relief to hand over responsibility to the ambulance crew. They exuded unflappable confidence, joking calmly with the frightened girl as they stowed her safely.

'You're the same age as my granddaughter,' said the older man. He was heavily built—could have been a useful bouncer at one time—with almost no hair. A gold stud glinted in one ear. He sat next to Cherie during the journey, timing contractions and providing a steady stream of reassurance. The girl did her best, even laughing weakly at his sallies.

'Haven't you got a lovely smile?' he remarked, offering oxygen. 'D'you know what you're having?'

'A baby,' panted Cherie.

He smacked himself on the forehead. 'Ask a stupid question.'

'It's a girl,' said Cherie, relenting. 'They told me at the scan.'

It *would* have to happen on a Friday. Imogen had plans for the evening: a hens' night for an old friend. Ten of them were getting together for the first time in years, and it was going to be a riot. Swaying in the back of the ambulance, she tried every number possible to contact the foster mother or Cherie's own social worker. But one—Ellen Bayley—was stuck on the motorway, waiting for the AA; the other had already swanned off for the weekend; and the duty team were busy with some more pressing crisis.

A midwife met them in the ambulance bay, introducing herself as Jude and taking a brief history from the bald, gold-studded paramedic. He fondly patted Cherie's hand, told her he was looking forward to hearing she'd had a bonny baby, then closed the doors of his ambulance and set off to the next emergency.

Jude was pushing fifty, Imogen reckoned, and had an air of solid experience. A square woman: square body, square shoes, square face.

'Glad you've come to support her,' she said pointedly, as they hurried behind Cherie's wheelchair.

'Um, I can't actually stay,' ventured Imogen.

'I think you can.'

'I'm not her social worker. I'm—' Imogen dropped her voice. 'I'm key worker for the unborn child. We've arranged a foster placement for both mother and baby, but if things don't work out we'll have to remove the child. So it's hardly appropriate for me to be the mother's birth partner.'

Halting abruptly, Jude regarded the social worker. She had the kind of mouth that turned down even when she was smiling. Right now, she wasn't smiling.

'You're not going to leave this kid to give birth *alone*, are you?'

Imogen hesitated, glancing into the delivery room. Someone was helping Cherie into a faded hospital gown. The girl stuck out her arms to be dressed, like a little child.

The midwife jerked her head at the lonely young figure. 'She's in care, right? So, *care* for her!'

Sighing, Imogen surrendered. 'Bang goes my night out.'

'Great. Welcome aboard. Sit here,' ordered Jude, patting the chair generally reserved for white-knuckled fathers. 'Just try to reassure her.'

What Imogen witnessed in that room, she would never forget. During eight years in her job she had seen much that was shocking and disturbing, and she often felt she had seen it all. But she had never come face to face with such raw pain, nor such stubborn courage. Through the agonising hours and into the night, Cherie barely screamed, although she made copious use of the gas. She seemed to accept the violent assault of it; seemed to withdraw into some private place in her own mind. But then, thought Imogen bleakly, Cherie King knew all about violence. Her mother and stepfather had taught her all too well.

Soon after midnight, Jude called in a student midwife. The two women worked smoothly together: preparing, checking. Imogen was fascinated.

'Head's there,' called Jude. 'You're doing brilliantly, Cherie.'

'Jesus, help me!' Cherie's voice rose high with panic. She was half sitting, her head thrown back. She dropped the gas mask. 'She's killing me!'

'Brave girl.' Jude was calm. 'One last time, darling. Here it comes . . .'

'I'm *dead*!' shrieked Cherie. On impulse, Imogen reached for her hand. The girl clutched blindly at her, squeezing with powerful, frantic fingertips. Imogen's eyes watered at the strength of her grip, but she held on.

Suddenly Cherie gave an inhuman cry, a wail of agony and triumph. And then the baby made its escape. Imogen saw a flash of glistening brown skin, and there was a new person in the world. A new, real person, who had been no more than a pale blue file in the cabinet in Imogen's office. The air seemed to vibrate with a thin bleating, like a lost lamb on a hillside. Something tightened in the social worker's throat.

'There we are.' Jude laid the baby—bloodied, slippery and still trailing its umbilical cord—on the young mother's stomach. Cherie's arms slid around the tiny body, and she held on as though she would never let go. She was sobbing convulsively.

'You've got a daughter!' Jude exulted, tucking a warm towel around the child. 'A beautiful, healthy little girl.'

'Well done,' breathed Imogen.

Still sobbing, Cherie pressed her lips onto the soft head.

The midwives began to bustle about, doing mysterious post-birth things. They took the baby briefly, 'to count the fingers and toes', and then returned her. They delivered the placenta without fuss and bore it away. Finally, the student brought tea and biscuits for the new mother before hurrying off to another delivery. But Cherie was oblivious. She seemed to be bewitched by the miraculous thing in her arms.

As the minutes passed, Imogen leaned closer to this brand-new human being, and closer still. Professionally, she often had to consider newborn babies. She could quote their needs, discuss their routines, reel off the symptoms of poor parenting. She'd sometimes arranged for their swift—and frequently permanent—removal from their mothers. But she had never actually seen such a new one before.

Cherie's baby, seeing for the first time, had shining eyes like pools of treacle. She had a mouth the size and shape of a polo mint, pouting at the strange air of the world. With awe, Imogen watched the rise and fall of a brave little chest that might breathe for the next hundred years.

'Are you going to try feeding her yourself, Cherie?' Jude smiled her encouragement. 'We can have a go right now, if you like. Be good for both of you, I promise.'

Cherie gaped at her. 'You mean . . . ? Gross!' She shuddered. 'She's gonna have a bottle.'

'Go on, give it a try,' urged Jude, pulling up a tall stool and perching on it. 'It's much easier than a bottle, no sterilising, and the good news is you get your figure back quicker.'

Cherie's heavy eyelids lowered defensively. 'No way.'

'It's the best start in life you can give her,' coaxed the midwife.

'*Jesus.* You know nothing.' Cherie sighed and stared up at the ceiling. 'The best start I can give her is to dump her on Imogen's doorstep in a cardboard box.'

'Silly talk, Cherie,' protested Imogen. 'You're going to bring her home to Ellen's, remember?'

Cherie's eyes overflowed. 'How can I look after her?' She wiped her face with the hospital gown.

'You're her mum, pet,' said Jude, rubbing the teenager's back in kind little circles. 'A girl needs her mum.'

But Cherie's face had grown blank, like an African princess carved in ebony. She gathered the baby closer, pressing the warm, downy head against her own cheek.

'I don't even *want* her to have me for a mother.'

Jude's eyes narrowed shrewdly. 'I think you're scared, Cherie.'

The princess turned her head away.

Jude sighed, pulled a biro out of her breast pocket, and ticked something on a clipboard. 'Bottle feed, then, if you're sure. And after a good night's sleep, you'll see everything differently. Have you decided what you'll be calling her?'

Cherie seemed ready, as though she had just this one gift for her child. She lifted her chin.

'Yeah. Grace Serenity.'

Jude's pen hovered over the page. 'Grace . . . what?'

'Serenity. S . . . E . . . R . . .'

The midwife nodded. 'I've got it. Okay. Lovely.' She scribbled, and then clicked her biro a couple of times. 'Now, your surname is King? D'you mind me asking, Cherie, what the father's name might be?'

Imogen's ears began to flap. Cherie had steadfastly refused to name the father. It was a problem, legally.

'Dickhead,' spat Cherie without hesitation. 'D . . . I . . . C . . .'

Imogen smiled, despite herself.

Jude held up a hand. 'All right, all right.' Carefully, she wrote something on a miniature plastic bracelet and then reached out and snapped it around the baby's tiny wrist.

'There we go. She's official now. Grace Serenity King.'

'Oh my God,' yelped Cherie suddenly. She was staring, horrified, at a spreading dark patch where her right breast touched the hospital gown. 'I'm *leaking*!'

The midwife laughed. 'It's the milk, pet. That's colostrum, with everything your baby needs. Your body's got more sense than you have.'

'I can't handle this,' said Cherie. Without warning, as though a switch had been flicked, she seemed to panic. She struggled to stand up. 'Get her off me, for God's sake. Get her off me, right now!'

Deftly, Jude lifted the baby. Cherie shuffled her legs over the edge of the bed and staggered, unsteady and distressed, crumpled in her hospital gown.

'I need a fucking shower . . . I'm filthy, look at me, it's disgusting, there's blood everywhere . . . I'm sticking to everything and there's . . . Oh my God, oh my God, I need to get out of here.'

'It's okay, Cherie,' said Imogen, getting up and laying a hand on the girl's shoulder. 'Calm down.'

But Cherie would not be calmed.

Jude settled Grace in a clear plastic crib. 'It's normal to feel grotty after what you've been through. Your body's in shock. I'll take you to the bathroom in a wheelchair.'

Wincing, weeping, Cherie stooped to pick up her overnight bag. 'I can walk,' she snapped, and hobbled painfully towards the door.

The baby seemed to sense her abandonment. She took several fast, furious breaths, filling her lungs. Then she cried out in a tremulous, lonely wail.

Cherie froze, as though she'd been slapped in the face. She turned, and Imogen saw that her cheeks were washed with tears. For a long moment her eyes rested on the helpless little figure in its plastic box.

Then she met Imogen's gaze.

'I need a shower, and a fucking *smoke*.'

*

Imogen gratefully accepted coffee in the nurses' room. She didn't feel like going on to join in the death throes of a wild hens' night. Not now.

'So.' Jude had wheeled Grace's crib into the room and was writing up her notes while Cherie had a shower. 'No idea about this baby's father?'

Imogen grabbed a biscuit from the tin. She felt odd, as though she'd had a glimpse of another universe. She thought it must be hunger.

'Cherie won't say. We think she might be protecting the guy because she was underage. She turned sixteen last November and—what's today?' Imogen glanced at her watch. 'First of August, but the baby's a couple of weeks early. You can do the sums yourself. It's a close run thing.'

'Who's your dad, little one?' Jude smiled down at the tiny girl who slept, snuffling and solemn, in her plastic crib. 'Maybe a married man. Wife, kids and a shiny BMW that he cleans on Sundays.' Her mouth twisted cynically. 'He won't want to know.'

After a thoughtful silence, Imogen sighed. 'I just hope Cherie can get herself together, you know? She's got the ability, but she's so erratic— fine one minute, off this planet the next.'

'Mm.' Jude nodded, fervently. 'As we saw.'

'She's damaged, poor kid. We all like her, but she's never known anything but abuse, neglect and a string of care homes. She's used every substance, messed with every kind of high-risk behaviour. The assessment was quite tentative . . . she might just cope, with a truckload of support.'

'I can see she's a handful. But my word, she's got guts.' Jude shook her head in admiration. 'What happens if she fails?'

'Well . . .' Imogen looked unhappy. 'We've got a Plan B.'

Jude bent over the sleeping baby, tucking the blanket more tightly around her. 'Adoption,' she murmured. 'Sad.'

When Jude went off to check on Cherie, Imogen leaned back in her chair and closed her eyes. Staff traipsed in and out, but she barely acknowledged them. She drifted, wondering what the future might hold for Cherie and her baby.

Jude seemed to be gone a long time. When she reappeared, she was in a hurry. Imogen heard the rapid footsteps and looked around as the midwife strode in.

'Cherie's gone,' said Jude flatly.

'What?' Imogen leaped up, immediately alert. 'She can't have.'

'Long gone.'

Imogen was thinking fast. 'How? When?'

'She told one of the orderlies she was nipping out for a smoke. She didn't have an overnight bag or anything, just a packet of cigarettes. Janet thought she needed a bit of time to herself. Showed her how to get out. Then she legged it.'

'She shouldn't have been allowed out alone.'

Jude's turned-down mouth made deep valleys in her chin. 'Cherie may be in care, Imogen, but she's not in custody.'

'Okay, okay.' Imogen half waved an apologetic hand. This was a mess. 'Are you *sure* she isn't still outside?'

'Quite sure. There's a patient down there, having a smoke, who saw her. Said she seemed heartbroken. She told him she'd just lost her baby. He watched her being picked up by a car.'

'A car?' Imogen was aghast. 'How on earth . . . ?'

'Crafty young madam must've called someone when she went for her shower. I suppose she's got a mobile phone?'

'She has.' Imogen glanced at her watch. One o'clock, give or take. 'Was it a taxi?' Perhaps they could trace the driver.

'Not a taxi. A young maniac, doing handbrake turns and fishtailing all over the car park. Screaming at Cherie out of the window. A black car, the man said. All jazzed up, with a sound system to wake the dead.'

'Oh God,' moaned Imogen. 'That sounds like Darcy Fox. He graduated straight out of the care system and into the criminal courts.'

'Okay, that's a start. D'you know where he lives?' Jude crossed to a telephone. 'Maybe we could send someone to pick her up.'

'Darcy?' Imogen gestured hopelessly. 'Pillar to post.'

'We have to get her back.' Jude stood at the window, scanning the lights of the city. 'She had a baby about an hour ago. It's dangerous. She needs care.'

Imogen dialled Cherie's mobile with fingers that were, unaccountably, shaking. No reply. She tried again. Then she sent a text.

'We *have* to get her back,' repeated Jude, urgently.

Imogen called Ellen Bayley, waking her up; she was home, but Cherie was not. She tried the police, who promised to look out for the car. Nobody had Darcy Fox's latest address. Perhaps he didn't have one.

The end of Jude's shift had long passed, but she made no move to leave. The two women stood together at the window, willing Cherie to return, listening out for a stereo to wake the dead.

In her crib, the new baby slept on, oblivious.

Shortly after one am, emergency services were called to an accident at a roundabout on the dual carriageway. A black Vauxhall Corsa had collided head-on with a lorry.

The police arrived first, sirens wailing, swiftly followed by the fire brigade and an ambulance. The Corsa was barely recognisable as a car. Its stereo was silent.

'Must have been going a hell of a lick,' remarked a fireman as the ambulance crew jumped out. He gestured through the shattered windscreen. 'There's nothing you can do for these two. Just kids.'

'We'll have to cut them out,' said his colleague. 'What a bloody mess.' And he strode off to organise the equipment.

The lorry had slewed sideways and was blocking the road. A couple of police officers stood talking to the shaken lorry driver; others were setting up cordons and directing traffic.

The older of the paramedics was a bruiser of a man, almost bald. A gold stud gleamed in one ear. He shook his head resignedly at the carnage and then leaned down to the driver's door, looking in. Street lighting and shadows swarmed across his face.

'Hang on,' he muttered, moving closer. 'That looks like . . .'

'What's up, mate?' asked his colleague.

The older man didn't answer. He straightened and ran around to the passenger side, squeezing himself between the lorry and what was left of the car's bonnet. The interior of the wreck was lit rhythmically by the pulsating lights of emergency vehicles. He eased himself forward, peering through the contorted space that had once been a windscreen.

'No,' he said, suddenly. His voice was high and splintered. It sounded almost as though he was in tears. 'Jesus Christ. No.'

Chapter One

I never asked for any of this.

The day started out pretty routine. You'd never guess my life was about to spin off the track and smash into the barriers. The radio alarm began making a racket, I dragged myself upright with my eyes glued shut, and Friday morning was off to a flying start.

I was brushing my teeth when out of nowhere there was Anna, standing beside me, all blow-dried and high-heeled and little-black-suited. She was watching me in the mirror. I didn't even have my lenses in yet, and I'd nothing on but a pair of boxers. You feel at a bit of a disadvantage when the world's all fuzzy and your mouth's overflowing with white froth. I saw her taking a long, sad look at my reflection, and wished I could fit down the plughole.

'My clock's ticking, Jake.'

I didn't like the sound of that, but I couldn't reply. Not without spitting first, and that really would have upset her.

She had layers of reddish hair and a pale, wistful face. Sometimes I thought she looked as if she'd stepped out of an elfin kingdom. She drew her eyebrows together as though I was one of her more difficult clients.

'My biological clock. Also my emotional and financial clocks. In fact, their alarms have gone off.' She reached across and pulled the toothbrush from my mouth, and I spat into the basin with as much dignity as I could manage, which wasn't a hell of a lot.

'Can't you just press the snooze button?' I suggested hopefully.

'I already have, Jake. Several times.' She rubbed her hand across her eyes. 'I've spent an entire night sitting in the kitchen, thinking. And

I need to know, right now. Are you, or are you not, going to show me some commitment?'

I turned off the tap. I was thinking fast.

'Probably. In the end,' I mumbled grumpily, like a teenager caught smoking. The fact was, I knew I'd wasted enough of her time.

She smiled miserably. She was wearing a touch of lipstick for the occasion. 'After four years, we both know you never will. I'm running out of time, and so are you, if you could only face up to it. You're not immortal, for all your blarney. Your half-time whistle's blowing, same as mine.'

'Look, you don't *want* kids, Anna,' I protested. 'You work about eighty hours a week. Where do kids fit in?'

She was a solicitor, a partner in a city firm, and there were weeks when I was lucky to see her before midnight.

She was staring directly at me now, not at my reflection, and her eyes were unnaturally bright. 'I'm sorry, Jake. I've tried and *tried* to discuss this, and it's got me nowhere. I want to have a family, I've never pretended anything else. I hoped we might talk about it last night, on the boat.'

I couldn't seriously deny it. Trouble had been brewing for months. Over the past year, recession had forced her firm to get rid of staff— people with families and mortgages. Guilt weighed on Anna, made her re-evaluate her life. And finally, yesterday had been her thirty-fifth birthday, and that seemed to have an awful significance for her. I'd thrown money at the problem, got her some pearl earrings and—on the advice of Lucy from work—booked a river cruise for dinner.

It was a sound enough idea, bobbing romantically along the Thames among the ripples and reflections, but it was all a bit of a disaster. Anna was moody and quiet, waiting for me to ask what was the matter. I hate that. Makes me feel guilty. So I didn't ask. I got canned instead, rolled home and fell asleep with my shoes and socks on.

'You've got another thirty seconds,' she said now, still watching me.

'Don't do this, Anna,' I said. 'Please don't do this.'

It was a long thirty seconds. Finally, with me busily drying my face and looking anywhere but at her, I heard her sigh. It was a long-suffering sort of sigh, like your mother makes when you've forgotten to tidy your room again.

'Okay. I hoped I'd never have to say this.' She took a long breath. 'I want you to go.'

I stopped drying my face. Looked at her.

'I know you'd carry on as we are for another four years. But I can't,' she insisted, blinking fiercely. 'I have to move on.'

'When?' It was a staggeringly feeble response, I know. But it all seemed a bit unreal.

'I'll be away for the weekend. That'll give you enough time, won't it?'

'Anna,' I said, taking a step towards her. 'Wait.'

'How much longer should I wait?' She watched me hesitate. Then she shook her head. 'It's no good, is it?'

'I'm sorry,' I said. Funny thing: even when you expect some kind of a showdown—even when you've brought it on yourself—it still comes as a bit of a kick in the ribs.

'Thank you for everything, Jake Kelly. Thanks for all the fun. And . . . everything.' Slipping one warm hand around my neck, she kissed me on the mouth. I found I'd wrapped my arms around her, and she leaned against me, her face against mine.

''Bye,' she whispered, and I felt her breath graze my ear.

Then she walked out of the bathroom. Her footsteps paused in the hall; I'd like to think she was waiting for me to call her back, but perhaps she was just looking for her keys.

I didn't call her back. It wouldn't have been honest.

Eventually I heard the front door slam and her footsteps on the pavement, fading away. It wasn't a cheerful sound.

''Bye,' I said.

The flat seemed to hold its breath. I sat down on the edge of the bath. I could still smell her scent. By now she'd be halfway to the tube station, stopping to buy a newspaper. She'd be getting wet, rain plastering down her hair, undoing all the blow-drying. I could easily grab some clothes and catch her up, but then I'd have to ask her to marry me.

I seriously considered this option. It was a perfectly valid one. She was a fantastic girl, Anna. Clever, confident and vivacious. Far too good for me. I could almost see the church doors flying open and my bride gliding radiantly through them with about five of her clumsiest and ugliest friends trailing along behind her, wearing shiny purple dresses and looking like fat fairies on a tree. I could actually hear the thunder of the organ. I'd fly my mum over, and she'd wear her best dress and sob happily in the front row.

But I couldn't bring myself to do it. The very thought of spending the rest of my life tied irrevocably to Anna—or anyone else, for that matter—made me feel claustrophobic. Perhaps I was a fool, because I gave up a hell of a chance that day.

I got dressed, turned on breakfast television and made some coffee. Then I began to wander around the flat in my socks, lobbing things into cardboard boxes, feeling lousy, trying not to dwell on what I'd just lost. She wanted me out, she'd have me out. Today. This was her place, after all.

I was pretty decent about it, if I do say so myself. I left the stereo and most of the CDs, although I couldn't resist the Van Morrison collection. It was odd to see just how entangled our lives had become. Depressing, really. We'd surrounded ourselves with objects and memories that belonged to us both. Who actually forked out for that Moroccan rug by the bed? Who owned the Balinese statue we'd brought back in our hand luggage? It had fallen out of the overhead locker and floored that air hostie. Served her right, stroppy sow.

I spent all morning packing up, and in that time I made some decisions. Rather monumental decisions, actually.

Life in the City was changing, fast and furiously. The financial world was barely recognisable; it wasn't a fun place to be any more, and I reckoned it could get a whole lot worse. I'd been thinking about getting out for a while. Anna just gave me that final shove.

I left a note, a short one, just saying thanks. It was pathetic. Then I piled the stuff into my car and let myself out—for the last time—into the rain, which put on a special performance to mark the solemnity of the occasion. I stood on the doorstep for a minute or two, jingling the keys to the flat from one hand to the other and wondering where the hell I was going to be sleeping that night. It felt a bit odd, after four years, to be posting my own door keys back through the letterbox and hearing them thud onto the hall carpet. Final. Not my home any more.

I didn't cry, though.

Obviously.

The rain paused for breath as I arrived in the City. I left the car in an underground car park and walked the rest of the way. I've never quite got used to wearing the suit and tie and shiny shoes; makes me feel like a confidence trickster—which is more or less accurate, I suppose. They were digging up Moorgate again, and I inhaled the life-giving tang of burning tarmac and exhaust fumes as I marched in through the mirrored doors of Stanton's.

I headed straight up to Delaney's office. My boss was pretty friendly, in his slithery Californian way.

'Jake! Pull up a chair. What can I do for you?'

'I'm afraid I've come to tell you that I'm leaving, Barney.' Jeez, I enjoyed those words more than you can possibly imagine. I still smirk at the memory.

He looked vaguely impatient, turning in his swivel chair, peering at me like a hungry lizard. Then he crossed his legs and switched on his reptilian smile.

'So, Jake. How much?'

'No, really,' I protested. 'This isn't a device to lever more money out of you.'

He sighed cynically. 'C'mon, Jake, I wasn't born yesterday. Let's cut to the chase. What's the figure we've got to match?'

'No, no, Barney.' He's gone mad, I thought. Does he seriously believe I'm here to make demands, in the middle of a financial meltdown? 'I'm really leaving.' I dragged a slightly scruffy letter out of my pocket, scribbled in the car park. 'Here it is in writing.'

I pushed the paper across his desk. He stared vacantly at it, his smile fixed. Then he flicked his tongue. I'm sure it was forked. 'Perhaps you'd care to tell me why, Jake? I presume you're going elsewhere.'

I laughed out loud. 'Else*where*? You think I'm jumping ship? Barney, wake up! Everyone's getting fired, for God's sake!'

I could tell he didn't believe me. He didn't live in the real world. 'Sure you don't just need a holiday?' He was going through the motions now. We both knew it.

'Quite sure.'

He tossed his head, huffily. 'Well. I'm afraid I can't rule out the possibility that you're defecting. So you'd better clear your desk immediately.'

It didn't look as though he was going to thank me for the years of loyal service.

I arrived at my corner three seconds before Kenneth, the security man, fetched up to escort me from the building. That's the Stanton's way, although I'd expected to be given a bit longer. It's the same in most investment banks, I should think. You've become a spy, potentially, for the competition. So once you're out, you're out, before you start stealing secrets. Kenneth planted himself beside my desk, raised his eyebrows at me, and then turned his uniformed back.

I opened the drawers and took out my things: half a packet of glacier mints, and a fluffy kiwi sent by Mum as a hint because she wanted me to come home. It lived zipped up snugly in a miniature felt rugby ball, and many a happy hour we'd spent with it in the office, practising drop kicks and passes. Only last month, Len Harvey broke a tooth after a truly spectacular tackle on my part landed him face down in the wastepaper bin. Mum would have been proud.

Len glanced up briefly from his screen and nodded at me. Like most of my ex-colleagues he was in his shirtsleeves, hair tousled, looking wild and desperate like someone in a casualty ward.

By contrast, at the next desk Lucy Harrison was yakking enthusiastically on the phone. It was as though she'd been filmed in colour against a black-and-white background. She'd been away earlier in the week, dealing with some family crisis; then straight on to Oslo for work. I was pleased to see her before I left. I'd finished my packing, but I waited to speak to her.

'Jake.' She glanced up at the clock as she finished her call. 'How good of you to put in an appearance.'

'Hi, Luce. All good at home?'

She flapped a hand, dismissively. 'Mad as hatters.'

'How about Oslo?'

'Waste of time.'

She began dialling again, but then spotted the security guy. He was standing still, legs apart, waiting with the patience of a very bored person.

'Is Ken your new bodyguard?' she asked.

'No. I'm out of here. Barney's sent him to stop me walking out with the desktop stuffed down my pants.'

She dropped her phone, rage in the bottle-green eyes. 'They haven't given *you* the push?'

'Nope. I jumped first, but it was only a matter of time.'

'But you're better than everybody else.'

'No, just more expensive.'

Her gaze fell forlornly onto the little black rugby ball I was holding. I lobbed it over, and she reached out and caught it with one hand.

'You can't slink off without buying me lunch,' she insisted, standing up and grabbing her jacket from the back of her chair. 'Shall we ask the others?'

I looked around at the familiar faces. I'd probably never see them again. And you know what? I didn't care. I shook my head, and she shook hers, too.

As we left, both our desk phones were ringing.

We had lunch in a wine bar on Finsbury Circus. I bought a bottle of something that cost enough to feed a Sudanese refugee family for a year, and drank most of it myself. Lucy seemed a bit distracted, and I wasn't on top form either. She was a very deflating audience, drumming her long fingers on the table and scowling at the crowd mobbing the bar. Normally she's engaged, lively, cheerily flirtatious.

The waitress arrived with Lucy's minestrone, my steak sandwich, and the largest pepper grinder in the world. It made me feel inadequate. When she'd gone, Lucy leaned towards me.

'Now. Tell me why you're going.'

I didn't need to feel guilty. I'd done right by the girl. Been her manager until twelve o'clock that day. In fact, I'd interviewed her for the job in the first place. She was clearly outstanding. The boys leered, said she was *outstanding*, all right. But it honestly wasn't about her Wonderbra bust—she wore little green blouses that matched her eyes—or her spectacular legs, or the nifty boy's haircut that showed the nape of her neck. No. It was the way she looked at the world. She seemed to find it all rather funny. She was bright too, complete with a scary degree and three languages. Next to her, I felt like a hillbilly, which of course is exactly what I am.

Lucy and I had one of those entertaining friendships with an edge. But I'd never laid a finger on her, honest. It would have been harassment.

Anyway, I'd been proved right. She was one of the best, and she didn't need me any more. I told her so.

She had quite a pronounced nose, but I always thought it was her best feature. It gave her face sophistication. She looked down it now, raised one graceful eyebrow and dunked her bread into her soup.

'Of course I don't *need* you, dickhead. Bloody ridiculous. I don't need a feckless drunken colonial like you, no matter how sexy your smile.' She gazed at my mouth for a few seconds, allowing herself a sinful little smirk. 'What I want to know is why you're going, *when* you decided to go, and why you didn't tell me? And what's the brilliant new career you're heading for, and should I be hanging onto your coat-tails? Because—whatever it is—I'll be better at it than you are.'

'I'm going to open a massage parlour.'

'Oh, good. Can I be the receptionist? Together, we could go far.'

'No. You're too indiscreet. Actually, I'm going to be a bum. Look at them.' I pointed to the yelling, sweating scrum at the bar. 'Flooded with adrenaline. They're ready to fight to the death even now, in the half-hour they've got away from their desks. And for what?'

She glanced at the killer mob. 'Money.'

'Lucy, the system's on the verge of collapse. There *is* no money any more. And anyway, I've made enough of the stuff. It's time I got out.'

'When did you decide this?'

'Six o'clock this morning.'

She blinked innocently. 'Oh, yes? You had a midlife crisis at six o'clock this morning?'

'Anna threw me out.'

'Ah.' She nodded calmly. 'Well, that was inevitable. A woman like that wasn't going to wait forever. Did you try to change her mind?'

I shrugged.

She leaned closer, raking me with searchlight eyes. 'Do you love her at all, Jake?'

'I don't know,' I said helplessly. Everyone knows I don't answer that kind of question. 'What does that *mean*, really?'

'Honestly! You've all the emotional acuity of a dishwasher. Haven't you ever been in love?'

'Not since I was ten years old.'

'Who was the lucky girl?'

'I had a Jack Russell. Sala. Means Princess. She was neat.'

She slapped my wrist. 'Idiot! I was serious.'

I was, too. But I laughed it off. Always do.

'Look,' I told her, 'it feels like a reprieve. My neck was on the block. The drums were rolling and a messenger came galloping up, waving the king's pardon.'

She was gazing at me shrewdly. 'I don't believe you for one minute.'

'No. Well.' I sighed. 'Anna wants kids.'

'That's pretty normal. Doesn't make her a psychopath.'

'Bloody hell, Luce, I'm too young to be a father. I'm not *ready*.'

She snorted. 'Jake, you're forty! You're wearing it well, I'll admit that. You're revoltingly fit, and you've a luscious mouth and wicked brown eyes that make women want to mother you, poor tarts. And there's that lazy antipodean accent.' She smiled, stretched across and tugged at my hair. 'But one day soon you'll find a steely strand in here, glinting treacherously.' She leaned a little closer, focusing intently on my forehead. 'Actually, do you *dye* your hair?'

'Certainly not.'

'What do they call that shade? Mahogany?'

I didn't like the way this was going. 'Well, anyway. I *do* feel reprieved. And I intend to make good use of it because, as my mother always says, life isn't a dress rehearsal.'

'Really? Does your mother treat her life as the final performance?'

I picked up the bottle and waved it at her, but she stretched a hand over her glass.

'Well.' I poured myself another. 'She made the mistake of marrying my father, and she might as well have thrown in her lot with the devil himself. Every day's been the same for the last forty-five years. She gets up at five. Then she bakes and cleans and sews and feeds the calves and does the garden and the washing and the accounts, while he roars around on a quad bike with a pack of dogs sprinting ahead and a dead sheep slung across the back with its tongue hanging out. Every so often he stomps into the kitchen, swears, scoffs all the food, and messes everything up again.'

I paused, tasting the hatred. Knocked back half the glass, but it didn't take the taste away. Never would.

'They're reckoned to be a real success story in the district. People say, "That Connie Kelly, she doesn't waste a minute of her life."' I shuddered. 'And they're right. She hasn't wasted a minute. She's wasted the whole bloody lot.'

'How far are they from a town?' asked Lucy.

'They're in the middle of nowhere, Luce. And I mean that absolutely literally. It's an hour sliding down a gravel track to a tar-sealed road, and you're still another hour from the nearest traffic light.'

'You're joking.'

'Wish I was.'

'Why haven't they been over here? You could pay.'

'Dad won't come, and I wouldn't see him if he did.'

'Why not?'

I scowled, and Lucy raised her eyebrows.

'Well, it all sounds very childish.' She poured herself some fizzy water. 'Still, I suppose now that you're single and unemployed you'll be heading home.'

'I can't. My place has long-term tenants.'

'Not home to Clapham Common, you idiot. Home to New Zealand.'

I shook my head madly, holding up both hands. 'Oh, no, no, no. No way!'

'I don't believe you. I've seen you sniffling away when the All Blacks do the haka.'

'Bollocks.' I took a bite of steak sandwich.

'It's *not* bollocks. You go all misty-eyed when Kiri Te Kanawa comes on the radio, too. I think it's time you went home, Jake. You *need* to. Make peace with yourself, and with your family, and buy a vineyard or something. I might even visit you.'

'Never. I couldn't live without the Northern Line at rush hour.' I paused, pointing at my cheek. The steak was a bit chewy. 'Mind you, I'm the only one left. When I first arrived there were sixteen of us flatting in three rooms.'

'How revolting.'

'They all went home in the end. All except me.'

She looked at me with a new interest. 'Seriously. What *are* you planning on doing? You must have a plan.'

'I don't. I know you can't imagine that, Luce, but I don't. In fact, that's the plan. Not to have one. I'm going to drift around the world, sitting outside cafés in a Panama hat like a pommy toff, reading thrillers.'

Lucy tipped back her chair, head on one side. She does that when she's thinking. In fact she was plotting, as it turned out.

'So. You're a free man, and you're no longer my boss.'

'Yeah. Your place or mine, darlin'?'

'In your dreams.' She regarded me steadily for a little time and then seemed to come to a decision. 'When does Anna want you out?'

I shrugged. 'I'm out already. My life is all packed up in the boot of a flashy car I never had time to drive and can no longer afford.'

'Where are you going to stay?'

'Not sure. Most of my mates are mutual friends. You know. I expect they all think I've strung Anna along.'

She nodded. 'Yes, well. No comment.' She reached over and pulled a bit of loose cotton off my sleeve. 'Look. I don't like to think of you sleeping in Lincoln's Inn Fields under a copy of *The Sun*. Might get bullied, pretty boy like you. I'm heading home again tonight, for the weekend—I mean *home* home, to Suffolk. You can come too.'

'I can't just—'

She waved an airy hand. 'No, shut up. My father will welcome you with open arms. There's only him and my brother there at the moment. In fact I'll phone right now and tell him.' She started rummaging in her handbag.

'Hasn't there been some drama, though? They won't want me clattering around the place.'

She smiled indulgently. 'It's just my brother, as usual. Little Matt's been getting himself into a bit of bother.'

'Off the rails?'

'Well, slightly. But he's a bright wee sod, he'll be fine. We've taken him out of boarding school and he's finishing his education locally, where Dad can keep an eye on him.' She drew breath to say more, but then she shut her mouth again, and I didn't ask. None of my business.

That's one of the bits of baggage I've inherited from my parents. They obsessively practised what they called 'minding their own business', to the point of insanity. The neighbour could have cut his own leg clean off with a chainsaw and be writhing on the ground, screaming, the lifeblood hosing out of his femoral artery, but they wouldn't take a look across the fence because it would be none of their business what he was doing on his own property. Seriously. The next time they saw him, hopping down the street on his one remaining leg, they'd pretend nothing had happened. All interest in other people, as far as my parents were concerned, was just nosy gossip. I could never quite throw that off.

Good old Lucy, I thought fuzzily, as she got out her phone. I was quite touched. We're great mates at work, but I hadn't expected her to invite me into her family home. It all sounded quite tempting. I imagined a freezer full of decent food from the local deli, and Old Man Harrison throwing open the drinks cabinet. I was curious, too. I wanted to see where Lucy came from. I should have known better—after all, we know what curiosity did to the cat. But I said thanks, and let her phone her dad.

And I suppose if I hadn't, none of this would have happened.

Chapter Two

She was in a hurry, and under siege.

The worst thing about being a clergyman's wife, Leila thought heatedly, is the way people look at you when you come in here. They count how many bottles you buy, and when you've gone they sidle over to the counter and mutter, 'Poor Mr Edmunds, his wife does let him down.'

She wasn't just the new curate's wife. She was the new curate's *black* wife. She was a curiosity. White elephant, black curate's wife. Things were expected of her, preferably lurid. Gossip was currency, in the parish.

She grabbed four bottles of red, more or less at random, and one of gin. The gin was expensive, but David's father lived for the stuff. She wouldn't be drinking any of this herself, though. Not tonight. Maybe not for a long time.

Resting her wire basket on the counter, she smiled at Dora Davies, behind the till. ''Evening, Dora.' She tried to sound friendly but brisk, a woman with no time to chat. Leila had been on her feet all day; she'd dispensed about two hundred prescriptions, meticulously checking each one for interactions and errors in the knowledge that a single mistake could prove fatal. She'd managed anxious customers—some tearful, some aggressive—and shopfloor politics. Finally she'd raced off, nipping into the off-licence on the way home for some last-minute shopping.

''Evening, Mrs Edmunds.' Dora wasn't about to let such a prize slip through her grasp. She began, with agonising care, to wrap each bottle in brown paper. Leila watched helplessly. What the hell was the point of *that*? She glanced at the clock behind Dora's head. Already after six o'clock, and they were coming at seven-thirty. *Please, please hurry up, Dora.*

The shopkeeper reached for the next bottle. 'Nasty weather we're having.' She tutted disapprovingly and smoothed another sheet of paper onto the counter. 'I've never known such a torrent.'

'Quite a downpour, wasn't it? Still, it's the time of year.' *For God's sake, who cares? Just hurry up.*

Dora hunted about for the sticky tape, musing in singsong Brummie. 'Actually, I got caught in it when I went out earlier. I had to go, though, to visit my mother. She's in hospital, did you know?'

'No, no, I didn't know. I'm sorry to hear it.'

'I looked like a drowned weasel by the time I got there. Water dripping off me in the ward.'

Five past six! This is a nightmare. I have to get home and cook dinner for six people, one of whom will be delighted when I make a mess of things. Please shut up, you hag.

'It's her hip, you know. Mother's been on the waiting list for . . . ooh, Alan, how long's Mother been on the waiting list? Alan? A year? No, love, much longer than that. At least two years, because Dad was still alive, and I know he passed away two years ago last month, even though it feels like yesterday. It got postponed five times, her operation did, right at the last minute. That's the NHS for you. I expect you know about all that, being involved in it yourself. Five times!'

'No! Five? Disgraceful. Er . . . don't worry about wrapping up the gin, Dora.'

Dora stopped wrapping altogether. Tucked her chins into her neck. Took off her glasses, very deliberately.

'Anyway. She tripped over the dog last night. Broke the other one.'

'Oh, no.'

'Lay on the floor all night, only Frodo to keep her warm.'

'No!'

'Milkman found her this morning. Luckily he noticed the curtains.'

Leila was trapped. You could not fail to show an interest in a woman of eighty-five who'd spent a long, painful night shivering on the floor with a broken hip. But it was now almost ten past six, and her pulse was going wild. She imagined herself hitting Dora on the head with a bottle before sprinting out. The security camera footage would be shown on the news, all grainy and blurred, with the headlines 'Clergy wife in robbery' and 'All for a bottle of gin'.

'Thank goodness for the milkman.' She reached into her handbag. 'How much do I owe you?'

Dora shook her forefinger. 'Wait a minute! You haven't heard the half of it yet.'

Nightmare. It's a nightmare.

'Milkman looks in through the windows, sees Mother lying there, thinks she's dead, which almost gives him a cardiac, calls the ambulance on his mobile phone. Then he breaks in. Glass everywhere!'

'What a hero.'

'Nah. Silly sod. You'd think he'd find the key under the mat, wouldn't you? Everyone keeps their key under the mat, don't they? She wouldn't let him anywhere near her because she was in her nightie, so he made her a cup of tea and sat down with his back to her. And do you know how long the ambulance took to arrive?'

Leila shook her head, hypnotised.

Dora paused for dramatic effect. 'Two hours.'

'No!'

Dora nodded, happily outraged. 'Two. You wouldn't believe it, would you? He had to sit there with his eyes averted for the whole time. Would've been quicker to take her on his milk float, as I told him in no uncertain terms. Well, she's not too bad now, considering. They've put her in a—'

'I'll ask David to call in. Which ward?'

'I wanted to talk to you about her medication, seeing as you're a pharmacist yourself. Because I'm not happy. I said to that doctor—'

'Dreadful! Dreadful. Really, Dora, it's appalling, but I'm sure they're doing all they can. I'll tell David, he'll visit her. Only I must go now because I've got people coming and the house is in *such* a state.'

Even to her own ears Leila sounded hysterical, but Dora appeared unconcerned. She replaced her glasses and began to slide the bottles into carrier bags.

'Looks like you're planning on sinking a battleship. Should've had the Chilean red. We've got it on offer, look. It's a lovely wine, that. You'd save . . . er . . . two, four . . . just a minute . . . you'd save about five pounds on this lot. D'you want to swap?'

Oh, God.

'No thanks, Dora. Honestly. Must go!' Leila giggled slightly wildly, handing over her credit card. 'Got the rector coming. Mustn't keep him waiting.'

Dora ran the card through the machine, glanced at the printout, then leaned over the counter, beckoning conspiratorially.

'Sorry, my love,' she whispered ear-splittingly, while all the other customers fell silent and pretended not to listen. 'Transaction declined.'

Six forty-eight. Leila had cleared a mound of ecclesiastical junk mail off the dining-room table—the overflow from David's study—and half-heartedly waltzed a vacuum cleaner around the floor. She'd answered the telephone four times, slammed a casserole into the oven and sent a text asking David to drop in at the off-licence to settle up with Dora.

Which was when the doorbell rang. Insanely jolly, that doorbell. Ping—*pong!*

Can't be them. Just can't be. Not yet.

The caller obviously liked the bell. Pingpongpingpong. Ping—*PONG!*

Leila wrenched at the door, peered suspiciously out and then smiled. A solid, olive-skinned child in leggings and a red-spotted tunic was just settling herself on the step. She had dark hair in a lustrous plait, all the way to her waist, and a large gap where one of her front teeth had recently been. And she was sniffling. The neighbours' daughter, six years old and already lonely. Her parents were Greek. They owned a restaurant and worked longer hours than anyone should have to.

'Jacinta!' Leila crouched down beside her. 'What's up?'

The girl stuck out her bottom lip. She was clutching a box, about four inches across. It was pink and heart-shaped, and it had a red bow on the top. She held it out, unsmiling.

'For me?' Leila took the box.

'It's Angel,' whispered Jacinta.

'Thank you, sweetheart. It's an angel, is it? Did you make this at school?'

'No. It's Angel.'

'Okay.' Expecting an angel-shaped chocolate, or perhaps a winged doll, Leila lifted the lid and peered in. Nestling in black tissue paper, glaring glassily up at her with a shining eye, lay a vivid orange goldfish. Leila nearly dropped the box.

'Gosh! It's um . . . Oh, I see. Did your fish die?'

Jacinta nodded. 'I found her in the tank. Floating on the top. Upside down.'

Leila stared down at the creature, mesmerised by its wide-awake eye. You'd think it was alive. Its body was still bright, but the long, wispy tail curled a little.

'Isn't she beautiful?'

'She looked nicer when she was swimming around,' lamented Jacinta. She reached out and stroked the tiny body. 'My sister's looking after me.'

'Daria?'

'Mmn. And she's snoggling with her boyfriend on the sofa and she said if I don't get my bloody fish out of the house she's going to flush it down the toilet.'

'Snoggling, is she? Shame on her!' Leila glanced surreptitiously at her watch, calculating rapidly. 'C'mon,' she ordered, straightening up. 'Shall we give your glorious Angel a decent send-off?'

Seven o'clock. They'd dug a grave by the hebe bush and lowered the coffin into it. They murmured a sombre goodbye, standing hand-in-hand in the light from the kitchen window, then hummed the theme tune of *Neighbours*. Not the most funereal of melodies, but it was Angel's favourite song, apparently.

'It's a shame David isn't here,' said Leila. 'He does a lovely funeral.'

With a tragic flourish, Jacinta threw a handful of soil onto the pink box before Leila buried it. Then, lest Jacinta's greedy gingercat should exhume the dear departed, they covered the little mound with stones.

'We'll make it into a rock garden in the spring,' promised Leila, leading the way back into her brightly lit kitchen. 'Little alpine flowers, and a cactus or two.' She reached into the freezer and dug out a Cornetto.

Taking a giant bite, Jacinta looked at the jumble of photographs on the fridge. 'Who's that?' she asked, pointing.

'My nephews.' Leila smiled proudly. 'Simon—he's eleven, very clever, like you—and Daniel, who's a little monkey. And the baby's a girl called Sade.'

'Where d'they live?'

'In London. But the boys are coming to stay here after Christmas. They'd love to play with you.'

'Okay. Can you and me make a cross to go on Angel's grave?' asked Jacinta, licking ice cream off her sleeve.

'Yes.' Leila steered her visitor towards the door. 'But not tonight. I've got people coming any minute. Tell your sister to stop her snoggling and make your tea.'

As soon as Jacinta had gone, Leila shot upstairs. She took the fastest shower in history (how did half the garden end up under her nails?) and pulled on a flowing black skirt and an emerald wraparound blouse.

The curate's house, a modern semi provided by the parish, was hopelessly cluttered. The piano, festooned with Leila's sheet music, was jammed into what should have been the study. There weren't enough shelves, and books lay in piles around the hall. Leila tripped over a box full of parish magazines as she scurried back and forth, trying to bring some order to the chaos, forcing gold hoops into her ears, all the while prattling distractedly to herself.

Catching sight of her figure in the hall mirror, she stopped. Pulled her stomach in and her shoulders back. Made a mental note to start a low-fat diet immediately. Almost immediately.

'It doesn't really matter, though,' she said aloud.

The woman in the mirror smiled warmly out at her. She had elegant cheekbones and even, white teeth. It didn't matter that David was late; it didn't matter that she'd gained at least a dress size in the last year and was now a trifle squeezed in a twelve; it certainly didn't matter that both the boss and the parents-in-law were due in a nanosecond, and the place looked like a bombsite. Because the miracle was happening, at long last. Someone was growing inside her, and life was about to change. This time she was sure.

Humming under her breath, she began to adjust the turquoise band she wore around her hair, retying the knot at the nape of her neck. When she heard David's long steps on the path she winked at herself in the mirror, flickering with secret delight. She wouldn't tell him yet. No. Not yet. There had been too many disappointments over the years of their ghastly rollercoaster ride. She'd do the test first, and then she'd wait a while longer, to make certain.

David burst in, a whirl of movement and vitality, and the house seemed to shrink.

'Sorry, sorry,' he spluttered, cheerfully and without a hint of contrition. He paused to hang up his coat, fair hair flopping over a broad forehead. Leila felt as though he'd recharged her just by walking through the front door.

'My beautiful wife!' Briskly crossing the hall, he draped his tall frame around her, running his mouth along one of the tight plaits that covered her head. 'Ah, my favourite silky shirt. What happens if I pull on this little bow at the back?'

Leila wriggled away, tapping her watch, trying to look severe. 'What time d'you call this?'

'Sorry! Got cornered by Dora.'

'You too?'

He scratched his long nose. 'Didn't make my escape until the queue of customers behind me was halfway down the High Street, rioting. I had to get a writ of habeas corpus.'

It's all right. Everything's all right. She put her hands on her hips. 'That wretched card had a nervous breakdown. Half of Birmingham was watching.'

'Oh, no!' Laughing, he kissed her. There was a fan of creases at the outer corners of his eyes, so that he seemed permanently to be smiling. It gave his face an ageless quality. 'I forgot to pay it off.'

She leaned happily into his warmth, prolonging the moment. Then, reluctantly, she whispered in his ear, 'You do realise that your guests are due to arrive in just under four minutes?'

'Blimey!' He was gone, thundering up the stairs, tearing off his dog collar as he turned the corner. It was a toy house, and a dolls' staircase. David, long-legged and athletic, could spring up it in three bounds.

'Your job this evening is to stop your father drinking too much,' she yelled after him. 'If he says anything smutty I swear I'll break that Roman conk he's so proud of.'

'Allow me.' She could hear David's chuckle, then a thud—shower door—and the splash of running water.

He was still upstairs when the doorbell rang. That will certainly be the in-laws, thought Leila sourly. Don't even have the decency to be late. I'll bet they've been skulking around the corner in their car, waiting for seven thirty-one. She dragged her most welcoming smile out of its box and glued it into position. She'd had plenty of practice at sticking on smiles, since David took this job. On the way to the front door, she checked her expression in the long mirror. It looked like rigor mortis.

Must look them in the eye. Must look them in the eye.

Throwing open the door, the curate's wife stood well back. Her face was alight with radiant welcome.

'Hilda! Christopher! How lovely!'

Eight o'clock. Angus and Elizabeth were late, of course. Bless them.

Leila had run out of excuses not to join the others in the miniature sitting room. There had never been open hostilities in her dealings with David's mother; never, in fifteen years. Instead, uneasy tension spilled into short bursts of sniper fire on both sides. It was exhausting. Blatant warfare might have been easier.

Lingering in the kitchen, she could hear David regaling them with that awful story about the coffin that floated when it was lowered into the grave. After the shocked laughter, she made out snatches of Hilda's voice. 'Monica's much in demand,' she heard, and 'Michael's been fore-casting this recession for years.'

Well, bully for Michael and bloody Monica.

There was an agenda, of course. David, like his younger brother and sister, had also been a source of pride until he gave it all up, well on his way up the management ladder in a tentacular agrochemicals company. Hilda was still grief-stricken at his abandonment of her ambitions.

Now her mother-in-law's sugary tones took on a strident edge. 'Leila? Aren't you going to join us? Can I help, at all?'

Bugger. Cornered, Leila blew out her cheeks and marched into the enemy camp, smile firmly fixed in place. Christopher leaped gallantly to his feet and stood to attention. He was every inch the dapper merchant seaman, weathered across the cheekbones, eyes a watery blue beneath the cloud-white sweep of his hair.

'You're working too hard,' he gushed, straightening his tie. 'Look at that, you're wasting away!'

'I wish,' said Leila.

She accepted a glass of apple juice and balanced on the edge of the sofa. She could sense Christopher watching her, a half-smile lifting his heavy brows as though they shared a little secret. He'd been handsome in his day, she grudgingly supposed. You could see the ghost of it still: the careful posture, proud features—strong, like David's—coarsened now by gin and boredom.

He leaned down to her. 'Got any—what d'you call 'em?—*gigs* coming up, Leila?'

'We've got a fiftieth birthday in Edgbaston tomorrow. Hospital administrator.'

'Wish I could be there,' sighed Christopher. 'I love to hear you sing.'

Hilda perched vigilantly in an armchair, legs neatly to one side like a little Persian cat. She looked powdered and tidy in a rose silk shirt, and not at all poisonous.

'You were a saint to allow David to go into the church, Leila,' she said, her voice dipped in syrup. 'You've had to make so many terrible sacrifices. Living *here*.' Her disapproval seemed to encompass the little house, the dingy suburb, the great heaving mass of the West Midlands. 'It's worse than the last place. And no prospects.'

David rubbed his nose, risking a surreptitious smile at Leila. 'Depends what you call prospects, Mum.' He held out a porcelain bowl. 'Cashew?'

'I mean *real* prospects, for your actual future,' snapped Hilda, ignoring the peace offering. 'Not airy-fairy celestial ones.'

Christopher crossed the room to the drinks tray, unscrewed the gin, and helped himself. 'Stop fussing, Hilda,' he said amiably, with a small wink in Leila's direction. 'They're bound for Lambeth Palace. David will make a very sporty archbishop.'

'Only a matter of time!' Leila was grateful for the vote of confidence. 'And I'm fine. My job's better paid here, actually, and there's far more back-up. There are three of us pharmacists on duty at peak times. I can normally work Saturday and have Wednesday off with David.'

'Kirkaldie's,' mumbled David, eating the cashews himself. 'Near New Street Station. Pretty hectic. Leila seems to dispense a lot of methadone.'

There was a cynical twist to Hilda's lips. 'Well, you won't starve, then.'

Christopher lowered himself stiffly into the seat next to Leila, suppressing a wince. 'I've taken up golf,' he confided, in an undertone. 'What d'you think of that?'

'Well . . . I've never played.'

'Don't.' He leaned closer. 'Boring people, pointless game.' He gestured at his wife, who was obviously listening. 'She makes me go. Gets me out of the house.'

The doorbell. Angus and Elizabeth. *Thank God.*

'Hello, hello!' Elizabeth bustled in first, turning to shake her umbrella out onto the step. 'Angus is parking the car—awful night—sorry we're late. Come *on*, Angus! Leila's standing in a howling gale!'

Elizabeth's voice was always a surprise; it didn't match the rest of her. It was deep, like a drag queen's, and had the huskiness of a chain-smoker, which Elizabeth wasn't.

Leila could see the rector's stocky figure rambling up the path, a newspaper over his head, bearded and grizzled and good-humoured.

Angus came from Inverness. Leila liked to picture him striding through the mist with a deer slung over his shoulders, or leaping to the bagpipes in a stone-flagged hall.

'Good evening, Leila.' Handing over a bottle of wine he shook himself, spraying droplets. 'Something smells good. Sorry we're late. Got caught in the off-licence by Dora.'

'You don't say. You're not late, anyway. We're just having drinks.'

'Oh, good!' Angus rubbed his hands together.

'You'd better come and meet David's parents.' Leila took Elizabeth's arm as they crossed the little hall. 'Brace yourself,' she whispered.

Chapter Three

I spent the rest of the day in the gym, and picked Lucy up in the early evening. The rain had cleared completely, and I had the roof down. Steam rose gently from the streets.

Lucy had changed into jeans and a soft, mushroom-coloured jersey. She greeted me with a whoop, dumped her bag in the back, and vaulted over the passenger door without opening it. I've never dared try that.

I forced my way into the traffic, and we sped towards the East End.

Actually, of course, we didn't speed anywhere at all. We inched along in a deep sea of humanity and carbon monoxide. It would have been quicker to walk.

London had its faults. It was grubby, cold for much of the year and had rows and rows of identical houses. In recent times the market munch had added a hefty dash of gloom. Yet on a warm October evening, when the bars were spilling out onto the pavements, and the smell of beer and fallen leaves and hot tarmac all mingled together— well, there was nowhere like it. I always hoped my mother could see it one day.

For the first twenty minutes or so, Lucy chatted merrily about her afternoon: how Len Harvey wanted my job, but she reckoned he was about to get the chop.

I turned the music down a bit. 'Your old man still working?' I thought I should get a bit of background, since he was kindly going to share his fridge with me.

Something unhappy flickered across her face. 'He was in the army. Retired early as a major, got the pension. He works from home now, translation work. Arabic, German. For pity's sake, don't bother asking him about it. Outstandingly boring. Even he nods off in mid-explanation.'

'So what *do* I talk about?'

'Gardening.' I couldn't tell whether or not she was serious, but she seemed keen to end the conversation. I wanted to talk, though. I was fizzing with freedom. Once we got onto the A12, I tried again.

'So they've been abandoned for the weekend?'

Lucy started flicking through my CDs. 'Actually,' she said, wrinkling her elegant nose at Bruce Springsteen, 'Deborah's been away for months. Dad's wife, Matt's mother.' She made her arm writhe like a snake. 'The venomous viper.'

'A journalist, isn't she?'

'Freelance. It's a sort of posh hobby, really.'

'So where's she gone?'

'East Africa. She went off to try and talk to some of the murderers who ran amok after the 2007 elections.'

'Wow! I'm impressed.'

'That's what she does, you see. She finds these people, then she gets their side of the story and humanises them for all the liberal lefty types. She hopes everyone will say, "So that's why they've been maiming babies all these years. Well, why didn't they *say* so?" Then they'll get their independence, or their share in the government, or whatever, and everybody will be happy.'

We'd stopped in a queue at some lights. The car in front of us was playing techno music at an unbelievable volume; I could actually feel the vibrations through my feet.

I was intrigued. I wanted to meet Mrs Harrison. 'When's she coming back?'

Lucy didn't seem to hear me. She was taking a keen interest in a pornographic advert for ice cream, up on a billboard. Then the lights changed, and we moved on. The boy racer in front accelerated away with a sound like Concorde taking off.

After about a minute she said, 'In fact, we don't know where Deborah is at the moment.'

'You mean she's disappeared, or what?'

'She found her perpetrators.' Lucy sounded casual. 'Wrote the piece. It appeared, in various forms, in a few rags. Then she sent Dad a postcard. That was ages ago.'

'And?'

'Well, and nothing.'

'Mobile phone?'

'Switched off. Or no reception. Probably both.'

This didn't sound good to me. 'So . . . are we worried?'

She crossed her arms, looking supremely unconcerned for her step-mother's safety. 'I suppose she may have been eaten by a lion in the Serengeti—there's always hope—but I'd pity the lion. More likely to be shacked up on an oil tanker with a Somali pirate whose body was made for love.'

'Like mine?'

'Like yours,' she said, and chuckled cruelly until London was behind us.

Lucy's father was waiting for us. I saw a lean figure in the shadows as we rolled around the turning circle outside their house. She jumped out almost before we'd stopped, and he hurried across and wrapped his arms around her. Anyone would think they hadn't clapped eyes on one another for years, the way they carried on.

I stood there, clutching her case and feeling like a complete pillock, until Lucy looked around for me. 'Dad, this is Jake Kelly.'

He took a brisk step towards me. 'Perry Harrison. Good of you to give Lucy a lift.'

He shook my hand and held on to it for a time, gazing into my face as though I'd come for a job interview. In fact I had, only I didn't realise it at the time. Even after he'd let go, I sensed him watching me. I assumed he was just trying to decide whether I was sleeping with his daughter or not.

As he led us into the house I found myself trying to work him out, too. Perry Harrison was certainly striking. Well into his fifties, I'd guess, maybe older. He still had plenty of hair, though, almost black

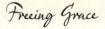

and shot through with streaks of silver. His eyes looked bloodshot and they drooped slightly at the outer edges, as though he was dead beat. He seemed to be wearing eyeliner, but I worked out later that his lashes were just unnaturally dark. It was hard to imagine him storming a desert fortress with a submachine gun on his shoulder, but he'd look perfectly at home in a painted caravan, with a gold earring and a slightly chipped crystal ball.

The house was outside a village called Coptree, in the depths of Suffolk, not far from the sea. The place was hidden up a narrow farm track overhung with trees. It was one of those seriously old farmhouses the poms go for if they can afford it: deep red walls and dark wood, and doorways that lean down and bash you on the head every time you go anywhere near them. The floorboards creaked and smelled of beeswax. They were wide and pitted, and so uneven that there were little blocks under the table legs to stop them wobbling. There were bookshelves everywhere, lining the rooms; there was even one in the downstairs bog, as I later discovered.

And there seemed to be a party going on next door. It was incongruous. You couldn't escape the music, just like the techno garbage from the car in London: *bommchukka bommchukka*. Funny thing, though. Lucy and Perry didn't seem to be able to hear it. They ignored it completely.

I was right about the fridge, I'm glad to say. It flew open as we walked in through the front door, and never got closed again the whole time I was there. Jeez, Perry could put it back.

He handed me a cold beer and we stood around in the kitchen while he chucked herbs into the chicken thing he was cooking. I tried asking him about the garden, and he bored on about his compost heap and how it was a hundred degrees in the middle. Apparently, this was a tremendous feat.

'I'll show you where you're sleeping,' he offered once the meal was in the oven. As we creaked up the stairs, the party next door sounded louder and louder, until I remembered that there *was* no house next door. We were in the middle of a bloody paddock. By the time we were at the top, I'd worked out that the racket was coming from one of the bedrooms—*bommchukka bommchukka*—but Perry behaved as though all we could hear was the chirruping of blackbirds under the eaves, so I did too. It seemed only polite.

He crossed the landing and led me into a room at the end of a short corridor. It had a beamed ceiling and uneven white walls, and smelled slightly of damp and mothballs. There was a fireplace, a broad window seat, and yet another bookcase full of authors I'd never heard of. Half of the titles weren't even in English. In fact, several were completely indecipherable.

Perry caught me peering at them. 'D'you read Arabic?' he asked, sounding hopeful.

I shook my head apologetically and stooped to peer out of the window. It overlooked a vegetable patch with a low picket fence, and a small orchard that merged into lawn. Across the grass, an old yew tree twisted itself out of the hedge. I could see fields and a wood beyond. The sun was just creeping away below a wide, floodlit horizon. It all looked very peaceful, but I could still hear that crazy music.

'I feel I've dumped myself on you,' I said.

'Nonsense. We keep the spare bed made up.' Perry paused to check whether the bedside lamp was working. 'Your bathroom's next door. Come down when you're ready.'

After he'd gone, I sat on the window seat and tried Anna's number on my mobile. I wanted to know how she was. After all, when we woke up that morning we were still together. And now our futures didn't include one another. I got her voicemail and left a lame message about how I hoped she was all right.

News travels fast. My message bank was all clogged with people telling me what a bastard I was, or what a witch Anna was. Apparently it doesn't do not to take sides in these situations.

I leaned against the window frame and watched a tractor rumbling up and down the stubble field, seagulls fluttering in its wake. A low mist was beginning to settle on the furrows, and the shadow of the yew reached right across Perry's lawn. I opened the window. The air smelled of leaf mould and earth.

It seemed only yesterday that it was Christmas, and now they were ploughing again. Spring and summer and harvest had come and gone, and I'd paid them no heed. Time was going faster and faster. Someone had their finger jammed on the fast forward button. Soon I'd be old, and then I'd be dead.

I'd better have another beer before my time ran out.

I was heading for the stairs when a door to my left swung open. The music was suddenly ridiculously loud, so bloody loud you'd have to shout to be heard above it.

A boy slouched out into the corridor. He was about seventeen, and absolutely vast. He wasn't fat, though: it was all muscle and physical confidence. I remember thinking he should have been in the First Fifteen at his school because no one would ever dare tackle him. He'd break their neck. Later, I discovered that he had been, and nobody did, because he certainly would.

White-blond hair curled over where his collar would have been if he'd had one, and his eyes were an extraordinary colour. I had an impression of blue and green and even yellow, edged with moody bronze lashes. His eyebrows almost met in the middle, his nose had been broken at least once in his life, and his shoulders were slumped down in that aggressively slobby way teenagers have. He was wearing a baggy tee-shirt and jeans, great wide things that were falling off him and showing stripy boxer shorts. A musky, dusty smoke billowed after him out of his room. I sniffed. I couldn't believe my nose.

He stopped dead when he noticed me, scowled as though I was nicking the silver, then stomped back into his room and slammed the door, muffling the music.

I found Lucy in the sitting room. She was balanced on a footstool laying the fire, with a glass of wine beside her.

'Jake! Come on in. It gets chilly when the sun goes down and the mist comes up off the estuary.'

'Can I help?'

'All under control, thanks. I've brought you another beer. There, on the table.'

I lowered myself into an armchair. It was made of worn, patched leather, and a little puff of dust flew up from it. 'I think I've just met your brother.'

She tore a sheet of newspaper in half, her lips twitching. 'Matt? Lucky you.'

'He's smoking dope in his bedroom.'

She pretended to look prim, but her smile widened. 'I'd be surprised if he wasn't.'

'Does your dad know?'

She just snorted merrily and carried on scrunching up newspaper. I looked around the room. On a writing table beside the fireplace I spotted a collection of photographs in silver frames, and I leaned over for a closer look.

There was a little dark-haired girl, presumably Lucy, sledging in the arms of an expensive-looking brunette. I held it up. The woman wore a ski jacket and wraparound shades. 'This your mother, Luce?'

She glanced up. 'Yep. That's Mum.'

I knew her mother was dead. She'd mentioned it once or twice, but I'd never asked her any more.

'I think I've told you,' said Lucy. 'She died when I was four.'

'D'you remember her?'

'Um, yes, in a shadowy way. She had a brain tumour and it all happened very fast. We were living in Germany at the time.' She piled kindling onto the paper, pressing it down. 'So we had a nanny instead of a mother.' The words were spoken with finality, as though the subject was at an end, but after a few seconds she added, 'And the nanny was Deborah.'

She flicked a lighter, holding it to the paper. Surprised, I turned back to the photographs. There was Matt wearing a waxed jacket and holding up two dead rabbits with a smug look on his face; Matt holding up a dead trout with exactly the same smug look on his face; and Lucy and Matt, aged perhaps eleven and four, on a beach. They were posing before an enormous sandcastle, and they both had smug looks on their faces. There was also a picture of Perry in uniform, looking rather distinguished.

Then I saw a photo hiding at the back, and picked it up. A youngish woman in a straw hat gazed warmly out at me, her mouth puckered into a smile, her eyebrows slightly raised as though she was laughing with the photographer. She had a little constellation of freckles scattered across her cheekbones, and wisps of fair hair escaped from under the hat. Behind her, I thought I could make out a white sail and brilliantly turquoise water.

'Wow! Who's this?'

'Which one? Oh.' Lucy yawned. 'That's Deborah. I took it, actually, a few years ago. We were on a sailing holiday in the Greek Islands.'

I took another look at the woman in the photo. She couldn't have been much older than thirty. Although she was tanned to a light gold, her nose was peeling slightly, just across the bridge, leaving a small white patch. It was a delicate nose, and her eyes were the same blue-green as the glittering water around her. Blue-green, with yellow flames around the pupils. Like Matt's.

'I imagined someone . . .'

'Older?'

'Well.' I stared at the freckled, smiling face. 'I certainly didn't expect her to look like *this*. She's a kitten.'

'Cat, more like,' Lucy said coldly. 'It's out of date. And it doesn't do justice to her innate ghastliness.'

'What's ghastly about her?'

'Where do I start?' Lucy picked up a poker, jabbing it moodily into her smoking pyre. 'She's the most dishonest and manipulative person I've ever met. Got herself pregnant, then Dad had to marry her. A cheap trick, don't you think?'

'Oldest in the book.'

'And now she's frolicking around Africa when she's needed *here*.' To emphasise the word, Lucy aimed a deathblow at a poor, blameless log. Sparks flew up the chimney.

The woman in the picture laughed out at me. I tried to imagine her—the scheming stepmother—arranging flowers and polishing the silver before setting off to collar an African bandit. I was still wrestling with this image when I heard a door slam, and Matt came clomping down the stairs. Even his footsteps were sulky. He slumped into the living room, ignoring us both, snatched up the TV remote, and threw himself full-length onto the sofa.

'Matt, I gather you've met Jake.' Lucy nodded in my direction.

'Uh.' He didn't even look at me. Straightened his arm, squinted down it and took aim at the television as though it were a pheasant and the remote was his shotgun.

Lucy clapped her hands impatiently, like a teacher. 'Say hello to Jake, Matthew.'

He honoured me with a single glance, in which he managed to convey the most sincere contempt.

'Uh. 'Lo.' He squeezed his trigger, and the TV sprang into life.

'It's like living with Neanderthal Man,' huffed Lucy, and stood up. Giving his leg a good-natured smack with a rolled-up newspaper, she headed off to the kitchen.

I made up my mind to try and have a conversation with this creature. After all, he was human.

'Hey, Matt, I see there's a photo of your mother.'

'Yeah?' He yawned, flicking through the channels.

'This one, here.'

Flick, flick.

'Looks like you.'

He didn't bother to break eye contact with the screen. '*Her*? Fuck off. My arse she does. Fucking nothing like me.'

I gave up. I really didn't need to get to know him. Perhaps he wasn't human at all. Instead, I settled back and stared at the screen too. I'm a bit of a channel flicker myself; I can watch four at once, no problem. Used to drive Anna spare.

Suddenly, on a sports network, I spotted the Big Match. I'd completely forgotten it was on. The All Blacks were playing South Africa that very night, and the first half was almost over. Hell, how could I have forgotten the Big Match?

'Stop there, mate,' I said. 'I really want to watch this.'

And he actually did. In the next hour or so we were almost companionable, in a monosyllabic kind of a way. I spent quite a lot of the time dancing around about an inch in front of the screen, screaming, '*Go*, man! Go, go! Yes!' while Matt craned his head around me and yelled, 'Lousy pass, you fuckin' cretin!' Lucy and Perry came in from time to time and watched too, and mouth-watering cooking smells floated in from the kitchen.

The Springboks played elegantly but not well enough, and they lost just in time for dinner. And it was then, as we sat around Perry's kitchen table, that my day *really* got weird.

Chapter Four

By the time they came to eat, David had wordlessly confiscated the gin bottle from his father. Christopher, however, had already downed enough to blind a newt. He'd slid into the bluff, old-sea-dog phase of his descent into drunkenness. As they crossed the hall he was holding forth to Elizabeth, in clipped, military tones, about the dangers of rounding the Horn in a gale.

Leila listened to his bluster with half-hearted sympathy. Retirement had been a sort of death for Christopher. He was rusting away like a derelict ship, beached and abandoned, lying on its shattered keel and dreaming of the glory days.

David swiftly surveyed the table. 'Corkscrew,' he muttered, and headed off to the kitchen.

Christopher darted into the seat next to Leila's, while Hilda sank down opposite and began to make conversation with Angus. 'Do you have a family?' she asked, arranging herself precisely in her chair.

Angus glanced at his wife. 'Indeed,' he replied. 'I have four. A gaggle of grandkids, too, who come and destroy the rectory every school holidays.'

There was something odd about the exchange. Curious, Leila was replaying it in her mind when Christopher began to whisper, his breath hovering by the glinting hoop of her earring. She edged towards Angus's comfortable bulk at the far end, but her father-in-law was not to be put off.

'You know what your lovely name means, don't you, Leila?'

Leila looked bored. 'Yes, I do actually, Christopher. You've told me several times.'

'Dark as night. Dark . . . as . . . *night*.'

Leila leaped to her feet and lifted the lid on the casserole. *The man is obscene*, she thought incredulously, as she snatched up the ladle. *Getting worse, too. I bet he was a southern plantation owner in another incarnation, harassing his slaves and fathering their children.* For several seconds she battled with her desire to spill a ladleful of scalding gravy onto his bald patch—she could see it gleaming, even though he'd brushed his hair across it. Ooh, sorry, Christopher! *So* clumsy. Still, they can work wonders with plastic surgery these days.

Looking up, Leila caught Elizabeth's eye. The rector's wife taught in the local secondary school. In fact, she was their longest surviving member of staff, surpassed in longevity only by the janitor, who was deaf and therefore had an advantage. Her hair was pewter-coloured and cut like a helmet, but somehow she managed to look young and alert. Her glance whisked from Leila to Christopher and back again, and then she winked. It was the merest flicker, but it made Leila smile.

'A stew!' tinkled Hilda, as David reappeared and began to open another bottle. 'Leila, I don't know how you do it, in that tiny kitchen. Is it a Caribbean recipe?'

Leila raised one eyebrow. 'I don't think so.'

'Mum!' David rounded on his mother, exasperation twisting the strong, spare lines of his face. 'You know perfectly well Leila isn't from the West Indies.'

'Nigeria, isn't it?' asked Elizabeth.

'Yes, Nigeria. Although I was born and bred in Peckham.' Leila regarded her mother-in-law mischievously. 'But perhaps we all look alike to you, Hilda?'

Hilda's Persian-cat eyes snapped wide open.

'Leila's father was a lecturer at the School of Oriental and African Studies,' David explained hurriedly, filling glasses. 'Magnificent man, Ayotunde. Terrifyingly clever. He's retired, but they keep asking him to come back and give guest lectures.'

Elizabeth played the game, carrying the conversation in her sandpaper voice. 'When did your parents come to this country, Leila?'

'In the sixties.' Leila handed her a plate. 'But they're still very much West African at heart. Civil war was brewing in Nigeria at the time . . . Angus, is this enough for you? . . . My mother lost a brother in the crossfire.'

'Have they been back?'

'Oh, yes. Often. Their families are still there, mostly. Mum and Dad follow the politics avidly, read newspapers online, keep in touch with everyone. And they're ardent supporters of the Nigerian football team.'

'They're going over soon, actually,' said David. 'For a cousin's wedding. When are they off, Leila?'

'Mid November, lucky things. They'll be gone about a month.' Leila replaced the lid on the casserole dish. 'Angus. Will you say grace?'

'Certainly.' Angus folded authoritative hands. 'Bless, Lord, this food to our use, and us to thy service.'

'Amen,' breathed Leila, sitting down. 'That's the starting gun.'

As if on cue, the trill of the telephone wafted gaily in from the hall. David winced, met Leila's eyes, then pushed back his chair and went to answer it. A short time later he stuck his head around the door.

'Gatecrashers at the youth club,' he announced, shrugging into an overcoat. 'Getting a bit out of hand. I'd better nip down.'

Angus stood up, but David waved him away. 'Please. Carry on.'

Leila followed him into the hall, sliding her arms around his waist, imprisoning him. 'What if I refuse to let you go?'

He chuckled. 'I'd look pretty funny, walking down the street like a mutant ninja turtle with you attached to my back.'

'Come home in one piece, then,' she grumbled, releasing him. She reached up to grip his nose. 'That's an order.'

'Don't worry,' said Angus, when she rejoined them. 'They won't mess with David.' He glanced at Christopher. 'Your son's already brought so much to this parish, you know. Started a football team, and they're queuing up to join.'

'I'm sure they won't mess with him physically,' Leila struggled not to sound petulant, 'but do they have to interrupt *all* of his meals? You'll help yourselves to the rice, won't you? That *is* a Nigerian dish, actually.'

'Oh, yes. I'll help myself, Miss Dark-as-Night,' crooned Christopher under his breath. 'If you'll step into the kitchen with me.' He reached across her to grasp the wine bottle, and his forearm brushed hers.

Leila swung round to face him, eyes glinting dangerously. 'Sorry, Christopher?'

He smirked uncertainly, and his glance darted to Hilda and back.

'I didn't quite catch that,' Leila insisted, her voice slightly too loud. 'Could you just repeat it for me?'

Christopher shrugged and looked sullen.

Angus intervened, diplomatically. 'You can both be justifiably proud of your son,' he remarked genially, slicing through the awkward silence. 'This is a pretty tough parish. The last curate didn't last the distance.'

'What makes it such a difficult job?' asked Hilda, covertly glaring at her husband.

'It's vast,' replied Angus. 'And like all inner city parishes there's poverty and racial tension and all that comes with it. The churchyard gets used by bored teenagers as a meeting place. They smoke, drink, sniff glue, get one another pregnant—all the usual things. We're fighting a losing battle against vandalism.' He paused, taking a mouthful of casserole. 'Delicious, Leila!'

After another moment's silence, Elizabeth took up the baton. 'Breaks people's hearts. They spend more than they can afford on a carved marble angel for their baby son or whatever, and it's smashed. Only last night, an old fellow arrived at the rectory in tears. He'd laid a bunch of red roses on his wife's grave—her favourite flowers—cost half his week's pension, and within hours they'd been ground into the dirt.'

'Ever catch 'em at it?' asked Hilda.

'Ah.' Angus held up a triumphant finger. 'Yes, the odd win. Last summer I caught some boys in the act of lighting a fire in a litter bin. Two ran away, but one stayed to face the music. That bit of courage changed his life. He's since joined the choir and become a legendary goalkeeper in David's new team. Quite literally, David is his hero.'

'Then I'd keep a very close watch on the church silver if I were you,' advised Hilda, with a knowing curl to her lips.

Leila met Elizabeth's startled eye. 'Hilda's a magistrate,' she explained.

Elizabeth's gaze ran over Hilda before she nodded, coolly. 'I see. Well, I don't think there's any need to lock away the silver. We trust Kevin. He's a good lad, getting confirmed after Christmas. Lovely voice, too.'

Hilda smiled. 'I admire your forgiving nature. But actually, he's an arsonist. And he always will be.'

By the time Leila brought in the fruit salad, Christopher had drunk himself into a wheezing, dangerous silence. He seemed to be sulking. Hilda, by contrast, had stepped smartly into her stride.

'People talk about education,' she mused, passing the cream jug across David's empty place to Elizabeth. 'You can't just take a child and educate it and hope it will behave differently. No. In my experience, it will always go back to its genetic roots.'

Elizabeth chuckled, but Angus looked appalled. His mouth actually fell open.

'Surely you don't mean that, Hilda? You're not suggesting that some folk have no choice but to be criminals? That they're trapped in their subculture, prisoners of their genes, whatever they do?'

Hilda blinked sunburst eyelashes. 'Well, of course they have a *choice*. They have a choice when they think about burgling a house, but they'll always choose to go ahead and do it anyway.'

'Whoa there,' cried Angus. He loved a debate. 'If they'll inevitably make that decision they don't really have a choice, do they? Actually,' he paused, cheerfully conducting an imaginary orchestra with his spoon, 'in my view, people are largely a product of their experiences. There's a genetic component in personality, I'll accept that, but experience is the make or break. If kids grow up in, say, Priory Park Farm—what a bizarre name for a sixties housing estate—their experiences may be pretty shattering. Some of them—not all—go off the rails. But they can change, with the right input. Is locking them up the right input?'

Hilda fluttered a pink-nailed hand. 'My point is that it doesn't matter what you—or poor David—do for them. You're wasting your energy. It's nature, not nurture.'

'Research doesn't really support you though, does it, Hilda?' Elizabeth was smiling bemusedly. 'Children who've been adopted—'

'Ah, *adoption*!' Hilda rested her chin on clasped hands. This was clearly her pet subject. 'I've seen it time and again. A young person from a good family, a *good* family, comes before us. He's got into drugs, stolen from his parents and mugged people. The family sit at the back weeping, the lawyers wave their arms around, and then it'll turn out he was adopted.'

At this, Leila slammed down her spoon.

Elizabeth glanced sharply at her. 'Children are adopted for all sorts of reasons, I believe,' she said hastily. 'No need to assume their birth family's bad in any way. Perhaps this isn't the time, though. Tell me, what brings you people to Birmingham? Have you just come up to visit David and Leila, or . . . ?'

Hilda seemed delighted to be asked this question. 'No, no. We're on our way down from the Lake District, actually. Staying in a motel tonight. Michael—that's our younger son—has a holiday cottage on Windermere.'

'You have other children?'

'For my sins! Michael and Monica. They spoil us rotten, can't do enough for us. We've just spent a week with Michael and his bride, Alicia.'

'How lovely!'

'Mm. They were married this summer. Stunning girl. And . . .' She glanced coyly at her husband. 'I think I could make the announcement now, Christopher? I've kept it secret all evening.'

Christopher shrugged with bad grace. His cheeks were a lace of red veins, his eyes heavy and bloodshot. He didn't look at all dapper any more.

'*Well*. We're so thrilled.' Hilda took a deep, blissful breath. 'Alicia is pregnant. Already! And it's twins!'

Angus and Elizabeth made enthusiastic noises. Leila knew she ought to rejoice for Michael, but she felt her insides twist into jealous little knots. She couldn't help it.

'Fantastic!' she said, placing a hopeful hand on her own stomach.

Angus cleared his throat. 'Will they be your first grandchildren?'

'Oh, no. Monica has two beautiful little ones. Freya and Charles. My goodness, I'm a proud grandmother.'

'She dotes on them,' wheezed Christopher, and showed his teeth with malicious satisfaction. He drained his glass, lowering it unsteadily onto the table. 'Spoils them like nobody's business. And *you* people—' he nodded with exaggerated courtesy in Leila's direction—'had better get on with it.'

Before he had finished the sentence Leila was on her feet, her chair smashing to the floor behind her. 'You know perfectly well,' she hissed, 'that we have been trying to *get on with it* for ten years!'

Mercifully, the front door slammed. The next moment David was in the room, rubbing his hands.

'Freezing out there.' He grinned at Leila, then focused upon her more intently, his good humour faltering a little. He stepped closer, eyes darting suspiciously between his wife and his parents. 'What's going on?'

Elizabeth spoke first. 'I wholeheartedly recommend the fruit salad, David. And charge your glass, because your parents have some happy news for you.'

In the kitchen, as she savagely jammed the plug into its hole, Leila's teeth fairly chattered with rage. 'The old *bastard*.'

'Shhh,' giggled Elizabeth, making an anguished face. 'Thin walls.'

Leila scowled, but she dropped her voice to a furious whisper.

'That wasn't tactless, it was completely deliberate. And as for her! She knows damned well we've been trying to adopt for years. Bitchy, even by her standards.'

'Mm.' Elizabeth shot a furtive glance at the door. 'He was all over you, and she was fuming. It was revenge.'

'It's not as if I encourage him,' protested Leila, pulling on a pair of rubber gloves with a snap.

Elizabeth picked up a tea towel. 'Is he—' She broke off, holding up a warning finger. They waited, listening, as the rest of the party crossed the hall. The sitting-room door shut, dulling the voices.

'Is he always so . . .'

'Sleazy?' Leila turned on both taps and then jumped back as a jet of water ricocheted off a spoon, soaking her shirt. 'Only after he's been drinking.

They tell me he was quite an impressive character in his prime. You know, a romantic, half-mythical figure who turned up every few months, bringing swashbuckling stories, and the smell of the sea on his clothes.'

'Ah. And then he retired, and lost all his magic.'

Leila squeezed out far too much washing-up liquid. 'One minute he's somebody. The next he's a nuisance, getting under Hilda's stilettos. No cronies down the local, no hobbies, no one.' She slid a pile of cutlery into the water. 'So he drinks. And the more his body crumbles into old age—sunspots, aches, fading hair—the more he tries to prove his virility. Ageing must be awful for the vain, don't you think?'

'Awful for everybody.' Elizabeth shook the soap suds from a handful of knives as Hilda's laughter jangled through the airwaves. 'I can't quite work *her* out, either. I don't think she's stupid, is she?'

'Not at all.' Leila heaved a dripping pot onto the draining board. 'She ran the family single-handedly as well as managing her rather posh dress shop in Northampton. And she's said to be very sharp as a magistrate. It's common knowledge that she liked Christopher best when he was sending pay cheques from twelve thousand miles away. She's nobody's fool.'

'Where's she from? There's a sort of lilt in her speech . . . I can't quite place it.'

'That's Tyneside.' Leila raised an eyebrow. 'She'd be horrified you've asked because she thinks she's cast off her roots. Her father was a ship builder. Asbestos got him. Her mum's ninety, broad Geordie, lives in a home in Gateshead.'

Elizabeth whistled silently.

'David's the apple of her eye,' muttered Leila, dropping her voice still further. 'Her eldest. She's never got over the triple whammy. First he married me—I'm hardly going to look the thing on the court and social pages, am I? Not quite the peaches and cream. More Death by Chocolate.'

'Delectable.'

'Then I failed to come up with the goods as far as grandchildren are concerned. Finally—and this was the last straw—David threw away his glittering career in poisons. She thinks I encouraged him.'

'And did you?'

'Certainly not! After all, *I* stood to lose by it financially, not *her*. And—let's face it—not exactly macho, is it, the dog collar thing? You're hardly the envy of all the other wives.' She thought for a moment. 'Except the kinky ones who like to dress up.'

'Tarts and vicars,' said Elizabeth, deadpan. 'Angus makes a great tart.'

They fell silent, moving quietly, listening to Hilda's tweeting. 'Dear Monica's throwing a party for our ruby wedding anniversary!'

'That's the sister?' asked Elizabeth.

'Monica.' Leila chuckled. 'She has a kind heart and a big, bossy bottom. She's a professional party organiser. Voice like a hospital matron.'

'A professional *what?*'

'Party organiser. People pay her to arrange their bashes from start to finish. If you pay her enough—and you'll need to take out a second mortgage—she'll do the marquee, the band, the flowers, the food, the portaloos, the staff, the photographer and a taxi for when Uncle Harold passes out. You name it, Pertwell Party Solutions will provide it.'

'Goodness.'

'She's flat out. I don't know whether Freya and Charlie have ever actually *met* her, but she buys them stuff instead.'

Leila paused, brow creased, hands resting in the grey warmth of the water. *Why bother? Why turn them out like biscuits, and then palm them off on a nanny?*

Elizabeth paused in front of the fridge, looking at the same photographs which had intrigued Jacinta. 'Are these your parents, on the London Eye?'

Leila gazed affectionately at the faces in the picture. Fola and Ayotunde, waving from their bubble, surrounded by their dynasty. Leila and David were just visible at the back of the group.

'Ah, that was fun. We took them up for Dad's seventieth.'

Elizabeth bent closer to the picture. 'They look so young. What did they say when you first brought David home?'

'A white boyfriend?' Leila shrugged. 'Race wasn't allowed to be an issue in our household. We were always proud of our heritage, but never to the exclusion of others'. The first time David came home he talked football with my brothers and African literature with my parents, and he's been one of the family ever since.'

'They know a good thing when they see one.'

'They do.' Leila smiled. 'Once—just once—Dad got all serious and warned us to expect hostility as a mixed race couple. And he was right, but it's been nothing we can't handle.'

Another silence. The draining board was almost empty before Leila spoke again. 'Actually, childlessness can be a greater barrier than race.'

Elizabeth was absent for a short time, pewter helmet bent over a wineglass. She seemed to be deep in some memory of her own.

'I know what you mean.' She ran her cloth carefully around the stem.

Leila tugged at the plug, watching the foamy water as it spiralled away. The hope had trickled away, just like the water: round, and round, and down the plughole. Glug.

'It's my fault, you know,' she said. 'It's an inescapable fact.'

Elizabeth had the sense not to protest at this.

Leila held out her arms. 'What's the point in having childbearing hips and page-three knockers if you can't deliver? Mind you . . .' She hesitated, eyeing her friend's calm features, and then put a finger to her lips. 'Shh, don't say anything to David . . . I'm pretty hopeful, at this moment.'

'Because?'

The sitting-room door swung open, and Hilda was in the hall: first her footsteps and then her curiosity. 'Have you two been kidnapped?'

Swiftly, Leila crossed the kitchen and switched on the kettle. 'No, no. Just making the coffee!'

Once Hilda was safely out of earshot again, Elizabeth raised her eyebrows. 'Because?'

Leila's eyes gleamed. 'I'm a day or two late and I feel . . . well, you know.'

'Do I?'

'Different. Very, very different. They told us it wasn't completely impossible, just increasingly unlikely as I grow older. We stopped actively trying ages ago.'

Elizabeth dried her hands, her keen gaze fixed upon the younger woman's face. 'Have you done a test?'

Unsmiling, sober, Leila rubbed her hands together. It was a gesture of anxiety, of longing, of terror. 'I've got one. I'll do it tonight, after David's asleep. Ooh! It would be unbelievable, after all this time. Unbelievable!'

The kettle began to sigh and gurgle. Frantically, as if wounded, Leila screwed up her eyes and squeezed the back of a kitchen chair.

'Touch wood. Touch wood. Maybe there is a God, after all.'

Chapter Five

Matt sat down at the dinner table without a word and started shovelling it in as though he'd just escaped from a health farm. Perry poured me a glass of wine and asked about New Zealand. He seemed to be going out of his way to be nice to me.

'I gather you're not planning on going back for a while?'

'Probably not.'

'D'you call home often? Feel free to use our telephone.'

'Not a lot.' I tried the wine. It was fantastic. 'Mum gets a bit emotional. I had to hang up on her one time because she wouldn't stop crying and it wasn't much of a conversation.'

'Why was she crying?'

'She hadn't heard from me for a while. Thought I'd been blown up by a terrorist or something. Silly woman.'

'Your poor mother!' Lucy was shocked. 'You should be ashamed, Jake.'

I was. Poor Mum. She was paying for *his* crimes. Three minutes later, I'd phoned her back.

Perry was watching me. 'When were you last home?'

'I don't go back.'

'What, not once in . . . ?'

'Seventeen years. I tell a lie: I went over when Gran turned ninety. The drums were beating and the whole family had to front up in their best bibs and tuckers. I stayed five days and it was as though I'd never been away.'

'That's lovely,' said Lucy.

'Not very.' I felt my jaw clenching. 'My old man was still a bastard.'

She laughed as though I was joking, but I wasn't. I have a picture of Dad in my head, and I take it everywhere with me, and I always will. He's frothing with rage, marching down to the kennels, with me hanging off his arm and trying to drag him back, and my feet swinging clear off the ground.

I hate my father. I'd like to kill him.

'Safe over there, though,' persisted Perry. 'No one wants to make war on New Zealand, holy or otherwise.'

I put down my glass. 'Perry, you don't want to be *that* safe. A cuddly hamster in a cage is safe. No cats to eat it, plenty of grub, nice wheel to run around on. He'll probably live to be about a hundred in hamster years. Doesn't make his life fulfilling. He doesn't wake up every morning tingling with zest for the new day.'

Perry's face had gone blank. I'd offended him, but I couldn't see how. Lucy lightly touched his hand.

'He doesn't mean it, Dad. Jake secretly longs to go home.'

I snorted, and Perry topped up our glasses. 'You come from the South Island?'

'Yep. The back blocks, under the mountains.'

'I gather it's very beautiful there.'

'Yeah, it's beautiful all right. When you're mustering sheep and you ride up the hillside just on dawn, it's pretty magical. Just the calls of the native birds. You don't want to come down again, ever.'

'Will you take me up there, Jake?' asked Lucy, half-seriously.

I grinned at her, helping myself to the salt. 'Then it hits you just how bloody still and silent it is, and you gallop away and hop on the first plane out.'

'When did you leave home?' asked Perry. He'd got up, and was messing about with a pudding in the oven.

'Left the farm at seventeen, headed off to uni. Jesse—my older brother—moved into the shepherd's cottage and became Dad's partner. He's the most eligible bachelor for miles around, but it doesn't get him anywhere because every girl with two legs and half a brain left long ago.'

'I never knew you had a brother.' Lucy was staring at me.

'We're not close,' I said. 'We were as little kids, but we went in different directions. Chalk and cheese. There's too much of my dad in old Jesse.'

'Do try the peas, I grew them myself,' urged Perry. 'And what do you intend to do now? Lucy tells me you find yourself a free man, unexpectedly.'

'Well.' I took a spoonful of his peas, glad to change the subject. 'I never intended to stay in London. I was twenty-three and planned on working my way around the world. But my temporary job at Stanton's turned into a permanent one, and the bonuses started rolling in. I just didn't have the balls to turn down all that cash. I sold my soul.'

'The good old days,' Lucy remarked sourly. 'Before the bonus became an endangered species.'

'So I stayed,' I said. 'And stayed, and stayed. Until it was nearly too late.'

'Too late?'

'Nearly. I've had a narrow escape, really, because I almost got stuck in Basingstoke with a wife and kids and a sofa to think about.' I shivered. 'Might as well be dead.'

The kettle was hissing merrily away on the stove. Lucy and Perry exchanged a glance, and I had a nasty feeling I'd said the wrong thing again. Perhaps Perry was born and bred in Basingstoke.

'This chicken thing is great,' I burbled.

'Thank you. It's very easy.'

I smiled. 'You sound like my mother. She always swears things are easy, then spurts out a recipe you'd need a degree in catering to understand. It's a funny thing though, because she hates cooking. She told me once: she hates cooking and gardening and sewing, and she always has. But she's done nothing else her whole life.'

Perry seemed to be deep in thought. Matt filled up his plate and started refuelling all over again: probably had the munchies, after that whacky baccy.

All of a sudden, Perry stirred. 'You know, Jake, I believe you could do me a service.'

'Er . . . ?'

He trickled another couple of inches into my glass. 'Yes, you could. I have a small difficulty, and I think you can help. It'll be . . . *entertaining* for you.'

'Sure. What's the problem?' I imagined that, perhaps, the light bulb in the bathroom had blown, and Perry didn't like to climb the stepladder.

'Lucy will have mentioned my wife, Deborah?'

Mrs Harrison, the harridan? 'Um, a bit. All good.'

Matt guffawed before making a grab for thirds. His father ignored him.

'Deborah was last heard of in Mombasa, but she hasn't made contact for some time. That in itself isn't so very surprising. She'll be busy, and communication can be tricky in these remote areas. But we need to find her. Urgently.'

'Why?'

'Do you mind if I don't tell you that? It's a private, family thing.'

'Is someone ill?' It seemed the most likely explanation.

Perry held up his hands and shook his head. 'You could be in Mombasa within days. It's not a large community; I'm sure you'll pick up her trail.'

'Why don't you go, then?'

Matt laughed again, until he choked. Lucy glared at him as though wishing she had a remote control button with which to turn him off. No one answered me, so I tried again.

'Seriously, why don't you go, Perry? I mean, isn't it a bit unusual, sending a total stranger to look for your wife?'

He got to his feet and started collecting the plates, and I stood up to help. I really thought he might be joking. Matt was still chortling away to himself.

Eventually, Perry shut the dishwasher and leaned against the stove. His cheeks were quite sunken, I thought, and he stared with a little too much intensity. It was a bit creepy, to be honest. But then he smiled, and his eyes looked wearier than ever, and somehow he had me on his side. For the first time, I could imagine him loping across the desert: the exhausted, charismatic officer whose men would follow him anywhere.

'I'd like to go myself, Jake, but I simply can't afford the time. I've several deadlines coming up. I also have Matt at home.'

I was shaking my head, trying to make it work properly. It was spinning a bit. I felt as though I'd been dropped into a play but didn't know the lines.

The telephone rang, and Perry exited stage left to answer it. Once he'd gone, Lucy leaned towards me over the back of her chair.

'Please, Jake. I know it's a lot to ask, but you've absolutely nothing better to do.'

'Thanks.'

'Well, you haven't.'

I pondered for a moment. 'I thought you said this was typical of your stepmother, and you hoped a lion had got her in the Serengeti?'

'You know damned well I wasn't serious about the lion.'

'No, I don't know. Have you tried the Kenyan police?'

She gestured impatiently. 'Do try to be realistic.'

'It's not me that's unrealistic. It's you lot. You're off your bloody trolleys. This is why you got me down here, isn't it?' The penny had finally dropped. 'To send me off to look for some globetrotting housewife so I can get her to come back and restock the freezer.'

'Yeah.' Matt slapped the table. 'We're running out of those meat pies she does.'

Lucy pushed herself to her feet, stood behind her brother, and rested her hands on his strapping shoulders. 'Please?' Brother and sister stared at me expectantly.

'Look, guys,' I whispered. 'What's the big secret? Is Perry ill? Is he dying? I can see he looks bloody rough.'

'You see,' Matt burped, gently. 'She makes this unbelievable strawberry ice cream. One bite and you're in heaven. I can't live without it.'

Lucy ruffled his hair.

'Gerroff.' He squirmed, dodging her fingers.

'You're all mad,' I said.

Perry reappeared a couple of minutes later. 'Don't decide immediately, Jake,' he rumbled generously, slapping me on the back. 'Take your time. You've got the whole weekend to think about it, and then we can book your ticket first thing on Monday morning. Okay? Now. Try a dram of *this*.'

I'd imagined he might be the sort to turn in early with a good book and a mug of cocoa, but he slammed a bottle of Scotch onto the table with an air of celebration. It was going to be a long night.

Chapter Six

The party broke up early. Elizabeth saw to that, hustling Hilda and Christopher down the wet path and into their car.

'*Phone me*,' mimed the rector's wife to Leila, and David could have sworn she held up crossed fingers.

Once they'd all gone, he slammed the front door and attached the chain. Then he pulled Leila down to sit beside him on the stairs.

'Right. What happened?' With one finger, he drew a line along the strong sweep of her brows. His own powerful hands seemed coarse beside the flowing planes of her face. 'Come on, spit it out.'

Leila's solemnity melted into a slow smile. 'Well, your father's a lecherous old sod, and your mother has all the tact of a charging bull elephant.'

'I know all that. But what . . . ? If I'd lit a match, the entire street would have exploded.'

'Well, first we were treated to Hilda's views on adoption. You know.'

'Oh, dear.' Sighing, he rubbed the back of his neck. 'Yep. All too well.'

'Then there was the news about prissy Alicia's twins.'

'Go on.'

'And as a little extra delight, Christopher suggested *we'd* better get on with it, too. He also spent the evening leering down my front, whispering sweet nothings.'

'Oh, for God's sake!' David's eyebrows drew together. He drew a long breath, holding it, letting the anger catch alight. 'Right, that's it,' he said, getting to his feet. 'Where are they staying?'

Leila didn't move. 'Settle down, Edmunds. You're too old for impetuous rages.'

'No.' David jerked the car keys off their hook. 'I've had enough.'

'It was half a bottle of gin talking.'

He strode to the door and then swung back to face her, his hair falling across his eyes. 'That's no excuse, Leila! He will not get away with insulting you.'

'He didn't get away with it.' Leila stood up, stretching. It was a feline, languorous movement, oddly serene. 'And I don't think he intended to insult me. I wish I'd never told you. I don't need you to gallop around on your white charger. I'm not a damsel in distress.'

David swore under his breath, then abruptly threw both arms around her, shutting his eyes, shutting out the world. She felt unbearably valuable tonight.

'What was the problem with the youth club?' she asked, and he felt the warmth of her hands on his back, under his shirt.

'No problem.' His resolve was weakening. 'Don't change the subject.'

'Come on,' she coaxed, removing one hand to tug at the keys in his fist. 'It's late, and we're going to bed.'

Upstairs, he hovered, eyeing her as she folded clothes and strolled in and out of the bathroom. She moved lightly, competently, butter-coloured lamplight caressing the smooth, high curve of her cheekbones. He rummaged for words.

'I keep telling you, Leila. It's *you* that's important, not the family we might have together. If no kids come along, I'll never have to share you with anyone. Lucky me!'

She threw him one bright glance and then began to sing to herself. David knew the song, a lullaby from Nigeria. She had a mellow, resonant voice, like espresso coffee. It made his throat constrict.

As Leila sang, a smile lifted the warm curve of her mouth. She seemed luminous with some secret pleasure, as though it was his birthday tomorrow and hidden in the cupboard she had the best present ever.

'You seem very pleased with yourself, Leila Edmunds,' he said. 'What're you up to?'

'Nothing, nothing.' She twitched out her earrings and dropped them onto the dressing table with a small clatter. 'I had a chat with Elizabeth. Cheered me up.'

David watched as she took out cotton wool and tipped lotion onto it. 'C'mon, I know you. You've thought of something, and it's made you happy. Quite a feat, after an evening like that one.'

Leila crossed the room and poured herself under the duvet. 'Can we *please* get some sleep? Your parents have finished me off.'

David scowled. 'I still think I should've—'

'And no doubt you'll be up at the crack of dawn, crashing about like a rhinoceros.'

'Oh. Yes, I will, I'm afraid. There's an early team meeting tomorrow.'

'Lights out, then.' She stretched up to flick the switch.

David brushed his teeth, changed and slid in beside her. He reached out to touch her face, but she was already asleep.

For a while he lay in the dark, drifting, letting time flow over him. She was still the same, really, after all these years and all this trouble; still the bossy, vital girl he'd first met beside the river.

His crew had rowed together for more than a season before they lost their coxswain: a Japanese postgraduate, light and competent; his father had gone bankrupt, and he'd rushed back to Tokyo.

The four put up notices and bribed every girl they knew—and the skinnier men—but no one would take on the job. The crew spent their evenings in pubs and student bars, drowning their sorrows and eyeing up Japanese postgraduates.

Then, one evening, Joshua had news of a breakthrough. 'Third year, pharmacy. Weighs less than eight stone, apparently,' he crowed, ordering another round. 'She's keen, and she's done it before.'

'But is she a hottie?' Rhys wiped the froth from his new, rather inadequate moustache. 'Yukio wasn't much to look at.'

'I hear she's gorgeous. Nigerian. Vocalist for the Bath Beat Chicks.'

'Wow. That girl?' Tom paused in the act of murdering a handful of peanuts. 'I've seen her in action. That *is* exotic.'

They waited at the river the following morning. Rhys had even put on a clean tee-shirt for the occasion, and Tom was fingering his designer stubble. She arrived on a man's bicycle, speeding up to the boathouse in a whirr of spokes and nimbly undoing her helmet as she leaned her bike against the wall.

'Now,' she announced, turning hypnotic, almost-black eyes upon them. The early light glinted on her bare shoulders. 'I've heard all about you four—your reputation goes before you. I'm here to cox, and under no circumstances whatsoever will I become a notch on that kitchen wall of yours. Got it? Good. Where's the boat?'

They fell in love with her. They couldn't help it. She was utterly in control, crouched in the stern. Her hair was twisted into dozens of braids that fell over her shoulders. They were held off her face by brilliantly coloured bands of cloth, revealing delicate ears. She wore inspired, off-the-wall clothes. For training, she sported flimsy white vests that glowed against the dark lustre of her skin. These tended to become transparent when she was wet, which may have explained the crew's cheerful insistence that training continue even when summer storms drenched them all. In those days she had an hourglass figure in miniature; David was sure he could have joined his hands around her waist. She was noisy, with a proud, confident energy, and she treated them with friendly disrespect, like brothers.

They were careful with her, though. Nobody so much as touched her, unless you counted that time on her birthday when they'd all picked her up and hurled her into the river. There was an unspoken rule: leave her alone. Don't rock the boat.

They met at the boathouse on glittering summer mornings, when ragged mist rose off the water and other students were just crawling into bed. Sometimes the coach would ride along the path on a bicycle, yelling. Leila folded herself into the stern, her chin up. Whenever someone lost the rhythm she'd know instantly and would hurl insults down the boat. David was mesmerised by the sweep of her eyes, gazing past the rowers, guiding them. At weekends they'd all go on to the pub afterwards and swap outrageous stories, sitting at picnic tables by the river. They'd nag her to sing for them, and—if they bought her enough Bacardi—she would.

Obsession crept up on David. It ambushed him. He became a loyal follower of her student band, the Bath Beat Chicks. He looked for her everywhere. Each time they met he had more to ask, more to tell, and afterwards agonised about whether he'd talked too much.

It was a summer that hummed with perfection. One morning, as they pushed away from the bank, he rested for a time and looked around him. The oars dripped calmly, their ripples shimmering under a milky sky. From the dank shade of the willows a family of ducks paddled importantly into the sunlight, and the air bubbled with the smell of weeds and warm mud. Leila sat facing him, laughing at something the coach had said. She alone looked sharply in focus, vivid in the smooth green eddies of the water.

With sudden clarity, David became aware of a new sensation. He felt settled, as though he'd reached some destination. He floated with hope. Presumably, he thought, this is happiness. Happiness. And it's because of her.

Leila caught his eye and smiled briefly, widely. He was in freefall. Then she looked away, but he didn't.

Later, when the others had hurried off to their lectures, he loitered beside his last-legs Beetle, pretending to adjust the wiper blades as she dragged her bicycle out from behind the boathouse. She wheeled it towards him, adjusting her helmet with one hand. The strap made her cheeks bulge. David took a breath and clenched his fists.

'Got time for, um, coffee, Leila?' It came out all right, he thought. Only a little squeaky.

She smiled again, and the sun glittered through the trees, dappling her face. 'I've got all the time in the world,' she replied calmly. Carefully, she set her bike on its stand. Then she stepped forward, took his face in her hands, and kissed him.

And that was that, forever.

They kept it quiet until the end of the season. They met in the evenings and strolled in the water meadows while clouds of gnats floated in the shadows; or drove out of town and hid in the gardens of little country pubs. But David had begun to worry. He'd deceived his best friends. In the last week of term he bought the other three a pint, and they leaned in a row on the bar, gazing at themselves in the engraved mirror behind the cash register.

'Look, guys,' stammered David. 'Um . . . got to tell you.'

'You and Leila?' yelped Joshua.

David nodded, his eyes wide.

The others guffawed heartily while Rhys slapped him on the back. 'Tell us something we don't know, mate. You've got the bug, you poor bastard. It's terminal, no hope for you at all.'

'Look. I'm sorry I didn't—we thought it would be best if—'

'Bloody look after her, or we'll break both your legs.'

'Yeah.' The others nodded. '*And* your arms.'

'And don't you go getting her pregnant,' snarled Tom. 'We'll never find another cox as good as her.'

David smiled, self-conscious and delighted. 'When we *do* have a baby, you three can be its fairy godmothers.'

The trio fell about. 'Poor little bugger!'

They married two summers later, at Leila's home church in Peckham. Joshua was best man. Tom and Rhys offered to be bridesmaids, but Leila said their legs were too hairy so they were witnesses instead. David's family turned up in force, oozing strained politeness; they knew their duty. His mother cried with ludicrous abandon during the ceremony, but then so did Leila's. It was the first and last time that the two women appeared to have anything in common.

At the reception, Joshua, Tom and Rhys persuaded Leila to climb up on the little stage with the band and sing 'Blue Moon'. At the sound of her voice, the rumble and chatter faltered. Heads turned.

'Classy,' whistled the band's vocalist, who'd hopped down and was standing next to David. 'Great delivery. Stylish interpretation. She'll have my job.'

The applause could have taken the roof off. Joshua got down on one knee and begged Leila to divorce David and marry him instead.

David kept a photograph of that day, on his desk. He'd balanced it between the in-tray and the telephone. Without turning his head, he could rest his gaze on Leila's slender form, dark shoulders vivid and smooth above the immaculate white lace of her dress, gold hoops lustrous in her ears. She was laughing, twisting towards him, the sunlight dancing on the graceful cheekbones and the curve of her eyes: a living, glowing sculpture. And he towered beside her, smiling dazedly, a giant to her elf. The scene seemed to shimmer, as if lit by her magical fire.

She wasn't quite so tiny nowadays, at the age of thirty-six. A little more matronly, perhaps. Then again, he didn't have a rower's body any more. And he was still crazy about her.

In those early days they'd easily saved enough for a deposit on a place in Finsbury Park. After all, they had two incomes and no children. One day they'd have a family. They'd even talked about names: Fola, Rose and Ben. But there was no hurry.

Now, in the dark, it seemed that those had been the last days of their youth. They hadn't seen it back then. Time is stealthy when you're young. It's cunning. It pretends to be asleep, but as soon as your back is turned, it leaps up and sprints towards death.

David reached for her hand under the covers. 'I need you,' he said aloud. He thought he felt an answering pressure of her fingers on his, as he sank beneath the surface.

She heard his murmur; felt his hand embrace hers.

He's like a child, she thought, listening to his breathing. When he wakes up—*bang!* Time to be awake. But the moment he lays his head on the pillow, he slides away as though he's never known trouble in his life.

It could be infuriating, especially during the IVF. Three rounds, three cycles of vicious disappointment. But every night David had cheerfully abandoned her, drifted away into his peaceful world and left her lonely and blind in the darkness. Once, overcome by his snoring serenity, she had punched him in the chest, and he'd yelled and sat up, knocking the lamp off the bedside table. She had felt a bleak satisfaction.

Tonight, though, was different. Five more minutes . . . yes.

Leila lowered one foot onto the ground then rolled out of bed, careful not to disturb the duvet, and tiptoed across the landing to the bathroom. The fluorescent light flickered on, and she blinked in the white glare.

She had left her handbag behind the door. There it was. She'd bought it in the Fair Trade shop, years ago; it was made by women in Bangladesh.

She opened it—with difficulty, because the zip was sticking—and her hand closed around the paper bag.

She slid out the familiar blue and white box. No need to read the instructions. She was an old pro at this. At one time it had become a sort of hobby, as though just carrying out the test made the miracle a possibility. But this time was special. This time, she *knew*. Well, she almost knew.

The world was already starting to glitter with the wonder.

Touch wood. Touch wood. She had to touch wood, now, immediately, otherwise something might go wrong. She looked around, panicking slightly, holding her breath until she'd touched some. Bath, shower, mirror . . . bugger, everything was plastic. Her eyes began to pop. The towel rail—surely *that* was made of wood. She clutched it with both hands and then let out her breath in a rush. It made her feel dizzy.

'Blue line, blue line, blue line,' she gabbled. 'If I say it twenty times without breathing, it'll happen . . . *blue line, blue line, blue line* . . . Dear Lord, if you make it happen I promise I'll believe in you once and for all. I'll join the choir. I'll do the altar flowers—how's that for a sacrifice? I'll start a Bible study group and not laugh at the nerdy types in socks and sandals who turn up. I'll give myself to you like David did, honest I will. I promise I promise I promise.'

She tore at the box, forgetting to breathe altogether. Her hands trembled in anticipation and dread.

Please.

The blue and white cardboard fell onto the floor with a dry clatter; empty, irrelevant.

Please.

She began the test. And waited.

And waited, her eyes fixed on the stick like a cat at a mouse hole. The rain exploded into celebratory applause, submerging the window, lending the nearest streetlight a wraithlike halo.

Blue line, blue line, blue line.

It loomed out of nothing. A blue ghost, for a breathless moment; then triumphantly distinct. Silently. Smoothly. And unmistakeably.

Chapter Seven

I mulled over Perry's request. Once the Harrisons had stopped drivelling on about their lost wife and mother, it was a good weekend. Perry spent most of it locked away in his study. Matt put a lot of effort into wrecking both eardrums in his bedroom, although he sloped off somewhere mysterious on Saturday morning. When Lucy and I strolled along the road for a pint in the Dog and Gun, I spotted him waiting at a bus stop.

'Where's *he* going?' I asked, jerking my chin towards the kid. He was propped up against the bus shelter, hands in pockets, kicking a tin can into touch.

Lucy glanced over as though she hadn't noticed him. 'No idea. Probably off to hang out with his hoodie friends.' She was looking very shifty.

'How old is he?'

'Seventeen going on seven.' She took my arm. 'Now. Let's talk about *me*.' As we went into the bar, she stopped to take off her beret and ruffle the dark, pixie-cut hair.

The pub had all the usual stuff. Massive leather harnesses, warm beer, big-boned barmaid in a tee-shirt that showed a lot more stomach than was good for her.

'Pint?' asked Lucy, taking out her wallet.

Out of the window—complete with fake whorls—I watched a bus pull up. After it lurched away, Matt was gone.

*

He didn't come home until quite late in the afternoon, when he smashed open the front door, thumped wordlessly off to his room and cranked his stereo up to full volume. He didn't even appear for the delectable feast Lucy and I produced that evening, so she took some into his lair. She stayed up there with him for quite a while, and came back down with an empty plate and a worried frown. Perry seemed determined not to comment on it, so I didn't either.

I was last to bed on Saturday night, staying up to watch a trashy film. After I turned the TV off, the world seemed deathly quiet. I could hear my brain ringing like a burglar alarm as I padded up the stairs in my socks. But while I was tiptoeing along the corridor, I caught a whiff of Matt's special smokes. There was a bar of light under his door. I hesitated, gathered all my courage—he was a big lad, Matt—and gave the door a tap.

I heard a creak. 'Uh?'

'It's me. Jake.'

Pause. 'Yeah?'

'Wanna share that spliff?'

The door jerked open, and I didn't know what to say, because the kid was crying. That isn't my thing at all. I expect I should have put a fatherly hand on his shoulder or something, but I didn't. My father's hand wasn't very fatherly.

After a moment, he stepped back to let me in. His grief was none of my business, so I took the easy way out and pretended I hadn't seen it. The window was open, but his room smelled like an opium den. There were posters on the walls of half-dressed girl tennis stars—quite eye-catching, actually—and model biplanes hung from the ceiling. He handed me the spliff and then crumpled onto his bed with one mammoth arm over red-rimmed eyes.

Sitting down on a denim bean bag, I had a go. It tasted just like the stuff Jesse and I used to grow at home.

'Where did you get this?' I thought that was probably a safe subject and wouldn't start him off blubbing again.

'Grew it in the greenhouse.'

'What, *here*? Doesn't your dad mind?'

'He's okay with it. Doesn't want me to leave home, so he has to be okay. My plants are five foot tall,' he rambled vaguely. 'It's Dad's compost that does it. Did you know . . .'

'That it's a hundred degrees? Yeah, I did.'

He sobbed and then giggled. 'It's hot stuff.' He was blasted enough to find that unbearably funny, and rocked around on the bed, holding his stomach.

It *was* hot stuff, actually. After a couple of minutes, I felt that crazy whizzing in between my ears. Dr Who's Tardis. I was well out of practice. I passed him the spliff and leaned back.

'Nice sound system.' I nodded at his deck.

'State of the art. I can lift the roof off this dump.'

'You'll go deaf.'

'Not until I'm as old as you, and then I won't care.' He lay flat, looking up at the ceiling.

And I remembered why I don't like being around teenagers. It's because they don't see me as I see myself. I mean, I'm in my prime. I may take a little longer than I did to focus on the instructions for a packet of spaghetti, but they're definitely printing them fuzzily these days. Have you noticed that? You have to hold your arm out quite a long way to read the writing. Some optician tried to tell me I needed reading glasses, but that's just bollocks. And I do occasionally limp a bit when I first get out of bed, just until my ankle joints start working properly; but there's an explanation, I'm sure, and it's nothing to do with my age. I'm only bloody *forty*, for God's sake. I'm not middle-aged. I did the London Marathon last year. I was a teenager myself, very recently. I'm really just one of them.

But they don't see it that way. You can tell from the way they can't even be bothered to look at you. Especially the girls. You're not an object of interest. You're old, like their dads. I hate that.

'So, Matt.' I was deafened by my own voice, very loud, so I whispered the next bit. 'You got a girlfriend?'

'What? Can't hear you.'

'Got a girlfriend?' The question sounded in stereo.

'Not really. Been shagging someone. You shagging Lucy?'

'Not really.' Pause. 'Not at all, in fact.'

'You going to?'

I shook my head, and it felt as though it might fall off. 'I don't think I'll get that lucky, mate.'

'Nah. Too old.'

'Thanks.'

He held out the joint for me. 'See that spider by the basin? It's been crawling up the wall for three weeks, but it never gets any higher.'

I squinted over at the basin. There was no spider; just a vaguely spider-shaped smudge by the towel rail. Matt's mind was playing tricks on him. Alarmed, I sat up straighter and pointed at him.

'Hey, Matt. Seriously. You're going to bugger up your game if you keep getting wasted. You need to give it a rest, mate.'

'I don't *have* a game. Got a neck injury last season. Surgeon says I can't play again unless I want to end up doing foot and mouth painting.'

'Bummer.' I had a feeling my teenspeak was at least twenty years out of date, but Matt seemed to understand it, because he nodded gloomily.

'Yeah. Mum doesn't get that. She says it's a stupid game and she's glad I couldn't even finish the season. She's a cow. She thinks shooting is mindless violence and fishing is for morons and everything I'm half good at is a waste of fucking time. She never even bothered to watch me play.'

'Fault on the right side, mate. My old man only ever spoke to me when I had a mouthguard and black shorts on.'

'He fetched up to your games, then?'

'Oh, he *fetched up*, all right. Maniac. Frothed at the mouth. Hollered. Swore. One time he smacked the ref.'

'Shit.'

'Gave him a bloody nose. Got himself banned. I was four years old at the time.'

'*Four?* You're kidding.' Matt laughed until he was crying again.

I cackled wildly too, but it wasn't funny. 'They start 'em young in the Antipodes. Small Blacks.'

'How the fuck d'you get boots for a four-year-old?'

'You don't. Bare feet for the little kids. We ran about on the frost with our toes practically dropping off, while Dad stood there in his farm jacket and two pairs of socks and nice warm gummies, screaming. And if I dropped a pass or missed a tackle, he used to belt me when I came off. It kind of spoiled the fun.'

'Did you pack it in?'

'Wasn't allowed to. I represented our region for eight seasons, made captain, then left home and never played again. Broke the old man's heart.' That's the reason I quit, even though I love the game. Just to piss him off.

Matt swore sympathetically, and shut his eyes for a minute—or maybe ten, I tend to lose track on these occasions. Then he stirred. 'What about your mum? She a cow, like mine?'

'No, mate. No. Poor old lady, she did her best.' I watched the smoke curling up and away. 'Tried her very, very best.'

He didn't comment. After a while, I heard my own voice.

'She gave me a puppy once for a surprise, for my birthday. Even though she knew Dad was going to go ballistic. Dogs aren't pets, in his book.' He *had* gone ballistic, too. Worse than usual. I'd hidden with Sala, shivering in the orchard. I passed Matt the spliff.

He inhaled, thoughtfully. 'You still got the dog?'

'Nah. I was eight, so Sala would be more than thirty by now. That's about two hundred in dog years. She'd have to be the oldest terrier in the history of the universe.'

Matt fell about laughing, and I pretended to. When he next spoke, he seemed to be having trouble getting the words out, as though his tongue had been injected with local anaesthetic. I knew the feeling.

'You goin' look for my mum?'

'I dunno, mate.'

'She has to get back here. She's needed. She's really needed. It's an emergency. Tell her she's needed, quick.'

'*Why's* she needed, mate?'

He leaned unsteadily across and grabbed me by the collar. 'It's life and death, tell her. Life and death. Bring her back.'

'I won't be going anywhere if you've throttled me.'

73

'Promise you'll bring her home with you.' He let go of me, sank into the pillows and shut his eyes again.

'Okay,' I said. 'I promise.' After a minute I pulled the duvet over him, stubbed out the spliff, and left him snuffling quietly.

I sat on the window seat in my room and looked out at the stars, and, my God, they were bright that night. They were as bright as car headlights. They were so bright, they looked as though they were going to leap right in through the window.

I don't remember getting into bed. That was hot stuff, all right. I remember the dreams, though. I wish I didn't.

Mum crept into my bedroom in the early morning light, because it was my birthday and Dad had gone to the sales. She had something hidden up her jumper, and a smile on her face. And I loved her more than anyone in the world.

She was older, now, and her body sagged a little. But she was so pleased to see me. She stood at the kitchen door, her arms held out, eyes creased and bright. But I put down the phone and left her sobbing on the doorstep.

Sala had been in the pig bin again. I could see the mess, as soon as I got off the school bus.

On Sunday morning, I woke to daytime gloom and a blackbird singing in the rain. I leaned on one elbow and looked out. On the lawn, a rabbit was nibbling at the grass, his ears twitching in the wet. He sat up, sniffing, then lolloped his way calmly through the picket fence and in among Perry's vegetables, where he began to help himself to cabbages. I had to admire his style.

I'm a fan of rabbits. My father and brother curse them and spread disease through their burrows so that they go blind and die horribly. We used to find their contorted bodies and throw them into the offal pit.

After a while, Matt's stereo sprang to life and the smell of cooking bacon seeped into my room. I liked being there. It was a bit like a home.

The rain kept up steadily all morning. Lucy and I went for a walk under an enormous umbrella, across the ploughed fields and through Coptree Woods. She was energetic and long-legged in gumboots and a waxed jacket of Perry's. When her fingers froze, she shoved her hands under my jersey.

If we were going to start something, that was probably the moment. But we didn't. Perhaps, when it came to the crunch, the age gap was too wide for both of us. For my part, although I'd pulverise anyone who hurt her, I knew I couldn't offer Lucy what she deserved. In four years' time she'd have been throwing me out, just like Anna.

She stood looking at me with those all-knowing green eyes. Then she smiled and touched my cheek. So we walked home, under the umbrella, like two good mates. Which is what we were.

Nobody mentioned Mrs Harrison again until Perry cornered me after lunch, as I was skulking in the sitting room. I'd been thinking about his suggestion, though. Going to Africa on a zany quest was a ridiculous idea, calculated to waste weeks of my life. But it seemed as good a way as any of avoiding the fact that I'd cocked up my life. I had no job, no girlfriend, no goal. I was rootless and drifting. My freedom was a vacuum.

And then there was young Matt. Even if I was under the influence of his hooch at the time, I'd promised to find his mother. He'd seemed so desperate.

Perry brought in a pot of coffee on a tray, and we sat opposite each other by the fire, a couple of old geezers in their gentlemen's club. Perry was a bit too exotic for the scene, somehow. He ought to be puffing on a hookah in the shadowy depths of a Middle Eastern café, plotting assassinations.

'So,' he began, fixing me with his kohl-rimmed eyes. I knew what was coming. 'Have you thought?'

I nodded my head, and then shook it. 'It's just crazy, Perry.'

'You're entitled to your opinion. But you'll do it?'

'Your wife does *want* to be found, does she?'

He held out his hands, like a used-car salesman. 'Of *course*, Jake. She loves us.'

'And you reckon she's in Mombasa?'

For just a second—less, maybe a hundredth of a second—I thought I saw a gleam in his eye. It's hard to describe. It was a flicker of some private party. But even as I watched him, I thought I must have been mistaken. He instantly looked as weary and haunted as ever. In that whole weekend, I only saw him smile about twice.

'We had a postcard from there. Hang on, I've got it.' He dug in the desk drawer and pulled out a postcard with a picture of two Arab sailing boats in a saffron sunset. Clearly, Perry didn't believe in sticking things to the fridge with magnets. He dropped it onto the tray.

'Go ahead.'

I looked down at the handwriting. It was a confident scrawl in blue biro; the sharp loops of a person in a hurry.

Lovely family,
   Got the piece finished and sent off. On another story now, one I've been after for years. Take care of yourselves.
   Love you all.
   Mum/Deborah

I squinted at the description printed underneath the picture. 'It says Zanzibar.'

He waved a thin hand, irritated. 'Yes, I know it says Zanzibar, man. But look at the postmark.'

'Ah, I see. Mombasa. Okay. But she'll be long gone by now, surely?'

'I don't think so.'

He knew more than he was telling me, I was sure of it. He wasn't just relying on a blurred postmark.

'Perry, I—'

'She's blondish. Slim, medium height.' He picked up the photo of her, the one taken by Lucy in Greece. Slid it out of the frame. 'Better take this. It's not the most recent, but it's a close-up. Ask in the post office, the police station, ask the taxi drivers. Failing that, try along the coast. I don't imagine she'll be in one of the big tourist resorts, so look off the beaten track. There are less accessible places. Extremely basic. Campsites. Backpacker lodges. *Someone* will know.'

'You've been?' I asked, suddenly suspicious.

'Not recently.'

'When did you—'

'You'll need to hire a vehicle out there. Use your credit card, and I'll reimburse you in full.'

'No you won't. The cost isn't the issue.'

'That's good of you.' He inclined his head. 'I suggest you leave your car and all your things here, and have your mail forwarded to this address.'

'Hold on, Perry. Whoa. I haven't agreed to go.' I held up my hands to halt his steamroller. 'I don't *get* it. I don't understand what all this is about.'

This time he did smile, very briefly, and I caught a flash of gold tooth.

'Come on, man. Where's your sense of adventure?'

Chapter Eight

The fiftieth birthday party on Saturday night turned out to be a good one. Leila's band—Dusty and the Defibrillators—consisted of two junior doctors from the Queen Elizabeth (keyboard and guitar), a student nurse (double bass), an administrator (drums), a GP (saxophone) and Leila. They played everything from Gershwin to Lloyd Webber via the blues—it was for fun, not for money, although Leila suspected that Patrick, the drummer, would have loved to give up his day job.

That night they were a success. The hotel's dance floor heaved with lindy-hopping fifty-year-olds and embarrassed teenagers, and Leila brought the house down with a husky blast of 'I've Got You Under My Skin' before the band took a half-hour break.

'Nice one, Leila!' Maggie lowered her sax into its case. 'Watch out, Ella Fitzgerald.'

Maggie's surgery worked closely with Leila's pharmacy; the two women were regularly in touch over the minutiae of prescriptions. It was she who'd dragooned Leila into the band.

'They're a fantastic crowd,' said Leila, looking around happily. The sun had risen on the world, tingeing her future with gold light. Leila had new energy, clarity of mind, and affection for her fellow man.

Maggie was thirty: plain, perky and almost divorced. Separation had made her rebellious, and this evening she wore a bowler hat, a black basque and jeans. She had wispy hair and an uncomfortable nose, but no shortage of admirers.

The band had their own table. Maggie turned a chair around, sat astride it and poured two glasses of fizzy wine. 'Cheers.' She had to shout above the music, as she handed a glass to Leila. 'Oh my God, someone's asked for "The Birdie Song". I thought this shindig was supposed to have a touch of class?'

Leila took the glass, sipped, remembered, and carefully put it down.

'Can't,' she said firmly.

Maggie stared. '*Can't*? You've not gone teetotal on me, you baggage?'

'Temporarily.'

'Why?'

Leila wriggled delightedly.

'You're not . . . ?' Maggie leaned closer, hazel eyes widening. 'You're *not*? . . . No! You *are*!'

'Shhh!' Leila's smile was dazzling as she put a finger to her lips. 'Top secret. I haven't even told David.'

Maggie leaped up, blasphemed merrily and spun her bowler into the air. It sailed onto a fan and began to have the ride of its life. 'This is the best news I've had all year. When did you find out?'

'Last night. It was one of those really early tests, which is why I haven't told David yet.'

'Oh.' Maggie's enthusiasm slipped a little. She ruffled her flyaway hair, calculating. 'So you're still only . . . ?'

'Four weeks. Max. I'll do another one soon, but it's all fine. I just know it is.'

Maggie bustled around the table to hug her. 'Sit down, for God's sake. Have an orange juice . . . here. How are you feeling?'

'I feel absolutely fantastic,' said Leila. 'And incredibly lucky.'

Maggie held up two sets of crossed fingers. 'Come in and see me at the surgery. This week. Promise?'

'Promise.'

'Monday. Come in on Monday.'

'Okay. Maybe. But that's enough about me. What about you? What's Harry been up to?'

Maggie shook her head. 'Poor old Harry has finally lost the plot,' she said pityingly. 'I got a solicitor's letter last week. They reckon I'm stashing about half a million quid in an offshore bank account.'

'Incredible.' Leila laughed. 'You wish!'

'It's this new boyfriend putting him up to it,' said Maggie, rolling her eyes. 'Paranoid Peter. If my husband had only had the sense to run off with a *woman*, we might have settled everything amicably.'

'Meanwhile the lawyers charge like car batteries.'

Maggie scowled. 'He's not even asking to see Toby. I had to insist that he take him tonight.'

'Oh, no.' Toby was Maggie's three-year-old son. 'How is the poor little man?'

'Confused. I never expected it to turn out like this.' Maggie picked at the lace on her basque. 'I knew we had to split up when I caught Harry taking a shower with the plumber. But I thought we'd do it with panache. With style. Be bestest of friends. All this aggro is so . . . mediocre.'

She downed her glass in one go, and poured another. 'If your David ever starts wearing Lycra shorts and going cycling, get a private detective. It's a very, very bad sign.'

'David would look *ridiculous* in cycling shorts.'

'So what's he really like, under all that lovely lanky charm? Is he incredibly holy?'

Leila's eyes danced. 'He was a womaniser of the worst kind when I first met him. Drank, swore, broke hearts and went to church on Sundays to ask forgiveness.'

'Until you came along.'

'Perhaps.' Leila looked slightly rueful. 'He's a real teacher's pet nowadays. Gets up at six every morning. Reckons he needs the space to pray.'

'What about you?'

'Oh, *me* . . . My family were pillars of the church. That's how I got into singing. Through gospel. I was the choir leader.' Leila smiled and then shrugged. 'But my faith seems to have slunk away, tail down, like an old alley cat. I'd be an atheist, but I'm too much of a coward.'

'Not a very good vicar's wife, are you?'

Leila leaned closer. 'I promised God I'd join the choir and do the altar flowers, if the test was positive. I even said I'd start a Bible study group. So now I've got to do all that stuff, just in case he exists.'

Maggie laughed extravagantly, choking on a mouthful of wine.

Suddenly, Leila giggled and pointed across the dance floor to where Maggie's hat had flown off the fan, to the delight of a group of young men.

'Look at that!' Maggie cried. 'They're using it as a Frisbee, cheeky sods. Hoi! That's *mine*, you thieves!'

A body builder type brought back the battered headgear, apologising. He had a square jaw and broad shoulders, and a white shirt with the sleeves rolled up to reveal hairy arms. Maggie looked him up and down, thanked him cordially and then winked at Leila. When he asked her to dance, she took his hand and let him pull her to her feet.

'Look after this for me,' she yelled, resting the hat on Leila's head.

Leila tipped it forwards so that it covered one eye, and touched her upper lip with the tip of her tongue.

'Very alluring. God, woman, *everything* looks better on you,' complained Maggie. 'Some people have all the luck.'

The luck held until Monday morning.

As soon as she saw the blood, Leila knew. She recoiled, gasping as though she'd seen a snake. She riffled with numb, shaking fingers through her handbag and took out another pregnancy test kit. It was the one that was supposed to be just for confirmation, before she told David. She went through the old routine. Waited. Waited, willing the line to appear. But this time the little window sneered at her, leered at her, cruelly, sickeningly white.

For a long time, she leaned against the basin of Kirkaldie's staff toilet in a cold sweat. She felt faint. Panicky. Finally, she splashed water on her face and dug her phone out of her bag. Mercifully, Maggie was between patients.

'Leila! I'm still hung-over from Saturday night, and I've got post-alcohol paranoia. Did I do anything disgraceful? Do I need to apologise to anyone?'

'No,' said Leila.

'Remember hairy Howard, the body builder? He's actually a physics teacher. Turned out his girlfriend had just dumped him. All he wanted was a shoulder to cry on.'

Leila couldn't speak. The ground was spinning away from under her feet.

'Anyway.' Maggie was cheerful. 'What's the problem, you bossy baggage? Don't tell me you can't read my writing again. When are you coming in, like I told you?'

'Um,' said Leila, and cleared her throat. 'Now.'

Maggie had half an hour free before evening surgery. She did a blood test. But there wasn't really any doubt.

'Be honest, Maggie,' said Leila. 'I just need to know.'

'Okay.' Maggie took a deep breath. 'Well. It looks like a chemical pregnancy.' She washed her hands at the basin. 'Probably never even had a chance to implant.'

'So . . .' Leila perched on a chair, hands twisting together. 'So my baby never existed?'

Maggie's face was pinched with sympathy. 'Oh, Leila. Yes, it existed. But very briefly.'

'And now it's gone?'

Maggie laid a hand on her friend's arm. 'This is very common. Incredibly common, but normally people never even know. Look, you're in no state to get yourself home. Let me phone David and ask him to come and get you.'

'No.' Leila blinked, hard. 'Please don't do that. I told you, he never knew. It was going to be a sur—' Her voice failed her, and she pressed her palm to her nose. 'A surprise. Sorry.'

Maggie handed her a wad of tissues from a box on her desk. She picked up the phone and asked her receptionist to bring in two mugs of tea. Then she bent tactfully over her computer, pretending to type up notes.

'Is it my fault?' asked Leila tearfully. 'Because I went out singing, and dancing, and . . . ?'

'No.' Maggie held up a hand. '*No.* Definitely not your fault. There was nothing you could have done differently. This pregnancy was never going to be viable.'

'I don't understand,' whispered Leila. After a few seconds' thought, she looked up at Maggie. 'I have poor . . .' She gulped. 'Sounds awful. Like a hen. Poor egg quality, apparently. I suppose that might fit with what's happened?'

'Yes, poor ovarian function and miscarriage can be related. But the thing is, Leila, *most* pregnancies actually end in miscarriage. Maybe as many as seventy percent. It's so early that people never realise. They just get their period, maybe slightly late, maybe bang on time, and they're none the wiser. You see? These very early tests . . . they don't always do us any favours.'

'Oh, I don't know.' Leila dabbed her eyes with the tissues. 'It was a miracle while it lasted.'

There was a gentle knock on the door, and Maggie went to collect the tea.

'I s'pose I can drink alcohol now,' sniffed Leila, with a twisted smile.

'Only got this stuff, sorry.'

'Thanks.' Leila took the mug and held it between her hands.

'I can refer you back to—'

'No. No, thank you, Maggie. No more referrals. No more treatment. I've been through all that. I've tried everything conventional medicine can offer, had natural treatments coming out of my ears. Even acupuncture. And my chances are . . . well. You know.'

Maggie finished the sentence. 'Worse, the older you get. Yes. Will you tell David this has happened?'

Leila thought for some time. 'I will. Once I've pulled myself together. After all, it's the closest he's ever come to fatherhood. Perhaps the closest he will ever come.'

'Perhaps.'

'I lost his baby.' Leila stood up and wandered to the window. 'How very careless of me, to *lose* a baby. Have I checked in lost property?'

Maggie smiled sadly but said nothing.

'My poor mother,' said Leila, still looking out through the window. 'I don't think I'll tell her I've mislaid her grandchild. You know, in my family's culture women are often known by the name of their first-born child. Mama-David, say.'

'So the mother is defined by the child, in a way.'

'In a way. Family is fundamental. Mum seems to struggle with our childlessness almost as much as we do. I try not to moan to her about it.'

'I'm sure she wouldn't mind if you did.'

'I don't want to make it worse for her.' Leila rested her head against the glass. 'You know, Maggie, if one good thing comes of this, it'll be that we finally let go of the dream. It's not going to happen. I'm not going to conceive and carry a baby to full term. I've got the message, loud and clear. It's adoption or nothing. Probably nothing, by now.'

Maggie twiddled a pen around her fingers. 'Have you heard anything?'

'From the adoption people?' Leila turned away from the window. 'No. It took two years to jump through all their hoops. That was two years ago, and there's been hardly a whisper since then, except that when we moved here we had to navigate *more* hoops.'

Maggie leaned closer. 'After a miscarriage—even a very early one like this—sometimes people need time to grieve. You might need to work through that, put adopting on the back burner for a while.'

Leila laughed shakily and sat down. 'You sound like the bloody social workers. That's how they talked about IVF.'

'Sorry.'

'I'm fine, really. I'll grieve for this baby—the baby that never quite was—but at least we hadn't started celebrating, at least we weren't out buying cots and car seats. And, Maggie, time is exactly what we *don't* have. It's been four years since we first enquired. I'm thirty-six. I'll be on a Zimmer frame soon. *Now*, more than ever, I'm ready. Just need a bloody miracle.'

'Is there an upper age limit?'

'Not officially. But there's no shortage of contenders for babies. If there's a choice, the younger couple will be picked for sure.'

'I don't see why they should. You're not old by modern standards.'

Leila shook her head. 'They ask the birth parents what they'd like for their children, then try to take it into account. They all want younger adopters. Understandably. David and I are probably as old as their own parents!'

'That isn't saying very much. I've got a twelve-year-old patient at the moment, due any time.'

'*Twelve*!' Leila's brow wrinkled in disbelief. 'That's the same age as Freya, David's niece. But . . . twelve? She's had no childhood! Isn't she scared?'

'Difficult to tell. She doesn't say very much.'

'Well.' Leila blinked and took a long breath. 'That puts my problems into perspective. Perhaps I should adopt your patient instead. Then I get two kids at once.'

The telephone rang. Leila looked at her watch. 'That must be surgery. I'd better get out of here.' She stood up, whisking her velvet scarf into a complicated knot. 'Thanks so much for . . . you know.'

'Drink tomorrow night?' said Maggie. 'I'll give you the results of the tests.'

'Okay. But we both know what the results will be,' said Leila. 'And—let's be realistic—we both know something else. That was my last chance.'

Maggie didn't even try to argue.

Leila made a dash past the receptionist with her curious, sympathetic eyes. She passed the main entrance to Kirkaldie's, which was just about to close, and wandered dazedly along the rush-hour street, letting the crowds wash around her, feeling utterly detached from them. She wasn't one of these people. She wasn't a part of their world.

Others couldn't comprehend the loss that is childlessness. Sometimes it made her whole existence seem pointless, yet people brushed it off as though it were a minor mishap. 'It obviously isn't meant to be,' they said, or 'There's more to life than children.' Aunts, doctors, perfect strangers on trains, all overflowing with apple-pie wisdom.

New Street Station. On autopilot now, she bought a takeaway coffee and checked the platform number. It wasn't until she'd shown her pass to the kind, moustached man at the barrier that she began to cry. And then, for some reason, she couldn't stop.

Chapter Nine

The Tanzania road had seen much better days. By now I knew every pothole.

South of Mombasa, I'd taken the Likoni Ferry and then set off through the rust-coloured landscape, houses and corrugated-iron stalls strung out along both sides of the road. And people walking. There were always people walking in Kenya.

I found the track exactly where I'd been told it would be—opposite a school. Turning onto it, I crawled at a snail's pace through banana plantation and scrub. It wasn't possible to go any faster, even in the solid little jeep I'd hired from some Ugandan Indians. The track made the main road look like the M1, and I endured at least twenty bone-shaking minutes of skidding and sliding and steering around holes that could have swallowed a bus. My back was sticking to the seat, and floating swirls of dust coagulated the sweat as it ran down me. I tried closing the windows, but the stuff seemed to seep in through every crack and the temperature rocketed; so I opened them again and wound a towel over my mouth and nose. And all the way, I wondered what the hell I was doing there.

I'd already wasted the best part of a fortnight looking for Mrs Harrison. I carried with me a hefty envelope from Perry, but I'd given up hope of delivering it to the bloody woman because she obviously didn't exist.

You couldn't say I hadn't tried. Day after day, I'd invaded the public buildings of Mombasa, reciting her name at bemused officials. I'd tried the post office, the police station and the hospital. I'd sidled up to street hawkers, taxi drivers and shopkeepers. I even asked a priest in the cathedral. They were all very polite. They all thought long and hard before shrugging.

So I'd climbed dutifully into the jeep and driven for miles along scarred and crumbling roads, hassling bar staff and hotel managers up and down the coast, feeling like a total jerk. I'd drawn a complete blank, and the whole thing had started to seem bloody silly, frankly. Perhaps it was all a complicated hoax.

Finally, that very morning, I'd rammed the envelope into the bottom of my bag and emailed Perry to tell him I was throwing in the towel. Sad for Matt, of course, but I told myself that he'd get over it. I'd wasted more than enough time. I was moving on.

I decided I'd have a go at Mount Kenya. The challenge would keep all that nasty reality at bay for another week or so. I was intrigued by this troubled, vibrant region; the place had cast its spell, and now that I was free of Perry's quest I thought I might get to know it better. With this thought, I'd checked out of the Durham Hotel. Then, deciding to have one last decent cup of coffee before I left, I settled myself happily on the hotel's wide verandah—wicker chairs, ceiling fans and bougainvillea. I leafed through my guidebook while a flock of tiny birds had a barney amongst the electric-blue flowers of a nearby tree.

Even though I'd given up, when the manager—Yusuf—brought my coffee himself, I collared him and asked the question, one last time. It was out of habit, really. I'd already tried the waiters.

When I mentioned the name, he frowned. 'Deborah Harrison,' he whispered. He broke the name up into six syllables and said each with great care. It made me feel sleepy. Eventually, inevitably, he shook his head. 'Sorry.'

Par for the course. Still, I handed him the photograph. He examined it for a full thirty seconds, holding it in one hand and, with the other, tracing a line around Deborah's silhouette. Behind us, the squabbling birds broke into a new round of hostilities.

Without looking up, and without any apparent surprise, he murmured, 'Yes, I know this woman.'

It came out so casually that for a moment I thought I'd misheard. 'You *know* her?'

'Well . . .' He inclined his head, thinking. 'The name is different.'

'Are you sure it's her?'

He handed back the photograph. 'There's a man who comes in here sometimes. Rod Jennings. He owns a campground out at Kulala Beach, off the Tanzania road. Beautiful place. One of the last they haven't ruined.'

'And you think this Jennings bloke might be able to shed some light?' I held up the picture, squinting doubtfully at the freckled, glowing face.

Yusuf shrugged. He looked very unhappy, suddenly, as if he wished he'd kept his mouth shut. His brow was creased with anxious wrinkles.

'The woman in that photograph'—he jerked his chin towards it—'looks exactly like Susie.'

'Susie . . . ?'

'Susie. His wife.'

The further I bumped down that hellish track, the wilder my goose chase seemed. I was tempted to turn back.

The dashboard had turned orange under a film of dust, and so had I. Then, between the trees, I spotted an indigo streak spilling along the horizon. The Indian Ocean. I cheered out loud.

The track opened out into a sandy clearing, littered with tents, mosquito nets and washing strung haphazardly among the trees. There were rickety picnic tables, a concrete shower block and watery, dancing light. Skirting the clearing, I parked next to a rusting white pick-up truck and sat for a few minutes, enjoying the sudden peace. My ears were ringing.

The occupants of the tents weren't much in evidence, except for a couple of scrubby-looking white guys, wearing sarongs and doing their washing on a slab of concrete underneath a tap. The water was gushing up over their clothes and spraying them while a crowd of monkeys cheered from the branches. On a low, wooden building nearby I could make out a cardboard sign: *Office*.

I was halfway out of the jeep when the office door opened and someone stepped into the bleached light. It was a white man of about my age, perhaps a bit older, wearing faded shorts and carrying a broad-brimmed hat. He was no tourist: he belonged here. It was unmistakeable. He had a sort of presence too, a poise that you don't see very often. He held himself with easy self-assurance. A young German shepherd padded quietly alongside him.

I leaned awkwardly against the jeep as he loped across, putting on his hat and glancing unhurriedly at me. He had bone-white hair, and the type of hide you could make into a shoe, the kind you get from living your whole life in the sun. I guessed he might be an inch or two taller than me. Thinner too, but I remember thinking that I'd want to have him on my side in a dark alley.

'Hi,' I croaked, with an ingratiating simper. 'Jake Kelly.'

'Rod Jennings.' He shook my hand, and I was tongue-tied. Faced with the guy, I hesitated to ask the question. I mean, how would it sound? *Hi, I'm after a woman who's somebody else's wife and they tell me yours looks just like her.* He was going to think I was a bloody blithering idiot. I'd be lucky if he didn't thump me.

In the end, he helped me out. 'You're after a room?' He spoke calmly, rather distantly. He sounded like a newsreader for the BBC World Service.

'Er, no.' I tried not to shift from foot to foot. 'Some friends asked me, while I was in Kenya, to try and find someone.'

He stood very still, watching me, an odd little smile twitching at the corner of his mouth.

I ploughed on, feeling sillier than ever. 'Um, a woman called Deborah Harrison. A journalist. Her husband last heard from her in Mombasa.'

He didn't react, so I pulled the crumpled photo out of my wallet. 'This picture's a bit out of date, apparently. Her husband's in his fifties. *Actually*—' I cackled desperately—'the manager at the Durham Hotel said it looked a bit like your, um, wife.'

One of Rod's eyebrows lifted, just a fraction. 'Who, Yusuf?' He took the picture out of my hands, regarded it sardonically, and then shrugged. 'Similar hair colour, I suppose. But no. Wrong woman, Jake. Susie's not technically my wife, but she's been with me, on and off, longer than I care to remember.' He handed the photo back, and a peaceful smile crossed his face, as though he *did* care to remember.

'Ah well.' I sighed. 'My hopes weren't high.'

'I'm afraid you're wasting your time,' he said, moving away to drop the tailgate on his pick-up. This is a small community, and we don't get many rogue English bluestockings.' He chuckled gently. 'But I'll keep an eye out, tell her to call home if I spot her.'

He began to load up the truck with crates of empty bottles. He seemed to be in a hurry, all of a sudden. 'Right then,' he called briskly, without looking around. 'You'll be off now?'

I picked up a crate. 'I'll give you a hand.'

'No need.' He glanced towards the beach. 'Thanks, but I'll be done in a jiffy.'

But I had nothing better to do, and he seemed to be in a rush, so I stayed. His parents still farmed inland, he told me over the clatter of crates. He was on his way there right now, because his father had slipped a disc and was yelling for help. He asked where I was going next. I said I hoped to get in some climbing, and we talked briefly about Mount Kenya. He didn't push advice onto me, didn't know it all, didn't tell anecdotes to show how clever he was.

Once we'd slung the last crate aboard he stood for a moment, wiping his hands on a rag. 'You'll be heading back to Mombasa, Jake?'

I opened the door of the jeep. 'Yep, I'm off. Probably make tracks for Mount Kenya first thing tomorrow.'

'Sounds good.' He waited until I'd started my engine, then swung easily into his seat. 'C'mon, Cheza,' he called, and the big dog jumped up behind, shaggy tail gently swishing.

I motioned to him to go ahead of me. This was his place, after all, and it was hardly fair to make him drive in a coppery cloud of my dust. Raising a hand, he began to rattle up the track.

We set out in convoy, but Rod was much gunnier at negotiating the obstacles—I supposed he could do it blindfolded—and as the minutes passed I began to drop further and further behind. Creeping around yet another pothole, I watched the pick-up disappear among the trees. Feeling mildly depressed, I stopped the jeep on a wider section of track.

I was hot. I had dust up my nose, sweat in my clothes. Insect bites. Heat rash in places I'd rather not think about. I imagined all that irritation floating away into the kind waters of the Indian Ocean.

'Bugger it,' I said, jamming the stick into reverse.

Five minutes later the jeep was parked in its original spot, and I was strolling to the edge of the beach. The sea spread itself out in bands of darkening blue, winking coquettishly at me all the way to the horizon. Just below the bar, where a group of palms leaned across the sand, three figures were bent over a board game of some sort.

I was in the water within seconds, and it felt like a warm bath. I lay in the pale, glimmering shallows, running my fingers along the seabed. The sand was the colour and consistency of my mother's sugary fudge. I swam out a couple of hundred yards until the creamy turquoise darkened, and then dived down to the bottom and scraped up a handful of fudge sand.

I think it was then that I decided to stay at Kulala Beach. Just for a night or two; just while I washed away the grime, and the frustration of my pointless search. I didn't intend to disappear forever, like the mythical Mrs Harrison.

Wading back through the shallows, I took a closer look at the group I'd spotted earlier. Two of them—a man and a woman—were battling over a soapstone chess set with frowning concentration.

It was the third figure who caught my attention. A girl with long silver hair like something out of a fairytale, and an absolutely mountainous bust. Seriously, it was spectacular. She wore a rather inadequate halterneck bikini—the skimpy little top simply wasn't up to the job—and a tiny skirt of tie-dyed cloth knotted around her waist. Around her neck, wrists and ankles were shells on plaited leather thongs. She was reclining on her elbows in the sand, drawing in it with a purple toenail, and pouting. I'd have said she was bored. She yawned, caught my eye and waved. Perhaps that *proved* she was bored. Anyway, I waved back. Then she pointed at a cold box beside her, held up a bottle of the local beer—Tusker—and beckoned me over.

Obviously I didn't need to be asked twice. Would you? I couldn't believe my luck. I was out of the water and across the scorching sand in about five seconds flat, rubbing my hair with a towel. She passed me the beer as I dropped down beside her.

'Hi,' she whispered, her head tilted close to mine. 'I thought you looked lonely.'

'I was.'

'My name's Karin.'

The bottle hissed happily as I prised off the cap. 'Jake.'

Her accent was European, perhaps Scandinavian. Things were looking better and better. She murmured, 'We have to be quiet as little mice, because Susie and Erik are *so* busy with their very important tournament.'

She rolled her eyes and jerked her chin towards the others. Their heads were bent over the board, and the man's brows were drawn together. He was bearded and earnest and probably ate mung beans. The woman—Susie—sat very upright on a driftwood log, smiling down at the field of battle, hands in the pockets of khaki shorts. She looked as though she smiled often; I could see the lines radiating from the outer corners of her eyes. Beside her feet lay a long row of the black pieces she'd already taken prisoner. There weren't too many left on the board.

Something made me look twice. She was in her thirties, I'd have guessed, and there wasn't much of her. On one tanned arm hung twisted copper bangles, the sort I'd seen sold on the streets in Mombasa. Her hair was bleached and tangled, pale honey streaked with beeswax. She'd hooked it back behind her ears. There was sand in her hair and on her cheek and up one arm, as though she'd been lying on the beach.

I stared, stupidly.

The leaves of the palms shivered in the first breath of evening. Still smiling, she glanced across at me and for a second she met my gaze. She blinked, and then the smile was switched off. I thought of a gazelle, wary and poised for flight.

Abruptly, she turned back to the board and moved one of the pieces. The sea breeze stirred her hair, tugging fretfully at her shirt. Her opponent lit a cigarette, shaking his head. He had only a few pawns and a bishop left, huddling loyally in front of his king. Karin was laughing at him. I felt her silvery hair brush my shoulder. Steadily, luxuriously, she drew one of her purple toenails along my calf. I should have been in heaven, but I hardly noticed because my mind was racing.

Susie's eyes glittered, the same blue-green as the sunlit sea, and there was a little constellation of freckles scattered across her cheekbones. Although she was tanned to a light gold, there was a small white patch on her nose where she'd peeled.

I knew that face. I knew it very well indeed. And I couldn't believe my eyes. I leaned closer.

'Mrs Harrison?' My voice sounded horribly loud. 'Deborah Harrison?'

Everything seemed to freeze. It was odd, like the silence before thunder. Slowly, very deliberately, she lifted her face and looked right into my eyes.

'No,' she said.

Then she lifted her queen, swung it like a mallet, and knocked Erik's bishop clear off the board and onto the sand.

'Checkmate,' she announced, standing up. And she walked away.

Chapter Ten

She'd tried to keep her chin up. Really, she had.

In the weeks following the lost pregnancy, Leila was as cheerful and efficient at Kirkaldie's as ever. She had time for everybody. She covered for another pharmacist whose mother had died, arranged birthday drinks for the boss, and mediated between two technicians who loathed one another. She even flirted valiantly with the mechanic at the local MOT garage, but he still failed her car.

But the bleakness slithered in, a chill draught under the door. It didn't lift; it didn't lessen. It drained her energy. It engulfed her in the dark hours and stole her sleep. She did her best to hide it from David— after all, he was bereft as well. He didn't need to have her burdens dumped on him.

When she looked at him she felt guilt. David would make the perfect father; but he was childless. And time was running out for him.

One Thursday, the pharmacy was ridiculously busy. Leila worked all day with barely a break, just a hurried sandwich for lunch, and there was still a queue at closing time. She managed to appear upbeat and energetic until the doors were locked behind her, but by the time she reached New Street Station she felt as though she had lead weights in her shoes. She trudged along the platform, past metal seats and timetables, towards the arch of tired light at the far end. There were the tracks, stretching away into open space, their paths ever parallel but never touching.

The station heaved with commuters. Leila leaned against her usual pillar, turning up her collar against the wind, winding her scarf around her ears. An ungainly figure came hurrying along the platform towards her. With a sigh, Leila recognised Jodie, a genial, frizzy-haired school leaver who worked at Kirkaldie's.

'Hi, Jodie.' She forced a smile of welcome as the girl skidded to a halt, bent double, gasping for breath. 'You nearly missed it this time. The train's just coming in, look.'

'Thought I *had* missed it.' Jodie sold shampoo and photo frames and sparkly lipstick. At seventeen, she was an odd mix of patronising maturity and irritating childishness. She lived with her parents in a suburb two stations beyond Leila's, and had adopted Leila as her train friend.

'Had to stop for passport photos,' she panted.

'Sounds glamorous.'

'I'm sodding off to Spain when I've saved up enough money, getting out of this dump. Going to get a job in a bar.'

Leila offered the girl a polo mint, shouting above the exuberant bellow of their train as it slid alongside them. 'Alone?'

'That depends on whether my useless boyfriend gets his act together.'

'What does your mum think?'

'Doing her nut.' Jodie pushed her tongue through the hole in her mint. 'Thinks I'll get trafficked as a prostitute.'

The carriage was rank and steamy. There was only one pair of empty seats, a little distance from the door, but Jodie was a very competent young woman. Aiming for the valuable spot with her elbows out, she barged past less determined commuters, plonked herself down in triumph, and signalled to Leila by furiously patting the space beside her. Leila slipped apologetically between her fellow travellers and sat down.

Jodie grinned. 'Got a seat, for once.'

'You certainly did. Another mint?'

Jodie pulled off her anorak as the train gathered speed, and continued to talk. Leila let her mind wander, features set in listening mode, as they rattled towards the suburbs. Sitting next to Jodie was like having your head in a metal dustbin while someone hammered on the outside with a spanner. Leila felt wearied by the sheer irrelevance of it. Mind you, the whole world seemed irrelevant, nowadays.

As they reached the high school playing fields, Leila hoisted her handbag, ready to stand up. Jodie seemed to have been waiting for this moment. She leaned closer, determination dimpling the cushioned expanse of her face.

'I saw you selling yourself a test a while ago,' she muttered conspiratorially.

Leila's fingers tightened on her bag, but she feigned blank incomprehension. 'A test?'

'You know. Pregnancy test. Sorry, I've been *dying* to ask.' Jodie was blushing now, a flood of mottled mauve seeping down her neck, and Leila felt a sudden fondness for her.

'Oh, that,' she exclaimed, as though light had finally dawned. She swept the back of her hand across her brow as if to show she'd had a near miss. 'Negative. Whew! Big relief!'

'Oh.' Jodie pouted. 'I was hoping you was banged up.'

'Blimey.' Leila forced a merry laugh, rolling her eyes at the narrowness of her escape. 'A rugrat! That's the last thing I need.'

The train swayed past the canal bridge and began to slow down. Leila stood and staggered, gripping the back of a seat. 'See you tomorrow.'

Jodie took out her iPod. 'Aren't you going to have kids, then?'

'Well.' Leila blinked. 'I've got a career.'

'I am.' Jodie stuffed in her earphones. 'Two. A boy and a girl.'

As soon as the doors opened, Leila fell out and into the blessed quiet of the evening. Jodie's moon face appeared briefly at the window, and then the train slid away.

Dusk was falling. Gloomy, and spitting with rain. The shortest way home was through the housing estate, and then across the canal and around the churchyard. Leila left the station, negotiated the main road and turned into the concrete desolation of Priory Park Farm. Pulling on her gloves, she made her way across the wretched play park with its defiant graffiti, threading a trail among dancing crisp packets and other detritus. The place looked like the set of a futuristic film. It was impossible to imagine that any child had ever played on the empty swings. Someone had systematically dug up the ground and thrown broken cement down the slide; the metal would be no good at all for sliding on ever again. It was pockmarked, twisted, hopelessly dented, with broken bottles scattered around its base.

She walked slowly. She mustn't cheat by hurrying past. On every side, despairing tower blocks reared over her with blank eyes, whispering, *What are* you *doing here?* Only a smattering of lights gleamed among the windows. These flats were half-empty, she knew, the glass broken and boarded up, and the smell of urine on the staircases made your eyes water. David came often, dutifully climbing the concrete stairs and visiting people whose doors opened onto bleak and windswept balconies.

As she passed beneath the furthest tower, she could make out a small child watching her from high up. Little hands gripped the bars and a pale, pinched face jutted forwards, jammed between them. She stopped, hopefully, and called to this other soul in empty space, but he turned away as if bored. And so did she.

The canal bordered the estate and touched one corner of the churchyard. She could smell the water before she could see it, oozing under the bridge. Plastic bags and shopping trolleys littered the grimy brambles on both banks. There were more miles of canal in the West Midlands, she'd read, than in Venice. It had sounded funny at the time. She paused halfway across the bridge and leaned on its cast-iron parapet, gazing down at the unmoving green.

What am I doing here?

The roadmap of her life bore no resemblance whatsoever to the reality of its landscape. Pregnancy used to be something inevitable, something for later. Fola, Rose and Ben. So careless. So *arrogant*. Precious years were wasted, waiting for the *right time*. The realisation that David and she were disastrously different—faulty—had trickled only gradually into their complacency, freezing the smiles on their faces. The thing they'd postponed so casually became their most desperate need.

Then began the frantic search for help: specialists and tests; diets, charts and thermometers. Scanning women's magazines, self-help books, medical journals; poring over the wackiest websites. When nothing else worked they invested their hopes in IVF, which for months dominated their lives. It would be their saviour. But it failed.

So they had whirled around and headed for adoption—sprinting now. A bewildering process. More waiting (*No, we won't consider you so soon after fertility treatment, come back in six months*), then a preparation group. And yet more waiting.

Time passing, squandered in the slowly turning wheels of the system. Birthdays celebrated with tight, frantic smiles. Friends peeling away, losing contact except for the guilty Christmas cards with their scribbled apologies. *Must try and get together this year. So busy. Molly's doing the ballet thing, Flynn's started school, loves soccer.*

Then the assessment: nerve-racking visits and complex, detailed forms; referees, as though they were applying for a job. Every aspect of their life was on show. Social workers poking and prying, as though David and she were criminals. Other people just *had* babies. They didn't need permission. They didn't have to be superheroes.

More waiting. Finally, the news came. They were accepted. They were in!

Or perhaps not.

'Prepare for a very long wait,' the social worker warned, sighing. 'You're on a good wicket, as a mixed race couple, but even so . . . Only about five percent of adopted children are babies, and only a fraction of those share your racial heritage.'

So they continued to wait, while the months and the years screamed belligerently past like express trains. Waiting became their obsession. Waiting, and waiting, imprisoned in limbo. Four years of waiting. At this moment, it seemed to Leila that the thing was hopeless. They were too old. They had missed their chance. She would never take her children to playgroup, never snuggle with them in front of *Postman Pat*. Never watch her son be a shepherd in the nativity play. Never go shopping with her daughter: hot chocolate and new shoes. Never, never, never. Her children were lost. Perhaps they were wandering somewhere in a hinterland, crying for her to find them.

The mushy-pea water under the bridge didn't even flow. It, too, was trapped in this sordid place. It looked solid. If you opened your eyes under there, you wouldn't be able to see anything at all. You could slide under the slime with barely a ripple, and it would close over your head. It wouldn't be difficult. You'd simply disappear.

The terrifying thought hung in her mind, wheedling and cajoling: *easy-peasy, lemon squeezy.* It would only take a moment, and she'd be off the rollercoaster forever. No more crashing down, down, sick and screaming.

It obviously isn't meant to be . . . there's more to life than children, dear; find yourself a hobby.

David. She felt a choking sadness at the thought of his bewilderment. But he would be better off without her, in the end. For him there were years to marry again, have a family, do birthday cakes and bicycles and tiny pairs of wellington boots. She leaned a little further over the parapet, stretching her neck to glimpse the murky shadows under the bridge. Her feet lifted up from the pavement and hung, toes clicking together in a vague little dance, as she wondered idly what it would be like, not breathing. It was said to be quite pleasant, once you gave in. Small lumps of stone broke off under her hands, sliding down the curve of the parapet and dropping noiselessly into the scum.

It won't take a moment. Over in a jiffy.

The world hung, suspended.

A lorry thundered across the bridge. The juddering blast of it shook the elegant old arches. Leila flinched, clutching the parapet and dropping her feet swiftly onto the ground. She watched the monster turn onto the main road. Then she slapped herself smartly on the wrist.

'That was bloody self-indulgent,' she scolded. 'Get a grip.'

'I agree,' came a dry, deep voice. 'But we've all been there.'

Leila whirled around, a hand to her chest. 'Elizabeth! Good Lord, woman, you just about gave me a heart attack.'

Elizabeth led a fluffy black dog on an extendable lead. 'Dora's mother's,' she explained calmly. 'Dora, at the off-licence? Her mother's back in hospital, and Dora's allergic to dogs. Guess which mug volunteered to take the hound?'

Leila bent to pat the black, snuffling creature, taking the opportunity to recover her cheerful mask. 'He's so *cute.*'

'Yes. But he smells worse than a sewage farm. And what drives Leila Edmunds to the parapet of the canal bridge?'

Leila tried to laugh. 'I wasn't *on* the parapet.'

They turned and started walking together across the churchyard, where mist spun and danced among the ranks of stones. Elizabeth took Leila's arm. The dog genially cocked his leg against a lichen-covered angel.

Eventually, Elizabeth spoke. 'David adores you, Leila—come *on*, Frodo! He doesn't want a brood mare. He wants *you*.'

It was some time before Leila could answer. She swallowed. 'It says in the marriage service, *for the procreation of children*. I've failed to deliver.'

'Oh, rubbish.'

After a minute's quiet strolling, Leila said, 'Perhaps we should look at international adoption.'

They'd come to the rectory gate. Elizabeth wound Frodo's lead around her hand. Her grey eyes were stern. 'Or perhaps you have to plan a life without children.'

'No! I can't imagine it . . . David's wonderful with children. He's meant to be a father.'

'Is he? David has much to offer the world. And so have you.' Elizabeth pursed her mouth severely. 'As a childless couple you have *more* to give, not less.'

Leila smiled.

'I haven't convinced you, have I?' Elizabeth looked exasperated.

'Not really.'

Elizabeth squeezed the younger woman's arm. 'Have a bloody big drink, Leila, and drown your sorrows. Sometimes oblivion is the only way out.'

Chapter Eleven

I sat on the edge of my bed and dug right down to the bottom of my bag. There it was, the envelope Perry had given me for his wife. Pretty battered by now. I sat for a long time, thinking, holding it in both hands. It felt different, suddenly. Heavier. Less ordinary.

And Mrs Deborah Harrison didn't want it. She didn't even want to *be* Mrs Deborah Harrison.

After she'd shot off towards the restaurant as though the place was on fire, leaving me to the mercy of Karin and her purple toenails, I'd hung around on the ruffled sand. Darkness fell and coloured lights flared along the terrace above us, and I lost three games of chess before I worked out that Erik and Karin were an item. That put a bit of a dampener on proceedings.

Leaving Karin and Erik to their sexual jealousies, I'd wandered off to arrange a place to stay. In the bar I found a grey-haired manager, Hamisi, who cheerfully led me through the trees to a round, thatched banda, perched on the edge of a little cliff above the gently breathing sea.

From the bar, I could hear laughter and the clinking of bottles. A couple of guys were smoking weed around a bonfire a little further down the beach, and someone was strumming a guitar. I sat on the bed and held the envelope. And I thought about Mrs Harrison. In the end, I made my decision. I'd found her. I must deliver her mail.

She'd gone to ground in the office. As I pushed open the door I could see her face in the lights from the bar. It was a ghost's face, gleaming red, blue and yellow as it floated on the shadows.

'He's sent you to bring me back, hasn't he?' she said. 'I've jumped bail, and you're the bailiff.'

'I've no idea what's in here. But I've brought it all this way.' I dropped the envelope onto the wooden table in front of her. 'So you might as well have it, Susie-Deborah.'

She didn't even glance at it. 'I'm not coming,' she said. 'There's nothing you can do to make me.'

'Someone's lit a fire on the beach. You could head straight down there and chuck that thing into it. I can tell Perry—quite honestly— that I didn't find anyone who answered to the name of Deborah Harrison.' I turned and was halfway out of the door when she called out.

'Hang on . . . have you seen Matt?' Her voice gave way a little. 'He's not ill, is he?'

'I honestly don't know,' I said. And I got out of there as fast as I could, feeling like a hired killer.

Believe it or not, I was still reasonably sober when I left the bar long after midnight. They were a friendly crowd, with their leather necklaces and hair tugged into rubber bands. We had the last round by candle-light. I said a warm goodnight to all my new mates—funny how quickly you make lifelong buddies over a few beers—and made a detour to the edge of the campsite.

The darkness around me was zinging with the hiss of cicadas. It was deafening. It sounded like the steam escaping from a giant pressure cooker. And thousands of creatures—frogs, I think—were making an almighty din out in the undergrowth. *Rawk, rawk, rawk.*

Yellow light flickered feebly through the mosquito screen at the office window. I pictured her alone with her battered envelope, in the breathless heat of that little room. When the door swung open, I was caught out. I mean, I must have looked like a complete weirdo, skulking around in the shadows.

'Ah,' she said quietly. 'The bailiff. Got your handcuffs?'

I began to edge away. 'I came to check you were all right.'

'All right?' She threw back her head, staring at the stars. 'Well, come in then. You can't do any more damage than you already have.'

She stepped back to usher me in, and our shadows loomed like bruises on the whitewashed walls. She was poised, like Rod. Her back was very straight, her head up, tendrils of hair luminous against the bronze of her collar bone. Yet she'd changed, already. She had lost her peace.

'You didn't get laid then?'

I smiled ruefully. 'Nope. Karin finally succeeded in making Erik jealous, and I became redundant.'

'She was onto a win–win, wasn't she?'

'I reckon.'

She sank onto a chair behind the table. The envelope lay in front of her. It had been opened.

'I knew you were trouble,' she said. 'I wanted to run the moment I clapped eyes on you. You stuck out a mile with your short back and sides, and your long stride. Much too purposeful. Purpose isn't a common commodity round here.'

'I've gathered that.'

She sighed. 'Tell me. How did you know where to look?'

'Your card. It had a Mombasa postmark.'

'Bugger.'

'And Perry seemed certain you'd be somewhere around here.'

'He worked it out.' She rubbed her face, a hand on each cheek. 'Had to catch up with me in the end. You can't run away, can you? A whale eats you up and spits you out, back where you started.'

I hadn't the faintest idea what she was talking about, so I just looked grave.

She regarded me tiredly. 'So. Who are you, mystery man? A private detective? Somehow I don't think so.'

'Jake Kelly.' It seemed a little late to shake her hand. 'A friend of Lucy's. I had a bit of time on my hands.'

'They sent you all this way, but they didn't tell you what's going on?'

'It's none of my business,' I answered staunchly.

'Oh, of course it is,' she snapped, waving a hand. 'Don't be bloody ridiculous. You're not a spy, working on a need-to-know basis just in case you get caught and tortured.' She spun the envelope across the rickety table. 'I didn't throw this into the fire. Maybe I should have done. But instead I opened it, and read it three times, and now it's too late. You must have had a teeny peek inside?'

'Actually, I resisted the temptation.'

'I bet you tried holding it up to the light, though.'

'Er . . .'

For the first time, she seemed to focus on me properly. Then she smiled, and her eyes slanted up at the corners.

'Thought so. Tip it out. Go on, tip it all out. You'll be astonished.'

I shook the envelope, and a pile of paper spilled out onto the peeling varnish of the table. On top was one of those chemist's paper sleeves with a stack of photographs inside. I picked it up. Looked at her.

She shifted restlessly. 'For God's sake, take a look.'

I slid out the photos and glanced at the first one, tilting it to catch the light. Then I held it closer, because I couldn't believe my eyes.

It was Matt. Matt, perched awkwardly on the edge of an armchair, looking muscled and clumsy and holding a tiny sleeping baby in a bubblegum-pink suit. It was a golden brown, this baby, with wisps of curly hair, and black eyelashes that reached halfway down very round cheeks. I could see one doll-sized arm. The wrist was no wider than Matt's forefinger. He could have snapped it with no effort at all.

Matt himself was hardly recognisable. This was not the sullen young gorilla I knew. He was looking down at the child with an intensity I could never have imagined in him. I couldn't fathom Matt showing such fascination for any human being, let alone one about ten inches long.

Baffling. I moved on to the next photograph, and the next. They were amateur snapshots, with the occasional red eye and fluffed focus. All were of Matt and the baby. Given the pink fluffy clothes someone had dressed her in, I presumed she was a girl. Even I could see she was cute, and I'm scared of babies.

I stared at the last photo for a long time. In it, Matt was feeding her with a bottle, and her shining eyes were open. They were huge, like a cartoon baby's eyes. She was looking straight up at Matt, and he was gazing down at her like a devoted servant. If I didn't know the boy better, I'd have said he loved her.

I looked up. Deborah was watching me.

'Who's the baby?' I asked.

She laughed sharply, unsteadily, moving her shoulders up and down as though trying to ease some pain. 'That's my granddaughter. She's called Grace. Adorable, isn't she?'

I suppose I should already have guessed. But, believe me, I hadn't. I was slack-jawed for a moment, trying to work it out. It took me a while. You may think I'm slow, but this woman—this *girl*—was totty, not Granny. She was younger than me, for Pete's sake.

'Who are the parents?' I persisted. 'Not Lucy? Have you got another child I haven't met?'

'God, no. Two was enough.'

'So . . . ?'

'Matt's the father.'

'Matt?' He couldn't be.

She nodded, patiently. 'Matt.'

I blinked, trying to believe her. 'And the mother?'

'She abandoned the baby. Then got herself killed, poor lass. She didn't have much of a life, according to what I've just read. Seems she was her family's scapegoat, and not much better off once she was in care. Perhaps Matt was the only person who was ever nice to her.'

'How old was she?'

Deborah smiled, sadly. 'Sixteen.'

I whistled. This was way outside my experience. 'Jeez. What a mess.' I looked again at Matt, adoring his daughter. It didn't fit. It didn't work.

'I spotted him sloping off on a bus,' I remembered. 'Would he have been going to visit this baby?'

'Probably. Apparently he gets to see her for an hour, twice a week. Has done since he became involved.'

'Doesn't sound like very much.'

'No. It's about to be reduced to once a week, then once a fortnight. Then not at all. They don't want him getting too *fond* of her.'

I couldn't imagine being fond of a baby. I certainly couldn't imagine Matt being so. I was still struggling with the concept of the kid as a father. I mean, the word *father* triggers utterly different associations for me. Horrifying ones. Power, rage, terror. Shut up at the dinner table, heads down, keep that bloody dog out of the bins, and for Christ's fucking sake stop snivelling or the other barrel will be for you, you little prick. *Father* is a dirty word, in my dictionary. Fatherhood isn't slouching around, listening to rap and wearing jeans at half-mast.

'Why shouldn't he get too fond of her?' I asked eventually.

'Because she's going to be adopted, and he won't ever see her again. In the end, he gets what they call a "final visit". And that's that. *Final visit*. My God. What a chilling . . .' She laughed shortly, swallowed, and shook her head.

I waited, embarrassed. I wasn't very good with emotions.

Finally, she blinked hard and jerked her chin towards the photographs in my hand. 'Those were taken by a social worker for what they call her Life Story Book. Isn't that sweet? Grace takes it with her. So she knows that she had real parents, once.'

'This is all news to you?'

'Oh, yes. If I'd known, I wouldn't have . . .' Feverishly, she started shovelling everything back into the envelope. 'I don't know what to do,' she whispered. She rested her elbow on the table, and her forehead on her fingers, and shut her eyes.

I sat, shifting awkwardly, until she opened her eyes and aimed a blast of turquoise light, right at me. I was a rabbit in the headlights.

'You should read this, since you're the courier. You have a right to know what you carried.'

I let her force the envelope back into my hand.

It's amazing how quickly you can sober up when you need to. After leaving Deborah, I followed a line of knee-high solar lights to my cabin. An hour ago I could have slept like a puppy, but now I felt as though I'd knocked back three double-shot espressos.

I ducked under my mosquito net. Vicious little bloodsuckers fluttered up and down, looking for a way in. Intrigued, but feeling like a peeping Tom, I tipped out the contents of the envelope and picked up the first thing that came to hand. Black ink on ivory paper.

My darling Deborah,

We need you back immediately. We have a granddaughter.

I enclose local authority documentation. They are already making preparations for the adoption of Matt's child. Deborah, whatever you are doing, it cannot come before this.

Get in touch. Please. For all our sakes. Matt needs you.

With my love,

Perry

Beneath the letter were reports, notes, and a chronology. They told the story of a girl called Cherie: neglected by her mother, terrorised by her stepfather, rejected by both. Then pregnant. And now dead. I read all this with my mouth open, trying to remind myself that it was real. I thought my own childhood was rough, but what had happened to this kid was off my scale. She wasn't three inches of newsprint in the evening papers. She was Matt's girlfriend, the mother of his baby. There was more misery and hopelessness in those pages than I cared to think about.

There was a long assessment of Matt. Let's face it, you wouldn't give the boy a puppy you liked. It was all summed up in a hefty dollop of poison by the social worker Imogen Christie, who seemed to be running this show.

The father is Matthew Harrison (known as Matt), now seventeen years old. DNA testing confirms his paternity. He lives with his father, Peregrine Harrison (known as Perry), near the village of Coptree.

Matt and Cherie met while both were attending Woodbury High School. According to Matt, it was Cherie who insisted that his identity be kept secret. Their relationship came to an end during the pregnancy. He tells me that he endeavoured to maintain contact with her but she refused.

To Matt's credit, he contacted the Department immediately upon hearing the news of the birth of his daughter, and of Cherie's tragic death.

At his request he was offered supervised contact at Fintan House twice a week. He has attended consistently, never failing to arrive in good time, and has been cooperative throughout. He has clearly become deeply attached to Grace, and wishes her to be placed with him.

I found myself gazing into space. So Matt caught that bus faithfully, twice a week, just to sit and hold a baby. And they were taking her away. Perry could at least drive him there, the heartless bastard.

A six-week initial parenting assessment of Matt has been carried out. The assessment team noted Matt's deep devotion to his daughter, and his ability to provide basic care for her while under supervision. However, sadly, it concluded that if she were placed with him he would struggle to meet her needs and would not be able to acquire the skills to do so within an acceptable timeframe.

Matt is a teenage male with no experience of young children, and has yet to complete his own education. His independent living skills are limited. His departure from his previous school was sudden. Enquiries revealed that he left voluntarily, but was on the point of permanent exclusion. He admits to using cannabis extensively. His present lifestyle is somewhat chaotic, and his attendance at school is erratic. He has significant emotional and behavioural difficulties himself and would be unlikely to put the needs of a growing child before his own. His offer to care for Grace seems to have been based on loyalty and guilt regarding Cherie, and an unrealistic image of parenthood.

Matt now reluctantly accepts this, and no longer seeks to put himself forward as sole carer. He does not, however, feel able to sign the form for consent to adoption.

The paternal grandfather, Perry Harrison, declined to be involved in the assessment process. The reason for this is not clear to me. When I discussed it with the family I felt that they were not being entirely candid. Both insist that the paternal grandmother, Deborah Harrison, is well able to provide care for Grace and that she will contact the Department immediately upon her return from overseas. She is, apparently, a journalist whose present assignment is taking longer than anticipated to complete.

I have had no communication whatsoever from Mrs Harrison. Her commitment must therefore be in considerable doubt, and her long absence indicates that her lifestyle is unlikely to promote the stability and security needed. Grace cannot wait indefinitely for her return.

At the recent case conference it was unanimously agreed that attempts to find a placement within Grace's birth family have failed. Her future needs to be secured without further delay.

In respect of Grace Serenity King, therefore, the plan is one of adoption.
Imogen Christie
25 October

Light dawned when I looked at the date. The Harrisons had just heard this news when I blundered onto the scene. This was the family trouble for which Lucy had taken time off. They'd needed someone to fetch Deborah. And fast. Step forward, Jake Kelly.

There were other documents. Procedural waffling. I skimmed through them, but I'd already got the gist. I stuffed the sheaf of papers back into the envelope and turned out the light. It was all very interesting but not my problem, luckily. I closed my eyes and listened to the rustling of a sea breeze in the thatch, and the shrill of a million insects, and the whisper of the waves, lovingly stroking the sand.

Didn't sleep, though. Not for ages. I kept thinking about Matt, sitting alone on the bus, looking forward to seeing a blob in a bubblegum-pink suit.

Chapter Twelve

David woke in the early hours, alert and jangling. For a time he watched Leila's sleeping face, and then reached out and touched her cheek. Maybe today things would be better. Or maybe not.

Was he losing her? For ten years they'd screamed in unison at the ups and downs, the sickening fairground ride. But this, now. This was different.

Some time before six he silently slid out of bed, dressed, and made for his study. He spent a little time in prayer, miserably seeking comfort, then turned on the radio—*Farming Today*—and tried to work. There was always plenty to be done. An accusing pile of unanswered letters sprawled untidily across the blotting paper on his desk, and ten unread emails lurked malevolently in his inbox.

Slouching at his desk, he gnawed the skin around one thumbnail and gazed, without seeing, at Jacinta's ginger cat on dawn patrol along the fence. He couldn't quite define what it was that so terrified him. There had been no row, no shouting match. They'd had one or two of those in the past. He'd almost welcome one, now.

The change had come, he thought, a few weeks ago, soon after that chemical pregnancy disaster. Since then Leila had begun to put a barrier between them, as though their tracks must inevitably diverge. She was drifting away. In his photograph the sun glittered on her wedding dress, and she laughed up at him. He'd been dazzled by her fire. But little by little, her fire had gone out.

It was growing light outside. Soon he'd take her a cup of tea, and hope she'd be herself again, and they'd be happy.

David had never been *born again*; there was for him no miraculous falling of scales or blinding flash of light, not even a satisfying near-death experience. He had never spoken in tongues or seen a vision. The idea—the call?—began as a brief tug, like a fish testing a line, barely recognised and swiftly rejected. But it came back. And back. For almost a decade it nagged and cajoled, refusing to leave him alone no matter how much he protested that he wasn't the type. There was no escaping it. Finally, at the age of thirty-two, he gave in.

'I've had a career. I've made lots of splendid money,' he explained to a dubious Leila. 'I've made it for other people, and I've made it for us. I can't run away from this any longer.' He insisted that it had nothing to do with their childlessness, but he knew she didn't believe him.

She'd agreed, in the end. 'I can see I've no choice,' she said. 'Go ahead, condemn us both to a life of poverty and servitude.'

He rested his forehead against hers, warm with gratitude. 'But think of our heavenly bank account.'

'Yours, David, not ours. It's not a joint account, I'm afraid. Mine's firmly in the red. Anyway, go ahead and start the process. If you're accepted, I won't kick up a fuss. But there are conditions.'

He raised an eyebrow warily.

'First,' she prodded his chest, 'no fish stickers on the car. Ever. That's not negotiable.'

'Done.'

'Second.' Prod. 'No stripy tank top.'

David looked faintly sickened. 'I don't think taking the cloth automatically transforms people into style disasters.'

'And I need to be at least a hundred miles away when you break the news to Hilda. She's gonna go into orbit.'

Leila was right on that score.

It had all taken time—application, training, curacy—but five years on, this parish in Birmingham was David's second curacy. Leila moved with him uncomplainingly, finding work as a community pharmacist in each new city. They leased out their house in Finsbury Park. The rent more or less covered its mortgage, but not the rates or the insurance, the leaking roof or the exploding boiler.

And the children had never arrived.

David rubbed his forehead. Anxiety clawed in his stomach. Outside, the street lights flickered off, angular silhouettes against a bile-coloured sky. Next door's cat ran along the fence and disappeared. Perhaps little Jacinta had called it in for breakfast.

Leila was stirring. The floor creaked, then she was on the stairs. David arranged his features into optimism, pushing his chair back from the desk. 'Hi! I was coming with your tea, I promise.'

'Morning.'

He heard the kitchen door, then a pause. She'd be flicking on the kettle. Her steps again, across the hall, into the tiny piano room. He trotted downstairs.

She hadn't even turned on the light. He could just make out her figure by the window, against the jaundiced dawn. She was wearing one of his sweaters, and it swamped her. He pressed the light switch.

'I was going to turn it on.' She sounded defensive. 'Just looking at the sky.'

'Sorry. Sleep well?'

A blindingly cheerful smile. 'Fine! Fine. How about you?'

He went over to her and found her hand. It felt dead. The clawing in his stomach became more insistent, a gripping of strong, pitiless fingers.

'Leila. What were you doing in here?'

'Looking for some music. Maggie wants to borrow it.'

'But what were you thinking about?'

She shook her head in brisk denial, her mouth contorted. He pulled her to his chest and wrapped his arms around her, squeezing.

'I love you,' he said.

'Ouch! Don't know your own strength, Popeye.' She pushed him gently away. There was a determined set to her jaw. 'Get along with you. It's after seven o'clock. You've got a meeting at the primary school at eight, according to the calendar. And I'm going to iron a shirt.' She headed back to the kitchen, and he trailed after her.

'Big day today,' he said, with unconvincing jollity. 'Showdown. Marjorie Patterson's coming round to discuss the treasurer's report. She's convinced that there's been some skulduggery.'

'Goodness.' Leila unfolded the ironing board. 'That woman's a slavering bloodhound.'

'Reminds me of my Aunt Phyllis.'

Leila laid her shirt on the board: Kirkaldie's uniform, in a harsh blue. 'How *do* you take it seriously? For years, you handled multimillion-pound contracts. Nowadays your hair's supposed to stand on end if there's a tenner missing from the vestry fund . . . D'you realise it's now ten past?'

David glanced at the clock, trudged upstairs, and turned on the shower.

Ironic, really, he thought bitterly, as he stepped into the steamy water. Physician, heal thyself. He was supposed to be the rescuer, the unshakeable listener, open all hours and never too busy for people's problems. He soaked up others' desperation like blotting paper. But he had nowhere to put his own.

He closed his eyes, letting warm streams run over his face. It was time to move on. It was time to face the inevitable. Today.

The confirmation class huddled around a dusty electric heater. At lunchtime, David had dragged the clumsy, sickly-green thing out of a cupboard and switched it on in an attempt to bring the chilled air temperature in the vestry up to a civilised level. Could have been donated to a wartime museum, that heater. It smelled of burning hair and had begun to make an unhealthy buzzing sound.

The three teenagers came straight from school, lumpy bags slung across their backs, uniforms rebelliously untucked. They made Ovaltine and clutched the chipped mugs to their chests as David read them the story of Samuel in the temple.

'Blimey.' Vanessa, the organist's daughter, sported black eyeliner, laddered tights and lots of thigh below a well-worn school tunic. Her Brummie accent deepened considerably when she came to these classes, and her vocabulary seemed to shrink. David suspected it was all in honour of Kevin, the arsonist-choirboy-goalie, who slumped ungracefully in his chair, as far away from the predatory girl as possible. At fifteen, Kevin had begun to grow so alarmingly fast that he seemed unable to catch up with himself.

David rested the Bible on his lap. 'Er, blimey, Vanessa?'

She crossed her eyes. 'Well, poor little sod. What was his mum *on*? She prays like mad for a baby, fuss fuss fuss, then when she finally gets one, what does she do? Dumps him at the temple. What a cow.'

'Well, I know what you mean,' mused David, scratching his nose thoughtfully. 'But Hannah had promised to give him to God, hadn't she?'

'Huh. That wasn't *his* fault.'

David persisted. 'And remember that he became a great prophet and kingmaker.'

Vanessa shrugged contemptuously. 'Lucky he didn't become a great smackhead, abandoned by his mum like that.'

'It does seem hard, I agree. You could call it an early form of adoption.'

The girl pulled her scarf across her mouth, raising sceptical eyebrows. 'You could call it a lot of things, but they wouldn't be very polite.'

'This all happened about three thousand years ago, Vanessa. Values were very different then.'

'Well, I can't see the point in having a kid if you're just going to hand it over to some old priest. No offence, Mr E.'

Smiling, David was about to read the next passage when Kevin cleared his throat.

'My mum shoved off when I was a kid.' He shifted his feet. 'Hadn't promised me to the temple, though. She just couldn't stand my dad.'

Vanessa stared, horrified. Her fringe fell across her eyes. 'Oh. My. *God*!'

'It's all right, keep your hair on.' Kevin folded his arms. 'Wish I'd never mentioned it now.'

'So where's your mum gone?' This was skinny, straw-coloured Kimberley, whose sister worked in the church office.

Kevin favoured her with a half-hearted grin. 'Dudley. Silly slag might have got a bit further than Dudley, if she was making a break for it.'

Both girls giggled, clearly relieved at the lightening in mood. David glanced down at the scribbled notes that lay in his Bible. He was wondering how to bring the discussion back to the theme he'd planned for the class: Listening to God.

Vanessa, it seemed, was in no mood for theological discussion. Scraping the sugar out of the bottom of her mug with a biro, she murmured casually, 'You planning on having kids, Mr Edmunds?'

Startled, he glanced up from his notes. 'Um . . . yes. We'd like to.'

Vanessa stuck the sugary biro into her mouth, and her Mary Quant eyes wavered towards Kimberley, as if for encouragement, and back to David.

'We heard you might be going to adopt a baby.'

He blinked. 'Yes. Well, it's no secret. We would very much like to adopt a child.'

Vanessa sat back in her chair. 'Have you prayed for one?'

David hesitated for a moment and then closed his Bible. 'That's a good question, Vanessa. You see, I don't think prayer is supposed to be treated as a sort of telephone ordering service.'

'Like dialling up a pizza?'

'Exactly. For me, anyway, prayer isn't about that. The Lord knows better than us what it is we need, so we don't need to go nagging him about it. We gather comfort and strength just by standing quietly in his presence. Sometimes, if we persist, we might catch a glimpse of that brilliance and power. But more often he speaks to us very quietly. So we must be sure to listen very, very carefully. As did Samuel, in the temple.'

His pupil ignored this blatant attempt to bring the lesson back on track. 'So can't we ask for stuff?'

'Er . . . yes, of course, sometimes. We can bring our troubles to him. And we should certainly pray for others. *Ask, and you shall receive.* But the answer doesn't always come in the way we expect.'

Vanessa nodded uncertainly.

'What about fostering?' Kimberley had lowered her mug to the floor and was leaning forward, regarding him with new interest. 'My aunty fosters kids. She's got three at the moment. You get paid and everything.'

'Fostering . . . well, we're far more selfish than your aunt, Kimberley. We want a child we can keep. I think it would be terribly hard to give them back, don't you?'

'Yeah.' The girl looked wise, nail-bitten hands stretched above the heater's crazed enamel. 'Sometimes it is. Aunty Trish says one little boy just about broke her heart.'

'Your Aunty Trish must be quite a woman.'

He decided to send them home early. After a day at school, he could hardly ask for a full hour's concentration. He watched the three as they banged out through the west doors. Vanessa had taken Kimberley's arm and was holding her other hand out to Kevin, teasing and laughing, desperate to catch his attention. David smiled and shook his head, and then turned into the tiny Lady chapel on the south side of the nave.

This corner of the church felt deathly cold after the relative cheer of the vestry. Stray shafts of light penetrated the dusty recesses of the little chapel, creeping through the stained-glass window, and David's breath billowed in clouds. A jar of gold chrysanthemums stood on the altar, tingeing the air with the last whisper of autumn.

He perched on the edge of the front pew. As each minute passed, the stillness gathered around him like a mist. It was rush hour outside, but the chaos could not infiltrate his silence. He ceased to be aware of the smell of damp stone, the peeling whitewash on the walls, or the plaques recording the names of long-dead families. He had entered the quiet room of his mind, and shut the door.

He was still there when Angus arrived. The rector gave no sign whatsoever of having noticed the tall figure of his curate sitting alone in the Lady chapel. He did not pause on his way up the nave. Instead, he headed into the vestry where he could be heard pottering about. David was on his feet and stretching the kinks out of his spine when Angus emerged again, turning off lights.

'I like the Lady chapel too,' remarked the rector, strolling up. 'Comfier kneelers.'

'Sorry.' David blew on his bloodless fingers, suddenly aware that they were numb. 'I forgot the time. Did you think I was a burglar?'

Angus held up a large bunch of keys. 'Not at all. I know you've had the confirmation class. I just nipped over to lock up, that's all.'

David forced his hands into his trouser pockets. He was in no hurry to move on. 'I was seeking a little guidance, maybe a little courage—for

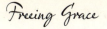

Leila and me. I think we've come to a crossroads, and I'm afraid it's a dangerous one.'

Angus stood very still, as though he had all the time in the world. 'How's that?'

'I'm quite worried about Leila . . . she's not herself.'

'Elizabeth's a little concerned too, actually,' admitted Angus.

David's gaze sharpened. 'Is she? Has Leila spoken to her?'

'Not in any detail. Elizabeth bumped into her last night in the churchyard. She feels she is at a low ebb. Still grieving, maybe, for the lost baby.'

David half turned, gazing up at the high, vaulted ceiling. 'We can't go on hoping for a family. It's all we ever do.'

Angus nodded and waited, watching his curate shrewdly.

David ran a hand through his hair. 'I'm afraid the problem is becoming destructive. It will come between us unless we make some tough decisions.'

'Such as?'

A long pause. 'I think it's time we gave up. I really do. I hope we can find other ways to use our time and our love, but we can't carry on as we are. We're living in limbo, and it's a waste of our lives. Frankly though, I'm afraid to broach the subject with Leila . . . I honestly don't know how she's going to react.'

'Not an easy task,' smiled Angus, and the two men began to stroll down the nave. 'Strikes me as a very determined woman, your wife. Beautiful, clever—and determined.'

'That's one word for it. I can think of less flattering ones.'

The rector led the way across the porch, clinking his keys, and they stepped out into a damp world of mist, eddying in the half-light.

'What have you got on this evening?'

'Nothing I can't miss,' grunted David, tugging at the heavy doors until they thudded together.

'Then miss it, whatever it is.' Angus locked up and dropped the keys into his pocket. He seemed to be deep in thought. 'Take heart, David. Remember Julian of Norwich? *All shall be well, and all shall be well, and all manner of things shall be well.*'

David managed an anxious smile. 'I'm not sure that applies to Leila and me. We're rather lower down the saintliness league table.'

Angus touched his curate's shoulder. 'You'd better get on home. Before you mislay your courage.'

Chapter Thirteen

I woke early the next morning. Habit of a lifetime. My mother was always up before dawn. I'd hear the crunch of her footsteps on the gravel outside my bedroom window as she went to water her veggie patch, and I'd roll out of bed and join her in the pale light, just as the first birds were stirring. That was our time, Mum's and mine, before the monster got up.

There was a bellbird that used to fly in from the bush to visit our garden, a little olive-green fellow with red eyes. He'd sit up in the rata and call, and his voice sounded like panpipes echoing in the hills. I don't think I've ever heard a sound so magical as our bellbird. I wanted him to build his nest in the garden, but he came only for the nectar, when the rata was in bloom. He'd bewitch us for a time and then he'd be off, back to the bush, with a rustle of wings. Mum said he didn't belong to us and he never could.

I pulled on last night's shorts and wandered out into the half-dark, peering across the gently moving sea. The darkness was thinning, like black paint in a pot of water. And it looked as though someone had lit an enormous fire just on the other side of the horizon.

I intended to hop down the little cliff and charge straight into the water. That would see off my hangover. I could already taste the salt in my mouth. But I didn't have the beach to myself. Someone was already there, standing in the shallows, facing east. Around her, little waves tumbled calmly onto the sand like a litter of kittens playing. She hadn't seen me. I sat down quietly, my legs hanging over the cliff, and we watched and waited together.

The distant fire pulsed and billowed as though fanned by a giant's breath. Then suddenly it broke free, and the sea glittered, and a path of dazzling light shot like an arrow across the surface of the water, straight at me.

Hundreds of times I've watched the sun come up, in all sorts of places. It's always like witnessing a great event, an epic moment in history. You can almost hear the roll of drums. But this time was extraordinary. This time, I felt as though the sun *was* God. (Incidentally, if my brother Jesse knew I'd said that, he'd immediately have me committed to an asylum so he could get the farm all to himself.)

Within a few minutes the sky was denim blue, and about a thousand birds were making a hell of a racket. The heat was already getting into its stride, and the horizon had begun to waver. Deborah stood silhouetted against the flashing water, a light wind rippling her shirt. Tangled between her shoulder blades, her hair was set alight in the low rays. The legs of her shorts were soaked. I noticed she hadn't changed her clothes; I'm willing to bet she'd never been to bed.

Eventually, she glanced back towards the campsite. A tall old guy was emerging from the trees, wearing ragged shorts and holding up two magnificent silvery fish in each hand. She waded ashore and greeted him in Swahili. There was a fair amount of nodding and smiling, and they both headed off to the kitchen to complete the deal. I watched as they wandered up the path, talking quietly. I kept them in sight until the white cloth of her shirt had disappeared behind the glowing ivory and green of a bush. As she passed, a chattering swarm of little yellow birds burst from the leaves.

It was as though she had been here all her life. These were her colours and her sounds; this was her air. It was difficult to imagine her making meat pies in a red and black farmhouse near Ipswich, with beeswax on the floor and mothballs in the cupboards.

After a swim I strolled up to the bar, where Hamisi gave me some coffee. You could almost smell the heat: dust, seaweed, and an exotic sweetness I'd noticed as soon as I stepped off the plane. Over at the campsite, people were wandering to the showers and back, or boiling kettles on paraffin rings. The pace was gentle, the light clear; it was like floating in a beautiful, drug-induced dream. Even the sea seemed to move in slow motion.

It couldn't last, of course. Progress and politics and human greed had to catch up eventually, even here, and tear it all apart. Kulala Beach couldn't hold out forever. Perhaps drought would destroy it. Perhaps disease, or riot, or war. Or maybe a concrete crop of foreign-owned resorts. They'd put up a barbed-wire fence, and armed guards would beat up the dignified old fisherman if he came near.

I took a bottle of water back to my private cliff among the trees, grabbed my map and guidebook from the cabin, and sat with my back against the door. Briskly, humming boldly to myself, I looked up Mount Kenya. I'd found Mrs H, now. My life was my own.

Yep. I was out of there.

I stared at the same page for half an hour, and I didn't learn anything about Mount Kenya. I was still thinking about Matt. And Deborah, thigh-deep in the waves at sunrise.

A small sound on the sandy path. A pair of bare, dusty feet. She'd showered and wrapped one of those pieces of tie-dyed cloth around herself—bright primary colours—with another one as a belt. She sat down on a rock, facing the sea. A wisp of honey-coloured hair was blowing across her mouth. I wanted to brush it away for her.

'Read it?' she asked.

'Yep. Every word.'

'And?'

'And I'm very glad it isn't my problem.'

She jerked her head down towards the beach. 'Come for a walk with me?' Her voice was clear. Uncluttered. Like the chime of our bellbird, up in the rata.

I bet we set the campers gossiping. We wandered through the luminous shallows, right along to the end. The foam stretched in creamy arches around our ankles.

'Are you still writing articles?' I asked, when the silence became embarrassing.

For a second she looked startled. I think she'd forgotten I was there. 'They're hard to sell, nowadays,' she replied absently, swishing her toes.

I found myself smiling. 'Humanising these people for all the liberal lefty types.'

'Ah, yes. That's Lucy talking, isn't it?'

A shoal of pin-sized fish scurried away from our shadows.

'I'm not a brilliant journalist,' she said suddenly. 'But what I was trying to do was show how atrocity *works*, in practice; how the unimaginable becomes reality. I wanted people to, you know, recognise the monster within themselves. So they'd be on their guard against it.'

'Not me,' I argued, picking up a shell and skimming it out to sea. 'I'm a lazy prick. Couldn't be bothered to summon up enough hatred.'

She didn't reply, just looked cynical. Her eyes matched the turquoise water.

'You must have had to hear some harrowing stories,' I said, forcing myself to look away and vowing to get a grip on myself.

'And so should we all. We're *all* responsible.' She glanced sideways at me, a small smile at one corner of her mouth. 'Even lazy pricks.'

I laughed. She scratched her nose, thinking. 'I know what people's images are of Africa. Child soldiers, starving babies, atrocity, corruption, AIDS.'

'Or pretty sunsets and the odd elephant.'

She nodded. 'Both are distortions. Reductions. Both deny the fun.' She held her arms out wide, a tightrope walker. 'The life. The courage. Anyway, this is my home. For a while at least, I want to be a part of it, not an observer. Which is convenient, because there's not as much work for freelancers as there was.'

We'd reached the end of the beach, and she began to clamber purposefully over the rocks.

'Hamisi tells me you've met Rod.'

'Er . . . mm.' I hauled myself up, scraped my shin on a razor-sharp rock, and swore under my breath as bright red blood cheerfully spurted out. 'Nice guy.'

'And I imagine you're wondering how Mrs Perry Harrison comes to be living on Kulala Beach?'

'Not really.'

She made her fingers into a pistol and aimed it at my head. 'If you say it's none of your business, I'll have to kill you.'

I jammed my hands into my pockets like a schoolboy, squinting up at the sky. The sun looked menacing now, like a vast white firework at the moment it explodes. And the colour was draining out of the day. Even the sea had faded to a rippling opal.

'No good asking me for advice. I'm pathologically shallow,' I said. 'Really. A night out, couple of beers, swap a yarn or two—that's all I'm good for.'

'I don't think so. If all that was true, you wouldn't be here.'

I watched Mrs Harrison—a flash of brilliant colour—leaping easily from rock to rock, unruly hair swinging across her graceful shoulders. I tried to imagine her with Perry, hosting Christmas drinks by the fireplace at Coptree. And I couldn't.

'Okay,' I called after her. 'What's the story?'

She stopped, poised on a massive boulder. Her mouth twitched, as though she'd just beaten me at a game of tennis and was trying not to crow. Then, abruptly, she disappeared.

Following her, I found myself dropping down into a perfect miniature bay, just a few feet across. The sand was flat, washed clean by the tide and shaded by bush that tumbled down to the edge. After the glare, it was a relief. She'd settled herself on a low stretch of rock, half covered by heavy vines. She tucked that strand of hair behind her ear.

'Your shin's bleeding.'

'Won't kill me.' I splashed seawater over my leg. 'Look, Lucy did fill me in a bit. Her mother dies, and before she's cold in her grave, you swan in like a sort of gold-digging Mary Poppins.'

She laughed, without amusement. 'I'd just turned twenty when I married Perry,' she said. 'And—yes—I was pregnant with Matt.'

'Not a crime.' I began to mess about in the sand with my big toe, digging up little shards of coral. Here I was on a tiny, isolated beach, with a fascinating woman dressed in nothing but a couple of bits of cloth. And all I did was dig in the sand with my toe. Pathetic. I was losing my grip.

'It *was* a crime, though.' She chewed her lower lip. A habit of hers. 'I threw up on my wedding day.'

'I know lots of blokes who've done that.'

She rolled her eyes. 'This was *morning* sickness, Jake, not morning after the stag night. It wasn't a fairytale for me, all lace and orange blossom and bashful blushes. They had to stop the car on the way to the registry office so I could chuck up. Not a great start to married life.'

'No, I s'pose not . . . And it's true about you being the nanny?'

'Oh, yes.' She sat up a little straighter. 'I became Perry's nanny within days of leaving boarding school. I was booked into a course in journalism, but Perry was an acquaintance of my dad's, and he was desperate for help because his wife had just died. So I flew out to Germany, where he was based. It seemed a good opportunity to improve my German and save a bit of cash.' She paused. 'I was only seventeen. Lucy was four.'

I tried to picture a small Lucy. 'I bet she was cute.'

Deborah lit up. 'Unbe*liev*ably cute! Very clingy, because she'd just lost her mother. She used to creep into my bed in the night and snuggle up to me.'

'Wasn't compulsory to marry her dad, though, was it?'

Her voice took on a new resonance. 'Ah, Perry. I was a dreamy, romantic soul, back then. I thought he was my Mr Rochester. He's almost twenty years older than me, you know.'

'Bloody pervert.' I dumped myself on the sand near the foot of her rock, picked up a stick and began drawing circles.

She sounded surprised. 'No. No, he's not that.'

'C'mon. You were a baby, for Pete's sake. Seventeen! Bloody hell, that's Matt's age.'

'True.' She thought about it. 'But Perry didn't show any interest in me at first. He was grief-stricken about his precious Victoria. Ate in the officers' mess and staggered home after I was in bed. For my part, I was completely infatuated within about three hours. He was an army officer—tall, dark and haunted. Very attractive combination. He became my whole world.'

'He has a certain charisma. Even I can see that.'

'He has.' She sighed. 'Anyway, to cut a long story short, after several months he seemed to wake up. We started taking Lucy out together, like a family. Once I'd put her to bed, he would be waiting on the balcony with a bottle of wine. And one thing led to another.'

'He pounced.' I threw my stick away. I felt unreasonably sulky, for some reason. 'On the balcony, I bet.'

'He did. My dream came true. But . . . well. I was pretty naïve. I mean—you know—it wasn't my first time, as they say, but nothing had prepared me for this. It was so grown-up. Such an onslaught.'

'Told you he's a pervert.'

'No, no. Not a physical onslaught. But emotionally . . . He was the subject of all my romantic daydreams, but at the same time it was over-whelming. He wasn't a callow youth of twenty who might move on after a week; he was an adult, a widower, a father. He kept saying how much he needed me.'

'That's heavy.'

'Intense. Suddenly, I was in deep. Ever been out of your depth?'

'I'm a good swimmer.'

She prodded me with a tanned, sandy foot, and I fought back a ridiculous urge to catch it in my hand. 'I hardly think that strumpet Karin turning you down last night counts as a life-changing experience, Jake Kelly.'

'How would you know?'

'Anyway,' she continued, ignoring me. 'We settled down like a family, the three of us, and I knew I ought to be blissfully happy, and I almost was. I was still in awe of Perry, still sort of mesmerised. But it wasn't light-hearted. It wasn't *fun*. As the months went on, I realised . . . he wasn't jealous, exactly, or possessive—he didn't beat up other men for talking to me—but he wasn't easygoing. Quite the opposite, in fact. He always wanted to know I'd be home when he got there. He used to phone and check before he set out. There was a sort of neediness that I hadn't expected and wasn't mature enough to challenge.'

She took hold of that errant strand of hair and began to twist it distractedly around her finger. 'And then he began to have . . . attacks.'

I was puzzled. 'Attacks?'

'Heart attacks, or so we thought. The whole drama. Fighting for breath, clutching his chest, screaming for me. I was sobbing in the ambulance, begging him not to die.'

'Jeez, that's awful.'

'It *was* awful. The doctors did tests. They said there was nothing wrong with his heart. In the end they . . .' She hesitated. Glanced at me and then away. Danced her fingers on her rock. 'Well, never mind. The upshot was that the army posted him here.'

'*Here?*'

'Yes. To Nairobi, actually. For a change of scene. To train some local troops the British Army way.'

My eyebrows went up. 'Hell. He never said.'

'Well, now you know. We all came—Lucy and me, too. I was still the nanny, officially, although Perry and I had talked about marriage. He was stationed in Nairobi for six months. Then he got himself sent to Colchester, and that's when he bought the house at Coptree.'

She leaned back on her hands, her face turned to the sun as though she'd talked herself to a standstill. It was a full minute before she spoke again, very quietly, very clearly. She might have been talking to herself.

'And it was here, in this beautiful country, that I met Rod. Eighteen years ago . . . or was it only yesterday? I'd gone for lunch with some army wives, all older women, at the Thorn Tree—you might have heard of it?—and some of them knew Rod, so he joined us. He came and sat down next to me, and we talked for hours. One of the others introduced me—Deborah Bridges, as I then was—but I told him to call me Susie.'

I was baffled. 'Why?'

She shrugged. 'A bit of rebellion, I suppose. My parents called me Deborah after my grandmother, and she was a mean, sharp-tongued old woman. Susan's my middle name, and I've always preferred it. I was Susie to my friends at school. It was only my parents' generation that insisted on calling me De-bo-*rah*.' She stuck out the tip of her tongue as though the word tasted sour. 'Perry came into their category. Rod certainly didn't.'

The sun had moved around. I shifted a few inches, into the shade of an overhanging bush.

'When the others left the Thorn Tree, we hardly even noticed. We were nose to nose. I told him all about Perry and Lucy, and he said it sounded as though I needed rescuing.' She shook her head in wonder. 'The army wouldn't have touched Rod with a barge pole. He can't take orders. He seemed so gloriously young—especially compared to Perry—and untamed. I couldn't see him commuting on the tube. You might as well imagine a leopard settling down quietly in Milton Keynes.'

'A free spirit.' I let my eyelids droop for a moment, remembering. 'I used to be one of those.'

'Aren't you still?'

I opened my eyes, and she was looking at me. 'Carry on,' I said.

'You're probably thinking what a faithless little whore I was.'

'Yeah. Best kind of woman.'

'Thank you.' She inclined her head. 'But it isn't true. Remember, I was still a teenager! My friends back home were students, young and silly, getting drunk on Saturday nights and stealing garden gnomes. But I'd shot out of school and straight into this intense, isolating relationship with Perry. I hadn't had the fun, the laughs, the dating and discos and falling in and out of love like a yoyo. Meeting Rod made me face the fact that I was suffocating.'

She shielded her eyes with one hand, gazing at a ship as it crawled along the horizon. 'We met again that evening, and again, and again. We *had* to be together, all the time. With him, I felt like a bird out of its cage, and I wanted to sing. He'd just bought this place, and he asked me to join him.'

'But you didn't,' I predicted confidently. I knew she hadn't come to live at Kulala. After all, she was Mrs Perry Harrison.

'But I *did.*'

I was perplexed. 'You left Perry?'

'Yes, and it was horrible. I told him I'd met someone else, and he went nuts. I thought he was going to have a heart attack—a proper one. I felt like a total bitch—and I was confused, because he'd been such a colossal figure in my life. Lucy held onto my legs all the way to the taxi, crying. Well, we were both crying. It was like leaving my own child. She was waving with both her hands, stumbling after the car like an abandoned puppy.'

'Poor kid.'

'You're so right. Abandoned by her mother, then by her surrogate mother. I hated myself for it, couldn't bear the misery I'd caused them both. For days I moped about like a bear with toothache, fretting over Lucy. It almost ruined everything. Then, one morning . . .' She trailed off. A cockerel squawked in the scrub, close by. It made us both jump.

'Um.' She laughed, self-consciously. 'You'll think I'm mad.'

'I already do.'

'No, but . . . okay. I stood in the sea and watched the sun come up over the horizon. Raging up. I imagined I could hear it, roaring like Aslan, stretching out to me across the water. I imagined he—Aslan, or God, or whoever—was giving me permission. What I was doing was right.' She flapped a hand at me. 'Loony tunes.'

'No, I wasn't thinking that.'

'Yes, you were. Anyway, there it is. I stopped moping and helped Rod and Hamisi get the place set up. Designed the layout of the bar, just as it is now, cantilevered over the beach. Rod and I slept under a mosquito net strung between the trees just where your banda is. Every morning we'd crawl out and run into the water. We were so happy . . . *so* happy.'

'I sense an "until" coming on.'

'Yes. *Until.* I suspected, feared, denied for months. Vomited.'

'Matt?'

'Matt.'

'Don't tell me Rod's his father?'

She shook her head vehemently, holding up an imperious hand. '*No.* That's the point. Perry is. I had to leave.'

'Did you? Why?'

'Imagine yourself, Jake, at the age of twenty-three. Your new girlfriend gets herself pregnant, and it's not even yours. What would be the decent thing for her to do?'

'Disappear?'

'Precisely. Rod values nothing more than his freedom. *Nothing.* That's why I love him—d'you see?'

I nodded uncertainly.

'If I'd told him about the pregnancy, he would probably have done right by me—whatever that means—but he would have resented me for it.' She shuddered. 'No. I couldn't ask it of him. If I went back to Perry, I could at least give my child a father—its *own* father. So I pretended my dad was ill, dying of cancer, needing me to nurse him through his last illness. It wasn't true at the time, but it became true a couple of years later, and poor Mum followed him. D'you think that was divine retribution?'

'Nope.'

'Rod was so calm. He didn't *need* me, you see? He drove me to the airport, walked me across the tarmac, said he'd be waiting. I didn't believe him.' She made a small, unhappy sound, smoothing the vivid cloth across her knees. 'Perry met me at Ipswich Station, and we never spoke about my little escapade. It never happened.'

I shook my head. 'Amazing.'

'It was lovely to see Lucy, but she looked quite thin and tired. She wouldn't let me out of her sight; even used to get up in the night to check I was still there. Getting her to school was a real problem. The teacher called it separation anxiety.' Deborah chewed her lip thoughtfully. 'I suppose she'd suffered too much loss in her young life. She knew that people sometimes don't come back.'

She gazed down the years, eyes unfocused. 'Perry and I were married a month later at the local registry office. Lucy was our bridesmaid, and she was in heaven. I squeezed myself into a size fourteen dress and all day long I grinned like a Cheshire cat. Pity the bride who smiles all day! Mum had a *lovely* time. Dad, bless him, looked utterly confused by the whole event. You can tell from the wedding photos. They went on a cruise later in the year, because it had been such a budget wedding.'

'They got a bargain.'

'Yes.'

'But you didn't.'

She gave a little shrug. 'Matt arrived when I was still just a child myself, really. Wow. Hell of a thing, your own baby. Quite a life-changer.'

'I expect the novelty wears off,' I said seriously. 'After a month or so.'

She looked shocked for a second and then laughed. 'You're absolutely hopeless, you know that? No, life is never the same again, Jake. Never.' The laugh weakened.

'Did you enjoy having a baby so young?' I was ghoulishly curious. I couldn't imagine a damnation more hellish than being entirely responsible for another human being.

'Would you?' She met my eyes, and then her gaze slid away to the sea. 'You have to efface yourself completely and become a non-person. It's too hot on this rock,' she interrupted herself, and slipped down to join me in my patch of shade. I made room for her. It wasn't flirtatious, the way she parked herself beside me. It was companionable.

She picked up a handful of fine sand, and let it drift between her fingers. '*Enjoy* isn't strong enough . . . it's a lot more fundamental and a lot less comfortable. You love them in a way you could never have imagined. Your happiness is bound up with theirs, forever. You feel constant anxiety for them long after they've stopped feeling any for you. Both Matt and Lucy.'

I was silent, guiltily wondering if that's how Mum felt.

'Anyway. The point is . . . Perry's not what he seems, Jake.'

This was too much, dangling such a snippet in front of my nose. I mean, I'm not made of stone. I grappled with my curiosity for a few seconds and then said, 'He's gay, isn't he?'

'Uh-uh.' She shook her head, smiling.

'Mainlines heroin? Wears a tutu? International terrorist?'

She drew her finger and thumb across her lips, zipping them up.

I tried again. 'He *doesn't* own a string vest?'

'Look, it was naughty of me to mention it. I can't tell you, all right? I've promised him, on my children's life. And I've kept that promise all these years. So stop asking.'

'Fair enough.' I scratched my ear. 'Mud wrestling?'

'Shut up. Let's just say that he had to leave the army.'

'Okay.' My imagination was working overtime. Maybe Perry was a spy?

She patted my shoulder. 'You can take it from me that life with Perry wasn't easy. But I'd made my bed, and the children needed me. I just got on with it. That's what you do, isn't it? That's what my parents did, and yet they gave me a wonderful childhood. I suspect most marriages are like that, to a greater or lesser degree.'

'Endurance courses.'

'Exactly.'

'But you're here now,' I reminded her. 'You came back.'

'I wasn't going to end up buried next to Perry in Coptree churchyard. I decided that once the children were independent, once Matt turned seventeen, my sentence would be up.' She dug out another handful of sand. 'I knew I could manage that.'

The grains trickled out of the hourglass of her fist, falling in a thin stream. 'I was a model prisoner. I wanted Lucy and Matt to have perfect childhoods. My birthday parties were legendary, my Christmas tree had real candles. But every lighting of them marked another wasted year. I had this imaginary world, Kulala. It was a sort of Eden to me. In my mind I'd walk along the paths, sink into the water. I became utterly obsessed by the idea of coming back. *Obsessed.*' She shut her eyes for a second. 'I had no other concept of my future. I tried to tell myself that Rod wouldn't be here, he'd be married and pot-bellied and living in suburbia. But still I plotted and schemed and dreamed of coming back.'

She poured the sand over my feet. It felt like warm water. 'After Matt went off to boarding school, I did a course. Journalism.'

'Finally.'

'Finally. Then I managed to land a slot on the local rag. I got on well with the editor . . . one job led to another.' She dusted the sand off her hands. 'Several years ago, I arranged to write a piece on the war crimes tribunal in Arusha. That's only about a day's drive from here. I flew into Mombasa and took a taxi straight to Kulala Beach. I remember being driven through the plantation, watching for my first sight of the horizon. And there was the Indian Ocean, right where I'd left it.' She smiled, remembering. 'And there was Rod. He strolled up as I climbed out of the taxi. "So, Susie. Your dad finally died, then?" '

I laughed, feeling oddly miserable. 'You had a lot of explaining to do.'

'I did. We spent days and nights just talking. Rod understood. After thirteen years, we picked up where we'd left off.'

'Did you get to the tribunal?'

'Mm. Wrote a couple of pieces. I only stayed three weeks that first time. Just a bit of home release. Matt still needed me. But I came quite often after that.'

'Arusha?'

'No. The world has a short attention span; it tired of the agonies of Hutus and Tutsis. The circus had long moved on. Somalia, Darfur, Zimbabwe, the Congo. I didn't try to cover those areas. I did quite a bit of work on nomadic life—which fascinates me—and the effects of long-term drought here in Kenya.'

An insect began to click and hum in the dry grass nearby. Clickety-clicket.

'And all the time,' she said, 'Rod and I were counting down the years—then the months, then the days—until I could come home for good.'

'Perry must have known what you were up to.'

'Never said so. I always made sure he was looked after. To say that I lived for my weeks here would be a pathetic understatement. This *is* my home. This *is* my life. In Coptree I merely existed, just got through the day. Here, I live.'

'But this isn't the real world. You can't stay here forever.'

She lifted a shoulder. 'Why not? I don't like the real world. It's going up in flames. Literally.'

'True.'

We had a minute's silence, thinking of the world that was going up in flames. And then I remembered Matt, crying in his room.

'Matt's still pretty young.'

'Come on.' She scowled, flicking a giant ant off her knee. 'Matt despises me.'

'He's just being cool.'

'No, really. He's barely addressed two sentences to me since his voice broke. All I get is grunts and that's if I'm lucky. I've nothing to offer my son any more. Nothing. Ever since he stopped being a cuddly cherub and became a muscled killing machine.'

'I think that's normal for boys his age. He'll grow out of it.'

'So they say.' She grimaced miserably. 'You never, ever stop loving them but it hurts, Jake. He looks at me as though I'm a mouldy sandwich. Walks away when I'm talking to him.'

'Little sod. I'll have a word with him.'

She stood up and waded into the criss-cross brilliance of the shallows. The light seemed to flicker right through her.

'We had a party for his seventeenth, after his exams back in June. Lots of girls, all gorgeous and all swooning over Matt. He must have had this secret, the pregnant girl. He did seem on edge. And I had *my* secret. I'd already got my ticket.'

'What did you do about money?'

'I'd been siphoning off funds into a separate bank account for years. About seventeen years, actually. I had a bit invested. There's no need to look as though you're sucking on a lemon.'

I was gawping at her. I mean, we all make mistakes. But stealing the housekeeping money for all those years—stashing it away from the very first day of your marriage—well, that's over the top. That's dishonesty on a pretty monumental scale.

She kicked a spray of sapphires into the air. 'Look, Mr Goody-Goody, there's no call for you to be sanctimonious. It was my money too. I spent my entire adult life working for that family. They got a free nanny, chauffeur, housekeeper, cook and cleaner. Bargain! So I gave myself the odd bonus. So what? I won't ask Perry for more. I could demand a share in his army pension, make him sell the house. But I won't. He's getting off bloody lightly.'

'He is—financially. So there you were, ready to go.'

'All ready to go.' She held up both hands in a gesture of finality. 'Filled the freezer, cleaned the place from top to bottom, got the cleaner to increase her hours. The Great Escape.'

'Why didn't you tell them you wouldn't be back this time?'

'Didn't tell them . . . ?' She looked scandalised. 'I *did*!'

My jaw dropped. 'They lied to me.'

'Of course they lied to you. Otherwise you wouldn't have agreed to come. I told them on the day I left. I didn't say where I was going, just that after I'd written my piece I wasn't coming back. Perry took it hard, as I expected. Matt just went out. And Lucy gave me an ear bashing.'

'She's not in your fan club, is she?'

Deborah looked unhappy. 'I've abandoned her twice, really. She's never forgotten the first time, and she may never forgive the second. I would have been in touch, you know. Once the dust had settled. But the sad fact is that my children couldn't care less if I emigrated to Mars.'

'You're wrong there. Matt literally begged me to find you.'

She splashed back up the beach and knelt down, looking into my face. 'Really?'

'Really.'

Her face fell. 'Well he would, wouldn't he?' she said bitterly. 'So he can play with his new doll, which really cries and wets its nappy. If I don't play too, they have to take her back to the shop.'

I let it go. The air was distorted now, quivering as though the sand was on fire, and our patch of shade had shrunk.

'Rod will be home by this evening.' She sounded desperate. 'I have to decide before then. Tell me, Jake. Advise me. What do I do? What I *want* to do is burn Perry's letter and stay here, where I've found happiness.'

'That's a very rare commodity, happiness. Very, very rare.' I meant it. I'd been searching for years, and the pot of gold always disappeared when I got closer.

'A great gift,' she agreed.

'So. Stay.'

'But then my grandchild will be given away to strangers, and Matt will never see her again.' She rubbed her eyes despairingly. 'He'll never forgive me. And *I'll* never forgive me. Those photos . . . Matt and his tiny daughter. Made me want to cry.'

It's life and death, tell her. Bring her back.

'Lots of kids get adopted,' I argued half-heartedly.

'C'mon, Jake. Be realistic. It may be a miserable existence, where nobody loves her. Paedophiles have even adopted children especially so they can abuse them.'

'That can't be very common.'

'But it happens. And she'd never be able to contact us. We'd never sleep easy again.'

Promise you'll bring her home with you. Promise.

She met my eyes. 'So must I start all over again? Another seventeen years in the slammer?'

'Matt could have her back one day,' I suggested doubtfully.

'I'll be her mother . . . I'll love her. It means nothing to me any more, that half-life of the privileged. Plastic friendships. Hairdos and aerobics and personalised number plates. Fussing about whether our darlings will be brain surgeons or concert pianists. People here—those women you can hear, chatting, pounding maize—they worry about whether their children are even going to make it through the latest drought. Their lives are *real.*' Her hand fastened on my arm. 'Help me, Jake! I don't know what to do.'

At first I didn't answer. I was watching the silver trail of a jet as it inched across the emptiness, and wishing I had a better answer for her.

'I know what I'd do,' I said. 'I'd develop a sudden urge to explore Outer Mongolia. I'm a gold medallist at running away.'

I felt her fingers tighten. 'Good plan.'

I sighed. It was no use. 'But I know what *you're* going to do, Deborah, and so do you. I think you made your decision sometime around dawn this morning. I don't think the sun gave you his blessing this time.'

She hid her face in her hands, and I laid an arm around her shoulder as she grieved. The heat seemed to breathe, like a sleeping dragon.

I heard her laugh. Or sob. Either way, it was a bitter sound.

'I wait seventeen years,' she said. 'And Matt forgets to buy a condom.'

Chapter Fourteen

David had something on his mind. She knew it, even before he'd hung up his coat.

Leila had arrived home first, to a darkened house. The answer machine was flashing hysterically, as usual, but she ignored it. She wasn't in the mood to be David's secretary.

She mustn't give herself time to mope. Rolling up her sleeves, she attacked last night's washing-up with determined energy. Sent an email to her brother. Sat at the piano and started getting to grips with a song Patrick had written for the Defibrillators. Nice rhythm, but the lyrics were pure schmaltz.

David called out as soon as he opened the front door, as though checking she was there. Unusual. And as he carried his bag up to the study his footsteps sounded oddly resolute and purposeful. There was no tuneless baritone this evening, no jovial gossip about Vanessa and Kevin, yelled from upstairs. When he padded back down the stairs—often he jumped the last four steps, landing with a cheerful thud that shook the walls, but not tonight—she was standing rigidly in the hall, waiting for him. He held out his arms.

'Evening, my lovely,' he said quietly, and drew her close to him.

'Something's up,' she insisted, stiffening. 'What's happened? Is it Mum?'

'No. There's no bad news.' He ran a hand around the back of his neck. 'Let's have a drink.'

She hung around by the kitchen table, watching unhappily as he uncorked a bottle.

'Look,' he began heavily. 'There's—'

Out in the hall, the telephone rang. David didn't move. 'For God's *sake*,' he snapped, flinging the corkscrew onto the table. 'They can leave a message.'

Amazing, the fretful desperation in the sound of a ringing phone. Like a baby, crying. Every ring was an accusation. It cried out eight times before the answer machine soothed it. In the sudden silence they stared at one another, afraid to look into their future. A vice had begun to squeeze the breath from Leila's chest. She watched his hands as he poured.

'Look,' he began again. 'There's much more to our marriage than having children.'

Leila froze as the vice tightened. There wasn't enough air. 'Meaning what?'

He lowered himself into a chair, reaching for her hand. She felt the distracted strength of his fingers, tangling with hers. 'I love you, Leila. I want us to be happy, and we can't be happy while we're yearning for something that may never happen.' His warm, dry palm drifted up her forearm. 'We can't carry on longing for a child.'

Abruptly, Leila sat down. She meant to take a sip to give herself time, but her wrist shook uncontrollably. Red wine spilled down her sleeve and onto the table.

'But we *do* long for it. There's no off switch.'

David moved his chair closer, searching her face with fearful eyes. He took her other hand also, embracing them both, holding them against his chest.

'I don't think this is worth it any more.'

She was silent for a good ten seconds, marshalling the hornet thoughts that buzzed furiously to the surface of her mind.

'Not worth it?' Snatching her fingers away, she spat out the words as though they were poisoned. 'After all we've been through? Everything we've had to put up with—the IVF, everything—not *worth* it?'

'Leila . . . I didn't mean that we should never have tried. I just mean that it isn't worth the constant stress. Not any more. It's making you so unhappy.'

'That's *my* problem.'

'Can't we take ourselves off the adoption register? Can't we have a *real* future, not a fantasy one? It's been so long. We have to stop dreaming.'

She was glaring wildly at him, the back of her hand pressed to her mouth. 'Stop dreaming.' She gagged on the horror. 'It's what we *do*. It's who we *are*.'

'It doesn't have to be.'

'Really?' She found herself on her feet, hating him, wanting to hurt him. 'What else have we got?'

The question hung maliciously between them. Leila strode to the door and then to the sink, trying to escape the despair. Sorrow was welling up in her throat, choking her. She had a frantic need to keep moving. She seized a dishcloth, held it under the tap and frenziedly mopped the draining board.

'Leila,' said David quietly, from behind her. 'Please.'

Her movement was arrested, the cloth dripping in her hand.

His voice had a hopeless precision. 'Do you think I don't mourn for the children we'll never have? Do you think I never imagine what they would have been like? My son, my daughter?'

She turned, startled. Never before had she heard David acknowledge his own grief. He looked weary suddenly, his eyes deep in their own shadows. She could see one—no, more—strands of grey, glinting in his hair. She'd never noticed them. How could she have failed to notice? David wasn't young any more.

Ashamed, she took a step towards him and opened her mouth to speak without knowing what she would say.

The telephone shrieked again, furiously, a child who would not be pacified. Leila jerked her head towards the sound, grateful now for the interruption. It would give her time.

'Go on, answer the wretched thing. We can't just leave it again. Someone might be in trouble.'

He caught the wretched thing at the seventh ring. 'David Edmunds.'

It was astonishing, Leila reflected bitterly, how the man managed to sound sincere and wise and concerned, even at a time like this. She wasn't listening to his conversation; she had not the slightest interest in which nagging fishwife was after her husband's time and energy. She stood in the middle of the kitchen floor, while her cloth dripped a pool of water onto the lino.

He wanted to give up. How could he want to give up?

And yet. There was something different about this call. In the hall, David was momentarily silent, listening. The very air seemed to grow watchful, to lean closer, to hold its breath. Leila let his words trickle into her consciousness.

'Linda Hooper,' he said. 'Yes, Linda, of course I remember. From the adoption team. What can I do for you?' Caught by a sudden draught, the kitchen door swung shut.

A small, beguiling hope began to flutter away somewhere under her rib cage, but she sternly ignored it. There had been too many fluttering hopes over the years, too many secret little pets of happiness, and they had all died horribly.

Then David was shouting.

It was probably bad news, Leila told herself. They'd been taken off the register. Too old, perhaps.

The kitchen door crashed against the wall as he launched himself into the room and grabbed her by the elbows. He was grinning like a gleeful schoolboy who has discovered where they keep the key to the tuck cupboard.

'They've found one! They've *found* one!' He was making less sense than a schoolboy, too.

'Found what, you ridiculous man?'

'A baby.'

'I don't . . .'

'A *baby*, Leila! It was that social worker on the phone—Linda. There's a baby girl needing a family right now, and we're top of the list!'

Leila began to wring her hands together, agonised by the possibility, trying not to believe. She was horribly afraid to believe.

'Aren't there others who want her?'

'Of *course* there are! But we're the front runners because she's mixed race. Also, we tick the box on the father's wishes—he wanted one or both adoptive parents to be professionals, apparently, and wasn't fussy about age. They've compared our assessment report—remember that thing, a gazillion pages of questions?—with the baby's. And we're the nearest match.'

They stared dumbly at one another. David was rolling from one foot to the other as if unable to be still. Leila lifted a hand to her cheek. The hope began to flutter more insistently under her ribs, drawing breath, unfolding its beautiful wings.

'Who's looking after her at the moment?' she asked. 'The parents?'

'No, no. Foster care. In another region altogether.'

'So how does it all work?'

'One or two formalities, a lot of faffing around, but Linda says she sees no reason why we shouldn't—'

'When?'

'I'm not sure about the timing. You can call her back tomorrow, she'll have gone by now. She's been trying to get hold of us all day, she said, left messages on the machine, gave us one last go before she knocked off.'

Leila stood stunned, wondering where the catch lay. There had to be a catch. 'Have the parents given the baby up, or what?'

'The mother's died.'

'*Died*? How?'

'She wouldn't tell me. And the father can't look after her but I don't know why.'

'Oh, poor man. He loses his wife—or whatever—then his child.'

'He hasn't agreed to give her up, but—no, no, Leila, wait, listen—he won't actually object. Apparently that's normal. People just can't bring themselves to sign on the dotted line. So Linda says there will have to be a short court hearing, a technicality. Then she's ours.'

She looked at him, her lips moving, trying to digest the news. David encircled her waist with his arms, lifting her off the ground. She was wide-eyed, blinking through uncomprehending tears.

'I can't believe it,' he shouted, spinning them both in a tottering, dangerous waltz. 'Can you believe it?'

'I can't,' whispered Leila, and no other words would come. The years of waiting pooled, spilled, shone upon her face. 'I can't.'

*

Neither of them wanted to sleep; the magic of it was too beautiful to waste.

They entwined in the dark, talking, planning, laughing quietly with excitement and relief. A small girl now shared their future. They swapped images of her: in a high chair at the table, or in a sandpit in the garden, or snuggled between them on the sofa. They planned her bedroom. They decided on her name. Through the open window, a new moon smiled serenely upon their happiness. Those were, perhaps, the most perfect, precious hours either had ever known. Neither would ever forget them.

Chapter Fifteen

The sun was mellowing by the time we walked back. Deborah shaded her eyes with her hands, gazing along the beach towards the buildings.

'I don't imagine Hamisi's ever tried to shirk *his* responsibilities,' she said.

'Hamisi? The manager?'

'Rod's business partner, actually. He's lost two children to AIDS, and another in a car crash earlier this year. He and his wife look after eight grandchildren, but I've never heard him complain. Not a murmur.'

'That's incredible.'

'He doesn't have the luxury of a choice.' She sighed. 'Not sure I do, either.'

After another fifty paces, she stopped. 'Rod's going to be . . . What am I *thinking*? How can I do this to him again?'

Only now did the obvious thought strike me. 'He knows you're Deborah Harrison, right?'

'Of course. Another me, in another life. The only lie I've ever told him was about my father being ill. But to him I'm Susie Bridges, and always will be.'

I whistled. 'He told me he'd never heard of you, never clapped eyes on the person in the photo. Wrong woman, sod off. He generously promised to look out for a rogue English bluestocking. I only came back because I wanted a swim.'

'Well. No offence, but I wish you hadn't.'

Rod's battered pick-up was parked under the trees as we walked up. His dog, Cheza, came galloping across as we approached, prancing merrily around Deborah with a big open mouth, making welcoming sounds and swishing his tail. I bent down to pat him. As I straightened up, Rod appeared in the doorway of the office, also looking for her, smiling cheerfully. Poor bastard. He stood very still when he saw me, as though I was pointing a gun at his head.

'You found her then?' he said quietly.

I put up my hands in a feeble gesture of apology. I'd never in my life done anything that affected other people. Not really. Just drifted along, trying not to do any damage, avoiding anything that mattered. My aim, I suppose, was to be irrelevant. And now I'd made a difference in the lives of Deborah and Rod, and I wasn't enjoying it at all. It was like being the Grim Reaper.

She walked straight up to him and put her arms around his neck, and I pushed off, feeling like a total prick.

Mission accomplished.

I didn't see Deborah or Rod again until that evening, while I was buying one last round for myself and my brand-new lifelong mates.

I'd spent the rest of the afternoon on and off a kayak, snorkelling along the reef. By the time the sun went down I'd made myself at home in the bar, facing out to sea and yarning with two Irish guys who'd pulled in that afternoon. They were on their way down the east coast in an incredibly old Land Rover that really belonged in a museum. They'd driven this dinosaur all the way from London and were going on down to Cape Town, but they needed some time out. One of them was getting over a bout of malaria, and they both had seriously dodgy stomachs—walked around bent over like old geezers. They planned to stop here for a couple of weeks, rest up a bit and replace the Land Rover's gearbox. After a bottle of Tusker, I offered to give them a hand. After another four, they asked if I'd like to come along with them, down to South Africa, and I said thanks, great idea, I'll seriously think about it.

That was what was on my mind as I went to buy the last round. Hamisi was pottering about behind the bar, calmly cashing up. Hamisi, with his grizzled hair, who'd buried three of his children. It was hard to fathom the scale of it, really.

'Where are Rod and Susie tonight?' I asked. 'Haven't seen them for a while.'

He seemed to consider me. Then he pointed with his chin towards the southern end of the beach. 'See the fire?'

I walked to the edge of the wooden floor and stepped down into the darkness. It wasn't really dark, though, because the sky was an explosion of stars. You could almost hear them crackling. The ocean looked as still and black as treacle, and the waves had luminous silver fringes in the starlight. The landscape was frozen, like a painting; like one of those bad-taste velvet pictures everybody had in the nineteen seventies.

Far away down the shore, near the rocks, was a small fire. I could just make out two shadowy figures, standing side by side in its glow. I heard a footstep behind me, and Hamisi was there, at my elbow. For some time we stood in silence, watching the distant flames.

'I think they have a lot to discuss,' he said, finally. Then he cast me a reproachful glance before turning and wandering wearily back into the dim light.

I looked back at the fire on the beach. The two figures had merged into one. Perhaps Rod had talked her out of it. But I doubted it.

The plane was waiting, floating on a shimmering lake of mirage, its steps already wheeled into position. There was going to be no miracle. It was going to take her away from here, just like last time.

We hung around awkwardly until the gate opened. I trotted off to buy a newspaper while Deborah and Rod stood drooping and hollow-cheeked, like a couple of condemned prisoners in the queue for the gallows. When the dreaded call came, they held on to one another as though trying to stop some giant hand from prising them apart. I turned my back, looking out at the distant thorn trees that quivered beyond the runway. The other passengers began to stroll across the burning apron, fanning themselves with their boarding passes and waving to their friends.

For a minute or more it seemed as though she might change her mind, now that the last moment had come. I wouldn't have blamed her. Then she was marching across the tarmac, her head up. She paused at the top of the steps and looked back at him. Slowly, the propellers began to turn and their breeze lifted her hair. She bent her head and disappeared into the cabin.

Rod and I shook hands as though we'd just played a round of golf. I had to force myself to look him in the eye. I liked the guy; perhaps he reminded me of the person I used to be—or could have been—before I sold my body and my soul for a flat in Clapham. But I'd brought him nothing but misery.

He leaned forward, shouting above the increasing din of the engines, and I turned my ear towards him.

'Bring her back if you can,' he yelled. 'Please.'

I nodded, clapped him on the shoulder and set off at a run across the apron and up the steps, and they closed the doors behind me.

My seat was next to hers, but she didn't acknowledge me as I slid into it. The aircraft slowly turned and taxied to the top of the runway where it paused, flexing its muscles, pawing the ground. I usually get a buzz out of that moment. This time, though, it didn't seem much fun.

The throttle opened, and we lumbered forward with a roar. She pressed her face against the window as the terminal buildings slid away and the landscape blurred with speed. I felt our wheels leave the ground before we banked, turning sharply.

Beneath the shining wing I could see Rod's unmoving figure, standing on the red earth, and the faithful Cheza beside him. They looked as though they'd wait right there until she came home again.

Deborah lifted one hand, just a few inches. I suppose she was waving goodbye. After all, she was leaving Susie behind. Again.

The journey wasn't a bundle of laughs.

We had to stop at Nairobi and Dubai. Once we were on the final leg I fell asleep, drifting in the drone of the engines. Mum waited at the kitchen door, holding out her arms to me.

Shortly before we landed at Heathrow I opened bleary eyes to find Deborah trying to prise my headset from around my neck. I hoped I hadn't been dribbling or snoring. By the time I swam to the surface she'd gone back to staring out of the window.

It was dusk. Our landing lights were ghostly flashes in the gloom, until we burst through the underside of the cloud cover and the wing was a dark shadow against the lights of London. Millions of lights, all the way to the horizon, with the black snake of the Thames twisting through them.

'Never fails,' I murmured, craning my neck to peer out. Deborah nodded silently, and for a while we sat and admired the bling. Then she wiped her eyes and turned her back to the window, a determined tilt to her chin.

'D'you like London, Jake?'

'Must do. I've lived here almost half my life.'

She looked surprised. 'Really? Why? Aren't your parents still alive?'

It was there again. The taste of guilt and hatred. 'Yeah. Sort of. If you can call it living.'

'So where do you call home, then?'

'Dunno. I don't use the word very often.' I really didn't want to be having this conversation. Memories had been clamouring at me lately: Mum's love, and Dad's barbarism, and Jesse, and Sala. I didn't intend to pursue the subject, so I took a keen interest in the duty-free magazine.

She wasn't letting me off that easily. 'Ever been married? You certainly aren't gay. I can always tell.'

I had to smile. 'Can you? How? No, don't answer that. Not married.'

'Girlfriend?'

I sighed, and slid the magazine back into its pocket. 'I'm on a sabbatical.' The seatbelt sign pinged on, and we dutifully fished under the little cushions and plugged ourselves in. Without thinking, I added: 'Actually, I was living with someone until a few weeks ago.'

'Oh.' Amusement flickered around the soft curve of her mouth. Her upper lip was shaped like a hunting bow. 'I hadn't thought of you as having your own life, somehow. You haven't talked about yourself.'

The hostie was coming round with a basket of those little boiled lollies some airlines hand out to stop your ears popping. 'Go on, take a handful,' she whispered invitingly, rattling the basket over my lap. I never turn them down.

Once she'd shimmied past, Deborah started up again. 'What's she called?'

I was still watching the hostie. 'Who? Oh. Anna.'

'I thought maybe it was Lucy.'

I just laughed at that. I reached down for my boots, hoping she might give up, but she harassed the back of my head. 'Isn't that why you came to find me? For Lucy? I imagined it was a sort of knightly quest to please the lady.'

I forced my heel into a boot. 'Sorry. Nothing so chivalrous.'

'She wouldn't be a bad catch.'

'She's also almost young enough to be my daughter.'

Deborah raised an eyebrow. 'That never stopped Perry.'

'Well, I'm not Perry. Actually, I came because Matt was in a real stew. I also came because I've made a complete screw-up of my own life and had nothing better to do. It was all a bit of a frolic. A treasure hunt.' I began tugging at my laces.

She tilted her head, briefly touching my shoulder with her nose. 'Thanks for flying back with me. I think I might have legged it at Dubai if I'd been alone.'

'No problem.' A sly, pesky little voice in my head kept nagging me about why I'd chosen to come back with her, but I wasn't listening to it.

'I needed to get some things organised, anyway,' I told her. 'I'm not ready for a long trip, haven't even decided where I'm going. I'll drop in at Coptree in a couple of days, collect my car and see how you're all doing.'

She shook her head firmly. 'When I emailed Perry, I told him we were *both* arriving on this flight. He's expecting you to stay.'

She must have seen the indecision on my face because she touched my hand. 'Please, Jake. I need a Peter Pan like you to keep me sane.'

'Er . . .' I wasn't sure how to put this. 'But you'll want the spare room. I mean . . .'

'Perry has slept in his study for years now.' She hesitated and then looked away. 'Long story.'

I was appalled. What a criminal waste. 'Bloody hell, Debs.'

'Yes, bloody hell.' She leaned back, resting her head against the seat. 'He won't confront me about where I've been, you know.'

'He might ask *me*.'

'Mm.' She chewed her lip, thinking. 'I doubt it.'

'Poor Perry.'

'Huh. You don't know him, Jake. He's cunning, like a panther. He'll take me lovingly in his arms, and we'll chat as though I've just come back from a weekend minibreak. It's our myth, our united front. We're a class act.'

We began another circuit. I could see the lights of other aircraft, stacked up and waiting to land. Our hostie swung efficiently down the aisle in her little skirt and jacket, checking all our seats were upright and glaring like an angry Rottweiler at those delinquent passengers who'd started getting their bags down. She smiled benevolently at me, though, and I noticed she'd slapped on some lipstick. She leaned over, checking that my seatbelt was properly adjusted—can't think why, because it obviously was—then reached up and pressed my overhead locker with long, manicured fingers, just to be sure it wasn't going to fall open.

Deborah was watching all this with amusement. 'I reckon you can get your bag down any time you like, so far as *that* hussy's concerned.'

'Nah. She's nice to everyone. It's her job.'

'Yes? Her, and Swedish Karin, and the skinny girl in the bank at Nairobi airport. They all start fluttering their eyelashes and sticking out their chests like pigeons. Don't pretend to be oblivious.' She looked me over curiously, and I tried not to squirm. 'You're essentially youthful. That's the appeal, isn't it? Brown eyes, long lashes, winsome smile.'

'After seventeen hours on a plane, I need a paper bag over my head.'

'The unshaven look's pretty rugged, actually,' she said, smiling.

'I never saw any girl in the bank.' Honestly I hadn't.

A suspicion seemed to strike her 'Tell me you don't play rugby? Oh God, you do, don't you? You're just the type.'

'Used to. I gather you think it's a stupid game.'

'Of *course* it's a stupid game. Matt got injured. It's what sent him off the rails.'

'He told me.'

'Did he? Well, I was relieved. You know that sound when two of them collide? The dull thud, and that sort of groan as all the air rushes out of them? Everytime I heard it I felt sick. They're so heavy, so fast, and so completely *insane*—like young male buffaloes.'

'Great, isn't it?'

'Three times I've seen Matt being carried off the pitch. Three! So I stopped going to watch. One day I got the dreaded call—it was his neck. I drove to hospital, speeding and sobbing all the way. Found him lying in casualty, white as a piece of chalk, still in his muddy shorts. He scowled at me as I came dashing in, and d'you know what he said?'

'What?'

'"What the fuck are *you* doing here?"'

I couldn't help but smile. It sounded just like Matt. 'That's what he says to everyone.'

'Oh, no.' She shook her head disgustedly. 'The nurses thought he was charming and delightful—they were eating out of his hands. Anyway, no more rugby for *him*. You'd think they'd amputated his leg, the fuss he made. He became quite impossible. All that animal aggression was poured into wreaking havoc at school. That's why we took him out. And that's why we're in this mess.'

I reckoned it was stretching the point, blaming the game they play in heaven for all the Harrison troubles, but I didn't say so.

She pulled on her own shoes. 'So you're definitely not in love with Lucy.'

'Don't think so.'

A minute later, she nudged me. 'Hey, Jake. D'you think Matt will have come to meet us?'

I didn't answer. The cabin lights went dim, and we began to descend into the Underworld.

'I hope I'm in time,' she said.

149

*

A stressed-looking Lucy was waiting at the barriers. No Perry. No Matt.

'Jake Kelly,' she said, kissing me on the cheek. 'You did it. You are a genius!'

'Lucy.' Deborah held out her hands. 'It's so good to see you.'

'Hello.' Lucy spoke sweetly, stepping out of reach. 'Had a lovely time?'

Deborah's arms fell to her sides. She looked around forlornly. 'Where's Matt?'

'You'll have to make do with the understudy, I'm afraid,' said Lucy. Then she took my arm and chatted all the way to the car park, ignoring her stepmother.

I wasn't going to sit in the passenger seat and be roasted by overheated emotion. Lucy was clearly furious with her stepmother for legging it. Deborah was in a stew because she'd had to come back. They could bloody well spend an hour stuck in adjoining seats, and sort out their differences.

'I'm sure you two girls have lots to catch up on,' I said, and shot into the back, chortling to myself.

The journey began in an arctic silence. Lolling against the window, I closed my eyes and gave in to the hum of the car engine as we slid out of Heathrow and into the Monday evening traffic. I was in the strangest sort of limbo. I had no job, no home, and no real plans. And here I was, a sort of unwilling valet to this tribe of complete barking maniacs.

I don't know what it is about cars. Unless I'm actually driving, I have to go to sleep. It's a sort of Pavlovian response with me. So I began to drift away almost immediately and watched the hostie stepping out of her uniform, smiling and whispering *Go on, take a handful.*

I opened my eyes, though, at Deborah's voice.

'I'm sorry I've hurt you, Lucy,' she said.

There was no reply.

After a minute or so, she spoke again. 'How's Matt? Is he coping with all this?'

'Nope.' Lucy's voice sounded brittle. I'd never heard her like that before. 'Dad phoned the social worker and told her you'd completed your, er, assignment and were on your way home.'

'And?'

'She said it's too late.'

Deborah put a hand to her mouth. 'No!'

Lucy nodded, flicking on her indicator. We were joining the M25.

'Yep. They've found a wonderful adoptive couple and told them they're getting the baby. They're delighted, and the plan isn't going to change now.'

'Oh, no.' Deborah sounded as though she meant it, and perhaps she did.

'Oh, *yes*.' Lucy seemed exasperated. 'You've really buggered things up, this time.'

'We must be able to do something?'

Lucy put her foot down and headed for the fast lane. 'Dad phoned that slimy solicitor, Forsyth, and he got onto them this morning. Told them they have to assess you and threatened to get a court order forcing them to do it. Said it wasn't your fault you were, um . . . not in the picture, it was all down to cell phones not working, and that as soon as you heard you got on the first flight home.'

'What did they say?'

'They're not very happy about it. Forsyth says you have *got* to be on their doorstep first thing tomorrow morning.'

'Have you met Grace?'

A pause. Lucy was messing about with the heating. 'I went once with Matt. She's stunning.'

'When can I see her?'

'Well, Matt's going in the morning. Maybe you could muscle in. You're so good at that.'

I saw Deborah run a hand over her face, as though checking it was still there. Lucy glanced over her shoulder at me, and I snapped my eyes shut.

'Why did you bring poor Jake back with you?' she hissed. 'Hasn't he done enough?'

'Yes, but he offered to come. Says he feels responsible.'

I almost sat up and let them know I was awake, but before I could say anything Lucy exploded.

'Jake? *Responsible*? He doesn't know the meaning of the word. You're screwing him, aren't you?'

'I assumed *you* were, actually. He's your type. There's just a hint of the untamed, isn't there, under all that self-deprecating charm? Just a little roughness around the edges.'

'We don't all behave like rabbits.' Lucy began to tailgate the car in front, jabbing her foot onto the brake every time we were about to collide. It was terrifying. 'You've made a fool of my dad. Now you're throwing your coils around one of my dearest friends.'

'I am not!'

'I saw you simpering up to him as you came through customs. Jake's not on the menu. Hands off.'

Deborah sighed. She sounded tired to her bones. 'Just grow up, Lucy, and accept that I'm not a wicked sorcerer with a magical talking mirror. I'm just a fallible human being. I make mistakes, quite a lot actually, but I muddle through as best I can. Christ! Mind that car!'

'Don't you tell me how to drive.'

The car in front pulled across to let us past—clearly its occupants valued their lives—then Lucy swerved back into the middle lane, narrowly avoiding a Porsche whose driver was talking on his mobile.

'Oh, I know *exactly* what you are.'

'What does that mean?'

'You conned Dad into marrying you—oh yes, you did. Money and status, that's what you were after. Then the novelty wore off so you started frolicking about, going for your dirty little holidays, all courtesy of his bank account. And then, *then*—and this is the icing on the cake—you abandoned him when he'd never needed you more. I can see through your baby-doll dimples. I've got no illusions about what you are.'

'And you're a spoiled little daddy's girl,' snapped Deborah. 'Why d'you think he's got me back here? Do you *really* imagine he gives a monkey's cuss about Matt's baby?'

Lucy glared stonily at the road. When she next spoke, it was in the sort of singsong voice people use when they're reading fairy stories to their toddlers.

'I'm sure you find it hard to imagine anyone having unselfish feelings, Deborah. But actually, Dad does. He cares about Grace. You, on the other hand, care only about Deborah Harrison, because you are dazzlingly self-obsessed.'

'I'm here, aren't I?'

'You had to be dragged back, kicking and screaming.'

'Well, what about you? You're her aunt. I don't see *you* offering to look after her,' persisted Deborah.

'Don't be bloody ridiculous. I've got a career. I've got a future. You haven't.'

One of them, I didn't see which, turned on the radio full blast. It was an organ recital, I think. The Porsche roared past, and Lucy swung smartly out behind him and fixed him in her sights, hunched and murderous like the Red Baron in a dogfight. No one roars past my Lucy and gets away with it.

They both shut up then and lapsed into silent seething; I was relieved, although I thought Lucy's driving was going to kill us all. There's something humiliating about being forced to listen to two women accusing one another of sleeping with you, as though the suggestion was a grave insult.

Ah well, I told myself, as I closed my eyes once more. This is not my problem. And I'm not in love with either of them. No way.

No way in this world.

Chapter Sixteen

Phoning her mother would be the best part. Fola must be the first to know.

They'd agreed to leave the news untouched until after the weekend. After all that had happened, it seemed too bright a joy, too much a thing made by enchantment; they were superstitiously afraid of breaking the spell. It was filmy, a web in the shimmering morning. If they reached out to touch it, the strands might shrivel yet again into nothing. So they hugged it to themselves, and for the first few days they told no one. Better not to tempt fate.

Leila took a week off work. There was so much to organise, and anyway work seemed irrelevant just now. All through Monday, she saved up the wonderful moment when she would let the news out of its box. She spent the day in the garden under a porcelain-blue sky, raking leaves and digging compost into the beds. Humming to herself, daydreaming, she planned how she would tell them. She practised the words she would use, pictured her mother's generous face fragmenting into joy.

In the allotments across the railway line someone had lit a bonfire, and Leila held her face up to the white smoke as it hung in the stillness. At half past three she heard a rhythmic creaking from the garden next door. Jacinta's swing. A minute later came the sound of talking-to-your-self singing, an aimlessly meandering chant.

Leila stopped in the act of pruning the roses. She stuck her head over the fence. 'How was school today, my friend?'

Jacinta jumped off the swing in midair, plait soaring, and ran to push her way through a hole in the fence.

'My dad caught my sister snoggling with her boyfriend on the sofa yesterday,' she announced smugly. Her round cheeks were flushed. 'Sent him packing. He put a big rocket up his bottom!'

'Oh, dear,' said Leila.

'Then Daria locked herself in her room and cried and cried. She said her heart was broken. So my mum's bought her a *gigantic* box of chocolates. Mum says they're just as exciting as a boyfriend and a lot less trouble.'

'Very true indeed.' Leila nodded solemnly. 'How's poor old Daria now?'

'She's very spotty. Can I do your garden?' asked Jacinta, looking critically around at Leila's neatly dug beds. 'I'm brilliant at gardening.'

'That's good,' said Leila, handing her a trowel. 'Because I haven't a clue.'

After a while the dew began to fall, softly soaking them. The bell ringers began their weekly practice, the sound glittering in the gentle air; a train grunted past, rattling its commuters home. As dusk was gathering, Jacinta's broken-hearted sister—a dimpled, red-lipped beauty, who always reminded Leila of Disney's Snow White—appeared over the fence, looking perfectly cheerful and calling Jacinta in for tea.

With her chatty companion gone, Leila couldn't hang on any longer. She left her muddy shoes on the back step, peeled off her gardening gloves and gave her hands a quick scrub. Then, with a sense of momentous occasion, she lifted the telephone. The smell of leaves and earth clung to her clothes as she dialled the familiar number.

She stood in the hall, listening to the ringing tone; she could picture her parents' tomato-red telephone hanging on the kitchen wall by the cork message board. They'd had the same board since Leila was a schoolgirl. Nowadays it hung overloaded, crammed with the wild primary colours of grandchildren's art.

She smiled as she waited, lips moving as she rehearsed her lines. Mum was going to go crazy. When she heard Fola's husky voice, she almost lost her own.

'Hi, Mum? It's me.'

A brief pause. Then, 'Leila!'

'Hi. How are you?'

'Fine, we're both fine. Except your dad's got a nasty twinge in his hip today.'

'Is he taking the glucosamine I gave him?'

'Yes, because I remind him every morning.'

'Are you ready for the trip to Nigeria?'

'Well, I've found our passports, which is a start. Is everything all right?' Fola sounded suspicious now, guarded, clearly wondering what this call was for. Leila knew her mother's morbid dread of unexpected calls. She feared bad news, had done for years, since the death of her brother.

'Everything is great, Mum. *More* than great.'

'Your big brother's here for supper, with the kids. D'you want to talk to him?'

'Maybe later.' Leila paused for one last, delicious moment. 'Hey, Mum. We're adopting a baby.'

'. . . ?!' It was a disbelieving yelp.

'We're adopting a baby.'

Fola squealed, a long '*Eeee!*' of delight, and Leila held the receiver a foot away from her ear, eyes squeezed shut, laughing silently. She could hear her mother yelling to the others, to her father and brother and anyone else who would listen: *They're getting a baby! A baby!* Sounds of general celebration floated down the line.

Isaiah must have grabbed the receiver: she heard her eldest brother's voice, precise and measured. 'Look out, Leila!' He had two already, and another on the way. 'You aren't going to get any sleep for the next twenty years!'

Then Fola again, breathless. 'When?'

'We don't know yet. There's a few legal things first—but quite soon, we hope.'

'Girl or boy?'

'A girl.'

'Has she got a name?'

'We haven't been told what name the parents have given her. We thought we'd like to call her Fola, Mum.'

Fola promptly started to cry. Leila could hear her gulps, and then her father's gravelly pleasure: 'Hey, Leila! You can tell poor old David to say goodbye to the easy life.'

Leila was shivering a little now, with the wonder. 'I'll tell him that. Sorry about your hip, Dad.'

'Oh, never mind about my hip. I don't even know why she mentioned it, never been better. You're going to be a mum, that's the important thing.'

'And you're going to be a grandpa—yet again.'

'So I am! Don't know what I've done to deserve such a fate. Oh, my goodness, your mother's gone completely mad, I'll have to call the doctor. She's crying and laughing like a cat that's drunk the whisky. She wants to commandeer the phone and tell everyone.'

'I'd better get off the line then.'

'We'll call you later, Leila, all right?'

'Right.'

'My darling daughter. This is a great moment. Remember it. Life will never be the same again.'

It *was* a great moment, the happiest Leila could ever have imagined. And yet, deep beneath the warm surface of her joy ran a thin, cold current of unease. After all the years, all the waiting, she felt there had to be a catch.

Forcing the thought away, Leila pressed down the bar, intending to dial again immediately and tell Maggie, but the thing rang, vibrating under her hands as though it were alive. She hesitated, suddenly afraid of bad news from the adoption team, bracing herself as if for a physical blow.

'Leila Edmunds speaking.'

'Ah, Leila. Good evening.'

Leila instantly recognised the authoritative tones of David's sister, Monica. Relief. 'Monica! What a surprise! How are you?'

'I'm very well indeed, thank you. I'll make this a quick one, Leila, because I'm just measuring up the Lord Chancellor's croquet lawn for a marquee.'

'Gosh.' Leila tried to sound awed. 'Er . . . big lawn?'

'Well, you know. The usual. I'm standing on the helipad as we speak. Now. I'm trying to get the final numbers together for Ma and Pa's do. And as yet I've heard nothing from you two.'

Catching sight of herself in the hall mirror, Leila glanced at her chin, then stared intently. There was a spot coming; she could see it looming menacingly.

'Their . . . er, do?'

Irritation crackled down the line. 'I canvassed your views months ago. The ruby wedding.'

Oh, bugger. They hadn't thought of an excuse yet. Leila swore silently and made belligerent faces into the mouthpiece.

Monica pressed on. 'I'm at the helm, because someone has to organise these things, and it's a thankless task, I can tell you. Just a minute . . .' She was still audible, but distant and wavery, as though she was holding the telephone to her chest. 'What's the problem? Can we please have some lights over here! No, no, *no*! The French doors won't arrive until tomorrow afternoon. Look . . .' The voice became more muffled for a few seconds, and then it was back.

'You still there, Leila? Yes. I'm sure everyone thinks I'm being managerial. But at least people might show just a little enthusiasm.'

'Yes, I see that. Sorry, Monica.' That spot was going to be a whopper. Leila turned her chin this way and that, screwing up her eyes. It gave her a childish satisfaction, somehow.

'Well?' insisted Monica. 'Can I put a tick by your names?'

There was no escaping this one. They were doomed.

'Of course.' Leila made a pretend crying face at her reflection. 'I thought David had already let you know. *Gosh* yes, count us in! Wild horses wouldn't keep us away.'

'Excellent. All right, that's a tick. Now, I rather hoped David might say a few well-chosen words, since he's so good at that sort of thing.'

'I can think of several well-chosen words to say about Hilda and Christopher.'

'Sorry? I'm losing you, I'm afraid . . . No, Louise. The corner of the dance floor is *there*, by that marker. See the marker? . . . You still there, Leila?'

Leila sighed. 'Yes, still here.'

'Sorry. It's a madhouse at this end. Incidentally, a thousand congratulations. I gather you're getting a baby.'

Leila's eyes widened. 'How did you find out?'

'Oh well, you know. Family network. Great news, anyway. *Fabulous* news!' Monica's voice was submerged, in a rampaging wave of sound. 'Oh God, here comes a helicopter. Must go.'

Leila hung up the phone just as David's figure appeared behind the glass door. He grinned delightedly when he saw her, and held his arms wide.

'Hello, my lovely.' He had a special Welsh accent he used on such occasions. 'Come over 'ere.'

Leila allowed him to envelope her, shaking them both in a little jig. She wondered where, amid all the celebration, he had filed her question: *What else have we got?* She'd never had to answer it, even to herself: saved by the bell, literally.

Sweeping the thought into a corner, she asked accusingly, 'Have you by any chance been talking to your mother this morning, David?'

The jig stopped. 'Er . . . I might have.'

'Hmm. Did you tell her about the baby? Think carefully before you reply.'

'It just came out. I was like a dog with six tails.'

'Soul of discretion, you are. Bloody radio Edmunds. I've just had your sister on the phone, banging on about the ruby wedding bash and congratulating me on the new arrival. You were going to wait until I'd told *my* parents, remember?'

'Oh, dear.' David put his arm around Leila's waist, steering her into the kitchen. 'So I was. I wanted yours to be the first to know too. But you must have spoken to them by now?'

'Yes, and they're wildly, frantically, sensationally happy. Peckham will be ablaze within hours.'

'Good old Fola.' David flicked on the kettle, frowning forlornly. 'Mum seems to think our child's criminal career is assured.'

'No! What did she say?'

David waggled his head and imitated Hilda's honeyed contralto. 'For heaven's sake, don't let this cuckoo into your nest, David. You don't know where it's been.'

Leila's eyes opened wide in outrage. 'You're joking!'

'I wish I was.' Petulantly, he ran both hands over his head so that his hair stood up on end.

'Did you tell her to sod off?'

'There's no point in trying to improve my mother, you know. It's a waste of energy. She isn't educable.'

'How dare she? Ooh, I wish I'd told Monica where she could stick her ruby wedding.'

David took off his jacket and hung it over a chair. 'It won't be the last judgemental remark we'll hear on the subject,' he remarked calmly. 'People have views, and they like to air them. And guess what?'

'What?'

The fan of creases around his eyes deepened, as he smiled. 'I don't give a toss. This baby is our own private miracle.'

It was midnight by the time David was ready for bed. Leila was reading a faded library book snappily entitled *Roses Around the Door? Case Studies on the Long-term Outcomes of Adoption*.

'Some researchers think adoption is a minefield,' she said. 'They say adopted children are more likely than others to have problems later. Depression, self-harm, academic failure . . . quite a list.'

'At last! You and my mother agree on something!'

Leila leaned across, walloping his nose with the book. 'That's not funny.'

David stuck out his lower lip. 'I think you've broken my fine, aquiline nose. I'm going to tell the social workers you've got violent tendencies.'

'Shush, I can't concentrate. This is actually quite serious . . . we need to work out our approach right from the start. I hope we're up to it.'

David bent to read the book too, pushing back his disobedient hair. 'Does this apply to people adopted as babies, though?'

'Um . . . less so, but yes. Some of them feel abandoned, or fantasise about the birth family. Our little Fola has a lot to deal with. Stop reading over my shoulder. It's really annoying.'

'But how would the same children have fared if left with their birth parents?' asked David reasonably.

'Fair point.' Leila carried on reading.

'How was Monica, anyway?' Noisily, David began plumping up his pillow.

'In hyperdrive. Wants you to make a speech.' Leila gave up on the book. She closed it and leaned on one elbow, reaching out to smooth his hair. 'I'll nip round to the rectory before work tomorrow and let them know the good news.'

David looked shifty. 'Ah.'

She gazed suspiciously at him. 'What do you mean, ah?'

'Well, I was there this morning, and I happened to let slip . . . ouch!' He rubbed his chest. 'I only had two hairs there, it took a quarter of a century to grow them, and you've maliciously yanked one of them out. That's a breach of my fundamental human rights. I'm definitely telling those social workers.'

'Is there anyone you *haven't* told about the baby?'

Smiling lazily, David lifted a hand and ran his fingertips down the graceful length of her neck. Her eyes glowed with an incandescence he'd feared was gone forever.

'You're beautiful,' he said. 'You're as lovely as you were the day I met you.'

'That's not what I asked.'

His fingers slid along her collarbone and underneath the red shoestring strap of her nightdress. 'You're going to have to share me from now on,' he warned. 'Better not waste any time.'

'True.' She caught his hand. 'So answer the question.'

'Okay.' He squinted up at the ceiling, pondering. 'Who haven't I told? I know. Dora at the off-licence. I'm leaving that to you. Ow! What did you do *that* for? That was my last one.'

Laughing, he reached out for her, knocking the faded book to the floor.

*

Leila lay wrapped in warmth, her eyes resting on the square of street lighting that glowed upon one wall. Each time a car drove past, the beam of headlamps tiptoed across the ceiling. She followed the ghostly glow on its course, waited for the driver to change gear before accelerating away. They always changed up just . . . *there.*

Twice she heard the siren of a police car and saw lights flash, sliding across the gloom. She listened—forgivingly, tonight—to gangs of late-night drinkers staggering home along the orange underwater streets. One group was clapping their hands and chanting a football song, breaking off into shouts of laughter before moving on. The stillness of the night seeped in behind them.

She closed her eyes. She could hear David's heartbeat as she rested her ear against his chest. She'd have to move soon, or they'd both get pins and needles.

As she tried to ease her head away he stirred, wrapping his arms around her. 'Don't go yet,' he whispered, his words slurring on the edge of sleep.

'I didn't mean it,' she said suddenly. 'David? Are you awake? It was a heat-of-the-moment thing.'

'No idea what you're talking about.'

'When I said . . . you know. When I asked what else we've got. I didn't mean it. I know what else we've got. I know how incredibly lucky we are.'

His arms tightened. 'Stop wittering.'

As his breathing slowed, Leila found herself smiling in the darkness.

Chapter Seventeen

We made it to Coptree by the skin of our teeth, and I couldn't get out of that car fast enough. It was like doing ninety miles on a rollercoaster.

Matt wasn't about, but Perry was waiting for us, dark-rimmed eyes burning with all their usual intensity. He folded his wife in his arms as though she'd just been away for a conference—exactly as Deborah had predicted—and she played the game too. Lucy threw me one sickened glance and disappeared.

Perry took my hand in both his own. 'We can never repay you,' he said.

'No problem,' I muttered. Then I lugged my stuff upstairs.

The landing was gloomy. There was no sound from Matt's stereo, but a band of light gleamed under his door. He must know his mother was home, but still he skulked in his room. I hesitated. I saw the kid in a new light now. Matt's life was a lot more complicated than I'd given him credit for. More complicated than mine, that was for sure. I dumped my bag on the floor and knocked as I walked in.

'Hi, honey. I'm home!'

He was slumped on his beanbag, wild-haired and broad-shouldered, headphones over his ears. I could just make out a tinny beat. He was nodding his chin in time to it. He glanced up at me, looked bored, and raised one hand. I sat down on the bed and waited. And waited. Eventually, he slid the headphones down around his neck.

'They're smart.' I nodded at them.

'Got 'em on eBay. Dad started complaining about my sound system.

I can feed about a hundred and twenty decibels straight into my ears with these.'

He pushed them back on, watching me defiantly with his vivid eyes. I reached over to the stereo and pressed the power switch.

'What?' he grunted, taking the headphones off.

'I brought your mum home.'

'Oh, yeah?' He knew already, I was sure of that. In fact, I was willing to bet he'd hidden by the window and watched her get out of the car.

'That's your cue, Matt. That's when you say, "Thanks, Jake."'

'Thanks, Jake.' He used a baby voice.

'Look, squirt.' I cuffed the top his head. 'Be grateful. I travelled about sixteen thousand miles for you, got bitten by three million mosquitoes, ate airline food for two days. And what's more, you knew very well your mum had left for good, and you didn't think to tell me!'

'Keep your hair on,' he mumbled, but he rewarded me with a faint smile.

There was a long silence. I wondered whether to go to bed, but I wasn't tired any more. Matt spoke first.

'What was Mum doing out there, anyway?'

'You'd better ask her.'

'Huh. She coming up to see me?'

'You could go down.'

He yawned. 'Nah. She wants to see me, she can come up here.'

'Suit yourself.'

He walloped the beanbag restlessly with the flat of his hand.

'So,' I said. 'You're a father.'

He sat up a little straighter. 'Yeah. Me, a father. *Fuck.* What d'you think of that?'

'I think the kid's lucky.' I had an image in my head: Matt, with his clumsy devotion, gazing down at his daughter.

He just looked at me blankly, didn't move a muscle on his face. 'The SS don't agree.'

'SS?'

'Social services.'

'Oh. Right.'

'They say I can't manage by myself. And they're right, the tossers. I mean, look at me, man.'

I looked, but I didn't comment. He pounded the seat again. Clouds of dust.

'I can't do it by myself. I need Mum. She's good at that stuff.'

'And what about your dad? Will he be a doting grandpa, take the baby out to the park every day in her pram?'

He raised his heavy eyebrows at me, smiling unpleasantly as if I'd just said something funny.

'No, really,' I persisted. 'I've spent weeks traipsing around the world for you lot. I found your mother and I brought her back, and now you're going to tell me what's going on. What *about* Perry? How come he never figures in anyone's calculations?'

Matt was still smiling, but he didn't look happy.

'Come on,' I said. 'Spit it out.'

He stared up at the ceiling, hands casually behind his head. 'Because he hasn't left the house in years, that's why. And I don't suppose he ever will until the day he's carried out in a box.'

I looked at him, my mouth open, trying to make sense of what he'd just said. He laughed foolishly, high-pitched.

'Yeah, I'll tell you. I'm sick of secrets. Secret, secrets, my whole life. School play? No Dad. "Couldn't your father make it, Matthew?" Boys and fathers cricket game? No Dad. "Couldn't your father make it, Matthew?" Biggest fucking rugby game of the decade? No Dad. "Do you actually *have* a father, Matthew?"' He glared with hot eyes, remembering. 'They never told me why. I couldn't understand why my own father didn't want to watch me play. Or see me at all. No one told me.'

I waited, fascinated.

'*She* still came, all right. Fussing on about how I was going to get injured. I worked it out in the end. On my twelfth birthday.'

'How did you work it out?'

'Mum was going to take me out to tea, so I was waiting for her in the school hall. I heard the housemaster, Gifford the Git, in his room. He was going deaf, had this loud bellowing voice even when he thought he was being quiet and discreet. He was telling Matron how he'd never met my dad. "Poor lad. I suspect the father has mental health problems." '

'That was a cock-up.'

'Yeah. Well, over scones and cream at the White Hart I had it out with Mum. She said okay, it was time I knew. She reckoned what Dad has is a most misunderstood condition. People call it agoraphobia, but that's very misleading, it's much more complicated, doesn't mean he's mad, blah blah blah. She said it had got so bad that he couldn't go out the garden gate. He'd totally panic, like he was dying. In fact, at first they thought he *was* dying.'

'Hell.'

'I did lots of solemn nodding and pretending to understand, but I didn't. Still don't, actually. I mean, what kind of a man hasn't the courage to go fifty miles on a weekend to watch his son captain the First Fifteen? A complete spineless weasel is the answer.'

Privately, I had to agree with him.

Matt clenched his jaw, still angry. 'And Mum. Why didn't she *make* him come?'

'Well, she couldn't really truss him up like a roast chicken and force him into the car.'

'Why not?'

I was stumped. He was off again, anyway. Now the cork was gone from the bottle, it seemed he wanted to pour everything out.

'She used to take us on holiday by herself. To Cornwall. Or visiting Grandma, before she died. This . . . *thing* had to be a secret, because Dad's so ashamed about it. We were never to mention it to anyone, not ever. Not even to Dad. It was a grubby little family secret, and we had to cover it up and pretend it didn't exist.'

'That must have been hard.'

'Other boys' parents were merchant wankers, like you, or cabinet ministers and surgeons and things. But they still managed to show up for matches. The worst thing, though, was that I couldn't bring anyone home. At school I was captain of sport, prefect, the lot. I was a bloody hero. But when I came home, I had to sit in this room by myself and play computer games.'

I grimaced. 'That's rough.'

'Then I got the injury, and that was a fucking disaster.' Matt glowered in disgust. 'I don't *have* anything else. Without the game, I'm nobody. Nothing. Just a boy with weird parents. So I started smoking quite a lot of hooch.' He looked at me and then away. 'I got a bit careless. Gifford the Git caught me selling some to one of the gardeners.'

'Jeez, Matt. Dealing!'

He waved a hand. 'It's okay, keep your hair on. Mum came down, just about sat on the headmaster's lap. Come to think of it, she was in his office for ages. I expect she got down under his desk and gave him a Lewinsky.'

I frowned. He'd gone too far. 'Watch it, mate.'

He looked vaguely guilty. 'Well, whatever she did, it worked. The police weren't called. I wasn't even expelled. Officially, I agreed to leave the same day. It was all hushed up, like everything else in this family.'

'So that's why you started school here?'

'Yep.'

'Big change. Posh boarding to local high.'

He shrugged. 'It's a well-known fact that all teachers are morons —doesn't matter where you go, they're all the same. I've stopped bothering with coursework and I'm going to fail the next lot of exams. I mean, what's the point? Serve my parents right. I sit at the back. Have a laugh. The teachers hate me, and the feeling's mutual.'

'I was like that.'

'I seriously doubt it, Jacko . . . Cherie was in detention with me quite a few times. The guys all claimed to have had her. They said she was anyone's. There was even a rumour going around that she'd walked into the boys' changing rooms, climbed up on a bench and auctioned herself. They said four of them clubbed together and put in the winning bid. I didn't believe that one, though. Some of them were horrible to her, you know?'

'Mm. I do know.'

'They used to make hand signals at her when the teacher wasn't looking. Really disgusting. I saw one of them put his hand up her skirt, and his mates were laughing. She was trying to pretend she thought it was funny, but I could tell she didn't. And I didn't do anything to stop them. I felt sick about it. So I started talking to her, just chatting. Carried her books. Sat with her in the canteen when nobody else would.' The knight in shining armour jerked himself out of his beanbag, slouched to the door and punched it. I winced.

He stood there, examining his knuckles. 'Cherie was a loose unit, but she was worth ten of those stupid giggling girls in her class. Had a hell of a rough life, violent stepdad and a bitch of a mother. Makes my family sound almost normal.' He scowled thoughtfully. 'She couldn't believe I wasn't just trying to get her kit off. I wasn't, honestly. I mean, we used to snog at the bus stop, but I didn't want to be like *them*. I wanted to show her I was different. I wanted to let her know there was one male in the world who respected her.'

He jammed his fists into his pockets, balancing on the balls of his feet like a boxer. 'You're wondering how I managed to get her knocked up if I'm such a gentleman?'

'No, I'm not.' I was, actually.

He began to stride up and down the room like a leopard at the zoo, pacing, pacing.

'We started on her sixteenth birthday. A year ago yesterday.'

'Yesterday was her birthday?'

He nodded bleakly. 'We took a blanket up into the woods. I bought her a ring for her birthday, an eternity ring, and a little birthday cake. She said she loved me. I thought . . .' He broke off. 'Well, never mind. We were using contraception, I'm not bloody stupid.'

I smirked. '*Every* time? I was seventeen once.'

'Well, most times.' He looked slightly red-faced. 'Unless I'd run out.'

'Ah.'

'They're hard to get, in a pissy little place like this. People know you. They know your *mum*. My old Sunday school teacher works in the local pharmacy—can you imagine strolling up to the counter and asking . . .' He giggled, embarrassed by the image. 'I used to get them from a machine in the bogs at the station. But we ran out sometimes, so we had to—'

I held up my hands. 'Mate, that's more than enough information.'

'It's okay, that's the end of the story. One day Cherie told me she was pregnant. I nearly had a heart attack. But then I thought, no, this is okay. I was proud.'

He gave the poor old door another clout. 'We had plans. We were going to move in together and look after it.'

'You *wanted* to be a father? If I'd got a girl pregnant at the age of seventeen, there'd be smoke coming off my trainers.'

Matt looked surly, heavy eyebrows lowered. 'It was my kid. My duty.' He stopped pacing for a moment and rumpled his bleached mop, thinking, trying to explain. 'Neither of us had anything to lose, you see. We had nothing better to do. Our lives were going absolutely nowhere. I'm a cripple, can't play rugby, good for nothing, and Cherie had fuck-all going for her, too.'

He was off again, the caged leopard. 'One day I felt Grace move. We were sitting in the woods.' He smiled lopsidedly. 'I even remember there were daffodils all around us.'

'Really? You actually felt her moving?'

He nodded, wide-eyed, still amazed. 'Like Cherie had a fish living in there. It was the coolest thing I've ever felt.'

'And that was Grace! Who chose the name?'

'Both of us. We went through the baby book.' He picked up two rolled-up pairs of socks from the top of his dresser, and started juggling them. 'You ever seen an ultrasound photo, Jacko?'

'Certainly not, except on telly, and I hope I never have to.'

He dropped one of the sock balls, stooped smoothly to flick it up, and continued to juggle. 'It's pretty clever, what they can do.'

One ball flew out of his reach, so I caught it and chucked it back. Then he threw me another one, and we tossed them backwards and forwards, two at a time. Matt had fast reactions, all right.

'You should try out for the RAF,' I suggested seriously. 'Be a jet pilot.'

He didn't pause in the rhythm of his catching and throwing. 'They don't take people with buggered necks.'

'Oh.'

'I asked them.'

'Oh.'

'They told me to sod off.' He caught both balls in one hand, lobbed them into an open drawer, and began to roll a joint. 'Look at this.' He paused in his rolling and reached into the drawer, pulling out a thin, shiny scrap of paper. 'This'll blow you away.'

I took it out of his hand and squinted at it; then I turned it the other way up and tried again. It wasn't anything. Just a black square, with a sort of grey smudged triangle across it, like a grubby windscreen after the wipers have been on. I looked at the back, hoping for a clue.

'Really clever, isn't it?' Matt said, happily. He was craning his neck to look. 'See how she's sucking her thumb?'

Light began to dawn. I focused on the thing again, and suddenly I got the point. It was astonishing. The ghostly white outline was—quite clearly, I now saw—the profile of a baby's face. And, with a little imagination, I could believe that the blur beside her mouth was a fist. It was like that mountain with Jesus's face in it. Once you've got it, it's obvious.

'Wow,' I gasped, as more and more of the grey patches formed into bits of baby. 'Unbelievable.' I looked up and caught Matt watching me.

'That's my daughter, four months into her life.' He took the flimsy image back with poker-faced pride. Slid it carefully into the drawer, underneath his socks. 'We broke up just after that. I took another girl out to the cinema—just a friend, really, but Cherie heard about it from the girlies' gossip network. She went berserk! Slashed herself all down her arms with a pair of nail scissors.'

'Shit! How bad?'

'She had to go and get stitches. Complete loose unit, you see? She finished with me. Said I was no better than all the others. She was obsessed with this idea that I'd been laughing at her behind her back. Maybe I could have got her to come round, but I was too scared and stupid.'

He raised an eyebrow, pretending to concentrate on his handiwork. 'She might still be alive if . . . Darcy Fox. What a total cretin.'

'Who?'

'I knew him at school.' Matt bared his teeth. 'Lucky he got killed too, or I'd be doing life for him right now.'

'What happened?'

'He picked her up from hospital. Out of his head on speed. Showing off. Another driver called the police, but they were too fuckin' slow. Fox takes a roundabout the wrong way. Hits a lorry'—he smashed his fist into his palm—'head on. My girl ends up in the hospital morgue, with our baby upstairs in maternity.'

I couldn't think of any words.

'I'll regret that trip to the cinema as long as I live,' he muttered.

'Wouldn't have made any difference, mate.'

'It would. She'd have phoned me instead of Darcy friggin' Fox.' He licked the Rizla very carefully, as if giving himself time. His hands were shaking.

'I went to her funeral,' he said. 'Never been to a funeral before.'

'I hate 'em.'

'I went and touched her coffin. Promised her I'd look after Grace.'

That's a responsibility, I thought. You shouldn't make promises to dead people. He stuck the joint behind one ear and began to rootle in the treasure trove again, dislodging socks and boxer shorts, spilling them onto the floor. Eventually he dragged out a crumpled wad of A4 paper.

'They said I could write Grace a letter,' he said, holding it up, 'in case she gets adopted. It's censored by the camp commandant, then it goes into a file. I've done five pages so far.'

I blinked. 'Hard one to write.'

'Yeah, well. I don't have to bother now, do I? Mum's back. Those dykes down the SS will love her. Ah, here's what I was looking for.' He shoved his letter back in with the underwear and pulled out a ragged, mustard-coloured object. He threw it to me, and I caught it.

It was the last thing you'd expect a teenage gorilla to be showing you: a knitted lion, about the size of a young kitten, that had seen better days. One eye was missing, and a new one had been drawn on clumsily in black ink. The mane and the fluffy part at the end of the tail were made of strands of brown wool, some of them unravelling.

But it had a happy, goofy look on its face, and it felt squashy under my fingers.

'Who's this?' I ran my fingertips across the soft mane.

'Frederick the Lion. I've had him ever since I was born. My grandma knitted him for me. I'm going to give him to Grace.'

Abruptly, he snatched the toy back and crammed it into the drawer. Then he lit up and sat down next to me, and we both stared at our feet. I was wearing desert boots, as I recall, and Matt was barefoot, his jeans frayed around his ankles.

He handed me the spliff. 'Um ... thanks for bringing my mum back.'

'No worries, mate,' I said, and inhaled. 'No worries at all.'

'She'd better not try coming in here. I'll fucking tell her what I think of her for going off. Selfish bitch.'

We both heard it then. Voices in the hall.

'Talk of the fucking devil,' said Matt hopefully.

Footsteps, gently creaking up the stairs. Then, so quiet that it might have been a bird under the eaves, a tapping on the door. Matt sat completely still, gazing vacantly at the ceiling.

'Go on, mate,' I whispered. 'Let her in.'

'*You* let her in,' he sneered, 'since you're such a frigging gentleman.' He took the spliff out of my hand, leaned back on his elbows and shut his eyes.

I was halfway across the room when the door inched open and Deborah's face appeared around it.

'Ah!' Matt breathed out a defiant stream of smoke. It rose past his nostrils in a herbal cloud. 'The prodigal mother.'

'Jake!' she hissed accusingly, her gaze sliding from Matt to me. 'What are you two doing in here?' She was sniffing at the loaded air.

I tried not to hop from one foot to the other.

She clicked her tongue. 'It's like having *two* teenagers in the house.'

'Just dropped in to catch up with old Matt,' I mumbled. 'Good mate of mine. I'm off to bed now, though.' I saluted him. 'See you, mate.'

'No need to go, Jacko.' He sounded anxious. 'Don't go just because of her.'

I suppose he wanted the moral support. I hesitated, hovering unhappily. Deborah caught my eye and nodded. Quickly, she crossed the floor. She leaned down and tried to hug him, but he went totally rigid.

'Hello, darling.' It sounded a bit forced; maybe she was nervous. Matt eyed her, his face expressionless, and she tried again. 'How have you been?'

He yawned and looked away, flicking his ash into a coffee mug.

Deborah crumpled onto the beanbag. 'Okay,' she croaked, 'I give up. You're very, very cross. Message received and understood. Well, so am I.'

'Why?' asked Matt, looking genuinely mystified.

'You managed to get a girl pregnant, right? I think most mothers would have views about that. You're welcome to sit there sulking if you want to. Go ahead. I'll be off to bed. You and Jake can blow your tiny brains out with that joint.'

'It all turned to shit here. You switched your phone off. You never emailed.' He dropped the last half inch of spliff into his mug. Then he got to his feet and started his restless roaming, up and down.

Deborah watched him for a little while, her head turning like a spectator at Wimbledon. In the end she snapped, 'For God's sake, Matthew, sit down. This room's too small for pacing. I'm sorry about the phone. It was stolen.' She glanced defiantly at me, but I kept my trap shut. If she wanted to tell whoppers, that was her affair.

Matt took a final swing at the door before launching himself onto the bed. He sprawled on his front, head over the edge, glaring morosely at the carpet.

'You're my bloody mother,' he said flatly. 'You're supposed to be here for me. Isn't she, Jake? She's supposed to be here for me, my own bloody *mother*.'

A smile tugged at Deborah's mouth. 'I saw some pictures of Grace.'

He lifted his head and met her eye for just a moment. 'She's okay,' he mumbled. 'Not a bad kid.'

'You visit her twice a week?'

He nodded. 'She recognises me. Imogen—she's one of the social workers—thinks so too. I give Grace a bottle. She'll drink the lot for me, four ounces, won't do it for anyone else.' He let his head hang down again. 'I'll never see her again if she gets adopted.'

'There's no chance of you keeping in contact with her?'

'Nah.' Matt sat up, teeth clenched. 'Lenora fucking Blunt—team manager down at the SS, ugly as sin—reckons I'd "destabilise the placement". She said it about fifty times. Eventually I asked her what the fuck that means, and she said, "It means you might cause trouble." Stupid bitch. Too right, I'd cause trouble. I'd go and get my daughter and bring her home.'

Deborah nodded. 'Yes, I can see—'

'Photos! If I behave nicely, I might get a photo every year. Big of them, isn't it?'

He looked extra fierce, like a toddler trying not to cry. Swiftly, Deborah got up and sat next to him. He hunched himself angrily away, his mouth a stubborn line, hands clasped together. I remembered doing that to my mother when she tried to comfort me.

'Don't worry.' Deborah stroked his powerful shoulder. 'We'll get her back.'

I edged closer to the door and then eased myself through it. As I closed it behind me, they were sitting side by side on Matt's duvet, staring at their feet.

Chapter Eighteen

It's odd. I can sleep on a plane or in a taxi—at uni I was famous for snoozing through lectures with my head propped on an upright pencil—but lay me horizontal between ironed linen sheets and my eyes snap open like starting gates. So there I was, tucked up in Perry's spare bed, listening to the murmur of voices from Matt's room. And wide awake.

I heard a thud, and grinned. He was belting that door again. Later on, I heard the door quietly open and close. Deborah, presumably, on her way to bed. I turned the pillow over and shut my eyes, and then opened them again. My future was an empty page, and it wasn't quite so pleasant a sensation as I'd expected.

Thoughts ricocheted exuberantly from one side of my mind to the other, yelling for my attention like a troupe of monkeys who've drunk far too much coffee. They were giving me a headache. For hours I lay there, listening dazedly to those crazy voices while my alarm clock smugly flicked numbers at me.

Nearly two am. Bugger this, I thought. There's nowhere lonelier than a sleeping house at two in the morning. I rolled out of bed, dragged on jeans and a jersey and headed for the kitchen, intent on raiding the fridge.

The hall was in darkness, but the kitchen light was on. Surprised, I put my head around the door, squinting into the brightness. Perry was sitting at the table reading, a bottle of whisky at his elbow. He looked up and smiled delightedly.

'Jake! Couldn't sleep?'

I slumped into a chair. 'Nah. Wide awake. I can't bloody believe it.' I made a pointless attempt to smooth down my hair.

He took off his reading glasses. 'Have some of this.' He fetched another tumbler and sloshed in a vast amount of Scotch. It's not really my drink—my father lives on the stuff—but Perry's was pretty drinkable, actually. It had a seriously expensive taste.

I peered over at his magazine. What does a man like Perry think about in the blackest hours of the night?

'*New Internationalist.*' He held up the article he'd been reading and gave me a thumbnail. I can't remember much now, except that it was full of uncomfortable truths about oil companies in Nigeria. Then he closed the magazine and fixed those gypsy black eyes on me—a little squiffily, I thought. I glanced at the bottle. Only about a third of the whisky was left, and I was willing to bet it'd been full at midnight.

'You know,' he began, too seriously, 'what I owe you can never be expressed.'

'Don't worry about it.' I hate it when drunk people are grateful. They're always so embarrassingly sincere.

'Well, don't rush off. Be our guest here. Least we can do. What are your plans?'

'Ah. That's a good question.'

He raised his eyebrows helpfully, topping up our glasses with impressive control.

'Thanks.' I nodded towards the bottle. 'This is bloody good stuff.'

His thin mouth lifted wistfully. 'That's the tang of the peat bog, and drizzle on the bracken. From the Isle of Jura. A wild, mystical place. You must go up there.'

'One day.'

'*One day* . . . So. What's on your mind?'

It was slipping down easily, that whisky. 'I met up with a couple of guys in Kenya. They drove all the way from London in an ex-army Land Rover. Took them months.'

'I had some friends who did that. People kept pinching their jerry cans, and they got shot at in Mali. They had a marvellous time.'

'I thought I'd give it a try.'

He nodded approvingly. 'Alone?'

'I'll probably find someone to come with me. From what I can gather, the trans-Africa routes are crawling with antipodeans all, as they say, "doing" Africa.'

'Is that really the term they use? How very irritating.'

'Very. My brother Jesse "did" Canada once. Took him all of three weeks. He calls it his Big Overseas Experience, poor bugger. Anyway, I'll sell my car and find some kind of four-wheel drive. And it won't be a bloody army Land Rover, either. No offence.'

'None taken.'

'I'm going to need sand mats and jerry cans and all kinds of gear, visas, and a carnet for the vehicle. I won't get away before the New Year.'

'Excellent!' He spread his arms. 'Then make Coptree your base. Come and go as you please. You can use the phone, the internet: make yourself at home. Your worldly goods are safe in the garage. Leave them there for as long as you like.'

I looked into my glass, thinking fast. On the one hand, I actually had nowhere else to go just then. Nowhere very convenient, anyway. But on the other hand, the Harrison family were—quite clearly—stark staring bonkers, every last one of them. They'd lied and they'd cheated, and sent me prancing off to Kenya on their secret mission. If I had an ounce of sense, I'd kick up my heels and be miles away before they roped me into any more of their wild schemes.

There again—and I couldn't for the life of me understand why this should be—I liked them, very much. All of them. And I was bothered about them too. Especially Matt.

'Thanks,' I said. 'That would be great.'

He allowed himself a brief, gold-toothed flash of satisfaction, raising his tumbler in a small toast. 'That's settled, then.'

I raised mine, half-heartedly. 'I've got various friends in London I can stay with for a while,' I explained, 'but it's a bit awkward just now. This girl I lived with—most people seem to think I treated her badly.'

'And did you?'

I made a despairing gesture with my hands. 'I just didn't marry her.'

'And you'd been together for how long?'

'Four years.'

He watched me with narrowed eyes. It was a funny thing about Perry: for all his faults, all his manipulation, you caught yourself wanting him to like you. There was something compelling about his stillness. I wanted him to understand.

'I don't want to get married, Perry,' I insisted. 'I don't want kids. That makes me a self-centred tosser, I guess. Childhood isn't what it's cracked up to be. I wouldn't wish it on anyone.'

'That depends, doesn't it?'

'No.' I took a gulp of whisky. 'And what's more I've never seen a married couple that were genuinely happy. My mother, for instance. She's had a pig of a life. The most exciting thing she's ever done is to stand between me and Dad's flailing belt.'

'And she put up with that?'

'Oh, yes. That's what you do where I come from. Put on a brave face and get on with it, even when your man's a howling butcher. My mum might as well have been a goldfish swimming round and round in a bowl all her life, for all the freedom of expression she's had. And that's a hell of a shame, because she's a good person.'

Perry twitched one eyebrow. 'That *is* a hell of a shame,' he said smoothly, 'but it surely doesn't mean the entire institution of marriage is flawed?'

It felt as though we were the only ones awake, anywhere in the world, in our brightly lit room; and even we weren't really awake at all.

I ran a finger around the top of my glass. 'From what I can see, getting spliced means being mildly unhappy, or possibly profoundly miserable, 'til death do you part. That's why people's mothers cry at weddings, I'm sure of it. They're in on the secret.'

'Secret?'

'They know it's really a funeral. A farewell.' I searched for the right words. 'The end of everything fun and easy.'

I knocked back the last of my drink, and he quietly refilled it.

'Married people were always on at Anna and me to get hitched,' I said. 'They didn't see why we shouldn't sacrifice ourselves to the great god Stability, like them. "So when are you going to get a ring on her finger, Jake?" Never used to shut up about it. They wanted us to be as disappointed and dismal as they were.'

Perry looked mildly amused, as though he knew something I didn't. 'You might be very lonely when you're old.'

'What kind of a reason is that to live in a fish tank?'

He inclined his head, gravely. 'I've married twice, of course. And I've been supremely happy each time.'

My jaw dropped. This bare-faced whopper was too much for me. I wasn't letting him get away with it.

'I don't want to offend you, Perry, but that isn't strictly true, is it? I had to go and shanghai your wife back from Kenya. And, as you very well know, I wouldn't have agreed to go if you'd told me the truth.'

He became absolutely still, the glass in his hand arrested in midair, watching me with eyes like glittering black slits. An owl hooted, out in the dark.

'Truth?'

'Yes,' I said savagely. '*Truth*. What you tell when you're not trying to mislead someone into travelling halfway around the world to do your dirty work.'

'Out with it, then, Jake. What, precisely, *is* the truth?'

Perhaps it was sleep deprivation or the effects of the whisky, or maybe it was indignation at the way I'd been duped. I found myself leaning forward, meeting his eye. 'The truth is that Deborah wasn't on an assignment, and you knew it. She didn't want to be found. The truth is that you didn't look for her yourself because . . .' I ground to a halt. Even Deborah hadn't opened the box on this one.

Perry raised his eyebrows. 'Because?'

'Well . . . you *can't*.'

He laughed without humour, showing his teeth like a yawning cat. His cheeks looked hollow tonight, and I reckoned he'd lost weight in the short time I'd been away. His shirt hung off him in artistic folds, as if he were an oil painting.

'Let's start with my anxiety,' he said calmly. We might have been swapping recipes. 'Since someone's clearly been so good as to enlighten you.'

'It wasn't Deborah.'

'It really doesn't matter who it was.' He played with the liquid in his glass. 'What do you know about agoraphobia?'

'Nothing,' I said. 'Absolutely nothing.'

'You believe it means fear of open spaces, I imagine?'

I'd started this conversation, but I wanted to stop him. He'd regret it in the morning. Perry, sober, was good company, if a little off-centre. Charismatic. But with about a pint of Scotch inside him, his intensity was a bit spooky.

'Forget it, mate.' I could hear my words slurring, despite my best efforts. 'Honestly. Forget it.'

'Now, where to begin . . . I was married before, as you know.'

I nodded dumbly, and he went on. 'Yes. I was married for ten wonderful years to Victoria. Her death came out of the blue—it was a matter of weeks from diagnosis to the end.' He shook his head, squinting at me as though he still couldn't believe what had happened. 'She was so *angry*.'

'I guess none of us know how we'd cope,' I said. 'I don't think *my* upper lip would be very stiff.'

'She didn't seem . . .' he began, and then stopped to knock back more whisky. 'She didn't seem to have space left in her soul for me. The last time she went to hospital, I carried her into the ward—like this, in my arms—and then I felt her turn away, as though I'd abandoned her because I wasn't coming all the way to death with her.'

He blinked, staring right through me. 'She wasn't conscious, at the end. There wasn't much to show she was alive at all. But at the instant of her death, the feeling I had of being abandoned was . . . One second she was still there, with me. The next, I was alone.' He looked dazed. 'She just wasn't *there* any more. The finality of it was unbearable. I wanted to run after her, like a child running alongside a train. D'you know what I mean?'

I could see Sala's head beside mine as I lay, snotty-nosed and sobbing, on the filthy ground under the dog kennels. Her kind brown eyes were already empty, turning opaque, and the farm dogs had gone deathly quiet. Dad said they were licking their lips because they could smell the blood and he was going to feed her to them, and if I didn't stop fucking snivelling he'd give me something to cry about. He said the other barrel would be for me. We were never allowed to cry.

'Yes,' I said. 'I think I do know.'

Then Dad stumped off to the house for tea and brownies, and I fetched a spade. It was hard to dig a hole in the stony ground. Her ears were still warm and soft when I lifted her in, and I wanted to stroke them for the last time, but I didn't dare because I had to cover her up before he came back. I lifted a spadeful of earth and tipped it into the hole, and Sala began to disappear, and I knew I'd never touch her again.

Perry was swinging the drink around in his glass. 'Once I'd buried Victoria, I relied on the bottle to keep me going.'

I glanced at the whisky bottle, almost empty now.

'You're right. I still do.' Perry sighed. 'God wasn't in his heaven. All wasn't right with the world. One time I had a real blinder. Got absolutely rat-arsed. Staggered home in the middle of the night, had to get up four hours later because we were going on exercise. Awful night. The dreams. The *dreams*.' He ran a shaky hand down his cheek. 'Victoria came banging on my window, rotting, raging. She'd come for me.'

I grimaced.

'She did that a lot,' he said. 'Anyway, when I arrived at the barracks I started to sweat and shake and . . . well, it was more than just a hangover. Had to sit down before I fell down. The medic said it was some sort of viral thing, sent me home. No problem.'

He stood abruptly and went to the sink, filling his glass with water from the tap. 'About a week later, same thing. It happened on the parade ground this time, witnessed by about a hundred men.'

'Hell.'

'I actually had a bizarre sensation, as though I was floating above myself. I thought I must be dying. Made a real spectacle of myself.'

'What was it?'

He shrugged. 'I felt . . . sounds stupid now . . . Victoria was doing it, calling to me to join her on the other side.'

'Was Deborah around?'

'Deborah was very young. Just the nanny, a friend's daughter. I didn't tell her. Anyway, the medics attached things to my chest and got me walking on a treadmill. They said I was fit as buggery. Suggested it was stress.'

He took a mouthful of water and made a face as though there'd been battery acid in the glass. 'Stress! I don't *do* stress. I don't *do* fear. I've spent much of my career on active service. Fear isn't something I have ever been afraid of, if you follow me.'

I followed him, but I wasn't sure whether I believed him.

He didn't wait for an answer. 'Anyway, the attacks stopped, and I almost forgot about it. I started spending more time at home, drank less, came to realise that Deborah was more than just a beautiful girl who loved my daughter.'

'A beautiful and very *young* girl.'

'Yes, young,' he agreed, sitting down again. 'But she wasn't a child. She knew what she wanted from life. She . . . I felt secure with her. She made me feel safe, with her youth and her vitality. I very nearly found happiness again. Then—out of the blue—*wham*!' He slammed his hand flat onto the wood, and I jumped. 'It knocked me right down this time.' He rested a hand across his chest as though he could still feel the agony. 'Good God, the pain . . . I was suffocating, I couldn't breathe. I believed my number was up, Jake. And I knew terror for the first time in my life. Pure terror.'

'Sounds like a heart attack, doesn't it?'

'I still wonder whether it was my heart, whatever these bloody people say. Had to be stretchered off, rushed to hospital in an ambulance—the hospital where Victoria died. Deborah was there, beside herself. Tests, tests and more tests. Nothing!'

He stared at me, wildly. 'It kept happening,' he said hopelessly. 'I longed for a diagnosis of some sort. Some explanation. I feared that I'd lost my mind. Eventually, the consultant told me he thought I was having panic attacks. *Panic* attacks!' He grinned austerely, like a skull.

'Doesn't sound very British Army.'

'Ah.' He paused, the whisky bottle in his hand. 'It's interesting, your saying that. In fact there's a fair old tradition of this kind of thing, if you go back to the old diagnoses of shell shock and battle fatigue and so on. You get some of it after every major engagement, even in modern warfare, although we don't shoot the poor bastards as deserters any more.'

He sloshed more into our glasses. 'So I'm not alone. I suppose my illness was triggered by personal trauma rather than military engagement, but the army didn't like to acknowledge it and neither did I. So it was put down as an episode of general ill-health, and I was posted to Nairobi.'

I wondered what the gospel according to Perry would be when it came to Nairobi. At the same time, he must have been wondering just how much I knew.

He sat for a moment, gazing into his glass.

'Nairobi.' He nodded wearily. 'All was well.'

My eyes just about popped out. All was *well*?

'With Deborah by my side, I could face anything. At the end of my posting, I asked to go back to England. We had Lucy's education to think of. I was sent to Colchester, and Deborah and I were married. Matthew was born. We were blissfully happy.'

I sat open-mouthed, awed by the scale of his whitewash job. Out in the hall the grandfather clock clunked, steadily.

'It came back, the bloody thing, in the end.' He spoke very quietly. 'Hit me like a bullet in the chest. At the barracks, inevitably. I couldn't go near the place any more. I knew then that my career was over.'

The clock whirred, and struck three. It sounded unnaturally loud.

'The *terror*!' he hissed. 'I'd become an animal. A lynx, say, cowering in a trap, waiting for death as the hunter approaches with his club. My rational mind would tell me I had nothing to fear, but the message simply did not get through. My brain was paralysed by terror.'

I knew that feeling.

'Most people,' said Perry, fixing his gaze on me, 'have never truly felt terror. Not in our molly-coddled society, anyway.'

'I guess not.'

Oh, no.

Oh, no. I can hear the quad bike roaring up the paddock. He's coming.

'You're at . . . oh, a drinks party, say.' He held up a clenched fist. 'Suddenly, dread. Panic. You're frantic. Make a complete idiot of yourself. Believe me, that's the last drinks party you'll ever go to.'

'I don't think I get it . . . *Do* you have a heart condition?'

'Not at all, according to the medics. Wish I did. No, it's all up here.' He tapped himself on the head. 'I'm barking mad, apparently.'

'I'm sure that's not right,' I said, a little insincerely.

He leaned towards me. 'Yes, I'm afraid it *is* right. I avoided anywhere connected with the army, since those places were the trigger. Avoidance worked for a short time, but it soon started up again. In the street, in a shop, in a theatre. Even sitting in a car. So I had to avoid those situations too. Now there's only one place it doesn't happen. Right here, in this house. So . . .' Sip, swallow. 'So here I rot.'

'Christ, you must be bored.'

'I have work—quite lucrative, actually, until the recent downturn—that can be done in my study. That's my cell. The garden is my exercise yard.'

'Isn't there any treatment?'

'I'm rattling,' he waved his glass dismissively, '*rattling* with anti-depressants and the Lord only knows what else. I've had bloody cognitive therapy and behavioural therapy and every other type of therapy, all with silly names. God. These people. They pretend it's so easy.' He emptied the last of the bottle into our glasses. 'No, Jake, for me there's no escape.'

'No escape? Ever?'

'Only one thing persuades me that my life is valid.' He knocked the glassful back in one, banged it down onto the table. 'Deborah. With her, I'm safe. Without her, I'm bewildered. But she's often away with her work, and I'm finding it increasingly . . .' He winced. 'I'm afraid even this house will become unsafe. And then . . .'

I waited.

He met my eyes. 'And then, I shall be finished.'

It was impossible for me to imagine such an existence. I sat looking at him, trying to understand. But I couldn't.

'I know what you're thinking,' he said. 'You're thinking that if I had an ounce of backbone I'd get out there. Just square the old shoulders and stride out through that gate.'

I held out my hands. 'I don't think I could live like this, Perry, completely imprisoned in my own home. Surely you could force yourself? A little at a time?'

He didn't answer. He seemed to be made of ash. I knew I'd said the wrong thing, and I didn't care. I remember thinking that the man needed to wake up to himself. I'd rather top myself than wander around my home like a ghost, only half alive, swilling whisky and popping anti-depressants until I rotted away.

'Now I understand why you sent me to bring her back,' I said, after a while. '*You* needed her. For yourself. It was nothing to do with that baby.'

He shook his head. 'How would Deborah have felt if I'd let her grandchild go?'

'I don't know, but—'

'Horrified.' He was rallying. 'Grace is our flesh and our blood! Try to imagine how it feels to be a grandparent. She's not just any baby, she's a part of us, you see. She must grow up with her family. There's no substitute for that.'

'But,' I argued, without thinking it through, 'you must be ready for a bit of peace and quiet by now, with your own kids grown up?'

Big mistake. Perry's chair scraped as he leaped to his feet. He was like Matt, pacing in his bedroom, agitated.

'Peace and quiet? Do you honestly imagine that I crave peace and sodding *quiet*? Good God, man! I've lived all over the world. I've led men into action, under fire, in eight different regions, in deserts and cities and jungles. I've been first down deserted streets, waiting for the sniper fire. And now I cower in the corner like an old dodderer in a geriatric ward, watching on a twenty-four-inch screen as the world explodes around me.'

Subsiding, he threw himself back into the chair. 'No, thank you. I'm *not* ready for a bit of peace and quiet.'

That shut me up.

The clock struck the quarter-hour. Perry jerked his head towards the door. 'It's all right. Go on, Jake. I know you're longing to get off to bed.'

'What about you?'

'I'll just stoke up the stove. Then I'll get my head down too.'

'Okay.' I pushed myself to my feet. 'Thanks for the drink.'

'Not at all. Any time. Thanks for your company.'

So I left him there, alone with his empty bottle, and sloped upstairs.

Mad, I thought, as I snuggled my head into the pillow and let the soft mists of Jura carry me away. *They're all mad.*

Chapter Nineteen

I didn't hear the creak of my door a few hours later. I never heard her cross the floor, either, or lower a mug down next to the alarm clock.

'Jake.' Fingers gently pinched my ear. 'Jake.'

Deborah was standing beside the bed, bright against the pale light of an autumn morning. She was dressed in proper clothes, I noticed: corduroy trousers and a posh, moss-coloured jersey. Proper pommy clothes, to go with the potpourri and polished floors. I missed the strips of tie-dyed cloth.

I peered at the clock, whisky-headed. 'Jeez!' I croaked. 'Half past seven! What is this? Boot camp? I could be snuggled down in a hotel room right now, with fluffy towels and *Do not disturb* hanging on the door.'

'Sorry. I brought you some tea.'

Her voice was clear as water. I felt grubby with her so close to me. I mumbled a vague thanks and reached for the mug—I don't touch the stuff, actually—and she sat down on the bed, somewhere near my knees. I could faintly smell her perfume. A warm, citrus scent, and maybe cloves.

I took a mouthful of tea, hoping it would scald the cotton wool off my tongue. 'Is anyone else up?'

'Lucy left two hours ago,' she said absently, staring out of the window. 'She says she'll phone you.'

I stretched my legs, smugly. 'She'll be at her desk by now.'

'I was hoping . . .'

'Yeah? Faithful hound, at your service.'

'I . . . um. I'd be so grateful if you could come with me this morning.'

I was suspicious. 'Come with you to *where*?'

'Children's Services. Fintan House. I've got to beard the dragons in their lair.'

'Well, I don't see what I've got to do with any of that. It's Perry you . . .' I wavered, remembering. 'It's a solicitor you need.'

She nodded. 'Stuart Forsyth. I've got an appointment to see him tomorrow. In the meantime, his advice is to get down to Fintan House and throw my hat into the ring.'

'Okay. Fine. Good luck.' I plonked my head back onto the pillow. The linen smelled of lavender. 'Let me know how you get on.'

'Perry can't come with me this morning. He's busy.'

What a whopper.

She reached down and shook me by the knee. 'He explained the whole legal thing to me last night . . . are you listening, Jake?'

'Nope.' I pulled the pillow over my ears, wishing I'd put a thousand miles between myself and this madhouse.

She dragged it off me, sat with it on her lap. 'Grace is being cared for by the local authority, but they have to restore her to her birth family if at all possible. That's their duty. Adoption is a last resort.'

'You'd hope so.'

'Quite. Well, they've tried, to be fair. Cherie died. Matt couldn't manage alone. Perry never came to the party. They didn't believe I existed, so they gave up and planned to have Grace adopted. They've even found a family.'

'Fast work!' I said. 'The thing's on the home straight.'

'Okay. Well, because Matt won't give consent, they've had to apply to court for an order. Without it, they're scuppered.'

'What if they *do* get their order?'

'It more or less casts her adrift. She'll go to the new family without any legal baggage. They call it a placement hearing. Nice, anodyne words, aren't they? Apparently it used to be called the freeing, because the child is cut free from her unreasonable, grasping parents.' Deborah laughed bitterly. 'An arresting idea: as though some judge could set a person free. I wish it was so easy. I'd apply for one myself.'

I ignored this stream of consciousness. It was too early in the morning. 'Sounds as though they've got everything nicely teed up,' I said.

'Mm. Well, they had until I appeared, like a bad penny. So now I've got to rush over there and show that I really do exist, and have only one head.'

I pulled the duvet up another few inches, trying to disappear. 'Great. And your clever lawyer can go along as well.'

She shifted fretfully. 'Stuart says it's better to front up without him. Looks less aggressive. I'm to smile sweetly and charm them into changing their plans.'

'Huh. I bet he's playing golf this morning.'

'Matt would like you to be there. He admires you.'

I wasn't giving in without a fight. This was going too far. Escorting the wretched woman back to Suffolk was one thing; being used as a surrogate Perry was another.

'I'm busy,' I said. 'I've got a trans-Africa expedition to organise.'

She jammed her hands under her knees, like a schoolkid. 'Please, Jake. Can't you just be a witness?'

I sat up and took another mouthful of tea—disgusting stuff—to buy some time. Outside on the lawn, I could see my friend the rabbit snuffling around in a patch of dandelions.

'Perry told me about his, um, fear thing.'

'*Really?*' Her eyebrows shot up. 'Ah, that will have been last night, in the dark hours. I heard your voices. It was the whisky talking.'

'Probably.'

'Now you know why he sleeps in the study. He can't . . . you know. It's a symptom. Not uncommon, apparently.'

Suddenly it all fitted. 'Why the dark secret?' I asked. 'Not such a disgrace, is it?'

'Dear, oh dear.' She looked sadly at me, shaking her head in disgust. 'That's just the kind of thing people say who've never lived with mental illness, Jake.'

'Actually, I have. I lived with my dad, and he's a total nutter.'

'And I bet you never told a soul.'

That shut me up, because she was right.

'So.' She began to pick at the embroidery on my duvet. 'What did you think?'

'About Perry? I thought, poor bloke.'

'Oh no, he's not. He's not a pathetic figure at all. He's all-powerful. I'm sure that isn't the impression he gave you last night as he wept into his tumbler.' She snorted. 'There he sits, lurking like a spider in his web, and we, poor insects, flutter blindly in. Then he sucks our blood. He doesn't tackle his fears because he doesn't *have* to. He has everything he needs right here.'

'No one would voluntarily box themselves up in their own home, Debs.'

'Look at you,' she jeered. 'You were in London, right? With a flat and a girlfriend and a job? Then, next thing you know, you're on a plane to Mombasa, searching for someone you've never even met. It's utterly surreal. And why? Because Perry asked you to!'

I considered this and then shook my head. 'No.'

'What d'you mean, *no*? That's exactly what happened.'

'I mean no, I didn't do it for Perry. I've told you, I did it for Matt. And also because my life is a train wreck, and I wasn't ready to face the fact.'

She fluttered a hand at me. 'All part of the game. Perry is astoundingly manipulative. He is the puppet master, and we jerk grotesquely on his strings.'

'I thought he was a spider in a web. That's a mixed thingy.'

She looked exasperated. 'Metaphor. Don't they have schools down under? You can't escape the fact, Jake, that you were his puppet. And you're still here. We all are. We're all trapped in hell.'

I tried the tea again. 'Have you asked Perry to come with you?'

She went back to vandalising the duvet cover. 'I did, just to upset him. The very thought of getting into the car can make him physically sick. By the time we reached the main road he'd be choking. He wouldn't look so bloody dignified any more.' She pulled out a long thread, dropping it delicately onto the floor with elegant fingers. 'I'm horrid, aren't I?'

'Yes.'

'Sorry . . . Look, Jake. Matt *so* wants you to come. Please.'

A bird scarer fired somewhere across the fields. The report echoed away into the distance, and a cloud of rooks took to the air, cawing furiously. Deborah waited, without taking her eyes off me.

'I'm not coming,' I said. And she smiled.

*

I disliked the place on sight. It did its best to look inconspicuous, hiding coyly in the middle of a row of other oversized townhouses. Victorian, I should think. Red brick. Lots of ivy. It sported a discreet little sign: *Fintan House*. There was a shrubbery at the front, but you could tell it wasn't just somebody's garden. It had that municipal look about it, and beyond the main building lurked a concrete and glass extension.

The three of us trudged up the wheelchair ramp to a solid wooden door. It was a desolate morning; the damp was creeping in under my collar, and I had an ache in one knee. Matt was an old hand. He rang the bell and grunted into an intercom, and the door clicked, letting us into a blue-and-brown-tiled hall with a wide wooden staircase curling up into the shadows. We stood there for a second. I felt like an extra in a horror movie, half expecting to hear wild evil-genius laughter and someone crashing chords on an organ.

The hall smelled of bleach and polish, like my old boarding school. I spotted a door to the right marked *Reception—All Visitors*, and from somewhere on our left floated a brisk female voice.

'Hi, there! Hi, Matt. Come on in.' A woman was waiting, holding a mug in one hand and jamming the fire door open with her foot.

Matt jerked his head towards her in greeting, and we followed her into a room with a high ceiling and long sash windows. Wooden partitions subdivided it; and behind one I glimpsed a guy with a harassed crewcut, hunched over a laptop.

The woman transferred the cup into her left hand and held out her right. She was around thirty, I'd have said. More or less blonde, with a little help. Hair in a long ponytail—it really *did* look like a pony's tail. Attractive, actually, although the barn-door chin was a bit disappointing. Engagement ring, quite flashy. Linen trousers. And tall: her eyes were almost on a level with mine.

'Mrs Harrison? Imogen Christie.' She spoke in a clipped, detached shade of Essex.

'Hi, Imogen.' Deborah didn't sound like herself at all. She seemed edgy and ingratiating, and once again I wished I hadn't come.

The social worker eyed her for a moment longer than was polite. 'Did you have a good flight? When did you get home?'

'Last night.'

'Just last night?' Imogen's appraisal flickered over me, and I felt like a cockroach in a bakery. Behind her, Crew cut's phone began to bleat.

Deborah took a nervous step away from me. 'This is Jake Kelly, a friend of the family,' she explained apologetically. 'Matt wanted him to be here today, since Perry couldn't come. I hope you don't mind.'

'I won't be any trouble,' I said, and put on my most appealing face.

My charms didn't work on Imogen. 'I'm not sure . . . The team manager, Lenora Blunt, will be available in a minute. She's making an urgent telephone call right now. Coffee?' She gestured towards a dusty kettle on a tray.

'Er . . . lovely,' said Deborah.

Crew cut had answered the phone but was still staring at his screen and jabbing at the odd key. Imogen picked up two of those glass mugs that make coffee look and taste like the run-off from a sewage plant. Opening a jar of brown talcum powder, she called back over her shoulder towards Matt, who was hanging around in the doorway, his hands in his pockets, looking surly.

'Matt, Lenora and I are going to have a chat with your mum upstairs. D'you want to come back in an hour?'

He scowled, mumbled something about going downtown, and slouched out. I heard the heavy front door screech shut behind him.

'If you'll excuse me for just a minute,' said Imogen. 'There's a waiting area off the hall.'

We parked our backsides on a wooden pew. There was a table with a pile of women's magazines, and Deborah began to leaf through one. I gave up on the muck they passed off as coffee and stood up again, stretching my knee.

The telephone rang in Imogen's office, and I strolled into the hall as she answered it. I wasn't being nosy, honestly. I was just bored.

'Hi. Yes, Lenora . . . *mutter, mutter* . . . got hold of the lawyer?'

There was a long silence until I heard Imogen shift abruptly; her voice sharpened. '*What*? Does he realise how far along the line we've got?' Pause. 'And he understands that the grandfather's never bothered to show up? . . . It's not good enough, Lenora. Where's Grace in all of this? . . . How are we supposed to carry out an assessment in four weeks flat? Does he realise how understaffed we are? My case load . . . yes, I agree . . . I mean, it's *us* who have to pick up the pieces.' Sigh. 'Oh, well, we're stuck, then. I'll wheel the grandmother up. Perhaps we can talk her out of it.'

She dropped her voice to a murmur. I caught the words *support person* and *come along to hold her hand*.

A thud—phone crashing down?—and Crew cut laughed and said something about a magic, reappearing grandma. There was a pause, for head-shaking I guessed. I scooted back to the waiting room, sharpish. Skidded across the tiles, fell down next to Deborah and snatched up a magazine. Seconds later, Imogen appeared at the door, chin jutting crossly.

We followed her linen trousers up the stairs and past a cupboard that was trying to be a kitchen. Deborah was staring straight ahead with a glassy expression, like a sleepwalker in a play. Eventually Imogen held open a door, and we trooped in.

The room was obviously intended for meetings—oblong table, whiteboard and a general air of underuse. A couple of cardboard files were stacked on the table. Facing the door, wearing a ghastly smile, was the weirdest-looking woman I have ever seen. This raven-haired creature would have been well cast as the housekeeper in a spooky nineteen forties film set in a sinister Estonian castle. She might have been fifty, or sixty, or eighty. It was hard to tell under all that makeup.

She stared, wide-eyed, before extending a bony hand. 'Mrs Harrison? I'm Lenora Blunt, team manager.' She had a limp voice, as though she were about to swoon, with an accent I couldn't quite place. I think it might have been eastern European, which fitted, somehow.

Deborah introduced me, and Blunt looked me up and down.

'I won't say a word,' I promised, and pinched my lips together with my fingers.

Blunt nodded with bad grace and gestured towards the table. We sat around it, and I tried to be invisible.

'It's very good of you both to fit me in like this,' said Deborah, politely.

'We've had to shuffle things.' The Estonian housekeeper waved an impatient arm; she was wearing a charm bracelet, and it jangled. 'This couldn't wait. We're working to a strict timetable, set by the court.'

'You're extremely late in the day,' scolded Imogen. She sounded like a plumber tut-tutting over your pre-war hot-water tank. I hate plumbers. They always make me feel less than a man. 'It's eight months since we discovered Cherie was pregnant. We've been planning for Grace ever since. And you turn up *now*.'

'How did that poor child manage to become pregnant,' Deborah seemed to be recovering her usual composure, 'given that she was in your care at the time?'

Lenora Blunt flushed. 'We can't fit them all with chastity belts,' she snapped, defensively. 'We haven't the budget.'

There was a brief, incredulous silence. Imogen threw her manager a look of pure contempt before turning back to Deborah. 'We've tried hard to find a place for Grace within both her birth families. No one came forward. Meanwhile, she's starting to bond with her foster carer. Adoption is tricky, Mrs Harrison. The younger the child, the better. Grace needs to move on.'

'I see,' said Deborah. 'Well, I can take her home today if you want.'

The social workers both shook their heads, with identical patronising smiles.

'You haven't been assessed,' said Imogen, and she almost waggled a finger.

Deborah looked unimpressed. 'No one assessed me when I had my own children.'

'We've found a match,' wailed Blunt, fingering a glass bead necklace the size of a small chandelier. 'It's an outstanding placement.'

'Lovely people.' Imogen tapped a blue file marked *Grace Serenity King*. 'Mixed race, of course. He's a vicar.'

I saw the steel shooting into Deborah's backbone.

'That's all very wholesome. But Matt is actually her *father*,' she reminded them sternly, folding her arms. 'You're not supposed to be social engineers. It isn't your job to churn out babies for childless couples, even nice middle-class Christian ones. Babies don't just grow on trees. They have families, with whom they belong.'

'Matt couldn't cope,' insisted Imogen. 'His heart's in the right place, I'll grant you. He's lovely with Grace. But he couldn't look after her.'

Deborah nodded. 'I agree. But *I* can.' She was magnificent, she really was; I wanted to applaud. 'Look, Imogen, Lenora. I'm truly sorry I haven't been here for your assessments, but I knew nothing about any baby.'

'You haven't kept in touch,' said Imogen, her sharp eyes flicking inquisitively from Deborah to me. 'Why not?'

'I was in a remote area. No internet.' Deborah put on a super-honest face. 'And my mobile phone was stolen.'

She caught my eye, and I gave her a schoolmaster frown—I mean, what a couple of monumental whoppers. Then the outer corners of her eyes lifted, and I forgave her.

'But I did write,' she said. It sounded a bit thin, frankly. She bit her lip ruefully. 'I know, I *know*. I'll admit I had my head buried in work. But the moment I understood the situation I took the first flight back. And I'll undertake to give up my work immediately. That's because I am absolutely, fundamentally committed to caring for this little girl.'

Blunt was trying to get a word in, neurotically spinning her bracelet. 'I wonder whether you appreciate the difficulties.'

'Difficulties?'

'Yes. You're the grandmother, not the mother. You're *not* of dual heritage, which puts all sorts of cultural and practical barriers between yourself and the child. Hair care, for instance. It's completely different.'

'*Hair care?*' Deborah stared, in disbelief. 'You're not seriously putting that forward as a reason for the permanent removal of a child from her family?'

Blunt blushed. 'Well, but it's a part of her cultural roots.'

'We *are* her roots! That's the point, Lenora. I'm trying to save her from becoming root*less*.'

Imogen leaned closer. 'The thing is, though, Deborah,' (first-name terms, I thought. We *are* getting chummy) 'that this will be more complicated than bringing up your own family. And you're . . . older, too.'

I had to chuckle at that.

'I'm thirty-seven!' Debs looked genuinely aggrieved. 'Nowadays lots of people *start* their families at my age. Lots and lots of people.' She pointed at me. 'Jake hasn't even found a mother to bear his children yet.'

'Look, Deborah,' insisted Imogen. 'Think about it. It will take so much commitment. *So* much.'

Deborah nodded. 'A baby is for life, not just for Christmas. I know that, Imogen.'

Or perhaps, I thought disloyally, a baby is for about seventeen years?

'I've done it twice before, remember?' said Deborah. 'Matt's sister, Lucy, wasn't mine, but I brought her up just as if she was. I've got buckets of commitment. That's why I'm here.'

Imogen narrowed her eyes. 'What about Mr Harrison? Why hasn't he been in to see Grace?'

'That's easy.' Deborah laughed gaily. 'Perry's agoraphobic. He's *longing* to meet her but he just can't travel. He's very competent with babies, actually. Come to our home and talk to him.'

'We have. He didn't tell us what you just have.'

'Of course he didn't. It's a feature of the condition. The shame, the secretiveness. Surely you know this? People sometimes go for years, hiding it even from their own families.'

Imogen nodded, thinking. 'That explains a lot,' she said slowly.

'So.' Lenora obviously wasn't giving up without a fight. 'The upshot is that you have a husband with mental health issues, a son with behavioural problems, and you saw fit to leave home for several months. Yours is a dysfunctional family, Deborah. How can we place a baby with you?'

I saw a flash of triumph cross Deborah's face. She leaned forward and looked Blunt square in the eye. 'My husband has a *condition*. A disability. Surely, Lenora, you aren't going to write him off on that ground? I don't think you're allowed to do that, are you? You've got to assess him like anyone else.'

There was a nasty silence. Blunt flared her nostrils. 'I'm just trying to—'

'Look.' Deborah had the ball now and she was sprinting away towards the line. 'We're her birth family. It's not a conventional nuclear family—whose is, these days? *But she will know exactly who she is.* You have a duty, don't you, to achieve that if you can? Right. Well, here I am: willing, healthy and able. You can't just shut the door on me. You aren't allowed to, and you know it. You have to assess me, properly and fairly.'

The social workers exchanged glances. Lenora had red spots on her cheeks, like a sulky doll.

'All right then,' sighed Imogen, and she opened a blue file.

Score!

'But we can't lose any more time, so we'll be taking a twin-track approach. We'll carry on with our adoption procedure while assessing you.'

Deborah had won. She could collect the cup and do a victory lap. And yet I saw her shoulders slump. A phone on the table trilled, and the sinister housekeeper answered it. She listened for a moment, whispered, 'Thank you,' and turned those anguished eyes on us.

'Grace has arrived,' she announced.

Deborah immediately stood up. Blunt swung her arm out in front of me like a lollipop lady.

'Just you, Mrs Harrison. Your, er, support person can't have contact with Grace. I'm sure you'll understand that.' She spoke to my left ear lobe. 'If you'd come back in an hour?'

Deborah gave me a faint smile. 'Go on home, Jake,' she said. 'Take my car. Here are the keys. I'm going to walk Matt back to school after this, and have a talk with his headmaster.'

Then she let them lead her away to become a grandmother.

Chapter Twenty

Leila's future was changing shape. It was like an animated piece of plasticine: unrolling, opening its eyes, squeezing itself into a bustling landscape of colour and fulfilment. Nothing looked the same.

On Tuesday she dropped in at work to explain the situation to her manager. Then she had an appointment with Linda Hooper, the social worker. Afterwards she met Maggie in a department store for coffee, ostensibly to brainstorm the Defibrillators' repertoire but really to discuss far more pressing matters. By the time they'd got up the escalator, Leila had relayed the gist of her conversation with the social worker. More meetings, more formalities, more proving themselves. But there was to be a baby at the end of it all.

'So.' Maggie slid their little plastic tray along the counter. 'You're a mother-to-be.'

Leila grabbed a blueberry muffin from the glass shelves. 'Eating for two,' she said.

'Quite right, love. Got to keep your strength up.' Maggie chose an alarmingly sticky jam doughnut, and got out her purse. 'Two large lattes, please. No, put away your massive sparkly handbag, woman. This is on me. Celebration time!'

They found a table under a potted palm. 'How d'you feel?' asked Maggie, unloading the tray.

Leila draped her coat over the chair back. 'I feel . . . ooh. How *do* I feel?' She sat down, scratching her head thoughtfully. 'I feel like the happiest woman in the world. I feel as though the clouds have rolled away from the sun and it's a brilliant blue-sky day, with . . .' She paused for a moment, and then finished with a lyrical flourish of her hands: 'With glittering frost on the grass and joy in the air.'

Maggie waited. She seemed to be expecting more.

'But there again . . .' Leila dipped her head as she broke up her muffin. She was wearing a midnight-blue cloth around her hair, and earrings the same colour. 'If I'm really honest with myself, I am sometimes a teeny bit scared.'

'Because?'

'First, because I'm waiting for the blow to fall.' Leila held up two sets of crossed fingers. 'Maggie, Maggie! Heaven doesn't come to earth.'

Maggie took a bite of sugar-laden delight, and her wispy locks fell dangerously close to the jam. 'Yum . . . they do the best doughnuts in here. Relax, Leila. Babies aren't heaven. They squawk all night. They whine all day. They vomit down your clothes and they trash your house.'

'Rubbish.' Leila picked up her coffee. 'Your Toby is tidier than you are.'

'Well, that's true. But sorry,' said Maggie. 'I shouldn't have interrupted. I know this is serious. You said that was the first thing. What's the second?'

'Well . . .' Leila's brow crinkled. 'It's all a bit like collecting a kitten or something. I'm not pregnant and bloomingly hormonal. My hair isn't shining, my bust isn't three times its normal size. I'm not sure I feel like a real mother would.'

'Mm, I've got you. You don't have heartburn, your ankles aren't swollen, your back isn't killing you, and your stomach doesn't enter the room three minutes before the rest of you.'

'Well, no,' Leila agreed. 'The social worker's talking about parenting classes. Preparation work. I'm happy to do it, of course.'

'Ooh! How d'you stand it? They are so bossy!'

'They *are* very bossy, but we're in no position to argue. David and I will do anything they say, anything at all, and be top of the class. But I reckon that's all window dressing. I can manage the practicalities, I think . . . We're adults, aren't we? But that's not the issue. What really matters is, will I be a proper mother to this little girl? Will I be able to replace her real mother? What if I'm just plain useless at it? What if . . .'

'Yeah? What if *what?*'

Thinking, Leila retied the blue band around her head. 'My body isn't set up to reproduce. It doesn't work. Agreed?'

'Yes and no.'

'Okay, take it a step further. What if that means my *mind* isn't, either? I'm not like other women physically, so maybe I'm not like them mentally or emotionally.'

Maggie looked at her, fondly. 'Well, you do stand out from the crowd. That's why I like you.'

'Maybe I'm not capable of true maternal feelings,' fretted Leila. 'I mean, how would I know?'

Maggie reached across and tapped her friend on the head. 'I come across many, many *real* mothers, Leila Edmunds, who are total bitches to their children. You don't want to know what savagery real mothers are capable of.' She shuddered. 'Sometimes I want to slap 'em.'

'And fathers too, I daresay.'

'When a child is killed, it's normally one or both of the parents. Did you know that? Parents can be very dangerous.'

Leila didn't answer. She was still fiddling with her hair.

Maggie burst out in exasperation. 'For goodness' sake, this is such total hogwash, Leila! You're a genius with kids. Much better than me—I've got no love for other people's. I hate it when Toby has a friend over. Whining and whingeing and blackmailing me into producing chocolate fingers. But you're so much fun with them. Toby thinks you're the best thing since Lego.'

'He doesn't have me as a mother twenty-four hours a day, seven days a week, for the rest of his life.'

'Look.' Maggie ate the last of her doughnut and licked her fingers. 'Stop all this soul searching. Doctor's orders!'

'Okay.' Leila ducked her head.

'Any child who gets you two is bloody lucky. End of story.'

'Thanks,' said Leila, smiling. 'Really. Thanks, Maggie. How *is* Toby?'

'Well.' Maggie twisted her mouth, noncommittal. 'He came home from his dad's on Sunday night, and he said, "Dad looked funny when he was kissing Peter."'

'How did you take that?'

'I tried to be very honest with myself. I had to think, "Now, how would I feel if Dad was kissing a Betty or a Barbara?"'

'And you concluded . . . ?'

'I concluded that I would be jealous either way. And since there is no future in jealousy, I am going to be grown up about it.'

'But Toby . . . d'you mind him seeing them?'

'Yes, no, yes . . .' Maggie shrugged. 'I don't think he was upset by it. Harry's relationship with Paranoid Peter is a fact of life like any other. We'd all better get used to it.'

'Whew.' Leila held out her hands. 'There you are, you see? The trials of motherhood.'

Buoyed by her conversation with Maggie, Leila drove home via the shopping centre and took a turn around Baby Planet. She couldn't resist picking up a glitteringly hypnotic moon and stars mobile that played the Brahms Lullaby, a nursery rhymes frieze, a set of tiny sheets, and an old-fashioned woollen blanket with blue satin edging. She stopped off at the DIY store for paint samples and ended up buying enough primrose paint for the whole study.

Suddenly the world felt like Christmas, but a thousand times brighter.

As she was parking in the street outside the house, Jacinta came bouncing up to the car. 'Got the baby yet?' She squinted hopefully through the windows as Leila climbed out.

'Not yet. She's going to be a Christmas present.'

'In Santa's sack?'

'Well, probably not. We've no chimney.'

Jacinta jumped up and down on an invisible pogo stick. Her plait bounced with her. 'I'm terribly ill. I wasn't at school today.'

'Not at school, eh? You look the picture of health to me,' said Leila, and Jacinta's dusky face broke into a gap-toothed grin of triumph.

'I forgot to do my homework,' she announced unrepentantly. 'Mrs Carpenter is a real dragon, and she would have torn me limb from limb and then eaten me. Mum said I could have a day off because school's not supposed to be a house of horrors.'

'Quite right,' said Leila, reaching for the first of her shopping bags. 'Run and tell her you're coming in for a visit, and then you can see what I've been buying.'

As they opened the front door David appeared, zigzagging comically across the hall under the weight of a bulging bin bag. Jacinta giggled.

'Hello, girls!' boomed David. 'How's your love life, Jacinta? Leila—don't go buying any baby clothes!' he gasped, dropping his burden at her feet. 'Jeepers creepers, it's heavier than it looks.'

Leila stared at the bag. 'What's this?'

'From Brenda Pollard on behalf of the jumble sale committee. They heard this morning from Angus—'

'The old gossip!'

'He's so excited, can't contain himself. He told them all about it, so they beetled off and picked out the best stuff they've got. It's all been washed and ironed already. Look.'

He sank his hand into the bag and pulled out a tiny scrap of woollen cloth. When he held it up, spreading out its arms, Leila could see that it was a stripy jumpsuit.

'Cute,' enthused Jacinta. She plunged in with both hands, pulled out five garments and laid them carefully on the floor in a circle. She sat among them, cross-legged, humming and examining each in turn. 'They're so *little*.'

'Do babies come that small?' Leila was doubtful. 'This one must be a doll's outfit.'

'Apparently they come even smaller.' David was still rummaging in the bag. 'Take a look at these snazzy things!' He held up a pair of red and white dungarees. 'They've got buttons all down the legs, see? What are those for?'

Jacinta wandered away and began to tinkle on the piano. Leila stepped forward and peered into the soft, dark recesses of the bag. She could smell the washing powder, and it breathed contentment and delight.

'Your mother phoned,' said David. 'They're off to Nigeria tomorrow, remember? And the wedding's on Saturday.'

Leila looked up from the bag. 'That's right. I'd forgotten it was so soon. I'll phone her back and wish them bon voyage.'

'Fola wants to buy us some sort of all-terrain pushchair so we can go striding across the Malverns.'

Leila laughed. 'To help me get my figure back?'

'She wants to know what model we'd like. There's a website. She says to give her a ring once you've had a look, and she'll order it before she leaves.'

'You know, I don't deserve my parents. Jacinta, are you going to help me carry all this stuff upstairs?'

The tinkling on the piano became a thumping. Chopsticks, now. David put his fingers in his ears and made a tortured face.

'I thought we could spend your day off tomorrow decorating Fola's room,' yelled Leila, over the racket.

'Fola's room?'

'Fola's room.' Leila jerked a thumb in a gesture of dismissal. 'You're evicted from your study without further notice. Have to make do with the piano room. I've got enough paint for two coats.'

'Oh, God. And so it starts.' David scrunched up his cheek as she kissed him. 'The husband is supplanted by the child. Discarded, like last year's Christmas tree. I've read about this kind of thing.'

'We'll get you a dog kennel to live in.'

'Okay. I'll start moving stuff downstairs.' David was bubbling over, still talking as he strolled into the kitchen. 'Brenda's daughter's got a cot we can have. She's dropping it off tonight.'

Leila followed him. 'I saw the adoption people.'

'Of course! How did it go?'

'Fine. They're working flat out, getting on with procedural things. No end of red tape and hoop jumping. Linda's made an appointment to come here next week, and they hope to introduce us to the baby once they've got this placement order. We'll need to go and stay nearby.'

'Where?'

'Dunno, exactly. Somewhere down south. We'll spend time getting to know Fola before we bring her home.'

'When's this going to happen?'

'The court hearing is listed for mid December.' Leila felt as though she were made of smiles. 'Four weeks to go! Angus will definitely let you have the leave?'

'Yep.' David peered into a tin of teabags, fishing out a couple. 'He's happy. Says he'll manage whenever we need time off. When do we actually adopt her, then?'

'We have to allow time for the dust to settle. Six months or a year.'

'It's all a bit of a learning curve.'

'The point is that once she's come to live with us, we can relax. They won't take her away unless we turn out to be Bonnie and Clyde.'

'Or Jekyll and Hyde.' David rubbed his hands together in anticipation. 'So we'll have a baby by Christmas. Scary stuff! Here you go.'

He turned, holding out a mug, but Leila was gone, dragging the rustling black treasure trove up the stairs and along the landing, calling to Jacinta to come and help.

A few minutes later, David stood at the foot of the stairs and listened. He could hear his wife opening and shutting drawers in a study that was now their baby's bedroom. At first she was chatting to Jacinta. Then she was singing: 'Summertime', from Gershwin's opera. David loved the wistful lullaby, and he'd never heard anyone who could make it resonate as Leila did. He sank onto the bottom step, resting his mug on his knees, wandering dreamily among the slow, sonorous cadences of her song.

The brilliance of sunset drifted into the hall, dancing across the dusty surfaces. The shadows seemed to glow. They were happy again, and young, and hopeful. Everything around them had been dipped in magic. Life was good.

Even the telephone seemed to respect their celebration. It rang only once, later that evening, as they were about to tuck into lasagne at the kitchen table.

'Mrs Thingummy,' said Leila, coming back into the kitchen. 'About the Diocesan Youth Event. She says she'll call back later.'

'Sorry,' said David. 'I should have switched on the answer machine.'

'No, it's all right. For once I feel warm and fuzzy towards her. After all, someone has to organise these jolly jamborees. Good old Mrs Thingummy. Three cheers, hats off. Where would we be without her?'

'Did you phone your mother?'

'Sure did.' Leila chuckled. 'She's in heaven. We're having a tartan four-wheel-drive buggy, deluxe model, costs more than a jumbo jet. I couldn't talk her out of it.'

'Are they all packed? What time are they off?'

'Isaiah's picking them up at the crack of dawn tomorrow. I've said my farewells. They'll be back just in time to meet their newest grand-daughter.'

'Ah!' David held up a finger before opening the fridge with a flourish. 'I almost forgot. Dora at the off-licence sent a bottle of Spanish bubbly to celebrate "our happy news".'

'Now I feel guilty for wanting to cosh her.' Leila opened the dishwasher and grabbed two glasses.

'How are they taking the news at Kirkaldie's?' asked David, watching the froth surge out of the bottle.

'The girls all want to be our nanny. Jodie intends to move in with us.'

David looked terrified. Leila laughed and laid her hand on his shoulder.

'Don't worry. She'll have to join the queue behind Jacinta. Manage-ment—well, I suspect they're relieved I haven't been there long enough that they have to give me paid adoption leave. Sales are down.'

David's nod was vacant. It was all too good. His mind had a puri-tanical, killjoy urge to spoil the moment.

'I wonder who she was?' he murmured, at last.

Leila blinked, uncomprehending, ready to raise her glass in a toast to their new child. 'Who?'

'The baby's mother. What was her story? What happened to her?'

'I hope we'll be told, eventually.'

'And what on earth has the father done that's so wicked he must forfeit his child? Is he such a monster?'

'Perhaps he killed the mother,' suggested Leila, half-seriously. 'He's doing time. That would explain everything.' A little pile of salt lay spilt upon the table. With one finger, she began to trace a pattern in the white grains. 'I'd like to meet him.'

'Really? I wouldn't.'

'I want to know who he is. I want to thank him for her. Linda tells me there's no plan to let him have continued contact with the baby.'

'So he'll be saying goodbye. Awful.' David's eyes flickered in guilt, processing the thought.

'It *is* awful,' agreed Leila, 'but there may be very good reasons. He might be a monster, as you say. Or else he doesn't want to know.'

David tried to picture the father. A drunkard, perhaps, who beat his wife to death. A drug dealer who gave her an overdose. Or a company director who'd seduced his secretary and wanted nothing to do with mother or child.

Leila brushed away the scattered salt.

'We might not get her at all, David. Something could still go wrong.' She stretched across and gripped the wooden servers he'd stuck into the salad. 'Touch wood. Touch wood. Sorry. You've got a superstitious pagan at your table.'

David watched her, and anxiety took a fresh grip upon his stomach. He didn't like to think about what might happen if this fell through. He stood up. Casually, as if by chance, he brushed his own fingertips along the wooden window frame, from one end to the other, and back again.

Chapter Twenty-one

The evening of the Fintan House meeting, Lucy phoned. Matt and I were playing a particularly violent game on his computer. Deborah still wasn't back. Apparently she'd told Matt she had things to do in town and would come home in a taxi.

'Sorry I missed you this morning.' Lucy's voice was warm and mellow; she sounded her old self again. 'I didn't think you'd appreciate me crashing in to kiss you goodbye at five am.'

'I'd appreciate your crashing in to kiss me at any time,' I insisted dutifully.

'Look, I really can't thank you enough, Jake.'

'No worries,' I said. 'Forget it. Please.'

'You will come and stay at my place when you're in London, won't you?' she asked. 'I can only offer you a sofa bed, but it's quite a comfy one. I'll actually be in Oslo again next week.'

'I spoke to Bill today. Remember Bill? He and Lottie have offered me their spare room. I've imposed on your family too long.'

'I think it's us who've imposed.' She had the grace to sound embarrassed. 'Now you know why we needed you to find her.'

'And now I know that back in October you couldn't have cared less whether I slept in Lincoln's Inn Fields under a newspaper and got mugged. I was just a gofer. A stooge. A runner.'

'A saviour.'

'Why didn't you tell me?'

'Sorry.' She didn't sound quite sorry enough. 'I was afraid you wouldn't go, since she didn't want to be found. And without Deborah, we were going to lose Grace.' She chuckled. 'She's quite a regal little person. Has mini tantrums if you don't do what she wants. She screws her face up and screams the place down.'

I gave up on being aggrieved, and suggested dinner when she got back from Oslo, and we picked a day.

'It's not the same without you at Stanton's,' she said. 'I'm looking for a new job. Delaney's a prick. Len Harvey's got your job. Dis*astrous*.' She gossiped chattily for a while, telling me exactly how disastrous poor Len was. I'm ashamed to say that I encouraged her.

'I'd better go . . .' she said, in the end.

I waited. I could tell she had something more on her mind.

'. . . But there was no need to escort her home.'

Ah. There it was. 'Didn't want her doing a runner, did we?' I replied lightly. 'After all that trouble finding her.'

'Jake.' A brief silence and then a sigh. 'Word of advice. Get out while you can.'

I tried to protest, but she interrupted me. 'She's brought my father to his knees.'

'I've got no heart to break,' I told her.

By the time I heard a car rumbling down the lane, it was late. We'd already had supper, and Perry had disappeared off to his study. I waited for her footsteps in the hall. I found myself glancing towards the door, wanting to see her. Five, ten minutes passed, but she didn't come in. So I went outside to find her. She was standing under the lilac tree in her long winter coat, staring bleakly up at the house.

For a moment, I lingered by the front door. A whisper of light, escaping from an upstairs window, glanced slantways across her face and shoulders; her eyes were in shadow, as though she was wearing a masquerade mask. Watching that motionless figure, I finally faced the fact that she made me feel very strange. It wasn't just physical desire.

Deborah's story was the opposite of mine. She'd sacrificed her youth, been an army wife, brought up children. She'd lived a lie, really, but she'd done it for more or less the right reasons. Me, on the other hand? I'd clung to my youth, avoided commitment, lived selfishly but honestly. I was even selfish in my honesty.

We were opposites. And yet, at some horribly fundamental level, I recognised something in her, a sort of kinship. A passion for freedom, perhaps. I felt as though she was a part of my past, and my future, and myself. I felt as though she was my home. But I couldn't have her. Never. I could put that idea right out of my head.

She didn't move as I walked up to her. She seemed stunned.

'I never want to go in,' she said quietly. 'And he never wants to come out. An agoraphobic, living with a claustrophobic. Impossible.'

'The Dog and Gun is beckoning,' I suggested. 'How about a swift one?'

'I've already had too many swift ones.'

She had, too. Her voice lacked its usual precision. 'I expect they do coffee,' I said. 'C'mon.'

She turned her shadowed eyes up to me. 'I still care about him, Jake.'

I took her elbow. 'Let's go.'

'Perry, I mean. But he doesn't make me happy. No, he makes me very *un*happy. I worry about him, and I want his approval. And I hate him.'

I steered her down the shadowy drive. 'Mind the pothole.'

'And I pity him, and I resent him because I pity him. He has a power over me . . . but it's black magic. That's why I had to get *clean* away.'

We walked along the road. Once in the pub, she folded herself into a window seat while I went to the bar. Same barmaid, bigger tee-shirt. When I returned, I saw that Deborah had closed her eyes. There was a deep line running vertically down the middle of her forehead. My mum used to look like that when she had a migraine.

I perched on one of those little plush stools and gestured to her coffee. 'Headache?'

'The prison gates are clanging shut.' She pressed a hand to her mouth as though she'd just been told she had a week to live. There were purple shadows like bruises around her eyes. 'Sorry, Jake. You hate it, don't you? Emotion. Not your thing at all.' She blinked slowly and forced an unconvincing smile. 'I gave myself a day alone, to think.'

'And? What did you decide?'

'She's beautiful.'

'She . . . ?'

Deborah's gaze slid past me to a hunting print on the wall. 'They had her in the back. A lime-green room. Ugh. Why *lime* green? There was a huge mirror, obviously a two-way job. I bet Imogen was on the other side, watching beadily and taking notes.'

'Jeez. Hard to relax when you're being spied on.'

'Mm. But Matt was there.' She smiled. 'Holding her in his big arms as though he was a butler and it was his duty to provide a comfy place for Her Highness to lay her royal head.'

I caught myself grinning goofily. I'd have liked to have seen that.

'Matt is so proud,' she said. 'He's *my* Matt again, you know? My son. The one made of pride, with his shoulders back and his chin up. Fatherhood has had quite a profound effect on him. *Mum, Grace . . . Grace, meet your granny.*'

'I suppose she looks pretty much like a baby?'

'One of her hands was clenched around his little finger.' Deborah held up a fist. 'Imperiously, like this. Dark eyelashes, fuzz of hair, mouth like a little red heart. She's perfect.' She cradled her cup. 'Well, except for the fluffy pink cardigan. Looks like coconut ice. It *has* to go.'

I chuckled at that, and she sighed into her coffee. 'I'd forgotten that baby smell.'

'Yuck!'

'No, no, it's *not* yuck, Jake. Just you wait 'til you've got one of your own. It's captivating . . . washing powder and milk and brand-new life.'

'Pheromones,' I said sourly. 'Even ants are driven by pheromones.' I wasn't enjoying this conversation. It was like hearing all about somebody's dream holiday in a place you couldn't possibly get to, ever. 'Was she asleep the whole time? Bit boring.'

'No. She smiled at me.' Deborah's tired eyes creased too, at the memory. 'Matt handed her over, and she lay on my lap, burbling and chewing her toes. Matt knows all about mixing bottles—can you believe that? He pottered off to the kitchen, and as soon as she started to whimper, he had one ready.'

'Man of many talents.' I downed the last of my half.

'He got me to feed her. Haven't done that for donkey's years—wasn't sure if I still had the knack. But she stopped squalling and started filling her face, looking up at me with those great big eyes. I could hear the air rushing into the bottle . . . I could have cried. It all came back. That feeling.'

'For God's sake, *what* feeling? Get real, Debs. You legged it from domestic life, remember?'

Her eyes weren't focusing at all; she was thinking about that wretched little pink blob. She seemed entranced.

'They're vulnerable,' she murmured. 'And they trust you.'

I had no idea what she was talking about.

'If Grace had arrived in ten years' time, I'd have been overjoyed,' she said. 'She's truly bewitching. It's just that she's . . .'

'A disaster?' I prompted heartlessly.

'A disaster.' She twisted her mouth. 'Precisely.'

There was a burst of laughter from the bar. Some sort of Celtic pipe music started trickling out of the loudspeakers.

'Matt's crazy about her,' she said. 'He asked me what I thought, and I told him she was the most beautiful baby I'd ever seen. And she is, Jake. She *is*.' Deborah nodded several times. 'I didn't have to lie. She's glorious. She's my family.'

She sighed. Drained the coffee. 'And she needs me.'

'Poor Rod,' I said.

Chapter Twenty-two

The call came when they were painting the baby's room.

They'd removed the study phone because it wasn't a study any more, it was a nursery. Leila balanced her brush on a pot and ran downstairs to answer it, while David rolled swathes of primrose onto the wall, whistling under his breath. She seemed to be a long time, so he knew it wasn't for him. Today was his day off, for all that was worth. They'd got up early to start painting; it was still only nine o'clock, and they'd almost finished the first coat.

Her footsteps as she climbed the stairs were slower than usual, and he paused in his whistling and stood among the pots and trays, facing the door uncertainly. When she appeared her face was blank. She stopped a few feet away, looking at him. Paint oozed from the roller in his hand, splattering onto the sheet they'd spread over the floor, but he ignored it.

'There's a problem,' she said, very clearly, very loud. Already, he saw the hopeless calm creeping back into her eyes.

'A problem?' Drip, drip.

'The birth family are putting up a fight. They've produced a grand-mother, like a rabbit out of a hat.'

They stood neither moving nor speaking, while paint splashed onto the sheet. David stirred first, dejectedly pressing the lid onto a pot and shoving the roller into a plastic bag. There was no point now. Leila bent to pick up her brush and dropped it into a bucket of water, and then began to stack the pots in one corner of the room.

David was attacking the stepladder with unnecessary violence, and much crashing and grinding of metal. 'Damn,' he muttered through clenched teeth, as it refused to fold.

'Yes. Damn.' Listlessly, Leila peeled off her overalls. She untied the scarf she'd used to cover her hair.

'So that's that?'

'The court thing is still on. We just have to wait until then. The grandmother might turn out to be hopeless. Maybe she'll have Alzheimer's or something.'

David crunched the stepladder into a new contortion. 'Do we go along? Do we get to have our say and show what nice people we are?'

'Oh, no. *We're* only the adoptive parents. *We're* only the ones who've got her room all ready, who want to love her and care for her for the rest of our lives. Why should we be allowed to participate? No, no, *no*! We have to be kept safely in the dark.'

'This is inhuman. He shouldn't be allowed to do this.'

Leila rubbed her hands on a rag. 'Who? The father?'

'Yes, the father. And the grandmother. What the hell are they playing at? Do they think this baby's a toy?'

'And them, too,' said Leila. 'The adoption people. They *promised* us he'd given up.'

Finally folding the ladder, David smashed it against the wall. A small piece of plaster fluttered to the floor, leaving a white hole in the new paint.

'We could always sue them for all this yellow paint,' said Leila bleakly, handing him the rag. 'You're going to have the jolliest study in the diocese. You'll have a nursery rhymes frieze, and a mobile that plays the Brahms Lullaby, and—'

The telephone rang again. It was a sort of leitmotif in their lives: the interrupted conversations, the unfinished sentences.

'Leave it,' said David.

'Oh, go on. It's your turn. Perhaps it's Linda again: Granny's turned out to be an axe murderer.'

David wandered down the stairs, barely finding the energy to lift the receiver.

'Ah, David,' he heard. 'Good morning. I'm *so* glad I've tracked you down.'

He knew the voice all too well: Marjorie Patterson, captain of the blue rinse brigade and treasurer of the PCC.

'Marjorie.'

'I need to have a word in your shell-like before the meeting on Friday evening, David.'

'This is my day off, actually.'

'Really?' Marjorie's charming hostess tones hardened a little. 'Well. Never mind. This will only take a few minutes.'

'Couldn't it wait until tomorrow?' He heard Leila trailing down the stairs and knew she was standing behind him, listening. He twisted around and crossed his eyes at her. She didn't smile. Her eyes bored into his, red-rimmed.

There was a small, irritated laugh; it rattled frostily in his ear. 'No, I'm afraid it couldn't. There's no time like the present. Now, do you have the agenda before you?'

'Er, no, and it'll take me a minute or two to dig it out. This isn't a good time, Marjorie. We're moving out of the study.' He ruffled his hair, distracted, distressed.

'I'll read the relevant section to you, then.' The woman was like a steamroller.

Leila's arm shot out and she snatched the receiver from David's hand. 'Marjorie?' she yelled. 'Are you *deaf*? It's his day off. It's his fucking day off, do you understand? One day, one miserable sodding day a week. So piss off and leave us alone for once in our sodding lives.'

There was an animated clucking from down the line, as though a fox had got into the chicken shed.

'I don't give a toss, you bossy old bitch,' snarled Leila, tossing her hair. 'Go ahead, make my day. Tell the fucking rector. Tell the Archbishop of fucking Canterbury, for all I care.' In the stunned silence that followed this invitation, she slammed the phone down.

She glared defiantly at David, whose hands were over his ears. 'Well, she deserved it.'

'Feeling better?'

'Much.'

David shook his head. 'You are truly magnificent. I'm delighted to see you've lost none of your fire. But you've also just destroyed my career, so I'll have to ring her back and apologise.'

Lips pursed, Leila folded her arms. 'You do that and I'm walking out of that door and never coming back.'

'Come on, Leila. You can't—'

'I mean it. You're a bloody slave to these people, David. They'll suck out everything you've got, every ounce of youth and energy. And finally, at the end of your working life, when you're just an empty, dried-out husk, they'll chuck you away. You'll eke out a miserable existence on a clergy pension, eating cat food, until one day the Meals on Wheels lady finds you dead and cold, propped up in front of *Neighbours*. Then they'll do a commemorative seat with your name on it and put it in the churchyard for teenagers to shag on.'

'All of that may be true, but I've still got to phone Marjorie back and grovel sickeningly.'

She shoved her hands into her pockets. 'Oh, God, *I'll* phone her.' As she dialled, she looked up at him. 'We've got to get out for the rest of the day, David. Please. I'll murder the next person who rings the doorbell. How about a walk up in the Malverns?'

'Lunch in that pub?'

'Ooh, yes. Let's be real devils. Hello, Marjorie? Look . . .'

Pulling the paint-splattered shirt over his head, David climbed the stairs, dragging his wounded soul. Each step seemed an unnecessary effort, as though it were barely worth the energy expended in lifting his foot. At this moment, right now, he felt he truly understood the pointlessness of his future—of all their futures, the whole human race. There *was* no point. There was no punchline to the joke.

He feared for Leila; for *them*, as a couple. In a little while he would put on a clean shirt and go down to her, and they would set out together. They must carry on. They *would* carry on. They always did. But first he needed to gather his strength, because this time he was utterly overwhelmed.

He sat on the bed, trying to see some other picture, trying not to care so much. After all, he had resigned himself to childlessness before they had news of this baby. Surely he could be resigned again. But he could taste only the loss. Loss for himself, for Leila. Loss of the happy Leila he had briefly regained. Loss of the future they had imagined for themselves. It was poison, acidic, burning in his throat when he tried to swallow. Choking, he reached out for—well, something. Just something.

I stretch forth my hands unto you; my soul gasps unto you as a thirsty land.

But for once he felt no friendly answering presence, no hand on his shoulder.

He raged at the unfairness. The cruelty. He demanded answers. But no answer came.

They walked hand in hand on the hills, just the two of them. It would, perhaps, always be just the two of them. They talked and talked, worrying and tearing at their loss, baffled by their sense of powerlessness. They had lunch in a pub that had once been brimming with character. Nowadays the place sported plastic beams, a flowery carpet and three gaming machines. Still, it did decent chicken and chips, and there was a table near the fire. They both needed all the comfort they could get. And still they talked endlessly, round and round the subject, until they were exhausted.

They'd just arrived home when the doorbell rang. David groaned.

Leila went to answer it, considering whether to yell, '*Piss off!*' and slam the door in the caller's face. That would set the old hens clucking. 'Have you heard about the curate's wife? She's actually gone mad, dear. Yes, completely off the rails. Sad, really.'

It was Elizabeth, waiting patiently on the doorstep, looking steady and composed. She was wearing a silk scarf dyed in the colours of a peacock's feather.

'Leila. May I come in?'

Leila nodded, stepping back to let the rector's wife slip past. 'I know what you've come about. Marjorie Patterson.'

'Let's go into the kitchen. I've brought a cake. It's okay, I didn't make it myself. Bought it at Saturday's Bring and Buy sale, so it's probably edible.'

David had rallied enough to put the kettle on. He stood by the bench, obviously trying to appear hospitable and succeeding only in looking strained. 'Evening, Elizabeth. How nice to see you. Tea, or something stronger?'

'Stronger, please. It's been a pig of a day. I had to cover for another teacher who's been sectioned—she's in the psychiatric unit, poor girl—and her class was . . . unspeakable.' Elizabeth shuddered and closed her eyes. 'Surprised she lasted as long as she did.'

David fished in the fridge with more bustle than usual.

'Marjorie complained?' asked Leila, drying three glasses.

'Inevitably. But I'm told you apologised.'

'Well, yes. But I was very, very rude to her.'

Elizabeth nodded, gazing at Leila with appraising grey eyes. 'So I gather. So I . . . *fucking* gather.' The word gained resonance, somehow, from the masculinity of her voice.

Leila grimaced, and Elizabeth shook her head. 'It's not worth it, Leila. I know you feel that your life isn't your own, that you are public property, constantly hounded by busybodies in flowerpot hats. I know, I've been a clergy wife long enough. If you wear jeans, you're a fast woman. If you wear a skirt, you're dowdy.'

'That's it! That's it *exactly*.'

'I'm a very dodgy character myself, you know. I'm not around to open the fêtes-worse-than-death, I make a lousy job of arranging the church flowers—twice left the tap on and flooded the vestry—and I refuse point blank to be Chair of the Women's Institute. They think I'm downright sinister. Half the female parishioners want to marry Angus themselves, thereby saving him from my vile influence.'

'The other half want to marry David, to save him from mine.'

Elizabeth inclined her head. 'It's a very strange life. But if you're going to last the distance . . .'

Leila puffed out her cheeks. 'Okay. Sorry. I'll send her a card and a box of chocolates.'

Elizabeth gave a sudden shout of laughter. 'I heard about it at lunchtime. Regaled them with the story in the staffroom, and they all rolled around. You've become a folk hero.'

David was standing very straight, twisting the corkscrew with distracted precision. 'We'd just had some bad news, you see, Elizabeth. Really bad news. The adoption might be off.'

'Oh, no!' Elizabeth leaned towards him, taut with concern. 'What's gone wrong?'

'The baby's grandmother has thrown her hat into the ring.'

'The *grandmother*?'

'Apparently,' sighed Leila, with an uneasy glance at David as he knocked over a glass. 'And we know the little girl deserves to be with her own family, if possible. That must be the right thing. We ought to wish this woman well. But we can't be that unselfish, Elizabeth, we just can't. We've been trying all day. And we . . . Well. Actually, we hate her from the very bottom of our hearts.'

David dropped the corkscrew. 'Why's she turned up now? Why not before?'

He gulped, searching in his jacket pocket, while Leila wrapped her arms around his neck. Then he pulled out a handkerchief and blew his nose, clearly determined to regain control. 'Sorry.'

'It's all right, David,' said Elizabeth quietly. 'You're allowed.'

David drew a long breath. 'All these people are playing games. Just games. We were painting the baby's room. Leila's handed in her notice. We've got the cot, and the blankets, and cupboards full of clothes and toys. In a way she was already a part of our family, d'you see? We were no longer just two, in our own minds. We were three. And now it's all . . . it's all a hoax. It's so cruel to Leila.'

'To both of you.' Elizabeth glanced from one to the other. 'Is this grandmother likely to succeed?'

'No idea.' Leila shrugged. 'The baby's not local, you see. Another mob has the care of her: they're the ones who have let this happen.'

'Which region?'

'We're not allowed to know. When Linda—at our end—gave them a piece of her mind they became very defensive and said it was down to

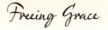

their legal department. *They've* told them they have to give the woman a chance.'

'So they've shifted responsibility onto some lawyer sitting in an office?'

'That's right. We don't really understand how it works, and nobody seems prepared to tell us.' Leila's eyes were bright with bewilderment.

'It's quite appalling,' said Elizabeth. 'Maybe you ought to get on to our MP.'

'Will he help?'

'Probably not.'

David was calm now. 'We've been talking about it all day. We wondered about going to a solicitor, or maybe taking our clothes off and chaining ourselves to the railings down at the town hall . . . just joking. We honestly believe that all we can do at the moment is wait, pray and—'

'—murder Grandma,' snapped Leila. 'Interfering old bag.'

'Unfortunately we can't actually do that, since we've no idea who or where she is.' David forced a smile. 'So we've decided to sit tight while they decide. But if there's any more cat-and-mouse games, we're not playing. We're going to tell them we're not having the baby.'

'That's very understandable.' Swiftly, Elizabeth glanced at the clock and drained the rest of her glass. 'I'll love you and leave you. I've taken up enough of your day—don't want Leila to tell *me* to piss off too.'

The two women paused on the front doorstep.

'I'm psyching myself up to phone my parents,' said Leila, peering out anxiously into the gloom. 'I'm dreading it. Poor Mum. She was as thrilled as we were.'

'They've already left for Nigeria?'

Leila nodded. 'This morning. No bad thing, really. Otherwise I'd go rushing down to Peckham and howl on their shoulders, and that wouldn't be fair.'

'When are you going to tell them?'

'I'll give them a day to recover from the journey. But I must do it soon—definitely before the wedding on Saturday—or Mum will have half of Lagos sending baby presents.'

'Your parents have lived,' said Elizabeth calmly. 'They will be more resilient than you're expecting. You concentrate on yourself and David.'

There was a pause. Elizabeth gazed up at the billowing brown velvet of the city night. 'Leila.'

Leila hovered politely, holding the door, wanting to return to David.

'I know you feel that this was your last chance,' said Elizabeth. 'I'm not going to suggest you'll get over it. We both know you won't.'

'Thank you.' Leila was genuinely grateful.

'But I think you will have a full life.'

'Oh.' Leila sagged as though under an immense weight, exhausted by the need to be understood. 'That's all very well . . . I accept it's irrational and mediocre and unimaginative to want a baby. But—'

'No.' Elizabeth held up a hand. 'No. That's not my point.'

'It's not something I can explain easily to you,' persisted Leila. 'You've had four children.'

'Not so, actually.' Elizabeth turned over a pebble with one toe. 'I'm not the mother of Angus's children.'

Leila stepped down onto the path, shutting the door sharply behind her. 'I don't think I quite . . .'

'When I was a young teacher,' said Elizabeth, 'I married a man called Guy Nelson. Dashing, dramatic figure. The stuff of Mills and Boon. But . . .' She hesitated and then smiled. 'Guy didn't want children. It was a stipulation of our marriage. Not negotiable. He insisted that he was too selfish, that the world was already over-populated, we would have richer lives without them, they would spoil our remarkable partnership. I was utterly crazy about this man, deranged, wanted nothing more than to be with him forever and ever.' Elizabeth turned away, looking at a pair of black plastic dustbins, shadowy under the hedge.

'We had a wonderful marriage: seventeen years of it. Guy was a brilliant engineer, and we travelled all over the world. Thailand, the Middle East, Australia . . . We lived the high life, I can tell you. Parties, yachts, far too much alcohol. Hard for you to believe?'

Some part of Elizabeth—of who she really was—fell into place in Leila's mind. The rector's wife appeared through a new lens, the flat image springing abruptly into three dimensions.

'No,' she replied. 'Not hard at all.'

'I stuck to my side of the bargain and we never had children. I very soon gave up trying to change Guy's mind. It wasn't good—I had three bouts of depression, diagnosed and treated. Broke my poor mother's heart too, but I adored the man—*adored* him—and we had a colourful, stimulating life.'

Elizabeth blinked at the dustbins, eyes narrowed in memory. 'I was forty-three when Guy fell in love with the daughter of a friend of mine. Candy. Inevitable, somehow, that she should be called something sugary. I was the last to find out, of course—everyone knows everything in these expatriate communities. Guy told me that he had to go because young Candy was the love of his life and their star signs were compatible and they were meant to be together.'

'*Bastard*!' Leila shifted suddenly, and pebbles ground under her feet.

'It gets worse,' said Elizabeth, meeting her eyes.

'They didn't.' Leila shook her head rapidly. 'No. Tell me they didn't.'

'Got it in one.'

'How many?'

'Three. All boys.'

Leila did a passable imitation of an erupting volcano. 'I hope you took him to the cleaners?'

'I got the house.' Elizabeth looked disparaging. 'Complete with mortgage and dodgy foundations. We hadn't saved much—too profligate. Guy kept his precious pension.'

Leila folded her arms censoriously.

'But spare the chap a little sympathy, Leila,' urged Elizabeth. 'He's a complete wreck, lost half his hair, going deaf, looks about eighty. He phones from time to time, moaning about how noisy and messy and expensive his sons are. Reckons he won't be able to retire until he's dead. Candy keeps making him go for facelifts and they hurt, apparently.'

'Good,' spat Leila.

Elizabeth's profile was mottled in the streetlights. 'It isn't easy,' she mused, head tilted as if listening to herself. 'It's not an easy thing to forgive. The aridity, you know. The loss. The loss.' She paused. 'I sometimes think my children were conceived when I was a child myself—conceived in my imagination—and now I've lost them. They've died.'

'Yes,' whispered Leila. 'I know exactly what you mean. It's a bereavement.'

'I can't pretend to be without regret.'

'I'm sorry,' said Leila, hating the limp words, wishing she had better ones. She imagined her friend, childless and abandoned in middle age. 'What did you do?'

'Reinvented myself,' replied Elizabeth, simply. 'Went back to teaching. I had little choice. I was certainly older, and I hope I was wiser. I lavished my time and energy on other people's children. It was a difficult time . . . my mother fell ill and I nursed her until she died. I met Angus several years later. A divorced vicar. Caused a sensational scandal. Of course, by then it was far too late to have a family of my own.'

'I'm . . .' Leila shook her head, defeated. 'I didn't know.'

'We don't broadcast it.'

'Where's Angus's ex?' asked Leila, overcome by curiosity.

'Paula.' Elizabeth grimaced in wry sympathy. 'She couldn't stand it when he went into the church. Well, d'you blame her? I certainly don't. Ran off with a rich farmer. It's all very amicable. Their children were almost grown up when we met.'

'The church let Angus remarry?'

'Oh, yes.' Elizabeth nodded. 'Quietly. We had a compassionate bishop. We've been married ten years.'

'It's not what I imagined,' said Leila. 'Not at all. I had you two down as solid and conventional. Christening photos, family holidays, silver wedding.'

'It's not what I imagined either.' Elizabeth chewed her lip, then gave a small shrug. 'My point is that you can still have a fulfilling life. And I *do* actually know what I'm talking about.' She gathered the peacock silk around her neck. 'And now I must go. You need to be with David.'

'Elizabeth.' Leila stepped forward, wanting to acknowledge the story somehow.

But the older woman waved her away. 'You two should get started on that cake.' She opened the gate and then looked back, grinning mischievously. 'You'll find she bakes a fine sponge, does Marjorie Patterson.'

Chapter Twenty-three

When I rolled out of bed, the house was unusually quiet. I stooped to take a look through the low window, rubbing a hole in the condensation.

Outside, the countryside lay unconscious in mist. Nothing stirred. No birds sang. The world seemed to be having a sleep-in. Beyond the garden, ploughed fields merged into white gloom. I looked down at the veggie patch where rows of cabbages crouched, lifeless on the damp earth. I felt like one of them. I had to get moving. I couldn't become a permanent accessory of the Harrison family.

Under the eaves, just outside my window, I noticed a row of rather ramshackle nests. I hadn't spotted them before. They seemed to be made of mud. Swallows, perhaps, or swifts, long gone. They'd be back. Mum used to say that swallows in New Zealand don't migrate. They don't feel the need to leave home, she said. It's the people who go away. And she smiled at me sadly from below her messy, unplucked eyebrows, as though she could see into the future.

I heard a soft crunch in the mist and Perry appeared around the corner, wearing green gumboots and a baggy jersey, wheeling a metal barrow. He was carrying a shotgun under one arm. Laying it against the picket fence, he stepped into the vegetable garden, took a spade from the barrow and began to dig energetically. I could hear the blade scraping into the earth. It was an alien sound, metallic in the limp stillness.

The man had incredible stamina. I wondered if he ever slept.

As I watched him, something stirred over by the compost heap. It was just a small movement, but I glimpsed it from the corner of one eye. It was my old mate the rabbit, peacefully lolloping across the grass. He was hidden from Perry by the fence, and didn't seem at all disturbed by the man's presence. Perhaps at ground level the fog muffled the sounds of digging. I watched him. He moved slowly, unhurriedly, his back end tipping up like a rocking horse with each hop, pausing every now and again to sit upright and twitch his ears. Suddenly, for no reason that I could fathom, he broke cover and raced for the hedge. I caught the white flash of his tail.

I didn't even see Perry move. I just heard the shot echoing away through the mist, and my rabbit somersaulted high into the air. I don't imagine he felt anything.

The man was a hell of a shot, I'll give him that. He broke his gun, walked over to the crumpled body and picked it up by the hind legs. Then he chucked it onto the back step where it lay, small and twisted, and he went back to his digging.

I pulled on shorts and trainers, took the stairs two at a time and stepped out through the back door, glancing apologetically down at my little furry friend as I passed. His brown eye was already glazing over. I'd seen *that* before.

Perry straightened and raised a friendly hand. His breath billowed into smoke. 'Ah, Jake. Good morning.'

'Hi, Perry. That was a bloody good shot.'

'Well, you know. One tries to keep one's hand in. I wasn't too bad a marksman in my day.' He lifted the spade again and drove it into the earth. 'When I was a child, I was very fond of Beatrix Potter's works. I sided with Peter, of course. But now I'm firmly in Mr McGregor's camp. The little blighters do so much damage.'

'Can I give you a hand out here?'

He shook his head. 'I need the exercise. You look as though you're off for a run? Well done. I'll have coffee ready in half an hour.'

He seemed a good man, I reflected as I pounded down the muddy lane. I liked him, and I enjoyed his company. Yet he killed without any guilt at all. And he lied, all the time. And so did she.

*

By the time I panted home, filthy and feeling more than a twinge in that bloody knee, the kitchen was warm and smelled of coffee and toast. Perry's cage was gilded, all right. I looked around for Deborah, listening for her footsteps. Funny how the place seemed different now that she was home from Kenya. More colourful.

'Where is everybody?' I asked Perry, spreading butter on my toast. 'Matt's at school, is he?'

'No.' He pushed the plunger down on the coffee. 'He and Deborah have gone into town to see the solicitor.'

She wasn't about to appear, then.

'Could I get online this morning?' I asked, taking the milk out of the fridge.

He waved the back of one hand towards the door. 'Absolutely. Go ahead.' He rubbed his hands together, brightening. 'Got your route planned?' Without waiting for an answer, he disappeared into the hall for a second and came trotting back with one of those enormous atlases, big as a tombstone.

'Let's take a look,' he suggested gleefully, opening the book up on the table. We both leaned over it. Perry traced lines on the page with one finger. 'You'll cross the straits, I assume . . . Morocco . . . look in on Fez, here. The Atlas mountains are extraordinary. I know them quite well . . . and over the border into Algeria just here. This'—he placed his palm flat onto the page—'is Sahara.'

I glanced at him. He was completely absorbed, as though he was planning this trip for himself.

'D'you want to come with me, mate?' I asked. It was a pretty crass question, I suppose, but I meant it. I'd have been happy to have him along. Honoured.

The lines on his face seemed to deepen. 'Bless you, Jake. No. But I'll be with you in spirit every inch of the way.'

Deborah and Matt arrived home as we were debating whether it was practicable to drive across the Congo, nowadays. Perry reckoned it was out of the question. The road was impassable and various militia were still causing havoc. He thought I should go through Angola. Deborah marched in, shot a vicious glance at the two of us

and raised her eyebrows coldly. I could tell straight away she was in
an odd mood.

'Ah. Biggles and Algernon, planning their next daredevil escapade.'
She dumped two bags of shopping down by the fridge. Matt drop-
kicked three more across the floor before disappearing upstairs. No one
suggested he should get off to school.

'How was your meeting?' asked Perry.

'Well, it's all going according to plan. Stuart's heard from Imogen
Christie. The assessment team—whatever that is—will roll up here on
Monday morning.'

'Darling! That's fantastic!' gushed Perry.

Deborah met my eyes and then looked away. 'Stuart seemed to find
the whole thing quite amusing. Says Lenora Blunt was apoplectic when
I turned up yesterday.'

Perry twitched the side of his mouth. It was almost a smile. 'You've
certainly put the cat amongst the pigeons.' He held out his arms as
though she was the cleverest, sweetest wife in the world and hadn't twice
tried to dump him for a beach bum. 'I knew they wouldn't be able to
resist you. Who can?'

She smiled, slightly flirtatiously I thought, and let him kiss her on
the cheek. I was open-mouthed. Last time I looked she was torn asunder
by her love for Rod. Now she was all dimpled and fluttery at an empty
compliment from Perry. Bloody women. Not that I cared. She wasn't
mine, and she never would be.

I'd had enough of the games and double-speak. It was all well beyond
me, so I grabbed my coffee and left them to their parallel universe.

In the study, I turned on Perry's state-of-the-art desktop and
waited while it warmed up, soothed by the familiar beeps and clicks.
I heard the door open and guessed who was there, but I didn't look
around as she padded across Perry's deep green carpet. She came and
stood beside me, but I ignored her. I busily scribbled notes while the
search engine was looking for *Niger* and *visas*. After a minute, she
started fidgeting.

'You're squinting at that notebook, Jacob. You need reading glasses.
I'll bet you're too vain to wear them, though . . . What're you doing?'

I peered at the screen. 'Visas,' I grunted, in the end. 'I'm planning on driving to Cape Town.'

'Can I come?'

I just laughed scornfully and clicked the mouse.

'Are you cross, Jake?'

Double click.

'For heaven's sake,' she breathed, exasperated. 'You're as bad as Matt.'

She wandered over to the window, pulling back the velvet curtains. The glass didn't let in much light. I could make out the drive through the murk. There was my car, faithfully waiting on the turning circle, all ready for me to make my getaway.

'He's my husband,' she said simply. 'We go back a long way. And we have a long way to go. How do you expect me to behave?'

I looked back at the screen, glaring defiantly. Out of the corner of my eye, I saw her rest her palms against the glass. I scrolled down, trying to concentrate on the job in hand, and then gave up and swung the chair around to face her.

'Look, Debs. It means less than nothing to me whether you go running back to Perry or not. I just find it sort of gobsmacking that you can slot back in and coo away like a pair of bloody paradise ducks. It just does my head in, that's all.'

There was a second's silence. Then she arched one eyebrow. 'Jake Kelly! Are you *jealous*?'

I could have hit her. My dad would have knocked her clean across the room. I forced a derisive snort, and turned back to the screen.

She took a step towards me. 'Which of us are you jealous of? Me or Perry?'

When I ignored her, she stormed over to Perry's futon and threw herself down. 'I come home, having bargained away my life, to find you two all cosily snuggled up over an atlas, droning on about the state of the roads in bloody Burkina Faso.'

'The Congo, actually.'

'You know what? I think you're flaunting your freedom on purpose. It's completely immoral anyway, thumping across Africa in a gas-guzzling truck, roaring past people who don't even have enough water. It's voyeuristic and obscene. Why don't you go on a bicycle? Why don't you find some voluntary work and do something useful for once in your life?'

'Ha! I don't need a lecture in morality from *you*.'

'Frankly, I don't care whether the pair of you go to Timbuktu or the devil.'

'Feeling's mutual.' I knew I was behaving like a child. I scribbled a couple of addresses and then glanced over my shoulder. 'You're still here, are you?'

'I've told you,' she said. 'We're all trapped in hell. The lot of us. I dream about burning the place down and killing us all.'

'Well, I'd appreciate it if you'd wait until I've left.'

And then she was standing at my shoulder. Citrus and cloves. I could feel her. I still can. It was like leaning against an electric fence.

'Don't be cross, Jake.' She reached out a forefinger, ran it along the line of my jaw.

I couldn't move. Couldn't even breathe.

'You have an extraordinary mouth,' she said quietly. 'Did you know? It's a work of art.'

The fingertip lingered on my bottom lip.

'Sulky,' she whispered. 'I love it.'

That did it. I shoved her hand away. Stood up. My head felt like a pressure cooker. 'Sod off,' I muttered through bared teeth. 'Just sod off.'

She dropped her hand. 'No,' she said calmly. 'You can't help. How can *you* set me free?' She turned away.

The door clicked shut behind her. Two minutes later, I heard her car swing out of the garage and accelerate down the lane.

I spent another hour staring at the screen before I shut it down and walked out to my own car. I pressed the lever to open the boot and then stood, gnawing at my knuckles, trying to work up the motivation to cart all my gear out of the garage.

'Stupid tart,' I grumbled, but without much conviction. 'Bloody mad as a March hare.' In the end, I went into the garage and lugged the first cardboard box out to my car. When I came out with my third load, Matt was waiting.

I raised my eyebrows at him. 'Shouldn't you be at school?'

'Study day.'

'Yeah? Your school seems very keen on study days.'

He shoved his hands even further into his pockets, doing a convincing imitation of a stroppy young bull. 'Friggin' study day.'

'Fine by me, mate. You can give me a hand.'

He watched as I dumped a duvet onto the passenger seat. 'What're you doing?'

'I'm leaving. Time for me to be off. I've got things to organise, you've got a baby on the way, and I think your mother's had more than enough of me.'

He didn't say anything, just lowered his eyebrows by about two inches and sunk his head between his shoulders. God knows how long he would have stood there, snorting and pawing the ground, if Deborah's car hadn't reappeared, looming up the drive like a red ghost in the mist.

She parked just behind me and hopped out, looking perfectly normal, as if I hadn't recently told her to sod off; meanwhile I whistled tunelessly under my breath as if her touch wasn't still setting fire to my lip.

She spotted the gear piled into the boot of my car. 'Jake! You're not leaving us?'

Something had got hold of me around the throat. I shoved a pile of pillows on top of the duvet, trying to stay angry. She shot a glance at Matt and then swiftly moved to stand between me and the garage.

'Look, I'm sorry, Jake. I behaved like a bitch. I was jealous of your freedom, jealous of who you are . . . jealous because you can go back to Africa, and I can't. I had no right. Please forgive me.'

'It's no big deal,' I mumbled. I probably looked a bit like a wounded bull myself. 'But it's time for me to move on. I have to camp on the doorsteps of all these embassies. You've got assessment people on the way.'

'I don't give a toss about them,' growled Matt. He grabbed the pillows and headed stubbornly into the garage with them.

Deborah leaned into the boot and retrieved a suitcase. 'Please, Jake? Stay until after the weekend at least. And leave your things here.' She glanced unhappily towards the blind, brooding windows of the house. 'We need your sanity.'

I wondered about her definition of sanity. I wondered when mine had deserted me. And—most of all—I wondered what the hell I thought I was doing, lifting my gear back out of the car.

Chapter Twenty-four

Deborah and Perry spent the next few days rushing about like a couple of hyperactive beavers. They sorted out their script; after a run of twenty years, the play was pretty polished. I heard them discussing it. Perry was going to be completely open about his condition, and sorry he hadn't come clean before. Deborah looked out some of her magazine articles just to back up her own story.

They thought of everything. Perry got up into the attic and chucked down a couple of cobwebby cardboard boxes full of old baby clothes and toys. Deborah said she'd put them up there when Matt grew out of them, meaning to send them to a jumble sale one day. It made me laugh, the idea of Big Matt fitting into those diddy little scraps. Deborah reckoned they smelled musty, and tipped all the clothes into the machine with about a pint of that disgusting stuff that's supposed to smell of spring flowers.

I caught her scattering what she called 'a few homely touches' around her bedroom. Trashy novels, magazines, slippers. Contraceptive pills artlessly left on the dressing table. The baby clothes were sitting in clean, fluffy piles on top of the chest of drawers, smelling gently of springtime.

'D'you think it looks a bit too *Home and Garden*, Jake?' she asked, spreading a hideous patchwork quilt on the bed.

'More like *The Simpsons*,' I told her.

Perry and I dumped the toys in the sink and scrubbed them, and then stacked them in a wooden toy box he'd been using to store seeds. I gave it a new coat of paint. On Sunday night he put on the breadmaker and set the timer for eight-thirty so as to flood the house with homely smells. It was a slick operation, I'll say that for them.

Monday came around at last, almost non-existent in another of those stifling sea mists. I was beginning to yearn for the sight of an honest frost and a clear blue sky. I offered to drop Matt at school on my way out through town, and he seemed happy about the idea.

It felt a bit weird, leaving. I reckon I'd become institutionalised. I needed to get away.

Perry came to the door to see me off. The smell of baking bread and coffee bubbled out from behind him, as though his home was a haven of warmth in a chilled, damp world. He was looking gaunt, with shadowy gullies in his cheeks.

He shook my hand. 'You won't be in London long, will you, Jake?'

'About two weeks, I should think. Depends on the visas, really.'

He nodded gloomily. 'Well, don't stay away on our account. There's always a bed for you here.'

Debs walked me to the car. 'Like my cardigan?' She held out her arms. She was wearing something seriously frumpy.

'No.' I threw my bag into the boot, then took a second look at the shapeless sack. 'Did you nick that off a scarecrow?'

She laughed anxiously. 'I keep it for gardening. It's supposed to be mumsy.'

I slammed down the boot lid. 'That's just bloody ridiculous.'

She poked her hair behind her ear. 'I've seen you watching all the rehearsals and painting of scenery with that twisted smile of yours, Jake Kelly. It's probably no bad thing you're not going to be here for the perform-ance. It'd be like having a schoolboy standing in the wings. You'd keep making rude noises and giggling during all my most moving speeches.'

'And pretending to chuck up into the fire bucket.'

'Mm. Make me fluff my lines. You're unhealthily honest, you know that?'

I folded myself into the driver's seat, and she stood at the window. 'I'll miss my conscience, though.'

I smiled at her. 'You can always phone, if you want. Dial-a-conscience. You've got my number.'

'I might even write. It's what I do, write to people. School friends, aunts, even my old German teacher.' She kicked my front tyre. 'Five letters to Rod, trying to explain why I won't be coming back to him. Haven't posted any of 'em.'

'Write to me, then,' I said. 'Good old snail mail.' I started the car up while Matt came sauntering out of the house and piled enthusiastically into the passenger seat. He was wittering on about V8 engines and torque. Then he pressed the button to make the roof slide down.

Suddenly I didn't want to leave. I looked up at Deborah, but there was nothing to be said. She kissed me on the cheek before straightening up and stepping away. I scrunched past her, through the gates and into a vague and misty world.

We nudged along for a few miles with the lid off, our road twisting through Coptree Woods. Cheerless vapour rolled around our faces, and the feeble beams of my fog lamps were throttled at birth. It was kind of spooky. I could smell leaf mould and rotting wood and, very faintly, a salty tang that I thought must be the sea. Eventually, the chill got through to my hands.

'It's a bit cold, mate,' I said, and pulled into the verge, narrowly missing a treacherous ditch the council had put there as a trap. Matt pressed the button again, then laughed delightedly as the roof unfolded itself and slid over our heads.

Letting out the clutch, I glanced sideways at him. 'You seem all bright eyes and two tails,' I said suspiciously. I'd never seen him so alert at any time of day, let alone at eight-fifteen in the morning.

Matt was examining the dashboard. 'The old folks made me bury my dope in the garden. I wasn't allowed to smoke any last night. Had to sleep in a howling gale to get rid of the smell. What does this do?' He jabbed at a button.

'Headlight wipers. Leave them alone.'

'What about this?' Jab, poke.

'Seat warmer, so you don't get a cold butt.'

'Wow! Look at this! That's so cool.' He leaned forwards, concentrating, and started messing with the music system. He twiddled various knobs and then flicked through my discs. 'Yeuch! Pink Floyd! Bob Dylan—you are *sad*, old man!'

I was stung. 'It's good stuff,' I protested. 'Put on some Dylan. Go on.'

He made an almighty fuss, but he did it, and I'd like to think he saw my point. As we puttered into the outskirts of town he pointed to a truck stop called Dana's Diner, perched on a roundabout.

'They do the best sausages you'll ever taste,' he announced hopefully. 'Wanna try them?'

'It's coming up to eight-thirty. Won't you be late for school?'

'Nah. I've got a free period first. Don't have to be there until ten. Anyway, I'll concentrate better with some of Dana's fabulous world-famous saussies inside me.'

He was certainly lying about his free period, I thought, but it wasn't my problem; so I turned in alongside the lorries. I could have driven clean under some of them.

'This,' Matt enthused as he hopped out, 'is a taste experience you will *never* forget. Her brother's a butcher, and he does them specially to his own unique recipe.'

It was one of those cafés you don't get anywhere else but in Blighty: a Formica haven, where they serve your tea in mugs. The sugar's in a bowl, not jammed into little paper tubes, and you don't need to worry about whether your boots are muddy or your overalls oily. A woman bustled out from the kitchen, holding a metal tray. She had an improbably blonde beehive hairdo and blue eye shadow, and she beamed tenderly at Matt.

'Be with you in a minute, Matt, love. The usual?'

'Yes, please, Dana, and the same for Jake here.'

She nodded and patted her beehive. 'You sit yourselves down. I'll be there in a jiffy.'

We found a table among the truck drivers, who slumped in various states of weariness. Dana slopped a couple of mugs of tea in front of us, hovering longingly over Matt for a few seconds before heading back to the kitchen. Matt watched her go, a wistful expression on his face.

'I used to bring Cherie in here.'

'Does Dana know about . . . ?'

'Grace? Yeah, I told her. She thinks I've got lovely eyes.' He smiled, faintly. 'Her husband's a stevedore down at Felixstowe docks. He's the Suffolk heavyweight champion.'

'Best you don't take *her* down the woods with a blanket, then.'

Matt chortled, ladling sugar into his tea. I watched him. The more I saw of Matt, the more he reminded me of *me*.

'You doing your A-levels next year, mate?'

He burped disdainfully, and I felt a little twinge of envy. I used to be able to do that to order, too. Gives me heartburn nowadays. Eventually he muttered, 'S'pose so. Might not even bother.'

'Which ones?'

'God, you're a nosy bastard. French, English, history, Latin.'

I nearly spat out my tea. '*Latin?*'

'They were hot on it at my last school.' He scowled, embarrassed.

I started to laugh. 'I'm sorry,' I spluttered, 'it just doesn't quite gel with your hard man image, somehow.' I straightened my face out. 'So . . . how's it all going?'

'It's not. They're all wankers, and education's a waste of my sodding life.'

'When did you decide it was a waste of your sodding life?'

Dana shimmied over, humming, and plonked a plate of heart disease in front of each of us. 'There you are, my love,' she said, 'and an extra sausage for my favourite customer.'

Matt picked up a knife and fork and dug in. His appetite was truly mesmerising; it was second only to that of my brother in his younger days. We were reverentially quiet for a good five minutes. Those sausages were the stuff of legend, I have to say.

Just outside the window a truck roared into life, and the table shivered. Matt swallowed a mouthful and mumbled, 'I was planning on being a journalist, once.'

'Yeah?'

'I used to run our school newspaper.'

'Really? Sounds fun.' I reached for the mustard.

'It was a bloody good newspaper. Honestly. Won awards. Anyway, I was all lined up to spend a year in Canada, working on a local rag. We actually had it all teed up through a contact of my old headmaster. I was going to play rugby for a Canadian team. I was everybody's golden boy.'

'What happened?'

'It all fell through when I got kicked out. Being a journalist was my big ambition—and don't you dare say I'd be following in my mother's footsteps. This is *my* thing, not hers. I wanted to be the best, you know? Incisive, questioning, all that stuff. There isn't enough of it. I was going to travel the world, make it my business to understand what makes it tick and who's messing it up. But it's all bollocks.'

'Why?'

'Fucking look at me, man! I'm not the golden boy any more.'

'You're not?'

He dropped the knife and fork, and began to tick off a list on his powerful fingers. 'One: buggered neck. Cripple. Can't use rugby to get me into a decent university. Two: drug dealer. Serious blot on copybook. Three: haven't bothered to go to any lessons this term. Not one. Teachers don't even know what I look like. If I *did* darken their doors they'd think I was a gatecrasher. Four: I'm permanently stoned and it's screwed my head.'

He pressed both hands on top of his hair and sighed resignedly. 'Five: got my girlfriend banged up and now I have a daughter. So school's even more fucking irrelevant than ever.' He retrieved his fork and stabbed a sausage. 'Sound like Britain's finest to you, Jacko? La crème de la crème?'

I looked at him, and then I put up a finger. 'One: you don't need rugby. You've got plenty going for you. Two: you sold a bit of hooch—but you didn't get nicked by the police, jammy sod. You got away with it, due to the intervention of your beautiful, charming and devoted mother to whom you should be very grateful.'

He laughed unkindly. 'You poor bastard! You're in love with my mother!'

'No, I'm not.'

'Oh yes, you are.'

I ignored him. 'Three . . .' I hesitated. He'd put me off. What was three? 'Oh, yes. School. You've got plenty of time to catch up, if you pull your finger out and stop making excuses. Four: you weren't stoned last night, and look at you. Your eyes are actually open!'

His eyes really were like hers, I thought. Sea-coloured, with tawny flames around the pupils, and curving up at the outer edges when he smiled. Dana was right.

I don't know what made me do it. I put down my tea and leaned forward, tapping the table bossily. 'Sort yourself out, mate,' I scolded. 'And then, if you want to, you can fly out and travel with me as long as you like. But only if you've passed your exams with flying bloody colours. I'll pay.'

He looked doubtful. 'Where will you be by next summer?'

'If I leave in the New Year and piss about, stop off and do a few things on the way, I'll have got to . . .' I counted the months in my head, 'about Tanzania, I should think.'

He stared at me from under his dolly-bird eyelashes. I laid both hands flat down on the table. Believe it or not, I felt as though I could actually do something for Matt. I felt like an uncle. It was a new sensation, I can tell you.

'Look. I promise you,' I insisted seriously. 'If you stop messing about and sort out your life, we'll travel together for a bit until you head off to college or wherever. You can text me in the meantime. Let me know how you're getting on.'

'Okay. Deal.' He pushed his plate away. 'You're off your trolley,' he said and looked out of the window. 'But you've got a nice car.'

'Not much good in the desert. I'm selling it this morning.'

'No! You can't!'

'I can. And I need you to come along and help.'

For a wonderful moment, he looked as though a weight had lifted off him. Then his face fell. 'And five?'

He'd lost me. 'Five?'

'On my list. Number five. Should've been first, really. I've got a daughter. I'm a father. Fathers don't fly out to exotic places to meet up with sad old hippies. They don't have fun, and they don't have a future. They get jobs in the local supermarket, stacking shelves to pay for the nappies.'

I drew quite a long breath. This was something I'd been wanting to say for days.

'Matt, you don't have to do this. There are people out there who *want* Grace. They're desperate. She'll always be your daughter, and when she's old enough she'll come looking for you. So you get to have your cake and eat it, mate. You pass on your genes without any of the hard graft. I'd do it myself, if it was always as painless as that.'

Dana appeared with a huge metal teapot and refilled our mugs. She must have heard my little speech because she winked at me, hissing, 'Go for it!' out of the corner of her mouth.

Matt didn't notice her. He was still staring out at my car, defiant among the monster trucks. 'Thing is, Jake, she's a nice little kid, is Grace,' he said. 'I quite like her.' He blinked and then looked down at his mug, apparently not surprised at the fact that it had magically refilled itself. He wrapped his fingers tight around the handle, but I could see the tremor in them.

'I didn't know what it would be like. I hadn't a bloody clue. I thought I'd be able to take her or leave her. But when I first picked her up, it hit me like a train . . . *Wham!*' He blinked, stunned. 'It's like there's a cord coming from her and pulling at me somewhere around here.' He pressed a fist into his solar plexus, fixing me with wide, haunted eyes. 'It hurts. It *really* hurts. I'd kill for her, Jake. I swear I would.'

I felt completely ignorant. Matt spread his hand protectively across his chest, still eyeing me.

'Maybe it makes sense for her to go to a better family,' he said. 'A normal one. Ours is bloody bonkers. Dad collapses if he steps out the front gate, and he drinks a bottle of whisky a night because he's so fucking miserable, and he can't live without Mum, but he hates himself for it.'

He's *right*, I thought, surprised at Matt's insight into his father. Perry's need for Deborah filled him with self-loathing. I hadn't thought of all that.

'And Mum. Huh. She was brilliant when we were kids, but she doesn't want to look after another baby. She doesn't even want to be here. I know that. I'm not stupid.' He shook his head. 'Which leaves me. And I'm not up to the job.'

I felt sorry for him. 'You're just young, that's all. You could be a great dad.'

He swilled the tea around in his mug. 'Maybe, maybe not. The truth is, I'm scared witless. Just like Cherie was. I reckon she couldn't handle it, you know? And I can't either. It's too big for me.'

'So . . . why not let the kid go?'

'I can't. I owe it to Cherie.'

'She'd understand. She ran away herself.'

'I'd never stop worrying. These people who say they want her, they don't even know her. They just want a baby, *any* baby. They don't love my Grace. When she gets a sore stomach and cries all night, they'll get frustrated and hit her. There's no cord attaching her to their chests.'

'But, like you said, if it's a more normal family—'

'How's she supposed to understand? She won't know who she *is*. She won't know where she belongs. She won't have a clue whether she looks like her mother or her father or her great-great-uncle.'

'That's true. No roots.'

'When the doctor asks if there's a family history of . . . shit, I don't know, flat feet or something, how's she going to feel? She won't *have* a family. She won't be one in a long, long line of flat feet, stretching away into blue infinity. She'll be all alone! Jesus Christ, Jake, how fucking sad is *that*?'

I was silenced, because he was right. We're all links in a chain. Even me.

He shook his head. 'No deal. Apart from anything else, she's Dad's only hope. With Grace at home, Mum and I will stick around. Otherwise, he's going to be alone. He'll go to pieces.'

I knew I was losing this argument. 'He'll get over it, surely?'

Matt hunched over the table. 'You don't know what it's like. He puts on a show for people like you. A bloody impressive show. But after Mum left, it was horrible. Lucy had to come home every weekend. Thank God for Lucy! He stayed up all night drinking, spent his days digging like a maniac in the garden, talking gibberish to himself. He stopped working. Stopped washing. Stopped sleeping. I used to hear him crying at night, down in the kitchen. It kept me awake. I had to get blasted just to blot out the sound.'

'Jeez,' I said. 'Perry seems very together to me. Stiff upper lip, polish your boots, don't mention the phobia.'

He sighed. 'Grace has given him hope.'

'So you can't give her up.'

'No way.' He thumped his fist onto the table. 'No *way*.' He got to his feet, and his chair scraped across the lino. 'Thanks anyway, Jake. But it's supermarket shelves for me.'

I dug out my wallet and paid the lovely Dana. She leaned across the counter as she handed me my change. 'How did you get on?'

'Fell at the last fence,' I said, grimacing.

She made an anxious face and pinged the till shut. 'Don't give up,' she breathed. 'He needs a bit of a friend, does our Matt.'

I put a hefty tip in the tin and followed my friend out to the car. The mist was starting to burn away, and I could see patches of stone-washed sky.

I reckoned one more morning's bunking off school wouldn't hurt, so I took Matt with me to visit the car sharks. They all salivated over mine, and I got a decent deal for it. We found an eight-year-old Land Cruiser that was in pretty good nick. Matt spent about twenty minutes under the bonnet, and then squinted at the pedals and the seat. He claimed that was the easy way to spot whether it had been clocked or not. When he emerged he seemed impressed, and I agreed with him. Dad used to have one, actually, and I'd done the maintenance. Dad wasn't welcome at the local garage; he didn't pay his bills.

We had a test drive and took the truck around to a Toyota specialist place I'd found in the Yellow Pages. I wanted them to look it over before I bought it. There was no one in the office. There never is. In the workshop, though, we could hear someone turning the air blue with curses before we spotted some legs sticking out from underneath a car. The mechanic pulled himself out on a little trolley and rolled to his feet, wiping his hands on a rag.

'Heap of junk.' He gave the bumper a kick and then turned to us. His face was covered in oil, and he looked about twenty-five. His name was sewn onto his overalls, barely legible through a layer of grease: *Jonty*. When I explained what we wanted, his face lit up like a beacon.

'Yeah?' He threw down the rag and strode out to the truck. 'I've done that. Cairo to Vic Falls. Eastern route.'

I recognised the accent. I always do, instantly, even after all these years. It's still the sound of home. It calls to me. I didn't mention it, though. There's a code of conduct. It's not cool to fall on someone's neck just because they come from the same tiny corner of the Pacific.

Jonty opened the door of the Toyota and made the bonnet pop up, and then he strolled around and leaned in. Matt and he had a fine old time, babbling on about head gaskets and rad valves and differentials.

'You talk like Jake,' said Matt suddenly.

'Yep,' Jonty grinned. 'That's because we're both from Godzone.'

'Where?'

'God's own country. Godzone. Aotearoa. New Zealand.'

'Why d'you call it that?'

Jonty met my eyes, and we both smiled. 'Because it is,' he said simply.

'Well, if it's so great, what are you doing here, then?' Matt sounded defensive.

Jonty put a hand to his chest. 'Following my heart,' he said. 'There's a nurses' hostel down the road.'

'That's not your *heart* you're following, mate,' I said, and he chuckled. Under the oil he had a freckled, lively face. I was willing to bet he did all right down at the nurses' hostel.

He winked at Matt. 'But Godzone it is, and always will be. Imagine a world,' he was warming to his theme now, 'where the women are all super fit and tanned and play netball in teeny-weeny little gym slips. Where you can ski, surf, and trek through subtropical bush all in one day. Where the sun shines all year round, there's no traffic, and nobody's ever so much as *seen* a queue. They don't even have the word in their vocabulary. A world where the scenery is so totally awesome that people don't even bother to talk about it.'

Matt looked sceptical. 'Is all this true, Jake?'

I thought for a second and then nodded. 'Yep. Pretty much.'

'So what's the catch?'

I didn't want to have this conversation. 'Er . . . dunno. What's the catch, Jonty?'

The mechanic was leaning right into the engine, his feet barely touching the ground. 'Catch? There isn't one,' he replied, straightening. 'That's why we're all homesick. That's why we all go home, in the end.'

He got down onto his back and slithered underneath the truck.

'Jake's not homesick,' insisted Matt. 'And he's not going back. You're not, are you, Jake?'

'Hell, no,' I assured him. 'Twelve thousand miles is only just far enough from my old man for comfort.'

Jonty reappeared, looking cheerful. 'You've found a good one,' he announced. 'Treat her right and she'll get you there and back five times. Treat her wrong and she'll dump you in the desert. Typical woman, really.'

Chapter Twenty-five

'It's going to be a nightmare from start to finish. It'll be awful getting there, and awful getting back, and *unbelievably* awful while we're there.' Leila turned her back so that David could zip up her dress.

'Now, now.' He took hold of the zip pull and tugged. 'There must be a bright side.'

'Isn't. Ouch!'

'Sorry. Did I pinch you?' He leaned down and kissed the injured patch of skin, and then raised the zip more carefully.

Leila stepped into her shoes. 'No, David, there isn't a bright side. It's two hours' drive each way, and I'd rather spend all day arranging church flowers than one minute in a marquee in Hilda's garden with that insipid Alicia, all blooming in her maternity smock.'

'You're ranting, my lovely.' David was crouched on the floor, peering under the wardrobe. 'D'you think it's going to be cold?'

'Probably. It's almost December. I wish we were going to spend the day with *my* family.'

David's head was underneath the bed, now. 'Oh, so do I! Let's find the time to shoot down to Peckham after your parents get back.'

'I might have to go by myself. Christmas isn't what you'd call a slack time for you holy types.'

'Um, have you seen my brown shoes?'

'On the kitchen table. I polished them for you.'

'What a woman!' cried David, springing to his feet. 'Did you find a present?'

'Got them an electric carving knife. I thought they could cut each other's heads off with it. And I got a gorgeous jewellery box for Freya, lined with burgundy velvet.' She stood in the middle of the floor, uncomfortable in her high heels, scowling forlornly. 'Do we *have* to go? Can't you develop a migraine?'

He clutched at his head and staggered theatrically, and then laughed. 'You look pretty spicy in that little red frock thing. Clingy, isn't it?'

Ah well, thought Leila. If I can't get out of going altogether, at least I can make sure we're extremely late. She reached over one shoulder to undo her zip, and then she stepped out of the dress.

So they left late, and arrived later because of the traffic, and Monica met them at the door.

'At *last*. What kept you?' Fussily, she brushed imaginary crumbs off David's jacket, and then peppered the air around them both with kisses. She had a long, well-scrubbed face and the same wilful light-brown hair as David. She'd clipped it up into a bun, but it was already escaping. 'You look fabulous as always, Leila. How d'you do it? I wish I had your flair. Can't stop! Bloody beef wellingtons haven't thawed, cream's gone off, chef's going bananas. Go on through and have a drink.'

She waved towards the back of the house, lifted a walkie-talkie to her mouth and began to snap orders into it.

Leaving their present among a pile of others on the hall table, David and Leila trudged reluctantly across the dining room and through French doors into the back garden. Hilda and Christopher's house was in suburban Northampton, postwar, with quiet neighbours, a pink concrete driveway and a laurel hedge. Behind the house, a garden stretched away towards school playing fields.

Today, on the back lawn a white marquee fluttered in the breeze like a mediaeval pavilion. David and Leila could hear chatter and laughter from inside, while a group of smokers had set up a private club by the greenhouse. Ignored by a flock of parents, children squabbled on the grass. Monica had laid on a bouncy castle to keep them entertained.

Under an awning a string quartet was playing quietly, but nobody seemed to be listening to them.

Hilda emerged from the marquee wearing a royal blue suit and a fixed smile.

'Aren't we lucky with the weather? A real Indian summer's day,' she gushed, brassy and anxious, steering Leila and David into the white cave. It smelled of mud and grass. A buffet was being laid out at one end by women in aprons. From a table in the centre, a three-tiered chocolate cake rose up like a piece of modern architecture. Garlands of sugar flowers twisted around each layer, and a large ceremonial knife lay ready.

A waitress shimmied up, carrying a tray loaded with champagne flutes, and Hilda waved distractedly at it. 'What'll you have? Alicia's being *so* good, only orange juice.'

Leila snatched up a glass and mutinously downed half of it in one go.

Hilda saluted gaily to somebody in the throng and then switched off her smile. 'David,' she breathed, leaning closer to her son's ear. 'Your father—' A sudden flash of welcome, a cheerful wave: '—Hel*lo*, Monty! Lovely of you to be here . . . Look, he's drinking *already*. I can't stop him. For my sake, keep an eye . . . today of all days . . .'

Pretending not to listen, Leila watched her mother-in-law surreptitiously. She's had her hair done, she thought, and felt an odd twinge of sympathy. It was streaked in flaxen layers, and the wispy, winsome fringe was carefully blow-dried to hide the creases of anxiety on her forehead. And she was wearing magenta lipstick. Poor Hilda; she tried so hard. Forty years of covering up.

A gentle, stooping couple in their eighties, old friends of the family, approached. Abruptly, Hilda became all pride and confidence: embracing them both, lying smoothly about how they hadn't changed a bit.

'David's going to be making a speech,' she told them, taking her son's arm.

David froze, gaping, and Leila giggled maliciously.

'Yes,' he stuttered. 'Yes, absolutely.'

Hilda left them, insisting that she had to circulate ('but *please*, David, do what you can, you're the only one with any influence'). David watched as the cheerful blue linen merged into a little twist of distant cousins. 'Blast.' Taking out his handkerchief, he blew his nose. 'You didn't remind me about the speech.'

Leila knocked back the rest of her champagne. The bubbles chattered and jostled one another all the way down. 'It's not my job to prompt you in your filial duties,' she retorted. 'I'd blanked it out. I've been in denial about this whole event. I'm not even *here*.'

'Damn,' sniffed David, stuffing the handkerchief back into his pocket. 'Got a bit of paper in your handbag?'

He hurried off to lock himself in the bathroom, leaving Leila to grab and knock back another glass. Across the floor she could see her father-in-law, angular in a striped blazer, being cornered by a woman in a green hat. Christopher glanced up, caught her watching him, and winked rakishly.

Shuddering, Leila picked up a handful of deep-fried mushrooms and made for the open air. A willowy blonde in a cloche hat and a flowery dress was floating around Hilda's herb garden, humming under her breath. She had an art deco haircut, short at the back and sweeping around her jawline.

'Yo, Alicia.' After two fast glasses on an empty stomach, Leila felt almost affectionate towards her sister-in-law. 'Double congratulations.'

Alicia smiled a slow, glowing smile. *Bet she's been practising that in the mirror*, thought Leila.

'Hello, Leila.' Serenely, Alicia picked a sprig of rosemary and held it to her face. 'Michael's just getting me some raspberry leaf tea . . . Come and smell this. It's heavenly.'

Leila plumped herself down onto a rustic seat, under an arch of honeysuckle. She accepted a top-up from a passing waiter. 'So. Well done. How have you been? You look as skinny as ever.'

Alicia laid a devoted hand upon her stomach. There was a small and ridiculously symmetrical bump, as though she had a mixing bowl stuffed up her skirt.

'No, I'm *vast*! I haven't felt sick at all, you know. No nausea, no heartburn, no tiredness—none of the things you're supposed to get. I'm so lucky.'

Leila felt an acid swell of bitterness somewhere under her ribs. 'You are,' she said. 'Lucky.'

Alicia bit her lip. 'I feel so awkward, you know, with you and David . . . I said to Michael, I wish we could keep it quiet until after the party. But I'm *enormous*! Everyone would have commented.' She wandered a little further away, her skirt swaying.

Leila scanned the garden, searching for a friendly face. The lawn seemed to be populated entirely by sweating, energetic parents and toddlers in designer dungarees, but there was no sign of Freya or Charlie, David's niece and nephew.

One tiny girl, keen to escape from a thug in a dragon costume, ran full tilt into Leila's legs, holding onto them for support.

'Whoops!' Instinctively, Leila reached down to save the child from falling, and found herself looking into a pair of brown eyes. 'Hello.' She ruffled the silky-smooth hair. 'Is that big old dragon bullying you?'

The child nodded dumbly, her dimpled hands warm and trusting, resting with familiarity on Leila's knees as though she'd known her for years. She was wearing an old-fashioned blue velvet dress with smocking. She blinked, and rubbed her nose. Then the chubby legs gave way and she sat down

'Pretty,' she said, grabbing a clumsy handful of grass.

Glad of the company, Leila slid off the bench and sat beside her, cross-legged. They made a small and rather uneven coronet of honey-suckle flowers, and Leila was just resting it on the child's hair when a brisk young redhead flurried up.

'Sorry,' she said coldly, snatching up the protesting little girl as though Leila were a convicted paedophile. 'My daughter's bothering you.'

'No, she's not,' Leila protested.

But the woman did not even glance at her before bustling away. 'I turn my back for five minutes . . .'

'Sweet,' chirruped Alicia, from the lavender.

Feeling profoundly irrelevant, Leila watched as the pair crossed the grass to join a gossiping gaggle, the child balanced casually as a handbag on her mother's hip. The flowers had fallen off her head. She was trying to reach for them, but her mother was too busy networking to notice. The parents stood in a tight knot of complacency with their baby slings and pushchairs, wiping noses and making cosy conversation about whether or not to immunise. They were members of an exclusive club, and Leila wasn't in it. No doubt they had smug, self-satisfied bumper stickers boasting about their 'Baby on Board'. For a moment, she hated them all.

And there was Michael emerging from the house, wearing a cravat and carrying a cup and saucer as though they were about to explode. No. Not now. It was too much. Leila was on her feet, desperate to avoid having to congratulate her brother-in-law upon his impending fatherhood, when her eyes rested upon the slightly stooped figure of Nicky Pertwell, Monica's husband. He was skulking with the smokers who huddled in guilty comradeship by the greenhouse. She hurried towards him, deftly avoiding the parents' club and Michael with his Semtex teacup.

Laughing, Nicky watched her progress.

'Leila. Thank God you're here. I thought you were going to let me down.' Nicky wasn't exactly good-looking. Not even elegant, really. He had an appealing, lopsided smile and an unhealthy pallor, and he never stood up straight. Perhaps he couldn't. Yet women—all women, even Hilda—loved him.

'Am I glad to see you, Mr Toad.' Leila let him kiss her genially on both cheeks. She wanted to cry. 'I've never seen so many happy families on one lawn. I'm afraid it's not helping my state of mind.'

Nicky stuck a cigarette between his teeth. He did look faintly amphibian, goggling through round, rimless glasses, and she had never met anyone so overtly camp in manner. Had he not been married to Monica, she would certainly have assumed him to be gay.

He flicked his lighter with a limp-wristed flourish and then snapped the brass lid shut. 'Where's David?' His voice had never quite broken, and there was a mild, friendly accent that Leila assumed was a remnant of his Manchester roots.

'He's dashed off to scribble down all the good things he can think of to say about his parents.'

'Did you give him a postage stamp to jot them on?' Nicky snatched two glasses from a tray as it sailed past, and handed one to Leila. 'Senior Management—I mean Monica—is in full tizz mode. Let's take cover in the kitchen. Far too many in-laws out here.'

Hilda's kitchen was large and chrome and surprisingly scruffy, with piles of junk mail and newspapers on every surface. It was cool, though, and Leila threw herself into a chair with a sigh. A bald chef was standing at the table, frenziedly stirring, while people in aprons ran around like ants.

Nicky dragged a handkerchief out of his pocket and began to mop his shining brow. His hairline was receding. 'Whew. So humid. Must be global warming.' He took off his jacket and draped it over a chair, and then held up his glass. 'This stuff's wasted on Hilda and Christopher. Pearls before swine. But Senior Management said I had to wheel out something decent.' Nicky imported wine. His business and Monica's had a symbiotic relationship.

'I suppose a lot of work's gone into all this?' asked Leila.

Nicky shrugged. 'Monica does these bashes all the time. It's routine for her.'

'She seemed quite uptight when I saw her.'

'Jumpy as a flea. That's because she's got no bookings. It's all dried up. Nobody can afford lavish parties nowadays. Or decent wine, for that matter.'

He picked up a bottle, squinted critically at the label, then filled two more glasses. 'Try this.'

Leila was staring at him, concerned. 'Nicky . . . are you in trouble?'

'Not yet. I could always go into the church.' Leila frowned, and he held up his hands. 'Stop worrying, Leila. We're not going down the gurgler. I think we've covered our bases. The day Monica has to sack her nanny, you can feel sorry for her.'

Leila let it go. 'Where *are* the children? I've got a birthday present for Freya in the car.'

'I expect Monica will summon them when she needs some matching accessories to go with her outfit.'

'Meeow!'

Nicky looked faintly ashamed. 'Nice girl, the latest nanny. Catalina. Chilean.' Tipping his chair sideways, he stretched an arm towards the kitchen benchtop and picked up a newspaper, as though anxious to change the subject.

'Gawd, look at this! Hilda gets *The Times*. Bet she doesn't read it. Let's have a squint at the crossword . . . er . . . got a pen? No, me neither. Oh, here's one. Now, seven down: of avuncular weed. Has to be an anagram. Has to be.' He wrote the letters in a circle in the corner of the page. 'Any ideas? We heard you had a disappointment, Leila, with the baby.'

The remark came without any warning or change in inflection, and Leila was caught off guard. Nicky didn't look up; he spared her that. She made an effort to sound breezy. 'We did . . . yes, we did. Never mind.' She coughed, trying to keep her voice level. 'Perhaps I don't need any accessories.'

'We were sorry,' he said. 'Monica and I. We were both so sorry.'

Leila didn't answer. His kindness had knocked the breeziness clean out of her.

'Any hope?' asked Nicky.

'Some. Not much. It looks as though dear old Grandma's going to get the child. But if she wanted her, why not say so before?'

'Have you been given an explanation?'

'Um.' Leila felt the tears welling up. 'There's a total news blackout. We know almost nothing about the birth family. It seems it's a hanging offence even to ask.'

'Frustrating.'

Leila laughed shakily. 'My mum's threatening to march into social services and give 'em a piece of her mind. They'd better get their tin hats on!'

Nicky felt in a jacket pocket and dragged out his cigarettes. They were rather squashed. 'Would your mother really do that?'

'No, she wouldn't.' Leila reached into her handbag for a tissue. 'She's pretty feisty, Mum, but she wouldn't actually make a scene like that. Anyway, she's in Nigeria for another fortnight.' She blew her nose as inconspicuously as she could.

Nicky was on the point of lighting up when he met the chef's stony glare. 'Whoops!' He placed a guilty hand across his mouth. 'Faux pas. Sorry.'

As he was jamming the cigarettes back into his pocket, the kitchen door was kicked brutally open and two children barged in. The eldest was half-grown, awkward and gangly. She had frizzy auburn hair and wore hipster jeans and a gold tee-shirt. She rushed at Leila.

'You *got* here!' she yelled jubilantly, squeezing her arms around Leila's neck. 'We thought you'd had a terrible car crash and your guts were spread all over the motorway.'

'Sorry, guys. Awful traffic.' Leila hugged the girl, swiftly wiping her eyes with her fingertips. 'Happy birthday for last week, Freya. How does it feel to be thirteen?'

'*Big* disappointment. It's no different from being twelve.'

Leila forced a chuckle. 'I love this gold top. D'you think it would fit me?'

'Might be a bit on the tight side,' snorted Nicky.

'Look,' groaned Freya, baring her teeth at Leila. 'Braces! Yeuch! Aren't they *disgusting*?'

'No, they're hardly visible,' declared Leila. 'And when they come off you'll have teeth like a film star.'

'We were all looking out for you from the spare bedroom window,' scolded Charlie testily, climbing onto Leila's knee. He was eight, small for his age and pale, with sticking-up hair. 'We waited for ages. Freya, Dad and me.'

'Oh dear, did you? I feel really, *really* guilty.'

Charlie shot a mischievous glance at his father. 'Mummy got extremely grumpy and said it was *bloody typical* of you and David to let the side down.'

Nicky spat a mouthful of wine back into his glass and wheezed with laughter, slapping his thigh.

'Shut up, Charlie,' said Freya. She elbowed her brother in the ribs.

'Ow! Well, it's true.' Charlie's eyes were wide with exaggerated innocence. 'She said quite a lot more as well.' He looked around. 'Where's David?'

'Writing a speech,' sobbed Nicky, still shaking.

'He promised he'd play football next time he came,' said Charlie. 'I'm going to hold him to that.'

Sensible heels could be heard, clacking on the tiles. Monica strode into the kitchen, and Leila was jerked back into reality. The day was to be got through: the celebration of fertility, the jollity, the inescapable grief.

'You two!' Monica's gaze swept across the scene. '*Here* you are. Poor Catalina's looking for you—run along to the marquee, quick. What on earth are you all giggling about?'

A platoon of girls in black trooped in behind her and began with military precision to fan out across the kitchen, collecting trays. Monica watched them and then clapped her hands for quiet. 'Right, are we ready to go? Good.'

The team clearly knew the procedure. They formed a line at the door and sallied forth, trays held high. Monica turned to follow them, pausing briefly in the doorway.

'Dad's drinking,' she hissed with an agonised grimace. '*Do* something, Nicky!'

Round tables were laid out in the marquee, each seating eight. Monica, who was in charge of the seating plan, had deployed the immediate family so that one Edmunds sat at each table, acting as a sort of local warlord.

Searching the name cards, Leila found that she was to preside over the younger generation—cousins and friends of cousins in their late teens; and for that she was grateful to Monica. At least she hadn't been stuck in the parents' club. She passed an entertaining hour listening to the youngsters' views on sex, war, and the latest James Bond film. Theirs was the only rowdy group, and the waiters enthusiastically tended their glasses.

Alicia was perched at the next table, listening politely to Christopher's only surviving uncle. The old man blinked his mauve eyelids in slow motion, like a tortoise. Alicia held herself very straight, a doll with a tranquil smile, taking saintly sips of her orange juice. Just watching this self-sacrifice made Leila stick out her glass for a refill. It was her little rebellion. It didn't matter what she ate or drank; *her* body wasn't a vessel. By the time they came to the coffee, she felt more relaxed than she would have believed possible. In fact, it seemed as though she was hardly there at all. She leaned back in her chair and let her eyes wander, although she had a little difficulty in keeping them focused.

Across the marquee she could see David, with Freya and Charlie to each side. He seemed to be telling them a long, complicated story, with much waving of hands and wild laughter from all three. Charlie was actually falling off his chair in his hysteria. David caught Leila's eye, waved, and patted his pocket to show he had the speech in hand.

And there was Hilda, making gracious little sorties around the tables, greeting old friends with feline tidiness: a lone figure in her brave blue. Christopher would not join her, although his wife glanced at him often with a tight, meaningful smile. She even jerked her head at him—a tiny movement, almost imperceptible—but he just beetled his heavy white brows, lounging in his striped blazer.

Twice Leila caught him watching her. The second time, she met his eye. *I'm not scared of you, you old bastard.* Fortified by wine she felt momentarily invincible, but the challenge backfired because Christopher appeared to be delighted. She yawned to show that she was bored, and looked away, but the sensation of his gaze on the back of her neck made her want to squirm.

Unfortunately, it was at this moment that Hilda paused to bestow a few minutes on her daughter-in-law.

'Leila.' She slid into an empty seat. 'I gather consolations are in order.' And perhaps she really meant to console.

Leila became dangerously still. *Don't you dare.* 'Consolations?'

'No baby.'

'Ah.' Leila sat back in her chair, pulse racing. 'No. No baby, Hilda.'

'Well.' The mother-in-law pursed her magenta mouth, sorrowfully kind. 'I'm sure it's all for the best.'

Fury was churning at the floodgates, boiling and bubbling. 'Excuse me? Why is it all for the best?'

Hilda shook her head, and the wispy fringe fluttered. 'You knew I had grave reservations about bringing a strange child into the family like that. Anything might have happened. *Anything.*'

Leila took a long breath. Then, quite deliberately, she opened the gates. The rage burst free in a glorious, foaming wave. 'David is miserable, Hilda,' she snapped, very loudly, and several people at the next table glanced around, eyebrows raised in amusement or surprise. 'Is your son's misery *all for the best*? He just wants to be a father.'

Hilda recoiled slightly. 'But my dear Leila, can't you see? This child would not have made him a father.'

'I don't think you *want* your son to be happy. Not unless he plays by your rules.'

A flush blossomed on Hilda's cheeks. 'Well, you know my views.'

'Oh, I do.' The wave was splendidly reckless now. It flattened anything in its path, annihilating their carefully built façade of cordiality. 'I do! Actually, Hilda, I've had just about enough of hearing your views. For fifteen long years, I've put up with your narrow-minded, self-serving drivel.'

Even as the words left her, Leila knew she would regret them. There was muffled laughter from the teenagers around the table, and it seemed as though a hush had spread across much of the marquee.

Hilda leaped to her feet. 'I will *assume* that's the alcohol talking.' She gripped the back of a chair, white-knuckled. 'Perhaps you'd better have another cup of coffee. Make it a strong one, Leila, will you?'

Someone was tapping their glass with a spoon, calling for quiet. It was Monica, standing on a chair, looking like a rather buxom statue of Queen Victoria. Hilda stalked back to her own table.

'Good afternoon, everyone,' bellowed Monica when the hubbub had died to a murmur. She beamed around at the crowd. 'It's *so* nice to see you all here to celebrate with my parents and remember that very special day, forty years ago, when they tied the knot.'

Leila felt increasingly nauseous; perhaps it was the clichés. Or the guilt.

'Anyway.' Monica simpered affectionately in David's direction. He'd made a paper napkin into a hat, and was pressing it onto Charlie's head. 'My brother David—who likes the sound of his own voice, being a clergyman!—has agreed to say a few words. After all, this is an extra-ordinary occasion, as we celebrate the long and successful union of two extraordinary people.'

There was a rumble of assent, and sporadic clapping. It seemed to come from far, far away. Leila felt a cold sweat gather ominously on her forehead. Pushing back her chair in a panic, she ducked under the open side of the tent and trotted across the lawn and into the house. She headed for the upstairs bathroom, away from inquisitive eyes. Tearing along the landing she made it with no time to spare, retching violently over the toilet.

Sounds of merriment trickled in through the open window. The crowd seemed to be laughing immoderately at David's speech. There were bursts of hilarity, and a cascade of applause. Hunched miserably on Hilda's bathroom floor, nausea had Leila by the throat. She'd forgotten how grim it felt. She vowed, fervently, never to drink alcohol again. At long last, she heard a toast to Hilda and Christopher. She imagined them cutting the cake in a parody of their wedding day, smiling for the photographer.

She was still crouching by the basin when David came to look for her. She heard the familiar footsteps thumping up the stairs, two at a time, and his worried voice at the door. 'Leila? You in there?'

'Um . . .' Shaking, she pulled herself upright and turned on the cold tap. 'Just a minute.' Water gushed into the basin. She bent, splashing her face and neck, and sloshed some of Hilda's Listerine around her mouth.

'You all right, Leila?'

Pressing her nose into a towel, she crossed to the door and opened it. David stood on the landing, his eyes bright with concern.

'What's happened? You look awful.' He laid a hand on her forehead.

'I'm not pregnant, if that's what you're thinking. I'm not in *the club*.'

He smiled gently. 'Never crossed my mind.'

'I've publicly insulted your mother and thrown up in her bathroom. I don't think it's possible to disgrace myself more comprehensively. I'm going to have to join the Foreign Legion.'

'Please don't do that.' Stooping, he rested his forehead against hers. 'It's hard sometimes, isn't it?'

'It's hard.' She shut her eyes, and they stood quietly together, taking comfort in one another until they heard footsteps in the hall below.

'Come on,' he said, taking her hand. 'Let's go home.'

To Leila's embarrassment, Monica was waiting for them downstairs.

'You might like to hang on to this,' she said, handing Leila a bottle of mineral water. 'Don't worry, nobody noticed. I think it was probably those wretched beef wellingtons. I should sue Pertwell's, if I were you. Let's hope the whole mob doesn't come down with food poisoning.'

Grateful for this generous fiction, Leila accepted the bottle.

Her sister-in-law nodded efficiently. Her hair had abandoned its clip. 'I'll see you off. David, why don't you nip ahead and fetch the car from wherever it's parked?'

As they made their way down the salmon-pink drive, Monica rubbed her palms together, as though wrestling with some dilemma.

'Look . . . I'm sorry. I gather my mother was extremely rude and tactless.'

Leila dipped her head, screwing up her face in pained recollection. '*I* was pretty rude to *her*. And today, of all days. Unforgivable.' She sighed. 'I seem to be churning out a lot of apologies at the moment.'

'No. What she said to you was quite ridiculous.'

'Even Christopher managed to behave better than me,' moaned Leila.

'Ah!' Monica looked smug. 'I put him on the teetotallers' table at the last minute. We were plying him with sparkling grape juice all the way through lunch.'

'That's a cunning plan.'

'Nicky's idea.' Monica's smile faded. 'I know I'm a bit pompous at times, Leila. It isn't easy, you know, being Hilda's daughter. I love her dearly, and she has many qualities I admire, but she was never the most sympathetic of mothers.'

Leila was taken aback. 'I suppose not.'

'None of us could ever match up to her expectations. The boys went off to boarding school. They had some other influences. I didn't.'

Fascinated, Leila watched her sister-in-law's robust profile. All the no-nonsense arrogance, the overblown confidence, was gone.

Monica raised her shoulders. 'Dad wasn't home much, but when he was around their incompatibility was exhausting. They're celebrating forty years of civilised dislike. They've actually made an art form of it.' The two continued to stroll. 'We've each dealt with it in our own fashion. I've tried to do the Right Thing. Married money, set up Pertwell Party Solutions, produced grandchildren.' She put a hand to her mouth. 'Oh, gosh. Sorry. That was crass.'

'Don't worry. Go on, Monica.'

'Well, Michael's become completely materialistic. Designer clothes, car and wife. It's the only form of self-expression he allows himself, and it earns him parental approval.'

'Ah. I get it!' Leila laughed suddenly. 'David's gone the other way, hasn't he? Black sheep, black cassock, black wife. He's thumbing his nose in style.'

They had reached the end of the drive. Monica stood stolidly on the pavement, gazing at Leila with a faint, admiring smile. 'Listen. Don't say another word about that row,' she advised. 'And for heaven's sake, don't go apologising. Promise me? I'll be cross if you apologise. She was well out of order.'

'So . . . we pretend it never happened?'

Monica nodded firmly. 'Absolutely. Don't give it another thought. I predict the old girl will treat you with more respect in future.'

The car drew up beside them and David jumped out, leaving the engine running.

'Thanks for a great day,' he said, hurriedly kissing his sister. 'Here's a birthday present for Freya—if you could pass it on? Say our goodbyes for us.'

Before they pulled away, Monica leaned down to Leila's open window.

'Well done, Leila,' she said, clutching Freya's parcel. 'Well done. And I truly hope the two of you will become parents soon. You'll be *so* much better at it than I am.'

Chapter Twenty-six

I spent the best part of three weeks in London, trying to prove to myself that I wasn't a fly in the Harrison web, all wrapped up and waiting to have my blood sucked.

Matt sent a stream of text messages, but nothing much seemed to have changed in Coptree. A couple of social workers had set up camp down there, and the Harrisons were all busy behaving like one of those grinning families in the toothpaste adverts. I decided I was well out of it.

I stayed with some old friends, Bill and Lottie, in Hammersmith. I kept out of their way as much as I could. They had a new baby, and all night long I heard it crying, and then doors creaking open and poor old Bill or Lottie padding patiently along the corridor.

They had a toddler too, called Florence. She was pretty cute, actually. I owned a greenstone key ring in the shape of two humpback whales. It was just a gimmick, made for the tourists who go whale-watching off Kaikoura. Mum sent it for my birthday. The whales were a mother and calf, and when you pressed the button their eyes would flash and you could hear this whale song. It was a love song, mother to child. It was an eerie sound, really, but when I showed it to the little girl, Florence, she was totally fascinated. She'd sidle up and pull the keys out of my pocket, and then plump herself down in a corner with her legs stuck out, and press the button. She used to sit there for ages, imitating the electronic cries and running her fat little finger around the outlines of the whales. Drove us all nuts. In the end I let her keep the thing.

I wasn't in the house much. I completely rejigged my finances and the tenancy in Clapham. I collected gear and visas and inoculations.

One of the jabs was in my butt, and the man-hating nurse used a bloody monstrous needle.

I caught up with a lot of people. Didn't see Anna, though. I tried phoning her, even dropped in at the flat one evening, but she wasn't there so I left a note. Just standing at the door—every scratch on its surface was like an old friend—made me feel screwy, as though I was living two lives at once.

Early one morning, about a week after I'd left Coptree, Florence came banging on my bedroom door. She waddled up to the bed, wearing pyjamas that made her look like Tigger, and smacked a letter down on my face.

'Postman Pat!' she squawked, and walloped me on the nose five more times with the envelope until I hid under the duvet. I heard her laughing uproariously, and surfaced just in time to see an orange-striped bottom disappearing around the door. Then I heard whales singing, out on the landing.

I knew the handwriting on the envelope. I'd seen it before, scrawled across a postcard with a picture of two Arab sailing boats in the sunset. Hadn't expected her to give me another thought.

Dear Jake,

I told you I'd write. Only rogue English bluestockings use real paper nowadays!

It's crazy here. Nothing new in that, I hear you say. The place has been crawling with busybodies of various shapes and sizes. Clipboards and serious expressions. They want Grace to visit us here so they can assess us looking after her. Our own granddaughter! How patronising is that? Nobody assesses other grandmothers who take care of their children, and I bet most of them aren't as capable as I am. Hamisi was looking after eight grandchildren—who assessed him? This is officious, bureaucratic and intrusive.

You have to hand it to Perry and me. We're giving the performance of our lives. If we were in a Gilbert and Sullivan (United Fronts, they'd call it) we'd keep bursting into song. Perry's the dashing military man, gallantly pulling out chairs for his interrogators. You'd never recognise him. He's all twinkly and self-deprecating. And I keep twittering away.

God, Jake, what is this about? Grace, of course. We must rescue our precious child. Did you see, there was a horrible story in the paper this week about foster carers who abused the children in their care— systematic cruelty over twenty years of fostering. Twenty! I'll spare you the details. It makes me shudder to think of Grace, all alone with nobody to protect her.

On the brighter side, Matt's a new man. He's stopped truanting and is trying to catch up on coursework. We're getting on so much better.

Well, I hope your arrangements are going smoothly. I hear you've got yourself a heroic new truck, simply bristling with machismo. Boys and their toys. Have you reconciled with Anna yet, down on bended knee? Go on, risk a little.

We look forward to your return, whenever that may be. Mealtimes are rather ghastly, as you can imagine, and we could do with a little cheerful normality.
With love,
Susie, or Deborah, or whoever I am x

I folded the letter and slipped it between the pages of my book, intending to read it again later. If they put their minds to it, maybe the Harrisons could pull this thing off. They were, after all, the baby's family.

I hopped out of bed and headed for the shower, wondering whether or not I was pleased to represent a little cheerful normality. Perhaps it was better than nothing.

I'd arranged to see a solicitor later that morning. It seemed like a good time to get a will drawn up, since I was planning to drive across the Sahara and various war-torn regions. It wasn't going to be very complicated. Mum got the lot, or my brother Jesse if she checked out first. Dad was specifically to be excluded from everything, whatever the circumstances. It would almost be worth getting myself killed in Chad or somewhere just to see the old git's face when he found out.

That same evening I had dinner with Lucy at an Italian near her flat. She was nipping down to Coptree the following morning, to see Grace and meet the assessment team. She'd been going home quite a lot, apparently.

'I'm slightly worried about Dad,' she remarked casually, her eyes determinedly on the menu. 'He's not in a very good place.'

I was concerned despite myself. Lucy was always a mistress of understatement.

'How's that?'

She squeezed some garlic bread between her finger and thumb. Her mouth had tightened a little.

'He went downhill fast when Deborah left,' she said. 'He seemed to improve when she first got back, but it was short-lived. In fact, now he's worse. He puts on a wonderful act for the social workers and then collapses.'

'Anything to be done?'

'Well, maybe he could try a change of medication. But he's refusing to see the doctor again.'

With an obvious effort, she changed the subject and began gossiping about Kenneth the bored security guard who had got himself onto a reality television show. This, I have to say, was riveting news. We forgot Perry for a while; we laughed and chatted just like old times, until, innocently tucking into my cannelloni, I mentioned that I'd heard from Deborah. Fatal mistake.

Lucy looked as though I'd laced her wine with paint stripper. 'You're not still hanging around her, are you?'

'I'm not hanging around anyone.'

There was a burst of applause from a group of young professionals at the next table. Stripy shirts. Loosened ties. Eating, drinking and being merry as tomorrow they might be sacked. One of them was opening birthday presents.

'Relax,' I said. 'I don't fancy your stepmother.'

'Jake.' She shook her head, sadly. 'You fool no one except yourself.'

'Bollocks.'

'You don't know yourself.'

'That's a mercy.' I leaned closer. 'Don't you feel even a little bit sorry for Deborah? She's never had the freedom you have, and her brain's just as good as yours. You probably owe your success to her.'

'Some of it, certainly. And your point is . . . ?'

'She had to give up her education and her freedom when she was just a kid. And now here she is, back where she started.'

'She made her bed. She can damn well lie in it. You just watch out she doesn't lie in yours, too. If she hasn't already . . . ?'

Exasperated, I dropped my fork with a clatter. 'Look, I've told you . . .' I stopped, suddenly baffled. 'Why the anger, Luce? It doesn't suit you at all.'

A waiter brought us salad in a square bowl, casting a longing glance at Lucy's legs. She thanked him in a spray of Italian and watched with narrowed eyes as he hurried away. Then she said, 'You have no idea.'

I waited, but she just attacked her pizza like George sighting the dragon. At the next table, they were arguing about the bill. Someone asked to see the manager.

'So tell me,' I prompted. 'If I've no idea.'

She tipped back her chair, eyeing me. 'She's left me and Dad before, you know.' Her chin was tilted, dark head high on her ballet dancer's neck. 'Yes, I see you *do* know. I was a tiny child. She slipped into the place of my mother, made me love her, and then . . .' She gave a little shrug. 'She left. I cried for weeks. I wrapped myself up in a curtain, hiding from life. I thought the world had ended.'

'But she was young. Much younger than you are now.'

'Is youth an excuse, Jake? Really?' She let her chair drop forward with a reverberating crash. 'The day she came back to us was one of the happiest of my life. Ironic, isn't it? She only scurried home because she was pregnant.'

'She missed you. She told me so.'

Lucy looked cynical. 'My father is worth a thousand of her. He forgave her infidelity, he forgave her betrayal. He did the right thing and he married her. Took her word for it that Matt was his. And was she grateful? Oh, no. She had to start going on her smutty holidays.'

'I don't think it was as simple as that.'

'Oh? Were you there?'

I met her eyes. There was a dangerous gleam in them.

'Well, I *was*. I didn't suspect a thing until a few years ago. Couldn't believe it when I found his letters.'

I was lost. 'Found whose letters?'

Her mouth curved, bitterly. The manager had arrived at the next table: a small, bald man in a suit. He was looking at the bill while a waiter hovered nearby.

'What's his name? *Rod*, that's it. Rod. How appropriate. Perhaps you've met him? No, don't answer that, I don't want to know. He writes a sizzler, does Rod. Ought to send them off to *Playboy*, make his fortune. I found lots of them in her desk. The pile hasn't grown recently. I expect he sends emails instead.'

Lucy knocked back her wine, lowered it to the table, glared at me. 'Right up to that moment when I found her little gold key and opened the drawer, I worshipped her. I thought she was the most beautiful, the sweetest, the cleverest woman in the world. Matt and I were her little team of cheerleaders. We thought she loved us as much as we loved her. And the whole time, we were no more than an *inconvenience*.'

'No,' I protested. 'No. That isn't right.'

'What other interpretation is there? All those years she brought us up, she was longing to be somewhere else, *with* someone else. Not with us or our father. All those years, she wasn't the person I thought she was. And as final proof of our irrelevance—whoops!—she's dumped us again.'

I considered whether I could safely repeat anything Deborah had told me. Probably not, I decided. I'd only dig myself into a hole.

'Did you have it out with her?' I asked.

'Of course I did. She never tried to deny it. She couldn't, could she?'

'I hope you didn't show these letters to Perry?'

'I spared him that. But he *knew*, for God's sake, he isn't stupid. He was vulnerable, her prisoner. But she didn't care, oh no. She just dangled her next trip to Africa in front of him with her pussycat smile.'

The group at the next table were finally paying the bill and standing up to leave. Lucy leaned forward, looking into my eyes.

'It was evil. He was down, and she kicked him, just for fun. Not once, Jake. Again, and again, and again. Year after year, she trotted off with her tail up like a bitch on heat. He was forced to wave and smile and chirrup, "See you soon, my darling, come home soon!"'

There wasn't anything I could point to as factually incorrect in all of this. But it wasn't quite fair, all the same.

'I think she has her own side of the story,' I argued. 'And Perry's symptoms began before they were even married.'

'Agreed. But if she had been loyal, he might have beaten them.'

'It can't have been easy to be married to him.'

She snorted. 'Do me a favour. There are plenty of women who would be delighted to take Dad on. He's cultured, he's dignified, and he's still a handsome man.'

I sighed. 'Even so . . . not easy, Luce.'

'I had to come home and be with him,' she said. The fine, clear eyes were brimming. 'Every time she went away. I watched my darling father disintegrate, and at the hands of a person I had once adored. How would *you* feel, Jake? Would you want to forgive?'

I thought about my own father. Jesse and I could tell when he was in a rage just from the way he thrashed his quad bike up to the sheds; just from the fury of the engine note. We used to hide in the orchard, and we could hear him yelling and Mum crying, but we couldn't protect her. Forgiveness wasn't on the cards, so far as he was concerned.

Lucy was watching me. 'No,' she said. 'I thought not. Well, neither do I.'

It was a week or so before Florence delivered another letter.

Dear Jake,

Well, it's been grim. The Gestapo have turned up repeatedly—as promised—and the novelty is wearing very thin, but I've been domesticated and steady enough to look after ten granddaughters. Grace comes here as part of the assessment, and she has stolen all our hearts. Her cot's in my room! Perry is sweet with her, seems genuinely head over heels. He picks her up at the first murmur and never wants to put her down. She's the only thing that lifts his mood.

As for Matt, I'd say they have a real bond. Grace lights up when he hoves into view. But it insults our precious time to have these people watching us. Turns our love into a spectator sport.

Someone called the 'Children's Guardian' showed up today. A scarily elegant Indian woman. Effortlessly authoritative. Her job, apparently, is to speak for Grace. That must involve some mental gymnastics, since the poor child's only four months old. Anyway, we got on rather well. I wanted to confide in her.

The court hearing is next Thursday. Stuart thinks the local authority will withdraw their application on the day. Then they'll 'place' her with us. That's Big Brother speak for letting us have her. There will still be some sort of order—Stuart did explain it all to me, but I got bored and started writing shopping lists.

Despite all this success, Perry's not doing well. He is sinking into one of the worst pits I've ever known. It's actually quite frightening. I've made about ten trips to the recycling with his empty whisky bottles in case someone pokes their big nose into the dustbin. Every evening the three of us sit around the kitchen table in a dour silence. It's just horrible, Jake. Sometimes I want to scream. Matt and I bolt down our food and take refuge in our bedrooms. I'm skulking in here now, while my adoring husband props himself up in the kitchen and breathes out fumes. I don't know when Perry sleeps, or even whether he does. I don't know how we can carry on like this.

Is this, then, to be my life? I've forgotten what normality is. Sorry to be so irremediably miserable. Could you come back? Please?

Love,
Deborah x

Well, I'd had enough of the Big Smoke anyway. On Friday afternoon, just as I was leaving Bill's, I had a text from Matt.

They liked Mum. We won. C U 2nite.

Chapter Twenty-seven

Leila sat at the kitchen table and wondered how she was going to tell him.

It had been a beautiful winter's afternoon and now the last light of a blue and yellow day blazed across the walls, glancing off her face and hands, making her hair glow. How could nature rejoice?

The radio was still on. She'd been listening to it when the call came, but now she was barely aware of its carefree chatter. A lorry had jack-knifed on the M25 and spilled its load, and the tailback was fifteen miles long because everyone was trying to get somewhere. All those people, all those weekends. So much irrelevance.

How could she tell him?

His key was scraping in the lock. She stood up, sickened by dread.

'Hello, my lovely!' he called cheerfully, using his Welshman voice. He was in a good mood, she could tell, and that made it worse. 'All well in the world?'

Standing in the kitchen doorway, she took a long breath. She felt as though she were hiding a knife behind her back. 'I'm afraid not really, Davie.'

He froze warily in the act of hanging up his overcoat. His hair fell across his brow, and he pushed it back distractedly. 'They've rung?'

She gulped, overcome. She shrank from saying it aloud.

David's eyes were shadowed depths in the dim light of the hall. 'They like her.' His voice had deadened.

Leila swallowed hard. 'The baby is to be placed with her birth family.'

David's coat missed its hook, scraping down the wall before crumpling in a desolate heap on the floor. He left it there. Taking a step towards Leila, he peered into her face. 'Is this definite, though? They've messed us about before. They might change their minds again.'

Bleakly, she shook her head. 'I don't think so. The court hearing's next Thursday. Linda says everyone . . .' A sob rose up in her throat; she forced it back, covering her mouth with one hand. 'She says everyone's agreed, and the hearing will take two minutes.'

'Two minutes.' David laughed shortly and then smashed his hand against the wall. 'Everyone's agreed, are they? Nice for them. I don't remember being asked.'

He sank down onto the stairs, eyes wide, staring straight ahead. He looked dazed, as though he'd just been coshed. 'That's it, then.' After a silence he added, 'Not unexpected.'

Inevitably, the telephone rang. Like a sleepwalker, Leila went to answer it. David pushed himself to his feet and limped into the kitchen. He hobbled gracelessly, on stiff legs, as if he had suddenly grown very old. Perhaps he had.

The voice on the other end was subdued and hesitant, as though the young man had been plucking up enough courage to call.

'Um . . . is Reverend Edmunds there? We'd like to organise our baby being christened.'

Not now. Not now. Leila's fingers seemed to lose their strength; the receiver slipped a little in her hand.

'Hello?' The voice gained confidence. 'Have I got the right place?'

No. This is definitely the wrong place. With an effort, Leila cleared her throat. 'Mr Edmunds isn't in, I'm afraid. Let me take your number . . .'

After the call, she unplugged the telephone from the wall. Then she moved to David's side, as he stood gazing sightlessly out of the kitchen window. The sun left them, creeping pitilessly away below a pale horizon. Shadows slipped gleefully into the room, and a draught numbed their souls.

David stirred, wrapping an arm around his wife's shoulders. 'Can we give up now, please, Leila?'

She looked out at the last of the light, bleeding away. 'Yes,' she said. 'Yes. We can give up now.'

And, very briefly, she meant it.

Chapter Twenty-eight

I got held up on the M25. Jack-knifed lorry, apparently, and something toxic all over the show. I fumed in the carbon-belching queue, wishing I had a takeaway coffee.

After about a decade without forward movement, I began to twiddle with the radio; hit the news—bad, all of it—and the weather. According to the very jolly weatherman, we were in for severe gales by the middle of the following week, a mother of a storm. And the odds were shortening on a white Christmas.

As the minutes passed I became increasingly aware of a twisting in my guts. I couldn't say quite why, but I found myself finger drumming and heel tapping like a hyperactive schoolkid. There was something about the tone of Deborah's last letter that I hadn't liked, especially when I remembered Lucy's recent anxiety. I had an uneasy sense that I needed to get to Coptree immediately. I wanted to see Debs—see them all. In the end I fished out a map and planned a cross country route from the next exit.

I opened the door of the truck and leaned out. Hundreds of red taillights, all arranged in neat, obedient rows. The night was settling into stillness and frost under a clear, city-glow sky. Butter wouldn't melt in its mouth. The jolly weatherman had to be wrong.

As soon as I spotted the next exit I barged my way across the crawling traffic, getting myself hooted at and not caring, keen to turn towards Suffolk. Once I'd left the motorway it was a convoluted route, and a couple of times I had to stop and check the map. But at least I was moving. And the closer I got, the faster I drove. By the time I reached Coptree Woods, I was flying.

Deborah's figure appeared at the front door as soon as I pulled up, and Matt was right behind her.

'Thank God,' said Deborah, as I jumped out and hugged her. She kissed my cheek. 'Thank God for you, Jake. We're going mad here.'

'Matt,' I said, clapping a hand on the boy's broad shoulder. 'How's it going?'

He grunted and shoved his hands into his pockets as they led me inside.

Perry appeared in the hall and shook my hand. He came with us into the kitchen and did his best to be a good host, but it seemed an immense effort for him. Deborah was doing a Stepford Wife impersonation over the stove. After ten minutes, the phone rang and Matt went to answer it. It was Lucy, checking in.

Without a word, Perry got up from the table and slumped out into the garden.

'So—what's wrong with Perry?' I asked, watching him through the kitchen window. 'I've never seen him so low.' I began to twist a corkscrew into a bottle. To thank the Harrisons for their hospitality I'd brought a case of pinot noir, imported from a small producer in Hawke's Bay. 'You'd think he'd be doing a jig on the kitchen table. He's won!'

Deborah turned away from the stove, compulsively winding that same strand of hair around her finger, and peered out into the darkness. We could make out Perry's thin frame as he dug violently in the mud.

'He won't talk to me,' she said helplessly. 'The better we do with Grace, the more incapacitated he becomes.'

'But everything's going to plan—*his* plan.'

She continued to gaze out at her husband. 'My leaving shocked him. He looked into the abyss.'

'He wasn't as bad as this last time I was here,' I said, trying to be matter-of-fact.

'No, he wasn't. Perhaps while he had a goal—finding me, getting me back—he continued to function. But now, even though we're all busy pretending, he's having to face the fact that I don't want to be here. And we're playing this grotesque game of Happy Families.'

Perry had stopped digging. He was resting his forehead on the handle of the spade. He looked defeated.

'I know he's suffering,' said Deborah. 'I know depression is torture, and it isn't something you can snap out of. But I have compassion fatigue, Jake. After so many years, it's hard to carry on caring. He will improve, you know. In a few weeks or months. He always does.'

I took her shoulders and turned her around, drawing her out of sight of the window. 'And you, Susie?'

She rested her head against me, just for a moment. Then she moved back to the stove and picked up a wooden spoon. 'I'm managing, Jake, really I am. I'm doing this for Matt.'

I had an image of Matt, dropping out of school, abandoning his future and stacking supermarket shelves into middle age. 'But . . . what if Matt's only doing it for Perry? And Perry's only doing it for . . . well, Perry.' I considered this idea. 'And for Grace too, I think.'

She smiled, stirring. 'It's no good, you know. Now that I've met that little girl, it is unthinkable to pack her up like a parcel and send her off into this . . .' she searched for a word, '. . . this *vicious* world. How can strangers be trusted to love and cherish her?'

I was silent. I saw her point.

'I thought I could escape,' said Deborah, and her spoon whirled crazily, round and round in its saucepan. 'But I never shall. I'm a life prisoner.'

For the next few days, Deborah rushed frenetically around the place, putting up a tree and lights and Christmas decorations. She spent hours arranging little clothes in drawers and making space for all sorts of plastic paraphernalia that I couldn't put a name to. She did her very, very best. But her eyes were blank.

The tanned and freckled girl I'd found, sitting on a piece of driftwood with her feet buried in the warm sands of Kulala Beach, that girl was gone. Susie was gone. I had forced her into exile. This imposter wore pearls, and a frown. And she'd done something awful to her hair. The bleached honey no longer tangled and twisted around her shoulder blades. It was ordered now, smooth and expensive, hanging in a lifeless curtain down her cheeks. She scurried all day, as though she was a robot and someone had wound her up with a key, and she couldn't stop.

I wanted Susie to come back. I knew she was still alive, still there, hidden under a mask of cashmere and lipstick. Sometimes I caught a glimpse of her in a musical lilt of the voice or a twist of the mouth. I wished I had left her where I found her.

Perry barely emerged from his study. When he appeared, his movements were slow; even his thought processes seemed to be dulled. He'd take a long moment to answer any remark, as if he had to drag his mind back from a land immensely far away. You could feel his lifelessness settling into your bones even when he wasn't in the same room. It was a paralysing mist that pervaded the house. I couldn't have stood it for long.

Imogen Christie paid one more visit—tying up loose ends, she said. I made myself very scarce that day; I gather Perry rose to the occasion, as ever.

I made it clear that I'd be leaving for good first thing on Thursday morning. Matt and Deborah were off to court in the afternoon, where a judge would rubber stamp the deal, and I wanted to be well away by then. There was nothing more I could do. This was not my family, not my home. I had to face the wreckage of my own life. And leave them to theirs.

Chapter Twenty-nine

Dusk. Sullen clouds raced across a tea-coloured sky. Leila hurried along the home straight, coatless, shivering, while delinquent gusts spat mouthfuls of freezing rainwater over her.

Tomorrow was the day of the court hearing. And she'd decided what to do.

She could no longer bear the inaction, the passivity. What did she have to lose? They were into injury time, she and David. If they didn't score now, they never would. So. She was going to telephone the social worker as soon as she got home. Make sure they weren't forgotten. Stir it up.

She had to negotiate an automated telephone answering system, and then wait while it played soothing music, and it all took time. In the gloomy hall, she glanced nervously at her watch. David would be home soon, and he wouldn't approve of what she was doing.

The music broke off, and she heard the familiar voice, rather cautious.

'Hello? Linda Hooper.'

'Linda.' Leila tried to sound pleasant and unthreatening, but her heart was stamping with big boots. 'It's Leila Edmunds here. You know . . .'

'Yes, Leila. I know. What can I do for you?'

Good question. Leila's resolve faltered. 'I just . . . I wanted you to know that we still want the baby. We're here, ready, waiting. Please make sure they know that. Please, *please* don't let them forget us.'

There was a defensive silence. Then Linda's voice, quite curt. 'We've done what we can, Leila. It's not our fault.'

'I know it isn't. I know that. But we seem so forgotten and sidelined and unimportant. I feel as though we've done something wrong—we're being punished in some way. *Did* we do something wrong?'

'No, it was the grandmother—'

'I want everyone to understand that we're still here, we haven't gone away. Please, Linda. Can't you do *anything*?'

There was another pause and then a heavy sigh.

'Look, Leila, I know you're very upset about what's happened, and the way it has been handled. I am too. But it isn't down to me. I have absolutely no say in this. None. It's all going to be ratified at about two o'clock tomorrow by some judge in Woodbury County Court.'

Leila's eyebrows shot up. 'Woodbury? You mean in Suffolk? Is that where they—'

Hurriedly, as though to cover her mistake, the social worker interrupted. 'Everything's already sewn up.'

'But . . . David and I, we never got a say. We never had a *voice*.'

'I'll be in touch, Leila.' With practised efficiency, Linda was ending the conversation.

'Wait! Give me the birth family's name. Just a name. Give me a phone number. Let me talk to them.'

'Out of the question.' Linda's voice had sharpened. 'Absolutely out of the question. You know that.'

'But—'

'Drop it, Leila! Drop it right now. If you want this department to work with you in the future, you'd better calm down. I'll pretend I didn't hear the suggestion you've just made.'

Leila hung up, deflated by the threat. Well, what had she expected? A miracle?

It was almost dark by now, and she hadn't turned on any lights. As she reached for the switch, she caught her breath at the sight of a shadow looming in the frosted glass of the front door. Whoever it was, he was standing close, peering in.

'Shit,' she hissed, recognising the figure. 'Not now.' Her pulse was still galloping, but her fright had turned to irritation. She looked around, irresolute, wondering whether she might get away with hiding. The shadow rattled the door.

'Let me in, Miss Dark-as-Night,' wheedled a hopeful voice.

Leila swore, squared her shoulders and unlocked the door.

'Christopher!' she mumbled unenthusiastically. *Sod off.*

'Ah, my little Leila! Just passing.' He was wearing an off-white mackintosh, like a flasher at a bus stop, and a plastic shopping bag dangled from one veined hand.

'Nobody's ever just passing Birmingham, Christopher.'

Her father-in-law bared his excellent teeth. 'Memorial service in Nottingham, tomorrow morning. Tragic golfing accident.' He slithered across the threshold, stopping just in front of her. 'I couldn't resist calling on my Queen of Sheba.' He pressed his mouth against her cheek, narrowly missing her lips. 'David out?'

Yuck. 'Yes. But I'm expecting him back any time. Cup of tea?'

'I thought something stronger.' He held up the shopping bag, and it clanked. 'I even brought the lemon.'

She eyed him with loathing; imagined her knee coming up and Christopher doubled over, wheezing in pain.

'It's cold in this doorway,' he said, hinting. 'There's a gale blowing up.'

Cursing to herself, Leila led the way into the kitchen, snapped on all the lights, and ostentatiously plugged in the kettle. Christopher slid off his coat and poured gin and tonic for them both, spilling some. He planted himself in front of her and handed her a tumbler.

'Come on. Have a proper drink with me for once, Leila. You don't want bloody tea. Tea's poison.'

She took a sip, and forced herself not to splutter. It was almost pure gin. He watched her with his faded blue eyes, smiling genially. Abruptly, she turned her back and began to scrub the draining board.

'Does Hilda know you're here?' she asked.

'Of course. I've no secrets from her.' She heard him swallow the rest of his gin, and the clink of glass as he poured himself a refill. 'Incidentally, I hear you insulted my wife at our party.' Clink, chink. Glug.

He stepped closer. 'Ooh,' he murmured, into her right ear. 'That *was* naughty.' And swinging an arm, he smacked her on the bottom.

It was not so much painful as utterly unexpected. And it was too much for Leila. After all these years, and at the wrong moment,

Christopher had finally gone too far. Whirling around she brought her palm across his cheek, hitting him with all the strength she could muster, and the shock ran up her arm and into her shoulder. The impact made a satisfying, whip-cracking sound.

'You are *repulsive*!' she yelled.

Christopher fell back against the table, mouth open in astonishment.

'Come on, now.' His eyes were reddening, but he forced a shaken laugh. 'No need to overreact.'

'You listen, Christopher.' Leila was breathing like a marathon runner; she felt powerful and in control as she took a menacing step towards him. 'And you listen carefully. This has gone on long enough. You're David's father, so I've let you get away with it until now. But you have to stop behaving like a total creep, or you will never set foot in this house again.'

'I was only . . .' He stopped, massaging his cheek.

'Yes, but you have no right.' She tapped her head. 'Think about it! To you it's a little harmless flirtation to pass the time, but it's insulting to me—and to David—and it makes you ridiculous. Where's your dignity, for God's sake?'

Christopher was still exuding hurt pride, but he was thinking. She saw a flicker in the watered-down eyes.

Behind her, the kettle boiled. Christopher pulled out a chair and sank into it.

Leila began to spoon leaves into the teapot. How eccentric, she thought, to be making a nice cup of tea when you've just clobbered your father-in-law. She watched him from under her lashes. He looked shrunken, suddenly, in his careful collar and jacket. She imagined him slowly dressing in the mornings: brushing his hair, knotting his tie, keeping up appearances; trying to look smart for another pointless day. She lowered the teapot onto the table and sat down opposite him, but he turned his head away. He's sulking, she thought. Well, let him sulk.

'I was fibbing,' he said.

'When?'

'Hilda doesn't know I'm here. Hilda knows nothing about me.'

Leila looked at him, trying to gauge his mood. He rapped the table with his knuckle. 'Her fondest wish is that I'll go quietly. She has a little leap of the heart every time a police car cruises past our drive. Hopes they've come with glad tidings.'

'Glad tidings?'

He smiled. 'Coronary, maybe. Or car crash.'

'Oh, rubbish, Christopher. Stop feeling sorry for yourself.'

'She's got her outfit planned, you know. Ever the optimist, is Hilda. Nice charcoal pillbox with a lace veil. Very tasteful. Hits just the right note.'

'I don't believe a word of it.'

'No, really. It's in her cupboard. I'm going to be buried in St Mary's churchyard.' He shuddered. 'Awful thought.'

'What, dying?'

'No, no! Rotting away in St Mary's churchyard among all those old, dead people.'

It was like meeting an actor backstage after the play, except that Christopher had not entirely lost the dissolute gleam in his eye. Leila poured tea and shoved the biscuit tin in his direction.

'Ours was a marriage of convenience,' he said, taking a HobNob. 'Not like yours.'

'I'm lucky,' said Leila.

He dipped his head. 'You are. Most people never find what you have. I hope you realise that.'

'I do,' said Leila. And as she said it, she knew that it was true.

'My son appreciates how bloody lucky he is. Never mind about the children thing. Children don't make you happy if your home's a cold place.'

Christopher reached for the milk, and she saw with a jolt of compassion that he had a tremor in his hands. How long had he had that? He poured very carefully, concentrating, placing the little jug back on the table with a small nod of triumph.

'There's a wonderful woman in Hong Kong,' he began. He stopped, mouth slightly open, thinking. 'She was always pleased to see me.'

'I'm sure lots of women—'

'No, Leila. Just the one.' He sighed. 'Just the one. A widow. She isn't beautiful like you are, but she is the love of my life.' He used the words entirely without irony. 'For ten years, Kimmy gave me happiness. Then they made me take a shore job and I couldn't see her any more.'

'Is she still . . . ?'

'Alive? Of course. Retired from her job at the university, but still going strong. We write. Email is a wonderful invention. We talked about my going to live there, but it isn't possible. Immigration, money . . . I'm too old to be an illegal alien. And Kimmy has grandchildren. She can't leave her home.'

Leila was lost for words. She imagined her father-in-law—younger, happier—hailing a taxi at the harbour gates, buying flowers from a stall, racing up the stairs of an apartment block. 'Couldn't you visit?' she suggested.

Christopher fiddled uneasily with his mug, eyeing her from under tangled brows.

'Oh, well . . . you know. I'm a doddery fool by now. I *do* own a mirror, you know.'

'But she must have grown older too.'

'Repulsive, you said. That was what you said, wasn't it? Kimmy sent me a photograph a while ago.' He touched his breast pocket. 'At the beach, with her grandchildren. She hasn't changed. Grey, of course. She doesn't dye her hair, never has. Grey suits her.'

He was reaching into the pocket when the front door rattled and a gust of damp air swirled into the room. Christopher dropped his hand and lurched to his feet as David appeared in the kitchen doorway, looking windblown.

'Dad!' David shrugged out of his coat. 'I saw your car.'

'I've been making a nuisance of myself,' said Christopher.

David's eyes narrowed.

'He has to be in Nottingham tomorrow,' said Leila quickly. 'Funeral. So he's staying the night.'

'Am I?' asked Christopher, bowing to her with a hint of his old flir-tatiousness. 'I am. Thank you.'

*

'*Hong Kong*,' breathed Leila, with a giggle of intrigue. She and David were huddled at the table, late that same evening. Their voices were muffled by the shriek and shudder of the gale.

'Doesn't surprise me,' said David, throwing a furtive glance at the door. Christopher was upstairs in the bathroom, but David dropped his voice still further. 'He never seemed to take much shore leave, especially towards the end. Must have been stopping off there instead.'

'D'you think Hilda knows?'

'I'd be astonished if she doesn't. She's pretty sharp. Poor Mum.'

Christopher's footsteps creaked down the stairs and into the sitting room where they'd made up the sofa bed. David shook his head in guilty admiration. 'How hard did you hit him?'

But Leila suddenly seemed oblivious, Christopher forgotten. She jerked upright, head tilted as if straining to catch a distant sound.

'Woodbury,' she murmured intently. '*Woodbury*.'

'Erm.' David scratched his ear, puzzled. 'What?'

Leila listened, alert, gazing into the distance as a furious gust flung itself against the window, beating its fists on the glass. Then, briskly, she pushed back her chair. 'There'll be trees down tonight. Power cables.'

'Somewhere in East Anglia, isn't it, Woodbury?'

'Forget it.' Leila leaned down and kissed him. 'I'm turning in.'

'I'll be right up,' said David. 'Five minutes. Just want to catch the news.'

At the door Leila turned, casually, as though a rather inconsequential thought had just struck her.

'Um, will you be needing the car tomorrow?'

Chapter Thirty

I spent much of Wednesday packing up the truck, ready to beat rush hour the next morning. I didn't see Perry at all during the day, but Matt stopped to give me a hand on his way in from school. That cheerful weatherman had known his stuff, when he predicted mayhem. A hell of a wind had got up. The boughs of the trees in the lane were doing a giant Mexican wave. I could hear them creaking and groaning, and bits of twigs and leaves started whizzing about. If you leaned forward with your arms spread out, the wind actually held you upright. Both of us were tottering around like drunken sailors, and I had to shout to make Matt hear me.

Just before dark everything took on this weird, nicotine-stained glow, as though we were wearing yellow-tinted goggles. The world seemed unnaturally bright and distorted. Then someone turned the lights out altogether and we felt the first spots of rain. I was afraid a tile might fly off the roof and plant us, so I parked the truck in a sheltered corner behind the garage and we staggered into the house. Between us we managed to force the front door shut, but the wind still wailed eerily underneath it like a desolate banshee.

Matt hung around in the hall next to Deborah's chocolate box Christmas tree, his schoolbag on his back. He looked like a man with a lot on his mind.

'So.' I cheerfully rubbed my hands, ignoring the banshee. 'You all ready for the big day tomorrow?'

He scowled. 'You could stay, you know.'

'No, mate. I value my sleep. Rugrats and sleep don't go.'

'Grace won't come here *tomorrow*! There'll be all sorts of pissing about first.'

'All the same. I've bludged off you people long enough.'

He swore, and shoved his hands into his pockets.

'You're going to keep texting me?' I asked, in my new, uncle's voice. He just grunted, so I tried again. 'Go to school today?'

He nodded sourly, told me I was as bad as his frigging mother, and trudged off upstairs. I felt oddly traitorous, because I was leaving and he couldn't.

Wandering into the sitting room, I found Deborah perched at her desk. It was one of those antique jobs, the desk, with a leaf that folded down. From the look on her face, I could tell she was trying to write to Rod. I didn't ask; instead I nipped into the kitchen, grabbed a bottle of Perry's Isle of Jura, and poured us both a hefty tipple. I reckoned it was called for on such a filthy, drowned-rat night. Our last night.

Deborah looked up and smiled as I balanced the glass beside her letter. 'Thanks, Jake.' She looked awful this evening, pinched and bruised.

I gave her shoulder a squeeze. 'I haven't seen Perry,' I said, unfolding a newspaper and plonking myself down in my favourite armchair by the fire. 'He okay?'

'Plastered already,' she said. 'No one else would be able to tell, but I can. I know him all too well.'

She returned to her letter, and we sat companionably for a long time. The gale worked itself up into a frenzy outside, screaming and sighing down the chimney, hurling handfuls of rain against the old windows. I listened to the scratching of the pen, and the gentle spitting of the fire, and tried not to wish that this was all mine.

It must have been well after six when I heard Perry's study door swing open and his measured footsteps in the hall. A moment later, he was striding into the room with a face like a death mask. I don't think he even saw me.

'I can't go on like this,' he said. His voice was clipped and flat.

Deborah shut her writing pad, double quick, and rested a hand over it while her husband crossed the room to stand behind her. I could see the silver threads in his hair, gleaming in the soft light of the standard lamp beside the desk.

She twisted around to face him. 'I don't know why you're so miserable, Perry,' she trilled brightly. 'We've won.'

He towered over her. 'Yes. But you didn't *want* to win, did you, Deborah? In fact, you don't want to be here at all.'

She blinked. Perry wasn't sticking to their script.

'Of *course* I want to be here!' She laughed, shakily.

Perry didn't move a muscle. 'Really? Who are you writing to?'

She picked up the pad and slung it into a drawer. 'My aunt,' she snapped, and slammed the drawer shut.

He still didn't move, just gazed at her with his panther's eyes. I'd have sworn he could see right through her face and into her mind. I'm sure he knew he'd lost her. She might live with him and care for his granddaughter, but he'd lost her nonetheless. I began to stand up, intending to sneak out, but something about Perry stopped me. I didn't like to leave her alone with him. In his present state, I thought him capable of anything.

'Shall we both give up lying for Lent?' he said.

She lifted a shoulder. 'It's not Lent. In any case, why change the habits of a lifetime?'

Perry stretched out both his hands, and for one awful second I thought he was reaching for her neck. I tensed, ready to spring up. I'd never seen him like this. He looked to be in physical pain, crabbed and angular.

'Please,' he croaked, as though begging for morphine. He dropped his hands, sinking onto a stool. 'I need reality. My feet don't touch the bottom of the lies any more. I'm drowning in them.'

A great mallet of wind pounded against the window, and the old house shook.

Perry shook, too. 'For pity's sake, Deborah. Help me! Let me hear some truth!'

His despair seemed to light some flame of anger in her. Perhaps his disintegration infuriated her, or perhaps his invitation to tell the truth was irresistible. I saw a hardening around her mouth.

'The truth hurts, Perry.' She folded her arms, raised her eyebrows. 'Okay. *Truth*. Where shall we begin? How about the unhappy fact that you have used our grandchild as a pawn?'

He ran one hand through his hair. 'No. *No* . . . I knew you'd want to save her.'

'Precisely!' yelled Deborah. 'My point exactly. I had absolutely no choice, did I? You said *fetch* and sent faithful Jake haring off to find me. Jake, your gundog. And here I am. You've got what you wanted, and I hope it makes you happy.'

'But *you* aren't happy.'

'Oh, I see. It's not enough for you to keep me rotting in this house. I have to *enjoy* it as well!' She began to laugh. It was crazy. 'Well, since you've asked for the truth, let me assure you that I don't enjoy it. It's like being walled up, actually.' She grabbed her glass and downed it in one. 'It's like being buried alive. You buried me alongside you when I was twenty years old.'

'No,' he whispered. 'No, Deborah.'

'And now you're going to bury Matt too. You're using a baby to trap him just as you did me. We'll be prisoners here, shut in with you until we've no life left to live.'

'Matt? . . . No.'

'And here's another thing that's true.' Deborah was letting loose half a lifetime of regret. 'I don't think you even like me very much, Perry Harrison. I think you *need* me, but you don't *like* me, do you? In fact, I think you find me utterly contemptible. After all, I'm nothing like your beloved Victoria.'

His eyes blazed with intensity. 'I *adore* you!'

'Oh, shut up.' She slammed down the glass. 'Actually I wonder, my darling. Did you really like Victoria, or was *she* a crutch as well?'

Perry sat for a moment, looking as though she'd just hit him squarely between the eyes with a carefully aimed slingshot. Then he stood up and walked out. I think he might have seen me as he passed, but he didn't show it. The door slammed shut behind him.

Deborah let out a long breath. She looked as though she might cry.

'I should *not* have said that.'

'No,' I agreed, folding the newspaper with a disapproving snap. 'You shouldn't. That last bit was well below the belt.'

'I've always been jealous of that woman. Always.'

I probably looked as though she'd used the slingshot on me too. I mean, how could Deborah possibly be jealous of Perry's first wife? When she next spoke, her voice was a little wobbly: the row had shaken her up.

'You haven't got a clue, have you, Jake?'

'Clueless,' I admitted, laying down my paper. 'Sorry.'

'All my married life she's been looking over my shoulder. Lucy's fairytale mother. Perry's perfect wife, who broke his heart.' She blinked, wiping her eyes on the heel of her hand. 'You can't fall hopelessly in love, at the age of seventeen, with someone fascinating and cultured and powerful, bear his son, raise children with him, share two decades of experiences, live with him through mental illness, be comforted by him when your parents die, and have *no* feelings for him.'

'But you left him, Debs.'

She stood up impatiently. 'Yes, I left him. He makes me terribly unhappy. But we go back a very long way together—can't you see that? We go back almost into my childhood, and he's an incredible man. I still admire him. I still . . .'

She walked to the door and pulled it open. A wild draught burst joyously past her and danced among the flames in the grate.

'No matter,' she said. 'This time tomorrow, we'll have a baby in the family.'

This time tomorrow, I thought, I'll be gone.

We had a surprisingly good evening, in the end.

Come suppertime, I ventured up to Matt's den and persuaded him to join us. Then I knocked on Perry's study door and he came out too. Perry and Deborah seemed a bit wooden at first, and they weren't looking at each other. I supposed that almighty ding-dong was still on their minds, but they were both too well-mannered to carry on slinging insults with me around. Matt stuck to Pepsi but Perry, Deborah and I got quietly canned, making serious inroads into the Hawke's Bay wine while the wolves howled outside.

We'd all brightened up by the third bottle.

Perry—who seemed to be making a mammoth effort—regaled us with stories of army cock-ups, and I told them about the time I ran with the bulls in Pamplona and very nearly got mashed. I'd been rescued by a Spanish policeman who dragged me over a fence by my hair. We laughed with the slightly hysterical, guilty jollity you get after a funeral. Even Perry laughed.

'Well,' I burbled eventually, holding up my glass and squinting at the three of them. 'Here's to you all, and thanks for your hospitality.'

'And here's to your death-defying expedition, you lucky bastard!' cried Perry, and tossed his back in one go.

'And to the future Mrs Jake, and all the little Jakes!' added Deborah, giggling wildly. 'Bring 'em to meet us.'

Matt ran out of steam and lurched off to bed first, and Deborah soon followed him. After that, Perry stopped laughing. He was sitting very upright, staring at nothing with his bottomless black eyes.

'So, Perry.' I carried our plates to the dishwasher. 'You did it. You've put your family back together.'

'Yes, I have, haven't I?' He opened a bottle of Scotch with the exaggerated concentration of the truly drunk person. I'd never seen him lose control like this before. Not really. As a rule, alcohol just made him more and more dignified.

'Marvellous,' he murmured to himself. 'Just … bloody … marvellous. What a bloody triumph. How proud I must be.' He poured us both half a glass of the stuff, spilling a fair bit onto the table.

I'd never get up the stairs if that lot hit my stomach; I just didn't have his capacity. I managed to put back a thimbleful, and then I smuggled my glass over to the sink and tipped the rest down the drain. What a waste.

'Going to court tomorrow, Perry?'

For a couple of seconds he looked right through me, as though there was something fascinating on the kitchen wall behind my head. Perhaps he was gazing into his crystal ball. Then I saw the flash of his rare smile.

'I doubt it, Jake. I very much doubt it.'

I said goodnight soon after that and headed upstairs, leaving Perry sitting straight-backed in his usual place at the kitchen table.

I made it to the landing without falling over. The wind had grown stronger if anything, and the banshee moaned in anguish around the front door. Matt's light was out, and the corridor beyond was in blackness. But a trickle of moonlight, seeping through a window, dipped the old boards of the landing in luminous paint.

I was just feeling my way towards my room when a floorboard creaked behind me. I turned towards the sound, straining my eyes. 'That you, Matt?'

It wasn't Matt.

I glimpsed her for a second as she moved from moonlight to shadow, her nightdress shimmering like a stream of mercury, and then she was beside me. She took my hands, interlaced her fingers with mine, and I felt the touch of her mouth on my cheek.

I heard the clear, warm voice over the banshee's lament. 'I wanted to say goodbye, Jake. I wanted to say thank you. You've been such a friend.'

Well, what could I do? What would anyone do, in the dark and the wailing wind? I couldn't run any more. The storm had caught up with me. Knocked me over. She was the only one I'd ever wanted, you see. I'll never understand her. I know that. But I'll never forget her either.

She drifted, slender and alive under my hands, and the world shrank until there was only her. I breathed in her warmth, and I kissed her. I felt as though my whole useless, aimless life was given validity in that moment, that single breath of time in the violence of the night. Perhaps I should have told her. She wouldn't have minded.

Then she slipped away, and I let her go. I had to. She wasn't mine. You can see that, surely? She wasn't mine, and she never would be.

I lay awake for too long, reliving it all in my mind, over and over again. Wondering how I'd let myself get hit so hard. I was at a loss. I had lost. I *was* lost. It was a new experience for me.

I finally managed to doze off, swirling dazedly down the whirlpool of sleep. I suppose it was the booze. Sometime in the night an owl screeched in Coptree Woods, and I remember opening my eyes for a few moments. The moon hung in a patch of clear sky, shining full onto my face. Through the window I could see the yew, stooped like a hunchback in the hedge. The world seemed breathless; the lost soul at the front door had fallen asleep, exhausted by her agony, and the trees were still. I closed my eyes, drifting, wishing like hell I hadn't let her go.

And Sala had been in the pig bin again.

I can see the mess as soon as I get off the school bus. Rotting scraps are scattered right across the yard.

He said he'd shoot her the next time she did it. I was scared, so I found a big rock and put it on the lid to stop her getting in. I check it every morning, make sure it's still holding down the lid, but today she's managed to tip the whole bin over and the rubbish is everywhere.

She's patiently waiting for me, running around in circles by the road gate. She meets my bus every day. It's the only good thing about coming home. I run from the bus and try to clean up the mess before he sees it, frantically shovelling the maggoty scraps back into the bin with my bare hands. Quick, quick. Jesse laughs at me, but he tries to help too.

Sala knows she's in trouble, but she doesn't care. She trots importantly off down to the kennels to boss the quad dogs about.

Oh, no. Oh no. I can hear the quad bike roaring up the paddock and through the gate. Dad sees the mess straight away and yells, 'Fucking filthy bitch.' He's in a rage, his face has twisted like it does, and he storms into the house. Jesse has the sense to disappear.

Dad's coming out now, heading for the kennels, and he's got his shotgun. He's walking jerkily, furiously, with his face pushed forwards, shoving cartridges into the breech. There are veins on his neck, like snakes. I'm hanging onto his arm, trying to pull him back, but I just get dragged along. Then he gets sick of me hanging onto him, so he jerks the butt of his gun into my face, and it really hurts. I have to let go because my nose is bleeding.

'She's only two, Dad,' I say, and I'm crying. 'She's only two, just a baby. She'll grow out of it soon. Give her one more chance.'

Sala's pottering about down there, chatting with the others, her stumpy tail wagging. He gives her a terrible kick in her stomach with his big boot and sends her flying almost under the kennels. She's yelping. She's wriggling in the dust, trying to get up. I grab at his arm again, but he throws me off and takes aim, and I'm holding onto his leg, screaming at him to stop. No, Dad, no, please.

Don't.

The shot, when it came, exploded into my brain with horrifying force. I was sitting bolt upright, ready to run for it, before I was fully awake. I felt sure it had blown my head away, so close and violent was the sound.

My heart was doing a crazy can-can under my ribs. Gasping, I stared wildly around me. Nothing moved. The white walls gleamed silently in the moonlight.

Gradually, as my breathing slowed, I subsided under the duvet. 'Bloody Perry,' I muttered, sinking my head into the pillow and closing my eyes. 'Lunatic. Shooting bloody rabbits at this time of night.'

I lay there for perhaps twenty seconds as the information filtered into my brain. Then my eyes snapped open, and I was out of bed and falling down the stairs.

Deborah. Please, no. Deborah had said goodbye.

The garden door stood wide open. Sprinting across the kitchen, I came to an abrupt halt as I reached it. For an endless moment I balanced on the step, peering out at the peace of the moonlit garden. Each blade of grass had its own shadow, and the hunchbacked yew crouched menacingly, silhouetted black against the stars. I didn't want to go out there. I didn't want to see what she'd done to herself.

I heard light, rapid footsteps on the stairs, and miraculously Deborah appeared in the kitchen. She was still in her nightdress, and her eyes looked white with fear. I sagged against the doorway. I couldn't get my breath.

'Is there an outside light?' I gasped, trying to take control of myself.

Wordlessly, she pressed a switch beside the larder door, and half of the garden was brilliantly floodlit. I stepped out, but she pushed past me. She hesitated by the picket fence, her head turning, looking around her. Then she gave a cry and threw herself onto the ground in the black shadow of the yew. I could see the silver glimmer of her like water in the darkness, and then, as I moved closer, I made out the terrible shape beside her.

I dropped down on one knee and put a hand on her shoulder, but she didn't seem aware of me at all. She was whimpering, frantic, and she had both her hands on what was left of his face. I had to force myself to look. Even in the strange black and white light, I could see that Perry had made a hell of a mess of himself.

Surprising, really: such an organised, tidy person. Perhaps this was his last great manipulation. I don't think there was anything left of the back of his head, and spread out behind him, gleaming sickeningly, were scattered substances that I'd prefer not to think about. They stretched all the way to the hedge. There was a smell too. I suppose forensic pathologists and serial murderers get used to that smell, but it still haunts me now.

I left Deborah in the moonlight with her husband of almost eighteen years, and went inside to make the phone call. When I was a kid I'd always wondered what happens when you dial emergency. But now I wished I never had to find out. I just felt sad. And I felt, somehow, that Perry should be left to lie in his garden.

The operator was efficient and calm, and she knew what to do. After I'd hung up, I grabbed some clothes from upstairs, and a blanket for Deborah, and went to be near her while we waited. She wasn't whimpering any more. She knelt beside him, stroking his chest and quietly talking to him. I draped the blanket over her shoulders and sank onto the wet grass nearby.

High above the woods I could see the lights of a jet, moving silently across a giant backdrop of stars. I remember thinking how odd it was. Just up there were pilots, and stewardesses in tight skirts, and people in complimentary bed socks watching the in-flight movie.

I was the last to see Perry alive. I had been his last hope. But I'd tipped his whisky down the sink and left him sitting all alone. I'd even kissed his wife, in the shadows. Shouldn't have done that. I wanted to put back the clock.

The ambulance arrived first, its lights flashing quietly in the grey calm of dawn.

'Dear God,' Deborah said when she saw it, and she laughed. It was disturbing, that laugh. She had blood on her face and hands. 'They've sent you an ambulance. Can they put you back together again, Humpty Dumpty, my love?'

I went to meet them, and they followed me round to the back garden in their uniforms, looking grave. They'd had trouble getting up the lane, they said, because of fallen branches.

As we approached, Deborah became agitated. 'Don't move him,' she hissed, guarding that horrible sight with her slender body. She glanced at me and then stood up resolutely, and the blanket fell off her shoulders. 'Jake. Help me. We must get Matt. Don't let them touch him while I get Matt. Matt must say goodbye.'

I looked at her and imagined young Matt, happy in the deep sleep of the teenager. 'Er . . . Deborah? D'you think he should see—' I stopped, gesturing at the appalling butchery. 'Shouldn't we at least cover him up?'

As I spoke, Matt appeared at the kitchen door in boxer shorts and a jersey. He looked wildly around: at me, and the uniformed men, and his mother in her silvery silk nightie, a dark smear across her face. Then he spotted his father, and he began to run. I tried to stop him, but he just put out an arm to shove me aside as though he was heading for a try. He thudded to a halt beside Deborah, crouched over Perry for a second, and then threw himself sideways. I thought he was choking. His eyes were stretched wide open as though in terror, as though he couldn't breathe. I took a step towards my young friend, but Deborah put her arms around him, and I heard him sobbing like a tiny child.

I walked away a little. I looked over the hedge and across the fields. The sky looked huge, and bruised, beaten to a pulp by the storm. And the sun was coming up over Coptree Woods.

Chapter Thirty-one

The sun was rising behind the tower blocks at Priory Park Farm. The sky hung suspended above the city landscape, soaked in a wild, reckless orange, as though a bloody battle was still raging among the clouds.

Leila lay in bed for a time, watching the sky and gathering her courage, until the early morning traffic began to rattle the windows. She wanted desperately to tell David what she planned to do, but he'd be horrified. He liked to play with a straight bat, did David. He'd never countenance this.

I'll tell him tonight, she decided, *when it's all over, one way or the other. He can't talk me out of it once it's all over.*

She slid out of bed, took a hurried shower—the hot water was a bossy friend, urging her to hurry—and dressed in the clothes she'd chosen the night before: a skirt, and boots, and the jade velvet jacket she'd bought for David's ordination.

David was up; in his study, presumably. She lingered, straightening her things and making the bed. She felt a compulsive need to be sure that everything was tidy before she left, as though she might never be back.

She was in the kitchen and checking her route by the time David clumped down the stairs. He was clipping up his dog collar.

''Morning,' she called, too brightly, covertly dropping the road atlas next to her faithful old handbag. 'Your dad's still dead to the world. Tea?'

He nodded sombrely, hovering beside her. 'I'll make sure I'm in this afternoon,' he said. 'I don't want you to come home to an empty house.

Actually, I don't want to be alone myself. Knowing they're making the order . . . knowing it's all over.'

'Oh, no.' She screwed up her eyes as if berating herself. 'That's why I need the car. We've got, um, a staff meeting after work, might need to give someone a lift home afterwards.' The lie hurt: it stuck in her throat. 'I'm afraid I'll be a bit late.'

'Yes. Yes. Of course. Best to keep busy.' David slumped into a chair.

She longed to tell him. She felt so lonely in her determination. Instead she asked, 'What did you pray for this morning?'

He chuckled self-consciously. 'Um . . . Lord, I don't want to sound pushy, but if a miracle can happen so that we may have this child, please let it happen, but not if you think she'll be better off with her own family, obviously, goes without saying, but please bear in mind that we will really love her, and we will cherish her, but if you have other work for us then you have only to show us the way, but on the other hand—'

'Stop, *stop*! I get the picture. You're so bloody *good*. Why couldn't you just cash in some of your heavenly credit and insist that the baby be delivered to us, immediately, by Securicor? You've given your life to the Lord. You'd think he'd do a little thing like that for you.'

David shrugged, looking sheepish. Leila lifted down a box of cereal and two bowls.

'D'you want anything to eat?'

He shook his head.

'Me neither.' She sighed, sliding the bowls back into the cupboard. 'You'd better get Christopher up soon, if he's going to make his funeral.'

David nodded, but she doubted whether he'd heard her. His eyes were bloodshot and puffy, as though he'd had no sleep. Unheard of, for him.

'We just have to get through one more day,' he said quietly. 'After this is over we can move on. We *will* move on, won't we, and make use of our lives?'

Leila crouched beside his chair, touching his cheek. 'Yes, we will.'

'Together?'

'Together.'

David ran a hand across his face, through his hair. 'There's an advertisement in the *Church Times* for a job. It's at a theological college in the Philippines.'

'Crikey.'

He tried to smile. 'If we're to be childless, we'll be free to do these extraordinary things.'

'Babies can travel in planes, David.'

'I know. I know. But there's all the hassle with inoculations and malaria and education. Anyway, I really think we should talk about this one. I've had a look on the website. I think you'll love it.'

'No harvest supper? No committees? No telephone?'

'I'm sure they have telephones.'

She kissed him. 'It sounds very tempting,' she said, and meant it. 'Whatever happens, we'll cope.'

She held her lips on his face for a moment, breathing, taking strength from the familiar warmth of him. It almost felt as though it was for the last time.

Finally, she straightened and stood up. She must do this, come what may. She would never forgive herself if she didn't make this final effort.

'I've got the mobile, if you need me.'

'Careful!' He stood up too. 'I've set it to play "Jingle Bells". Couldn't resist. It won't sound very professional if it goes off in your meeting.'

'We could do with a bit of light relief.'

In the kitchen doorway she hesitated and then turned back.

'David.' Anxiety was writhing in her stomach. 'I shouldn't go. But I have to.'

'No! I wish you'd stay here with me.' He smiled, pushing her towards the front door. 'But I've got a mountain of things to do, and so have you.'

'It'll all be over by tonight,' she said.

Chapter Thirty-two

Perry had done all the washing up, stacked everything with fanatical precision, and dropped his last empty bottle into the recycling. And he'd left a note, in his sharp handwriting. It was written in black ink on a sheet of watermarked paper, folded into an envelope and addressed to *Deborah, Matthew and Lucy.* He'd positioned the envelope exactly in the middle of the kitchen table where it still lay, patiently waiting.

Deborah stood barefoot on the cold kitchen tiles while the people in uniforms swarmed around her like wasps at a picnic. She stared at the envelope. Eventually she opened it, read the note, and handed it to me without a word.

> *Now we are ALL free.*
> *For God's sake, cremate me and scatter the ashes in a raging gale.*
> *With so very much love, and sincere thanks for all that you have given me.*
> *Perry/Dad*

I didn't like to see her in her silky nightie, surrounded by all those uniforms. It wasn't right. There were goose bumps on her arms. So I fetched one of the jerseys Mum had knitted for me, and pulled it over her head. It hung down to her knees.

'I'll be comforted by your mother's knitting, then,' she murmured vaguely, and moved to stand with folded arms at the window, watching as the wasps ruined Perry's lawn. They turned blind eyes towards Matt's horticulture in the greenhouse, though, and that was a good thing because he was running quite an impressive operation out there.

I fielded the swarm as best I could. Was it me who had found Mr Harrison? Yes, it was. Could I describe the events of the evening? Er, yes, I could, with one or two small omissions. They didn't seem to suspect what the press call *foul play*, though; they were just following procedure.

Deborah asked me to telephone Lucy. I couldn't refuse.

I shut myself in Perry's study and dialled the number for Stanton's. Was Lucy Harrison available? Yes, she was indeed! She was right here, at her desk. There was a pause, and then a click as I was put through.

'Jake Kelly, by my troth! You're up early.' Lucy was in a good mood, brisk and cheerful. She thought her world was still intact. And I had to tell her that it wasn't. It wasn't at all, and perhaps it never would be.

'No,' she whispered. '*No.*'

And then I had to tell her where it happened, and how.

'Dad,' she breathed. And there was a long, long silence. I imagined her hunched over the desk, turning her head away, trying not to let the others see.

'Lucy . . .' I said, but I had nothing to offer her. There was no comfort I could give.

When she next spoke her voice was fractured, barely controlled. 'Thank you, Jake.' A pause for breath. 'Good of you to—'

She couldn't finish the sentence. And I was cut off.

In the kitchen, Matt was reading the note. He sat and looked at it for a long time. Then he folded it carefully and laid it back on the table. He glanced at me, heaved himself up and left the room without speaking. I could feel the vibrations of his footsteps on the stairs.

Deborah hadn't moved from the window where she was still looking out at the yew tree. There was a huge amount of activity out there. The wasps had even put up a little tent.

'He's ceasing to be Perry,' she said. 'Can you feel that, Jake? Slowly, steadily, he's becoming something that isn't Perry. Soon he'll be just a crumpled shape in the mud.'

Eventually they took him away, and that's how he left the place for the first time in years.

When Matt reappeared, much later, he'd showered and was wearing a smart grey suit. He'd put on a tie, and shiny black shoes, and brushed his wet hair. He crossed the kitchen in three strides and stopped in front of Deborah. She turned her head, but it seemed difficult for her to focus on him.

'Get dressed, Mum,' he said, and then he reached out and touched her face. I'd never seen him do anything like that before.

Finally, she seemed to recognise him.

'Ah,' she said. 'My handsome son. My brave, handsome son.' She fingered his lapel. 'In your Sunday suit from when you were at school.'

'You have to get dressed, Mum,' he insisted, gently.

She looked up at him and past him, as though she was dreaming. 'Why?' she asked. 'Why ever would I do that?'

'We're due in court at two o'clock,' he said. 'I need you to come with me. We've got to get this done before they find out what's happened.'

She looked at him for another ten seconds, and you could see the comprehension seeping into her brain. Then she nodded. 'We've still got our baby to think about, haven't we, Matt? Well done. All right.'

The last of the swarm was ready to leave by then, taking Perry's note and his gun and a lot of little plastic bags containing bits of him, and promising to be back for formal statements the following day. I saw them out and then washed and dressed. I felt as though I had been awake all my life.

I paused on my way back downstairs. Deborah's bedroom door was half open. I hesitated and then knocked.

'Debs,' I called. 'Are you all right?' Well, what a bloody meaningless question.

'Come in.' She opened the door wider. 'Yes, do come in, Jake. I'm almost ready.' She was fully dressed, blow-drying her hair.

'Do you know,' she clicked off the hairdryer and began to hunt around on her dressing table, 'I've just been watching Perry's blood flowing away down the drain. It must have been splattered all over me.'

It was, too.

'It's a very odd thing,' she said, pulling her hair into a ponytail. 'I don't feel as if any of this is happening. My mind has almost completely shut down.' She laughed unconvincingly, lowering herself onto a stool in front of the dressing table. 'It had to. How else could it function, when I'm being choked by Perry's despair?'

'Debs . . .' I took a step towards her.

'Despair. I can feel it, Jake. I can feel it. Like a cloak of icy water.'

She began to stroke makeup onto her face, gazing into the mirror, and I watched her reflection. Women have a particular expression that they use when they're slapping on the potions. At least, the ones I've known do. It's a sort of pout, and they flutter their eyelashes at themselves. But Deborah didn't have that look at all, not today.

'I was asleep when he did it, Jake. I swear I was.'

'I know that,' I said, misunderstanding. 'I was the first one downstairs, remember? I *know* you were asleep when he did it.'

'I was dreaming about Rod, God forgive me. But I have a vivid memory of Perry doing it, all the same. As though I was there. I can see him, right now.' She stretched one hand towards her own image in the mirror. 'Yes. Yes. I can see him quite clearly, standing under the yew tree, getting . . . getting ready. He's forcing the cold metal into his mouth, and he's staring straight at me. He has such desperate eyes.'

I was silent. She picked up a tiny bottle of scent and rubbed a drop onto each wrist. I could smell the citrus, and the cloves.

'There.' She met my gaze in the mirror. 'I don't look like a widow. I don't even smell like a widow.' She stood up. Turned around. 'But I feel like one, all the same . . . Will you drive us? Of course you will. Loyal, dependable Jake.'

'Are you sure you want to do this?' I couldn't believe she and Matt planned to swan off to court and pretend everything was fine. Looking back now, I reckon they were anaesthetised by shock. 'Why not postpone the whole thing? This is ludicrous.'

'And have them find out what's happened? I don't think so.' She slid into a pair of shoes, balancing with polished fingers on the baby's cot. 'No. Our adoring public is expecting us, and the show has to go on.'

And what a show it turned out to be.

Chapter Thirty-three

Today, road works were more than an inconvenience. They were the end of everything.

Leila had driven without stopping for hours. Getting out of Birmingham had taken far longer than she expected, and then there had been one nasty snarl-up after another. Her ears felt muffled, her mind roaring in sympathy with the constant drone of the engine. An empty bottle of water lay on the floor. She'd drunk the last drops two hours ago, but hadn't dared to stop for more. She was fast running out of time.

The clock on the Renault's dashboard was her implacable enemy. She averted her face, afraid to catch its eye. She'd jammed the map between the steering wheel and her lap. The next junction was to be her exit for Woodbury. Its off ramp beckoned, clear and smooth, just yards away; she could actually read the tantalising signs. Yet here she sat, hopelessly trapped in a long line of gently revving engines, forced to stare at the soot-blackened rear of the lorry in front. It sported an irritatingly jolly picture of a family eating breakfast, with the legend *Paddy's Poptarts* bouncing across their heads.

She would never, ever eat one of Paddy's poptarts, as long as she lived.

She squirmed in frustration, hands dancing a wild jig on the steering wheel. Among the traffic cones stood a group of men in orange jackets, all watching one steamroller. She'd begun to fantasise about leaping out of the car, charging down the road and grabbing one of them by the throat.

'Please,' she prayed, squeezing her eyes shut. 'Please help me. I'm sorry I said those things about you. Please, please, *please*.' When she opened her eyes, she saw that the needle on the fuel gauge had begun to twitch maliciously, hovering over the *E*.

From her bag came the electronic trill of 'Jingle Bells'. She reached out, fumbling distractedly as the tune grew more strident and insistent. Finally her fingers closed around the phone's curved edges. At the same instant the ringing stopped, as if throttled, in mid jingle. She squinted at the missed call message, twisted her mouth regretfully, and then turned the phone off and rammed it back into her bag. She didn't want to speak to David now. Any more lies and she'd choke.

Paddy's Poptarts lurched into gear and ponderously thundered forward. Leila let out her clutch and crawled close behind it, as if trying to hide behind its bulk. They inched past the workmen and their rows of plastic cones. One of the orange jackets—the one holding the stop sign—actually waved to her, and she wrestled with the desire to wind down her window and scream obscenities.

Suddenly, without ceremony, they were through. Hundreds of drivers surged away, accelerating joyfully like fish released after an angling competition. Leila headed for her exit and darted down it. Swinging onto a roundabout, she forced herself to glance at the clock just as a vicious red light began to flicker on the fuel gauge.

Oh, God. Why didn't I leave more time?

She held the map against the wheel, scanning it while keeping one eye on the road. But nothing looked as it should. Maybe the bloody map was out of date. Maybe—heaven forbid—this was actually the wrong town.

She passed a petrol station, but she didn't stop. Instead she turned into what proved to be an industrial estate, where warehouses stretched away into a grey horizon. A person could drive around and around this hinterland forever and never see a real human being nor a blade of grass. Perhaps this was hell. Perhaps she would never escape.

The red light on the fuel gauge was unrelenting now. This was a nightmare. It had to be.

*

The Harrisons' solicitor, Stuart Forsyth, was waiting for us outside the courtroom. It was in a brand-new building, all pale wood and fittings in a corporate blue. Forsyth exclaimed heartily when he saw us, and then advanced on Deborah and pummelled her hand, looking extremely pleased with himself as though it was he personally who had charmed Big Brother.

Once she'd managed to get her hand free, Deborah introduced me as a family friend. Forsyth gave me a swift once-over, obviously weighing up whether I was shagging her or not. He was about fifty, with a particularly spivvy line in braces and an unnecessary amount of grey hair like a clump of tussock grass sitting on top of his head. I bet he had a comb in his back pocket. And he fancied Deborah, there was no doubt about it. *Join the bloody queue*, I muttered under my breath. *You've got no hope, mate. None.*

'No Perry?' he boomed amiably, and didn't wait for a reply. 'Never to worry.'

At the mention of his father, Matt stiffened and turned away. It went right over Forsyth's head, though. He was much more interested in impressing Deborah. I had the impression he wasn't expecting her other half to turn up, but I bet his silly hairdo would have stood on end if he'd known where Perry actually was at that moment.

'Excellent.' He rubbed his palms together. 'Follow me into a conference room. I've already bagged one.'

I parked myself on a row of blue seats in the concourse, but Deborah and Matt both emphatically jerked their heads at me, so I stood up again and resignedly trotted along behind.

'Don't tell him about Perry,' hissed Deborah out of the corner of her mouth. 'What he doesn't know, he won't feel duty bound to pass on. He'll find out soon enough, but by then . . .'

We followed Stuart the Spiv into a dim little room with a tinted-glass wall. It still smelled of new carpet, but someone had already broken a chair and scribbled on the table, *Judge Cartwright fucks horses*. Through the smoky glass I could see people gathering. A gang of three—two men and a woman, all in dark suits—were huddled together just outside. More lawyers, no doubt. I couldn't see into any of the other conference rooms because of the funny glass, but I did spot Imogen Christie in the distance.

Forsyth wanted everything to be done properly. He insisted on explaining at great length all the ramifications of the deal they'd struck. In plain English, it meant Grace could come home. The whole thing was typed up, ready for the judge to approve. Deborah assured him that she understood, but his words seemed to slide off her. Matt sat rigidly upright, his face a determined blank. I was proud of him.

'We've got Judge Cartwright,' the Spiv announced, smiling broadly. 'Cannonball, we call her. But I don't imagine she'll be firing at anyone today!'

Two o'clock had come and gone before a cuddly type in a black gown bustled in. An organiser of ceremonies, by the looks of her clipboard. 'You ready, Mr Forsyth?' she asked.

Spiv slammed both hands down on the table. 'We certainly are, Mandy. Early bath today! It's all agreed. We've even typed up the order.'

Mandy tapped her clipboard. 'We've not finished this morning's work. Listing office gave us an emergency injunction before lunch, and it's turned into a real can of worms.' She looked a bit smug. I don't think she liked Stew the Spiv any more than I did.

There was a good deal of tut-tutting and head-shaking at this. 'I'm going to make a complaint about that new listing officer at the court users' meeting,' fussed Forsyth, interlocking manicured fingers pompously across his stomach. 'It's the third time in as many weeks, and it isn't good enough.'

Mandy looked very happy. 'Mm. Her Honour says to tell all parties it'll be two forty-five at the earliest.'

Forsyth checked his watch and stood up, turning to Deborah. 'Disgraceful. Well, you'd better go and get yourself a cuppa, Mrs Harrison.' He swung open the door. 'I'll use the time to have a word with Marcus Watson, the barrister who's here for the local authority. Tie up loose ends.

Cafeteria's on the fourth floor—avoid the doughnuts at all costs.' He nodded importantly and bustled away in a flurry of loud braces.

There was silence in our room.

'This is surreal,' croaked Matt, and pressed his face down onto the table. Then he lifted it, squinting at the graffiti. 'Didn't Catherine the Great do that?'

Through the glass wall I watched Forsyth and a taller man—Watson, presumably—strolling up and down the long waiting area. The other guy looked weary and a bit threadbare, and he needed a haircut. They pretended to be talking very solemnly, with their heads together and their hands clasped behind their backs, but I bet they were discussing the footie, not a little girl whose future was all carved up.

'Come on.' I dragged myself upright and put out my hand to pull Debs to her feet. 'Let's sample the local café culture.'

The three of us took the lift upstairs. On the second attempt, I persuaded it to drop us at the fourth floor.

As things turned out, we got more than a cup of tea in that cafeteria.

Even as she reached the town centre, she knew she must be too late.

But ahead of her, like a heavenly mirage, floated the court building. It was a monstrous block of stone and glass, a coat of arms swirling majestically above the main entrance. There was nowhere obvious to park, so she swerved into a bus stop, running one wheel up onto the kerb with a sickening metallic thud. The drivers behind her burst into a chorus of sanctimonious hooting, but she didn't care.

There wasn't time to lock up the car. Lunging for her handbag, she charged across the pavement and up a flight of steps before exploding through the heavy revolving doors.

In an echoing lobby, two security guards lounged against a pillar, their heads bent over a crossword. They straightened as she whirled up, regarding her with faint curiosity.

'I'm *late*,' she pleaded, as the younger one languorously pretended to search her bag.

The elder of the pair ran a metal detector half-heartedly up and down. Then he stood back, taking in her obvious agitation. 'Where are you supposed to be, love?'

Leila's eyes flickered. 'I'm . . . I don't know. It's an adoption.'

The guard jerked his thumb towards the lifts. 'You want the second floor. There's only two family judges sitting this week, and one of 'em knocked off at lunchtime.'

Waiting for the lift was out of the question. She pounded up the stairs, the heels of her boots ringing on the concrete, breath coming in gasps.

There were several people on the second floor. Most of them wore suits and carried lever arch files, and they completely ignored her. Leila walked quickly past while studying them obliquely and trying to slow her breathing: a spy, creeping behind enemy lines. There was no sign of anyone who looked remotely like a grandmother, black or white.

Then a middle-aged woman, comfortably overblown, emerged from one of the courtrooms. She was draped in a gown and held a clipboard.

Taking a long breath, Leila approached her. 'I'm looking for the adoption,' she whispered, coughing because her voice was suddenly hoarse.

'Adoption?' The usher looked blank, glancing at her clipboard. 'We haven't got . . . you mean the placement?'

Leila nodded.

The woman shot her a shrewd, kindly glance. 'You the mother?'

'No, no.' Leila tried to look as though this was all in a day's work to her. 'I've got an urgent message for . . . um, the grandparents. It's very important indeed.'

The usher seemed to relax. 'You're in luck.' She smiled, contentedly tapping the clipboard with a biro. 'They're running late in Court Three, haven't even started yet. Family's up in the cafeteria.'

'Where—?'

'Fourth floor.'

Seconds later, Leila stepped into the lift. For a long time she hesitated, her hand hovering over the buttons. Now that she was so terrifyingly close, every instinct urged her to bolt.

Get a grip, girl, she told herself, and jabbed her finger at the panel.

The doors slid shut, imprisoning her. The metal box shuddered, groaned, and began to rise inexorably upwards.

There was no turning back.

Chapter Thirty-four

We sat at a table in the windowless space of chrome and Formica, staring at our untouched drinks. Half an hour earlier, we'd stepped out of the lift and stood in a bewildered huddle on the concourse. The fourth floor seemed to be deserted except for a woman in a white cap who was aggressively wiping the cafeteria's glass counter. When she spotted us she started rubbing extra fast as though to prove she was extremely busy.

'We've finished doing food,' she yelled.

'Oh.' None of us knew what to do next, and she took pity on us. 'I can do hot beverages. Or a snack out of the machine over there.' She jerked her head at one of those tall, glass-fronted robots that drop your crisps into a well; you have to reach through the flap for them, and it always swings back and traps your hand.

We crossed the concourse and Deborah lowered herself onto one of the metal seats. Her movements seemed uncoordinated. 'Coffee, Jake, please,' she said faintly. I looked at Matt, but he shrugged. He followed me to the counter and leaned against it, his hands jammed into the pockets of his suit, while I negotiated with the scary soup dragon.

I glanced at him. 'You okay, mate? You look a bit crook.'

The poor kid couldn't keep still. He pushed himself off the counter and furiously scrunched up his hair with both hands, as though his head was about to explode.

'*Fuck*, Jake, why are we here?'

I wanted to put my arm around his shoulder. Wanted to tell him it would be all right. But it wasn't all right.

'Matt,' I said. 'You don't have to agree to this. It's not too late. You can change your mind.'

His eyes looked all screwed inwards with some kind of pain. They were burning holes into his brain. He took a step away, and then swung back as though he had more to say. I waited, but he shook his head without looking at me and slouched off to throw himself down beside Deborah.

Our drinks went cold, as we sat there. No one spoke. I think we were all huddling over our images of Perry—ghastly, guilty, grieving images. I think we'd forgotten where we were, and why.

We'd forgotten Grace.

And that was when I heard the lift grinding up to our floor, stopping with a soft *ting*.

I was the only one facing that way. Deborah and Matt had their backs to the lift, and anyway, they were both on another planet. So they never noticed when a woman stepped out and stood on the concourse, looking hesitantly around. I remember thinking dimly that she was quite a headturner. She was black—much more so than Grace—and she had a great figure, curvy and confident. She was wearing a long jacket, like a very trendy highwayman's, rather swish boots, and a little kilt thing that stopped well short of her knees. A green band was tied around her head, holding back a mass of braids.

I watched as her eyes fell upon our group. There was something compelling about those eyes. I couldn't stop looking. She took a firm hold of her handbag, as if it was a riot shield, and began to walk steadily towards us. Her footsteps sounded like hammer blows on the silent concourse, and the kilt swayed jauntily along with her.

'I'm closed, love,' came a bellow from behind the counter, but the woman completely ignored it. Her eyes were fixed on Deborah now, as she came to a halt near our table.

'Excuse me,' she said quietly. She had a rich voice, like dark chocolate. 'I'm sorry to bother you.'

Deborah stared blankly at her for a moment; then her gaze slipped away, as though this intruder did not exist. Matt didn't even look up.

The newcomer took a step closer. She was older than I'd thought, somewhere in her thirties perhaps, and she had a fight or flight look about her. I noticed she had incredibly pretty ears. They were small and tidy, with heavy gold hoops in them, and they somehow set off her face.

'*Excuse* me,' she said again, and this time there was an insistent edge to the chocolate voice.

Deborah blinked, turning on a polite, empty smile. 'So sorry. I was miles away.'

'Are you the grandmother in the case in Court Three? The one about the adoption?'

Deborah peered at her as though trying to lip-read. 'Yes,' she said and nodded. 'I suppose I am. Are we needed already?'

The woman gripped her bag with both hands—it was big and colourful, this handbag, with embroidery and tiny mirrors all over it. She stood speechless for several seconds, gazing from one to the other of us with her Egyptian goddess eyes. Then she took a deep breath.

'I'm Leila Edmunds,' she said. 'That doesn't mean anything to you, I imagine. I'm the one who wants to adopt your granddaughter.'

There was a silence. Deborah frowned uncomprehendingly. 'But you can't be. You don't know who we are, where we live. You can't *possibly* be.'

The woman—Leila—glanced around, as if nervous of listening walls. 'I *am*, though. I found out which court it was. I've driven from Birmingham to get here . . . I thought I was too late.' She was shaking visibly.

'Here.' I made room for her on my side of the table.

She perched at the edge of the seat, looking me over anxiously. 'You're the grandfather?'

'God, no!' I was appalled.

She wrinkled her forehead and turned uncertainly to Matt.

'Yes,' said Deborah firmly. 'That's the father. And Grace doesn't need to be adopted. We can take care of her perfectly well, thank you.'

'I'm sorry.' Leila nodded, her eyes filling. 'I shouldn't have come.'

Matt seemed to stir, then. 'Why *did* you come?' He looked at her with a sort of hopeless desperation, as though she was the last lifeboat and now she was sinking too. 'You'll be in very big trouble with the SS if they find out. They'll take you off their list of adopters. You're a rebel.'

'I know.' She fished a bit of bog paper out of her bag and blew her nose on it. 'Sorry . . . I'm very strung up, such a long drive, and roadworks, and then getting lost . . . My ears are ringing.' She squeezed her eyelids shut but the tears poured out anyway, and we all sat like shop window dummies and stared at her.

'I thought that maybe if you met me, you'd see I'm not an ogre. And I'm not a fool.'

She dabbed defiantly at her cheeks with that soggy little bit of paper. She rested her nose on it, thinking. Then she seemed to regain control, facing Matt and Deborah.

'I've risked everything to come here. I came to tell you that I will care for your little girl, and I will love her always, and I will not let you down. She'll know who she is, where she's come from. You won't be forgotten, I promise. I've been going over and over it in the car, thinking what to say. And now none of it seems right.' Her gaze came to rest on Deborah. 'I wish you could meet my husband, David. You'd trust *him*.'

Deborah sighed. 'Does he know you're here?'

Leila didn't answer, but I thought I saw a guilty smile sweep around the edges of her lips.

Deborah picked up a little packet of sugar and began to twist it. 'I expect you and he both think that having a baby will solve all the problems in your lives, maybe in your marriage. You imagine that it will bring you closer together. Yes? Am I right?'

'Perhaps.'

'Well, it won't. Believe me, Leila. Once you've been up three times a night every night for six years, you'll know what I mean. Once you've been yelled at and spat at and told to sod off by your own child, you'll know.'

Leila held up her hands. 'I helped to raise my youngest brother.'

Deborah touched her own forehead in a gesture of exasperation, or perhaps pity.

'It's not the same . . . Leila, I've brought up two children. They look very sweet as babies, especially when they're asleep. But then they start encroaching on your life. They are everything, and the mother is nothing. *Nothing*. She pours her entire being into them. They take without thought or thanks, they expect to be heard and respected and worshipped, but they give absolutely nothing back.'

'*Thanks*,' said Matt, looking shocked. Leila was watching Deborah intently with those exotic eyes. There was a determined, rebellious lift to her chin.

'When they are your own family,' Deborah persisted, 'you can just about pull it off. You may occasionally feel like throttling them, but you don't because they carry your genes and you have an irrational obsession with them. A bond. Love. But I don't see—I really, really *do not* see—how you could do it for a child who is completely unrelated to you; a child who has simply landed on your front doorstep like a bottle of milk.'

What about Lucy? I wanted to protest. *She wasn't yours, but you loved her.* I kept my trap shut, though. Deborah's current relationship with Lucy was hardly a fine example of the genre.

Leila clutched the toilet paper in one clenched fist. Her eyes were narrowed, now, and they focused sharply on Deborah's face. When she spoke, we all listened.

'Irrational? Was your love for your children irrational?'

Deborah pulled back her head, glancing at Matt. 'Well, no. Of course not.' The packet of sugar split under her hands.

Leila pressed her advantage. 'How long will it be before this baby, too, begins to encroach on your life?'

Good shot, I thought. Bullseye. Deborah took a long breath, but Leila didn't give her time to reply.

'I can't have my own children, you know? I can't . . . I'll *never* have my own. The one I adopt will *be* my own. She will be the little Leila, the one who will share the rest of my life. She will be a part of me, and I'll spend every waking hour with her that I can, and we'll become as close as any mother and daughter can be.'

She looked at Matt. 'I promise.' She pressed her palms together as if in prayer, and dipped her head. 'I promise. I *promise*.'

'I don't know you,' said Matt and yet he stared at her, clearly fascinated. 'I wouldn't even buy a second-hand stereo from someone I didn't know. Once Grace has gone, we'll never hear from her again. We'll never know if she's all right.'

'Okay, then!' Leila began to fumble with her handbag. 'Bloody zip!' she fumed through gritted teeth. 'Come *on*.' She managed to force her hand in, and dragged out a pen and a dog-eared diary.

'*Here*,' she cried, vehemently, tearing a page out of the diary and scribbling across it in big, loopy letters. 'Here's my address, and my telephone number, and my email. You can have my shoe size, too. You can have anything you want.' She flung the page across the table. It was a challenge.

None of us moved.

Deborah recovered herself first. 'You're being silly. You don't know us. We might turn up one day and snatch the baby back.'

'I'm prepared to take that risk.'

Jeez, you had to admire this woman, Leila. What a stonker. She sat there regally, her chin up, looking Deborah full in the face.

For an age, Matt looked longingly at that scruffy piece of paper. We all did. Grace's future was poised, waiting for his decision.

He didn't pick it up.

The lift was at it again, whirring fussily up to our floor and coughing up the Spiv. He stepped out, tapping his watch.

'It's quarter to, Mrs Harrison,' he called, with determined jollity. 'Quarter to three. Back to the grindstone!'

The three of us got to our feet in a slavish little show of obedience. Leila didn't move, though. She hugged her handbag, staring wordlessly from one of us to the other.

'I'm sorry,' whispered Deborah. 'It was brave of you to come.' Then she turned away. 'Yes, Stuart. Lead on.'

Spiv stood back to let us into the lift. I hesitated by our table for a few more seconds, desperate to say something—*anything*—to this woman. She sat defeated, tears pooling once more in the darkness of her eyes. She'd shown more courage than I could even imagine, and yet I couldn't think of a word to express my admiration. Not a single bloody word. In the end, I put out my hand. She looked startled, but slipped hers into mine and we shook politely, like two business people at a meeting. Then I legged it across the concourse and into the lift.

'Just in time,' sang the Spiv, maliciously letting the doors go so that they trapped my trouser leg. 'Whoops . . . never mind, no damage done. Who was the lady?'

'No one,' I muttered, with my calf stuck to the doors.

He looked snide. 'I wish *I* could befriend dark and mysterious strangers in cafeterias.'

'Well,' I said, forcing Deborah to catch my eye. 'She seemed like a hell of a woman, to me. One in a million.'

As the lift slowed, I spoke again. It was on my mind, and it had to be said. 'In fact, I reckon I'd trust her with my most precious possession.'

Matt's eyes darted briefly towards me, but he said nothing. When the doors opened he was staring at his polished shoes.

As it turned out they still weren't ready for us in court, so I excused myself and scurried off to the bogs. The first lot was closed for cleaning—there was a terrifying troll in there with a mop—so I trotted downstairs and found some more. Apart from a platoon of cleaners and a couple of security guards doing the crossword in the lobby, I didn't spot another soul. Perhaps our judge was the last one working. God, I thought. What a day.

Back on the second floor, the Harrison contingent were closeted in the same little room. I didn't want to join them, and I knew I wasn't needed. I slumped on the blue seats outside and retied my bootlaces, barely stirring when the door swung open and Spiv shot past me. I paid him no attention; I was thinking about Perry, and then about Leila Edmunds and her long, lonely journey, all for nothing. I wondered how she'd find the heart to get back into her car.

There seemed to be a fair amount of activity around me. A couple of the lawyers wandered past.

'This is turning into a real pain in the arse,' complained the woman, with a glance at her watch. She was a sharp-faced brunette with silver fingernails, modelling the latest in Italian suits. 'At this rate, we'll miss the fast train back to London, and tonight's chambers Christmas party.'

'Complete cock-up all round,' agreed the threadbare man. He pushed his glasses further up his nose, slightly nervously. 'Have you seen Mrs H, though? Most unlikely-looking granny I've ever clapped eyes upon.' He growled appreciatively, and I considered getting up and socking him. 'Foxy! She should be modelling scent or something.'

His colleague yawned. 'Well, the father's the black sheep of a middle-class family, isn't he? This is a posh cock-up, not your common or garden one.'

They spotted me then, and started talking earnestly about the weather. I imagined Grace in her bubblegum-pink suit. Perhaps she was bouncing in one of those swing contraptions, gurgling merrily, not a care in the world. And she was causing a silver-nailed barrister to miss her Christmas party.

Meanwhile, Spiv was rushing in and out, bursting into other meeting rooms along the concourse and gabbling away. He reminded me a bit of the White Rabbit in *Alice in Wonderland*, racing around in a dreamlike state of anxiety. I wondered what had got him into such a tizzy.

Just as I was thinking we'd have to pitch tents and light a campfire, Mandy the usher bounced out through the swing doors of the court, throwing back her head like a cockerel and crowing, 'Re K! All parties in re K!'

The door of our room opened immediately, and Deborah and Matt trickled out.

'That's us.' Deborah nodded towards the usher.

Spiv planted himself in front of my seat and took hold of his braces. 'I've had a word with the other parties,' he intoned. He was sweating a little. 'No one objects to you coming in as a support person. You can sit in the public area, so long as you understand the rules of confidentiality and don't interfere.'

'Jake *never* interferes.' Debs smiled down at me. 'It's against his religion.'

'No way I'm going in there,' I objected, stubbornly crossing my arms. 'I'll just wait for you.'

'Suit yourself,' said Spiv. He strutted away through the double doors, tossing his tussock grass.

Deborah watched him go and then sat down beside me. 'I don't know how I'm getting through this day,' she said quietly. 'I feel as though I'm drunk, and at any moment I'm going to start giggling, or screaming, or both. And Matt is even closer to the edge.'

I glanced up at the unhappy figure of my young friend, wearing his best suit, his bleached tangles carefully brushed out. He looked so young. So lost. A schoolkid who had fallen over and scraped his knee. As I watched, he pressed his eyes into the palm of his hand, and I felt a bloody great jolt somewhere in my chest.

Debs squeezed my arm. 'We need you to look solid and dependable in your homespun sweater and desert boots. We need you to be in there as our friend. Please.'

And before I'd even found the strength to argue, we were in.

Chapter Thirty-five

Leila had reached the end of the road.

She was alone. The fourth floor was completely empty now, the lights turned off. There was no sound except for a vague electrical hum from the drinks machine. Even the cook had locked up her kitchen and gone home to her family.

She was frozen, isolated, in this void. There was no one to eavesdrop on her grief. It felt as though nobody else existed in the whole world. Some catastrophe had wiped them all out: perhaps nuclear war. When she finally stepped out onto the street there would be no traffic, no *Big Issue* sellers, no schoolchildren at the bus stop, no gnarled old ladies walking their dogs. Nothing.

For almost a decade she had lived in limbo, forever waiting, hanging on, suspending her decisions until the arrival of the children who were to join them. After every disappointment, she'd dragged herself up and made a new plan. It had become her career. It was what defined her. And this had been her final effort. She had risked everything, even David's trust. She had done her very, very best. And she had failed.

On the table in front of her, between three untouched plastic cups of coffee, the crumpled page of her diary lay rejected. It had been her trump card, but it had done no good. She covered it with her fist and stuffed it into a pocket.

The baby's family were not as she'd imagined. Not at *all*. They were real people. Distracted, perhaps, and oddly melancholy, but real. The man—the quiet uncle, in whom she'd sensed such unease—had even shaken her hand. They were not mad or drunk or evil or filthy. They wanted to keep their baby, and who could blame them? The little one was a part of their family. Leila had no place in her life.

Perhaps they were already telling the authorities she was here. Perhaps she would be confronted on her way out of the building, taken into a little bare room and forced to confess. They would never let her have another chance. Well, so be it.

Half an hour passed, and she'd long run out of tears. With a tremendous effort, she pushed herself up from the table and wandered towards the lift. She'd failed, and she was tired. She was almost too tired to put one foot in front of the other. She wanted to be home with David. The lift murmured softly to her and deposited her in the lobby. The older guard was still there, packing up his newspaper. No nuclear catastrophe, then. He glanced up at Leila as she passed.

'Did you make it, love?'

Leila stopped, and half turned towards him. 'Yes,' she said. 'Thank you. But it didn't help.'

She pushed through the revolving doors. Starlings were gathering above the roof of the Station Hotel across the road. She stood for a short while, her head turned longingly towards the neon sign that glittered cheerfully above the hotel's broad sweep of steps. She imagined taking a cheap, anonymous room and staring at mindless gameshows on the television. She wished she could run away, disappear, escape from the rest of her life.

Instead she forced her steps towards the bus stop where the Renault crouched, abandoned at a time—so long ago, it seemed—when she'd still had hope. At first she moved like a sleepwalker, barely conscious of the world around her. But as she drew closer she looked up, and her gaze sharpened.

Then, with a cry of indignation, she began to run.

Walking into the court was like being beamed into a spaceship made of polished wood and blue tip-up chairs. Spiv steered me into the cheap seats at one side and led Deborah and Matt into the dress circle. Their seats were arranged in rows, each with a desk running along in front of it. Forsyth and two other suits set up shop at the front, and their teams were parked behind. There seemed to be an awful lot of people in there. I found myself wondering whether it was all strictly necessary, just for one minuscule blob in a fluffy pink babygro.

I heard other footsteps and shufflings, and Imogen Christie slid past, carrying her blue file and giving me a cool nod. There was no sign of Lenora Blunt, but on the far side I spotted a well-groomed woman in flowing silk, who I guessed was the Children's Guardian. She looked just as Deborah had described her.

I wondered whether Cherie was there too. Watching us.

Mandy bustled up to the front. 'Everyone here?' she clucked, and the lawyers in the front row all nodded and coughed and pushed bits of paper around, as though the future of Grace King was remotely important to them, which I'm quite sure it wasn't.

We heard the judge coming long before we saw her. I swear I felt the beat of a military marching band; then in she thundered, shaking the ground, and everybody leaped to their feet. I was a bit slow off the mark, mind you, but luckily she didn't notice.

Jeez, you wouldn't want to meet this monster on a dark night. She was a one-woman artillery battery in a power jacket and pink lipstick. Deborah began to giggle, silently, unnaturally. I could see her shoulders shaking.

When the rest of us sat down, Marcus Thingummy—the weary, threadbare one with the bad-hair day—remained reluctantly upright, and the Big Gun smiled lovingly down at him. She looked almost maternal. I had the impression they went back a long way.

'Yes, Mr Watson?' She had a northern accent, quite strong. Lancashire, maybe. It only added to her presence.

'Your Honour, I appear on behalf of the applicant local authority in this application for a placement order in respect of the child, Grace Serenity King. The father is Matthew Harrison, and he is represented by Mr—'

'—Yes. Thank you. I know who's here.' Cannonball held up a hand to stop him. 'I've seen your helpful summary, Mr Watson, in this rather tragic case. And I understand that the local authority will be withdraw-ing its application? Having read their assessment, it seems to me that Mr and Mrs Harrison are both *very* capable people.' She shot Deborah a kind, encouraging smile.

The barrister's hair was standing straight up, as though he'd seen a ghost. He rocked back on his heels and then forward again, and cleared his throat. Then he slid his hands into his pockets and jingled some loose change. 'Er . . . no.'

I just about shot out of my seat. What the hell did he mean, no?

The Cannonball raised her eyebrows about a millimetre, and the temperature dropped by at least twenty degrees. The kind, encouraging smile was a thing of the past.

Poor old Watson held up one hand, as though waving a little white flag. 'Until fifteen minutes ago, that *was* the intention. The local authority was to withdraw its application and consent to a residence order in Mrs Harrison's favour. We'd even drawn up an agreed order for Your Honour to approve.'

The Judge pressed her pink lips together. 'Yes, Mr Watson. I know you had. I've *seen* it.'

'Mm. But at the eleventh hour Mr Forsyth has received instruc-tions—*clear* instructions, from both his clients—that they do not oppose the adoption plan. Indeed, they welcome it! It seems therefore that we are all agreed, including Mrs Midya, the Children's Guardian. You will find a copy of the original care plan at page fifty of your bundle.'

Cannonball leafed through the pages of a file in front of her, read for a moment, and flared her nostrils. 'I see. And is the proposed adoptive family still available?'

'They are, indeed. Very much so. A twin-track approach has been adopted in the planning of this case.'

'Don't give me jargon, Mr Watson. Give me facts.'

'Sorry. Er . . . we've just spoken to their team. If you agree, the plan is to inform the couple immediately. Today. We propose to commence introductions as soon as can be arranged, and have Grace placed with them by Christmas.'

'Hmm.' Cannonball blinked dangerously and then took aim at Spiv, who shot up and stood to attention, stroking his luxuriant locks with one nervous hand.

'Well, Mr Forsyth? What's it about? This is all very extraordinary.'

Spiv scratched an ear and looked perplexed and I couldn't blame him. I was bloody perplexed myself.

'It is, Your Honour. Very. I've spent a good deal of time just now ensuring that both the father and grandmother understand that they are burning their bridges. They're quite adamant.'

'What about the grandfather?'

'He has never been a party.'

'Some people, Mr Forsyth, might think it a disgraceful waste of public resources to carry out a detailed assessment of grandparents who then throw in the towel.' She flapped a dismissive hand, and he ducked gratefully down behind the parapet. Took a surreptitious glance at his watch. Shot his cuffs.

Slowly, menacingly, the great sights swung to rest upon Deborah, and I shrank lower in my seat in an effort to be invisible.

'This is right, is it, Mrs Harrison? You want to withdraw your application?'

Deborah gazed down the barrel without flinching. 'Yes, that's right,' she replied, bold as brass. 'I do. We feel it's better for Grace.'

'And is that view shared by the father?'

Matt nodded miserably.

'And what about the grandfather?'

Deborah didn't hesitate. 'He's right behind me.' To my horror, she motioned in my general direction. *Jeez, Debs!* I mouthed furiously, trying to hide behind a concrete pillar. I was spared, though. Cannonball barely bothered to waste her contempt on me. She merely flicked a nasty glance in my direction, sighed, and picked up a pen.

'Anyone else want to say anything? What about the Children's Guardian—Mrs Midya? She's entirely satisfied, is she? Does she need more time?'

'No thank you,' said the silver-nailed woman, rising briefly to her feet. 'In the circumstances, Mrs Midya supports the local authority's application.'

Once she'd sat down there was a long, uneasy pause. I could hear the lawyers shuffling their feet, tying up their papers, getting ready to make a dash for the fast train. I could hear the hum of a vacuum cleaner. I could hear the ticking of a clock above the door.

I almost thought I could hear Cherie, weeping; but perhaps it was only the squeaking of a chair.

Judge Cartwright began to speak fast and very clearly, as though dictating a business letter. 'The local authority has made an application for a placement order in respect of Grace Serenity King,' she said.

I'm afraid I lost track after this. It all became a blur of legalese; the history of the thing, assessments and adoption panels, checklists and time-tables, something called Parental Responsibility, and what the Children's Guardian thought. I was watching Matt. He'd turned completely white, poor kid. Almost blue, actually. Sitting bravely to attention, straight as a soldier; losing the most precious thing in his world.

When I next tuned in, Cannonball seemed to be winding down. '*Most* unexpectedly, and very late in the day, the grandmother wishes to withdraw.' She took several fiery breaths in order to glower at Deborah. 'I imagine she has her reasons, but I deprecate her timing. In any event, I give her leave to do so.'

She glanced regretfully down at Matt. 'The father is not by himself in a position to give the child a home, nor will he be within an acceptable timeframe. Greatly to his credit, he accepts this. He does not actively oppose this application although he feels unable to consent. I am able to dispense with his consent because the welfare of this child demands it. Her welfare also requires that her future be settled without further delay. In the circumstances, I find that adoption is in the best interests of this child.'

She halted, as though gathering momentum for the final swing of her axe. The death blow. They should have brought her a black cap to wear.

For too long, we were all suspended in a horrible echoing emptiness, waiting for the blade to fall. Deborah took Matt's hand. There were tears on his face. I swear I could actually taste his loss. The dry, recycled air seemed to vibrate with it.

Then down came the axe. 'I therefore make a placement order in favour of Woodbury Borough Council, authorising them to place the child, Grace Serenity King, with prospective adopters. There will be no order for costs.'

The judge stood, nodded curtly at the assembled company, and marched out.

So. It was over, just like that. One baby, signed, sealed and delivered.

Good luck to you, I thought. *Good luck, Grace Serenity King.*

The building seemed to be shutting down for the night. The lights had dimmed, the corridors were silent.

Imogen Christie collared Matt and Deborah in the lobby. She wanted to talk about their final visit. The social worker seemed quite subdued, which surprised me. She certainly wasn't celebrating. I reckoned old Imogen was human after all.

'I don't want a final visit.' Matt looked ready to punch someone. 'It might upset Grace.' I didn't believe for one moment that it was Grace he was afraid of upsetting.

'It's your only chance, Matt,' urged Imogen. 'There's no more contact after this.'

'Come on, Matt. I'll go with you.' Deborah rubbed his shoulder. 'We *must* say goodbye.'

'Um, Imogen.' Matt forced a hand into his jacket pocket—which had been bulging a bit, come to think of it—and pulled out something lumpy and yellow and ragged. He held it against his chest. 'This was mine. Give it to her, will you?'

Imogen stared dumbly at the young father and then down at the object he was clutching. It was that goofy lion.

'Name's Frederick,' said Matt. 'I brought it along, just in case.'

Deborah pressed a hand to her mouth and shut her eyes. Imogen still didn't move.

'*Take* it, for God's sake,' Matt snarled, forcing the moth-eaten thing into her hands.

Words seemed to fail Imogen for a second or two, and I don't imagine that's happened very often.

'I probably shouldn't tell you this. But I was there,' she whispered finally. 'At Grace's birth.'

Matt stared. 'You were there?'

Imogen nodded, sucking her lower lip and cradling Frederick. Matt watched her dumbly, processing the information.

'Cherie was so brave,' said Imogen. 'I wish I had half her courage.'

'Did she hold Grace?' asked Deborah, and there was a wobble in her voice.

'Oh, yes, she held her. Wept over her. Loved her,' declared Imogen, shaking her head for emphasis. 'But she was overwhelmed, and she knew it.'

'I wonder what she'd think of me now,' said Matt quietly. He shifted his feet. 'Giving up. Breaking my promise.'

'She'd understand, Matt.' Imogen took a step closer to him. 'Cherie wanted the best future for her child, better than her own, and so do you. Right now, she'll be cheering you on.' She grabbed poor Matt and started hugging him like a grisly bear. I don't imagine *that's* happened very often, either.

I felt like an intruder. I told Matt and Deborah I'd collect the car and meet them at the main doors.

Out on the darkening street, another little commotion was bubbling up with much revving of engines and tooting of horns. Someone had parked a car slap in the middle of a bus stop on the main road. It was a green Renault, bit of a rust bucket really, and the poor thing was stuck at a crazy angle with one wheel up the kerb. Rush-hour traffic was heaving around it, like sheep in a race.

A yellow tow truck had arrived. Its driver had already attached a winch to the car's back end. And hopping about in front of him, arguing vehemently, was the woman in the kilt. Leila. I couldn't believe my eyes.

'For pity's sake,' she was yelling, waving her hands around. 'I'm begging you. Just give me a parking ticket. I don't have *time* for this.'

'Sorry.' The tow-truck driver seemed cheerful, happy in his work. 'More than my job's worth, love. You can follow me, if you like, and collect your vehicle from the pound.'

'How the bloody hell can I follow you when you've taken my car?'

He began to whistle a merry tune. For a moment I thought she was going to slap him, but then she started wrestling with the zip on her handbag. 'I've got a credit card,' she said. 'I can pay now. Or a cheque. How much?'

He shook his head, still whistling. 'You'll have to do it down at the pound. That was a shocking piece of parking, love. Shocking.'

I found myself standing beside her. 'Cash?' I asked, fishing out my wallet. 'You wouldn't refuse cash, would you?'

Leila's head came round, and she stared at my wallet. She looked disorientated. The tow-truck man broke off his whistling and examined me suspiciously.

'Well now,' he said slowly, 'I can take cash. Not a bribe, mind you, it's all accounted for.'

'Of *course* it's not a bribe!' I tried to look scandalised. 'How much?'

Everyone has their price. His was pretty steep, actually.

When he'd gone, Leila reached into her rust bucket and then turned to me, clutching a chequebook.

'Thanks.' She produced a biro. 'You shouldn't have done that, but thanks. I'll write you a . . .' She leaned against the bonnet and began to scribble. 'I've left your name blank. It might bounce first time,' she warned, handing it over, 'but keep trying.'

I thanked her and crumpled the rubber cheque into my pocket, knowing I'd never bank it. In fact, I planned on destroying it as soon as possible. It gave away far too much information about where Grace was going, and that wasn't good for anyone.

Glancing up, I saw Matt and Deborah outside the revolving doors of the court building. I waved, and they spotted me and started down the steps. Leila saw them too. She muttered something about being in a rush.

'Don't go.' I put a hand on her arm. 'Please. Wait.'

Deborah's pace quickened as she approached. 'Ah, you're still here,' she said, looking at Leila. She sounded fraught but determined. 'That's wonderful.'

Leila made a disgusted face. 'It's not wonderful at *all*, actually. This isn't a social event.'

'I agree.' Deborah looked searchingly at her and then her lips twitched. 'You got a phone on you?'

'Er, I think so . . . yes, I have.' Leila began peering into that useless handbag.

'Well, I'd keep it switched on if I were you,' advised Deborah. 'I suspect you'll be getting a rather interesting call, any minute now.'

Leila finally found her phone and tugged it out, looking puzzled. She switched it on, and it came to life with a small flurry of notes.

Deborah watched her and then rested a hand on her arm. 'Drive carefully, Leila,' she said soberly. 'Please. We need you. And I think you should tell your husband what you did today. He'll forgive you. You are a truly remarkable person.'

Leila didn't pull away; she just stood there, gazing at Deborah in bewilderment.

Matt had been pacing round and round in little circles, muttering to himself and scrunching up his hair. Now he stepped right up to Leila, very close. He was about twice her weight, I'd say, but she stood her ground.

'You take good care of her,' he growled, looking her square in the eye. She must have thought we were all completely off our heads. Then he suddenly grabbed her arm and tugged it wildly up and down, like the handle of an old water pump. '*Bloody* good care! She's priceless.'

'Come on, Matt,' said Deborah. 'Let her go. She's got a long drive ahead of her.'

So we left Leila Edmunds standing there in the deepening twilight, gaping after us as though we had just spoken to her in Martian.

As we crossed the road, dodging between two murderous juggernauts, we heard the unmistakeable electronic tinkle of a mobile telephone, playing 'Jingle Bells'.

Chapter Thirty-six

David tried to ignore the silence. It was different today; there was a profound emptiness in the house that he had never felt before.

Evening was winning the battle outside, and the corridor beyond his study door had faded into shadow, but Leila wasn't back. Well, he had no right to miss her. He could hardly expect her to lighten his darkness. It was just that he wished she was there.

He'd tried to call her this morning, once Christopher had left; and again at lunch time, but she must have nipped out for a sandwich because there was no answer. When he'd tried yet again, the phone was turned off. Perhaps the battery was flat. Yes, that would be it. Happened all the time.

He'd had to go out again, in the afternoon, to see a schoolboy in the hospice. It had been a difficult visit. Awful, really. The young man, exhausted by suffering, had reached some kind of acceptance. He was ready to let go. Perhaps he'd walked alongside death for so long that it had lost its terror. But his parents were in agony. David had felt himself the lucky one, being childless.

He'd anxiously checked the answer machine when he came back, but there was nothing from Leila. Two from Marjorie Patterson, two from the church office, and a recent one from Linda Hooper. The social worker sounded businesslike, ready to confirm the bad news.

Hello, it's Linda Hooper here. I'll try your mobile.

David called her back, but her line was engaged. Well, not much point, really.

Now he sat chewing the skin around his thumbnail until it began to bleed. He was supposed to be writing a sermon, but it was going nowhere. On the wall around the window frame he could see cheerful primrose brush strokes, lurid from their days of hope. The ragged lines told their own story. When he'd made *that* one, they'd been happy. *That* long, joyously untidy sweep, right along the sill, had been made while Leila was answering the telephone. It was the cut-off point.

On an impulse, he lifted the receiver and dialled Leila's work, hearing the studiedly languid tones of Jodie's telephone voice. 'Kirkaldie's, New Street branch. How may I help you?'

'Hello, Jodie. It's David Edmunds here. Could I have a word with Leila?'

There was a long pause. Then, 'Leila's not here, Mr Edmunds.'

'She's knocked off early? Isn't there a staff meeting?'

Jodie muffled the receiver for a moment, as though whispering to someone. He waited, watching Leila glittering in her white lace on their wedding day.

Jodie was back. 'Um, Mr Edmunds . . . Leila never came in today. She phoned and said she had a migraine.'

David's stomach abruptly, spontaneously, filled with ice. Dread—he did not want to analyse it, face it—pumped through his veins. He looked at his watch and then up at the window. His own reflection stared back at him from the inky glass.

'No problem,' he stammered. 'Thanks, Jodie.'

Never came in . . . ?

For a bewildered whirl of time he struggled to think rationally, mechanically lacerating his bleeding thumb. Panic flickered in his brain, threatening to shut it down. Where would she have gone? Perhaps she'd left him, in the misguided belief that he would be better off without her.

I shouldn't go. But I have to.

Perhaps—no, surely not—she'd made a terrible choice, driven by despair. Heaven forbid. *It'll all be over by tonight*, she'd said, and now the words took on a horrible significance. She had seemed so anxious, so tender.

No. He was overreacting. She would never do such a thing . . . Yet in spite of himself his mind filled with unbearable images: Leila's broken beauty on the railway line, solemn policemen knocking at the door.

It'll all be over by tonight.

Oh God, oh God, where should he start looking? The hospitals? The police? He was breathing fast. Sweating. Eight hours, she'd been missing. A frightening expanse of time.

'Leila,' he cried into his hands. 'Where are you?'

The phone rang. It seemed to bore through his brain like a dentist's drill. He'd snatched it up before it had time to draw breath.

'Hello?' He could hear the desperation in his own voice and shut his eyes, praying silently.

Whoever was at the other end of the line, they were in trouble. He heard a series of choking gasps.

'Who is it?' he demanded, his words sharp with anxiety. 'Leila?'

'David.' Her voice was overflowing, singing with emotion.

He clutched the receiver with both hands, breathlessly relieved. Of course. It was all perfectly obvious. Linda Hooper must have called the mobile, confirmed the bad news, and poor Leila had hidden herself somewhere to grieve in peace.

'It's all right, my lovely. Where are you, Leila? Come home. I need you.'

There was another gasp, and a sob that he recognised, this time, as laughter.

'I'm in Suffolk.'

David actually shot out of his chair, one hand raking distractedly at his hair. 'You're *where*?'

'Suffolk. Woodbury, actually. I'm out of petrol.'

'I don't . . . What the hell are you doing in Suffolk? For God's sake, stop playing games. This isn't funny.'

'I went to court.'

There was a prolonged, slow-motion heartbeat as this statement sank in. And then, at last, David erupted. It was too much. 'Bloody *hell*! How could you be so *stupid*?'

'David.'

Livid, he ignored the interruption. 'Do you realise I thought you were—I can't believe you could be so deceitful and irresponsible and—'

'David. Shut up for a moment and listen.'

But his fury had flared out of all control. 'No, Leila—*you* listen!'

'We've got a baby.'

His mouth hung open, like a cartoon character. He was silenced, the white heat of his anger entirely vapourised. Leila's voice pressed on, sweet and melodic now, delight bubbling through it.

'Did you hear me? We've got a baby. The court made a placement order. She's to be our child.'

'Our . . . ?' David sank slowly back onto his desk chair. 'How did you do it?'

'You won't approve.'

'Probably not.'

'I'll tell you the whole story when I get home. There's a petrol station just along the road. I'm going to put some fuel in both myself and the car, then set off. I should be home by about nine.'

David closed his eyes. Took a breath. 'When will she . . . ?'

Leila's words seemed to shiver. 'Next week. They want to meet us, tidy up their paper trail. They'll gradually introduce us. And then we bring her home. What do you say now? Stupid, deceitful and . . . what was it?'

'After all this time,' said David. He felt overwhelmed, suddenly, by the long years of waiting. It was as though these years must be confronted and acknowledged before they could be left behind. His mind throbbed as the accumulated sludge of misery was stirred by a powerful tide of joy. It threatened to drown him. His mouth moved, soundlessly.

Leila's voice again. 'I can't hear you. Hang on, I'll just . . . Hello? Are you still there?'

Pathetic, thought David furiously, as he rubbed his sleeve across his eyes. Absolutely pathetic. A grown man, crying.

'David?'

'I'm here,' he whispered at last. 'I haven't gone anywhere.' He heard her soft laughter.

'I know. It's nearly too much, isn't it? It really hurts.'

He swallowed painfully, his throat overburdened. 'Leila . . . just come home.'

Chapter Thirty-seven

I was the getaway driver.

Matt stretched out along the back seat, both arms across his face. Debs sat beside me with her eyes closed. I kept glancing at her. Now that she'd stopped pretending, she looked as pale as death.

'D'you need anything?' I asked. 'Shall I stop at the chemist?'

She half opened her eyes. 'No, drive on, James,' she murmured drowsily.

The bell was clanging as we came to the level crossing, and its barriers were just going down. We seemed to sit there for about a year before the train came snorting self-importantly around the corner.

Ah, I thought, this looks like the fast train to London. The lawyers, and perhaps the judge too, would be all cosy in the buffet car, downing a hard-earned gin and discussing the case. I could imagine the silver-nailed woman in her black suit, smiling sardonically. 'Something very fishy about the whole event, if you ask me.'

The last carriage shot past us with a deafening hiss, and the barriers clunked up.

A couple of miles down the road I heard Deborah whisper, 'It was you.'

I did a double take. 'What?'

'You. You made your cryptic remark in the lift, then shot off. It was so *true*, what you said. Matt let poor Stuart get out of earshot, then he said, "Jake's right."'

I didn't comment. I was wondering whether it was really me, or whether Matt had already changed his mind.

'So we went into a little huddle on the stairwell. I pretended to argue with him, but my heart wasn't in it. I think he'd been battling with himself all morning, and Leila—with your help—showed him the way out. She truly, *desperately* wants Grace, and he no longer believes that we do. He says Grace will be lucky to have Leila fighting in her corner.'

'Well, I think he's got a point.'

'Mm. I played devil's advocate because I didn't want to feel guilty later. I needed the decision to be made for the right reasons.'

'And nothing to do with Rod.'

'Yes. Yes, exactly. Matt reminded me about Perry's note: *Now we are ALL free.* That's a very careful, very specific choice of words, don't you think? Matt is convinced that Perry *intended* to spring the trap. That's why he . . . you know. Did it.' She trailed off into silence.

'Matt's a good father,' I said. 'He did the right thing. He let her go.'

And so was Perry, I thought. In the end, he was. He cut through the knot in the only way he could. He let them all go.

When she next spoke, even her voice was pale. 'That woman, Leila . . . I think she will do a good job, if anyone can. She cared enough to break the rules. She was even prepared to have us hanging around her neck forever.'

Our road crawled into a tunnel of trees at the edge of Coptree Woods. Shadows slithered across Deborah's face, and her eyes seemed to sink into their sockets.

'I wish I could have got to know her,' she said quietly. 'I feel impoverished, because I never shall.'

It was after dark by the time we drew up at the house. I think we all felt strange about being back there. It radiated hopelessness, somehow.

There were lights on in the hall, and as we climbed wearily out of the car a lean figure appeared in the doorway. For a surreal moment I thought Perry had come out to meet us. Then I saw who it was.

'Lucy,' I called, taking a step towards her. As I moved closer, I heard a muffled cry before she hurtled across the gravel and collided with me.

Poor Lucy. She must have been waiting all afternoon, alone in that house. She must have been alone there when the darkness came. Perhaps she'd gone out onto the back lawn and found what the wasps had left behind. I put my arms around her, and she pressed her face against me. I could feel her shoulders shaking. We stood like that for a long time. To be honest, it made me feel better, too.

I stayed with them until after the funeral. They asked me to, and it seemed right. There was no need for me to hurry away any more. There would be no baby howling through the nights and absorbing all their time and love. So I was with them when the undertaker came to ask stupid questions about what sort of wood they wanted for the coffin, and which fabric for the lining. I was there when Stuart Forsyth arrived to discuss the will, and Deborah had to grovel to him for not telling the truth in court. I was there to take down the cot and stash it in the attic.

I was there when Matt and Deborah set out for their farewell visit with Grace.

Eventually, the coroner released Perry's body. There was no suspicion that his death had been anything other than suicide. He'd been on anti-depressants for years, living his half life: a wild black panther in a cage at the back of the zoo. He'd known exactly what he was doing, and made an efficient job of it. Well, you wouldn't expect anything less of the man.

They burned him on the following Thursday. The undertaker warned us that the crematorium would be squeezing us in between two others. It's a peak time, he said, as though everyone rushes to get their dying done before Christmas.

The army sent four massive young soldiers to act as pallbearers, and Matt and I helped them carry Perry into the chapel on our shoulders. The coffin was much heavier than I expected. I imagined Perry, the ultimate in dignity, jolting around in there. I was relieved when we were able to put him down.

It's grim, you know, the carry-on down at the crematorium. They had this electric organ, and the sound it made was truly tacky, like something at a fairground. Lucy looked stunned. Deborah got sort of hysterical giggles, more sobs than anything. She managed to hide it behind the handkerchief I lent her. My mum always nagged me to carry a large, clean hanky at all times. 'In case you meet a girl who's crying,' she'd say. I'd obediently made it a habit all these years although I'd never bumped into any crying girls. But now, at last, good old Mum was proved right. I made a mental note to tell her, next time I phoned.

When the coffin started sinking in slow motion into that terrible pit, to the jolly accompaniment of the hurdy-gurdy, it was like something out of *Star Wars.* I swear I could see smoke rising from the black depths, and then I needed my hanky back because my nose was running. Bloody hay fever.

The undertaker had hired some caterers, and we had an after-match bash in the church hall, which was all decorated with holly and tinsel ready for a Christmas disco. People who hadn't seen Perry for years said nice things about him. Superb leader, brilliant in the field, admired and trusted by his men. You can imagine the kind of stuff.

I took Matt away early, though. We'd both had enough. We wanted to be home.

'I'm so fucking *sick* of saying goodbye,' he snarled, as we drove away from the crematorium.

I glanced at the muscled figure hunched in my passenger seat. He looked older than I felt. And he was just a kid. By rights he should have been rattling on about which girls he fancied, or which band had broken up, or how to download a ringtone. But he wasn't. He was a son, mourning a father. And he was a father, mourning the child he'd lost. And he was grieving for the child's mother, too.

I drove on, into the woods.

'He was my dad,' he said. 'To them he was friggin' Lawrence of Arabia. But he was just my dad. I should have been there for him. I should've . . .'

I pulled over, sliding to a halt in the mud. 'He was a soldier,' I said. 'He weighed up the situation, and he came to a decision. It wasn't your fault.'

Matt fumbled for the door handle and just about fell out. He slammed the door behind him, and the violence of it made rooks wheel above the trees. I hopped down and walked around to his side. He was leaning against the truck, both hands spread out on the roof.

'I feel as though Grace died too,' he said, gulping. 'But there's no grave to put flowers on.'

I rested a hand on his shoulder. 'No, mate. She's not dead. She's still your daughter.'

'Going to see her . . .' He was battling for control. He pinched the top of his nose. Then he turned and sank down in the fallen leaves, his back against the front wheel. 'Hardest thing I've ever done. Hardest thing. I had to say goodbye to my little girl with them watching me.'

He lost it completely then. He covered the back of his head with his hands, a boy soldier under mortar fire, and the great shoulders began to heave. I knelt on the damp earth beside him, and waited. It was peaceful, in the woods.

'She was beautiful,' he whispered.

'Always will be, mate.' I said. 'Always will be.'

In those first few days after Perry died, Lucy stayed with us at Coptree. She was in a hell of a state. Couldn't sleep, wouldn't eat. Sometimes she'd just go and sit at Perry's desk.

She spent hours holed up in Matt's room too. I'd hear their voices, late into the night. One time, she came and perched on my bed. She talked, and cried, and my hankie came in useful again. She could hardly stand to be in the same room as Deborah: she still blamed her, at least partially, for Perry's despair. Debs tried to talk to her, but met a stone wall. It all made for a bit of an atmosphere.

They had to blow up eventually, and it happened the morning after the funeral. Lucy was leaving. She planned to catch up on urgent work at Stanton's, then spend Christmas with some old friends. When I came downstairs for breakfast, the war was already raging in the kitchen. I stood in the hall like a complete muppet, my hand on the door handle, wondering whether I should try to break it up.

Lucy was insisting she was going to take Perry's ashes and bury them in her mother's plot, and have Perry's name added to the headstone, and Deborah was saying no, Lucy most certainly *wasn't* going to do that, they were going to scatter him in a gale like he'd wanted. Lucy started shouting that no, Perry would want to be with Victoria, because she was the love of his life and Deborah was just a fancy whore who'd betrayed him and driven him to suicide; he and Victoria, she said, must be together in death.

Then I heard Deborah laughing—she sounded a bit mad to me—and she yelled, 'How sweet! Like bloody Heathcliff and Cathy!'

All of a sudden, the door handle was wrenched from my hand—just about dislocated my wrist—and Lucy came shooting out and barged into me, nearly knocking me over.

'I'm going,' she gasped. She wouldn't look at me.

I turned to pick up her bag from where she'd left it in the hall, but she growled, 'I can carry that myself,' and stormed past me and outside.

I followed her. It was cold and perfectly still. The lilac tree looked as though it had frozen to death. She'd stopped beside her car, staring up at the clouds with bloodshot eyes.

'Sorry, Jake. Sorry.'

I looked up too. The sky was pallid and heavy. 'He was tired of being ill, Luce. He wanted it to end, for his own sake and everybody else's.'

'But she still could have lifted him out of it. If she'd loved him enough.'

'Forgive her. She did her best.'

'But if I don't blame her, I have to blame myself . . . And even *him*. How could he do this to me? How could he? He didn't even say goodbye.'

'Nobody's to blame,' I said firmly. But I was thinking about how I'd left Perry alone, poured his whisky down the sink.

She buried her face in the wool of my jersey, and her voice was muffled. 'I can't cope, Jake. I can't see my way through, I can't imagine how life can go on . . . This is too big for me.'

After a few minutes she dragged a tissue out of her sleeve, blew her nose, and smiled wanly at her own distress. She was far too pale.

'Better go,' she whispered shakily.

'You shouldn't drive,' I fussed, but she shook her head.

'I'm okay now,' she said. 'Really, I'll be fine. Maybe I'll say sorry to Deborah, and we'll talk . . . but not today.'

I opened her car door for her.

'Thanks, Jake.' She laid a hand on my hair. 'Each one of us owes you thanks, including Dad. I saw you weeping for him at the crematorium. That's something I never thought I'd see.'

'Hay fever. All the lilies.'

'Ah, of *course* it was. You've even led the prodigal son back onto the path of righteousness. I can't think how you managed that.' She kissed me solemnly on both cheeks, slid into the car and started the engine. I shut her door.

'So. Tell me. Which of us were you in love with?' she asked, through the open window. 'Which of the four of us?'

Smiling, I shook my head. 'All of you.'

And in a way, it was the truth.

'But what about *her*? The viper?'

'Deborah Harrison is . . . how did you put it? The most dishonest and manipulative woman I have ever met.'

I wasn't expecting her to believe me, and she didn't.

'You're not fooling anyone.' A tear meandered its way wearily down her face. She reached out a knuckle to nudge my cheek. 'Poor Jake. She got you, didn't she? After all these years, Jake Kelly finally got bitten. There's no antidote.'

I didn't argue with her.

She wiped her face and laughed sadly. 'Go home, Jake. Go home. Go and buy that vineyard. There aren't any snakes in New Zealand, are there?'

She let out the clutch, and I stood back as she swept regally by in a spray of mud and gravel. I watched her car as it disappeared between the trees. My friend, Lucy.

Go home, Jake.

I didn't know Deborah was beside me until she spoke. 'I don't think Perry would want to end up in an army cemetery, do you?'

'Probably not.'

Just above us a group of seagulls swirled around, mewing like cats. Debs squinted up at them. 'But what do I know? I'm just a fancy whore.'

'True.'

'Well, thank God that's all over. We've got past the dreaded funeral.' She linked her arm through mine and we began to stroll down the lane, away from the house, like two old twerps in a National Trust garden.

'Coptree without Perry,' she said with a strange little laugh. 'He had extraordinary power. The place seems insipid without his presence.'

I knew exactly what she meant.

'I don't feel guilty, you know.' She glanced at me. 'I know I'm supposed to feel desperately guilty, but I don't. I feel darkened. I feel horrified. But Perry died because his life had become intolerable. And that wasn't my fault. I think the seeds of his end were sown before I ever met him.'

'I don't reckon he blamed you, Debs.'

'Ah, but Lucy does.'

'Not really.'

She patted my arm as we wandered on. 'Feels like snow.' She stretched out one hand as though to catch the first flakes. 'Look at that overloaded sky. And tomorrow's Christmas Eve.'

I didn't answer. I was wondering what it would be like to grow old with this woman, to potter arm in arm every day under the changing colours of the trees.

She twisted suddenly, staring up at me, and I couldn't look away. 'Jake. You've been more of a friend than any of us deserve.'

'Well, maybe. Also your page boy, bodyguard and bit of fun at the top of the stairs.' I was having trouble keeping the bitterness out of my voice.

She squeezed my arm. 'I'm so sorry. It was unforgivable. Actually . . .' She smiled, and I felt a tug of longing. 'I'm not sorry.'

'Doesn't matter. Didn't mean anything at all.'

That was my moment, I suppose, but I could no more tell her the truth than I could fly to Mars on a vacuum cleaner. I had my pride.

We reached the top of the lane and she leaned her back against a gate, swishing a wind-felled branch, slicing the tops off nettles. I stood on the verge with my hands in my pockets, scuffing my feet in the long grass and trying not to contemplate just how empty my future looked.

'I've been negotiating with Matt's previous headmaster,' she said. She mimicked the man's weighty tones. ' "In these, er . . . *unique* circumstances, we're prepared to take him back." '

I was surprised. 'Back to boarding school? Matt?'

Swish, swish. 'His own idea. He'll be better off there, with his friends. Normal boys who haven't fathered children, haven't seen their dad blown into pieces. Matt and I have become far closer but he needs routine, away from this house. He's hopelessly behind with his course-work—may well have to retake a year—but he's motivated. Thanks to you, I suspect.'

I looked at her and then down at my shoes. 'So. You're free to go back to Kenya.'

'Soon. There's the winding up of Perry's estate to get underway.' She smiled to herself, and suddenly she was as I first saw her, sitting on that piece of driftwood. It's hard to define exactly what made it so. A lightness around her eyes, I think. Susie was back. 'Rod's waited eighteen years. He says he thinks he can manage a little longer.' She chucked her stick over the gate and took my arm. We turned back up the drive.

And so they abandoned me. I wasn't needed any more.

Back in my room, I phoned Anna at work. I was lucky; she hadn't yet knocked off for Christmas.

'Hello, Jake.' She recognised my voice before I'd said two words, and sounded resigned, accusing and warm all at once.

'Er . . . hi. You busy?'

'Wildly. What can I do for you?'

Now, there was a question. I didn't know. Anna was my comfortable past. In the familiar voice I heard affection and sanity and fun. Anna didn't lie to me; she didn't come weighted down with unbearable burdens. She was reassuringly predictable.

'I'm going to Africa,' I told her. 'Overland. In a four-wheel drive.'

'Really?' She sounded genuinely intrigued.

'Want to come with me?' I wasn't serious. Obviously not.

Silence. 'Oh, Jake. You're too late. I'm sorry.'

'Oh. Well, it was just a thought. Um . . . why too late?'

'There's someone else.'

I should have been delighted for her. I should have been waltzing around the Harrisons' spare bedroom, scattering congratulations like confetti. Anna was a magnificent girl who deserved to be happy. But I didn't feel very delighted. In fact I felt as though she'd just kicked a soccer ball into my stomach: even she no longer needed me.

'Oh, good,' I mumbled. 'I'm, er . . . Well. That's great. Anyone I know?'

'I don't think so. Philip O'Neill, from the squash club.'

'That was quick.'

'Well . . .' She chuckled, embarrassed. 'He was waiting in the wings.'

'It's okay. I had my chance, and I didn't dance.'

'He's taking me to Venice for Christmas. In fact—what's the time? We're flying out of Gatwick this afternoon.'

I looked out at Perry's yew tree, hunched under a ghost sky, and I felt lonelier than I had ever felt in my life before.

'Well.' I swallowed. 'That's great, Anna. Marvellous. I hope you have a really fantastic Christmas.'

There was a slight pause. When she spoke again there was—I like to kid myself—a tinge of regret in her voice.

'You too, Jake. Happy Christmas.'

It was only a couple of hours before I heard from Lucy again. I was in the High Street, picking up one or two presents for the Harrison clan, and she sent a text. I was so pleased to hear from her, that's the funny thing. I'd been wondering how she was doing, back at work.

So I smiled. Stopped on the pavement, breathing out icy mist, while shoppers edged around me, looking hopefully up at the swirling sky and talking about white Christmases. And I read the message three times.

Your bro called Stanton's. Phone home 2day. Urgent.

I couldn't understand it at first. Couldn't get my head around it at all. My *brother*? I hadn't spoken to Jesse in years. Couldn't imagine him spending twenty dollars on a call, just to wish me all the blessings of the festive season.

I found a bench on a ragged patch of green and tried to remember Mum's number. I always struggled to remember it, even though it hadn't changed in living memory. It came back to me in the end, though, and I listened to the series of clicks and whistles as my little plastic box connected with hers.

I heard the ringing tone, and smiled as I imagined it jangling away in the hall, and Mum trotting through, drying her hands before picking it up. Mum always sounded eager. She'd never despaired. Dad wouldn't answer the phone even if he was standing right by it. That was her job, as his butler and cleaner and cook and gardener and punch bag. She always got to it on the fifth ring.

One. Two. Three, four.

'Hello?'

It wasn't Mum's friendly, hopeful voice. It was a man. I was startled for a moment, wondering if I'd made a mistake with the number.

'Er . . . Who's that? Jesse?'

'Yeah. Hi, Jake.' He sounded the same as ever. Flat, bored, unimpressed. He'd be standing in the hall in his socks, his gumboots waiting for him at the kitchen door, his farm dogs doing disgusting things in the yard.

'Hi,' I said. 'I got your message.'

There was a long silence. Long enough for me to remember that Jesse wouldn't be in his socks. In fact, he shouldn't be there at all. It was midnight in New Zealand.

'Jesse . . . what are you doing there?'

I could hear his breathing. 'Mum's in hospital. She's checking out.'

I felt flames of panic rising in my chest. There was no air. None at all. 'What d'you mean, checking out?'

'Hasn't got long. A week. Two, maybe. But she could go any time.'

The world darkened and twisted, and I had to screw my eyes shut. 'What's wrong with her?' The echo of my own fear bounced back from the satellite, mocking me.

'She's been crook for months. Wouldn't see a doctor.'

'I didn't know,' I said.

'No. Well, you're not here, are you?' A brief, accusing pause. 'We had to call an ambulance a couple of nights ago. She'd lost the plot. They opened her up, tumours everywhere, bowel's blocked. So they didn't bother doing anything much. Just sewed her up again.'

I couldn't think. Couldn't understand it at all.

'You still there, Jake?'

I breathed in, and out, forcing my brain to engage. 'Yes, still here, mate.'

He grunted. 'They've got her on morphine. Hopefully she'll see Christmas.'

I still had my eyes shut. I couldn't bear to look at the daylight, and flashing Santa with his sleigh, and McDonald's across the road. I felt the first gritty touch of snowflakes on my bare hands.

'You coming?' He didn't sound bothered.

'Um.' For some reason it was difficult to speak. I seemed to have something stuck in my throat. 'Of course I'm coming, for God's sake. But I don't want to see *him*. I hate that bastard. He's killed her.'

'Dad? Christ, get over it, Jake. He isn't a monster any more. He's just a sad old git with watery eyes and a hearing aid. He forgets everything, dribbles into his tea, can't even dress himself without her to help him. I have to wheel him into the bloody hospital. He's lost it, hasn't stopped crying. It's horrible.'

Good, I thought. *I hope he suffers until the day he dies, like she has.*

'Okay,' I said finally. 'I'll hire a car, drive straight to the hospital from Christchurch. Tell her I'm on my way, she has to wait for me . . . you hear me? Tell her I'm coming back.'

The line crackled. 'Better get a move on.'

I must be getting a bit clumsy. I dropped the phone, and it clattered onto the concrete under the bench. I had to sit with my head in my hands, just for a minute, just until the dizziness passed, and I was still having trouble with my throat. It really hurt to swallow.

I looked up and saw a couple of kids with skateboards and bobble hats standing there, staring at me as though I was a sad old wino. One of them wordlessly picked up my phone and handed it to me, and I thanked him, pushed myself up onto my feet, and lurched off down the street.

There was a travel agent on the corner, and I found the staff at their desks, looking out at the thickening snow. They couldn't believe their luck when I walked in. Could they book me on the next flight to New Zealand? Was the Pope a Catholic, sir? Just one problem. No seats left in economy. Never to worry! They'd fit me onto business class at twice the cost.

I packed a bag, and Matt and Deborah drove me to the airport, but none of us found much to say. I had so much to tell Mum; it filled my mind.

We were short of time. Heathrow was crazy, as usual. Once I'd checked in—a slick operation, thanks to my business class ticket—we had barely fifteen minutes for that awkward cup of coffee, the one nobody really wants but feel they have to have, all of us compulsively watching the departures board and making feeble conversation about the connection in Singapore, and how long I'd be in the air because the whole journey was more than twenty-four hours, and whether it's quicker via Los Angeles.

And sorry about your mother, Jake.

Lucy came dashing up just as we reached security, where I'd have to say goodbye. I heard the clatter of her heels over all the airport chaos. She looked dishevelled. Her beret was jammed on at a very eccentric angle.

'Thank God I've caught you,' she panted. '*Jake.* I'm so sorry. Your mother.'

I hadn't expected her. 'How did you know?'

'Deborah phoned me. Look, there must be something I can do to help. Something. Anything.'

'No,' I said, straightening her hat. 'There's nothing.'

'Call me when you get there,' she insisted, kissing me. 'Any time of day or night. Don't try to be brave.'

Matt stood, frowning and looking staunch, as I shook his hand. 'I'll take care of your wheels, mate,' he muttered.

I slapped him on the shoulder and then met Deborah's eyes. I knew every freckle of the constellation, every wisp of the wild honey hair.

'You were right,' I told her. 'You can't run away. A whale eats you up and spits you out, right where you started.'

She stepped forward quietly, and rested her cheek against mine. I can still feel it.

I wanted to say more, to all of them, but I couldn't think of the words. So I turned away. Handed over my passport. Then I looked back at them for the last time. They were standing side by side, watching me. Three pairs of eyes.

'You've no idea,' I said suddenly. 'No idea what you've become.'

They waved and nodded. They smiled a little sadly to see me go. But they didn't belong to me, and they never would.

I stepped behind the screen.

Chapter Thirty-eight

By four o'clock on Christmas Eve, the streets glittered in a diamond twilight. Down at the pedestrian precinct, shop fronts were still extravagantly lit. The council had parked a giant, slightly grotesque model of Father Christmas in the middle of a roundabout, and he waved a sinister yellow hand at the traffic seething past. In the church, the rector and his wife were preparing for a candlelight service, with the doubtful assistance of the confirmation class.

Angus pottered cheerfully along the pews, distributing candles on small clay saucers, four to a row, while Kevin rehearsed the lesson he was to read. The boy paused in his rendition of the story of the shepherds, draping himself over the lectern and squinting into the cardboard box Angus was carrying.

'Where d'you get those little flying saucers, Rev?'

Angus glanced up at the lanky teenager. 'As a matter of fact, these are clay birds, Kevin. My brother and his family in Scotland are very fond of shooting. These do the job rather well, I think.'

'Wicked!' Kevin jumped down for a closer look.

Beside the pulpit, Elizabeth was struggling with the Holy Family. 'Mary keeps falling over,' she complained. 'What on earth's happened to her since last year? She's had one too many down the King Herod, I think. I'll have to prop her up against the manger . . . Vanessa, see if you can get Baby Jesus wrapped up in swaddling clothes, would you? I've brought some torn-up pillowcases.'

The organist's daughter held up a doll, doubtfully. 'It's not newborn, though, is it? Just about shaving, this one. 'Cept it's a girl.'

'Nobody will notice in the candlelight. The mice ate last year's Baby Jesus, unfortunately.'

'Where's Mr Edmunds been all week?' Vanessa grasped the doll in expert hands, winding cloth around its unyielding plastic legs. 'Funny time for a vicar to take a holiday, right before Christmas.'

Unaccountably, Elizabeth—who was not deaf in the slightest—didn't seem to hear her. 'I'm *sure* we used to have more oxen than this . . . Bloody mice . . . Kimberley, how are you doing with those fairy lights?'

In answer, Kimberley flicked a switch at the foot of the pulpit, and an arch of brilliant colour sprang into life around the wooden stable. At the same moment, someone turned the handle of the heavy west doors; they clunked, rumbled and then creaked open.

'Oh, well *done*, Kimberley. Lovely!' Elizabeth stepped back to admire the tableau. 'There. I think we've done it. Just needs that baby, Vanessa.'

But Vanessa had stopped swaddling the Baby Jesus. She wasn't even looking at the Holy Family. She'd turned to see who had come in, and was peering down the gloomy nave towards the font.

'It's Mr Edmunds,' she cried, delighted. 'Hi, Mr Edmunds! Where d'you think you've been, skiving off while we do all the work?'

There was no reply. The little group fell silent, watching David's tall figure as he made his way swiftly up the nave. There was something ominous about his hurried gait.

Quietly, Angus lowered his box onto a pew. 'Everything all right, David?'

The curate halted by the altar steps, his hands in his pockets, eyes deep in a shadow of their own. Elizabeth stepped forward, her brow creased. Behind her, Vanessa, Kevin and Kimberley huddled close together, watching anxiously.

'David, what's happened?' asked Elizabeth, her voice rising as she searched his face. 'Where's Leila?'

'I'm glad you asked me that,' replied David, soberly. 'Because I'd like to introduce you to someone.'

They heard the ring of heels on the worn stone floor a second before a figure emerged from behind the font.

Later, Elizabeth and Angus would agree that they had never before seen Leila as she was that evening. Eyes glittering, she walked steadily up the nave. And close to her chest she was holding something: a wriggling bundle, wrapped in a blanket.

'*Blimey,*' gasped Vanessa.

With a flourish, Leila reached down to draw back the folds of wool, and pandemonium broke out. Elizabeth sprang forward to kiss Leila, Angus laughed and grasped David's hand, while the youngsters crowded around for a closer look.

'Oh, my God!' Kimberley was beside herself. 'Are you adopting her? She's *gorgeous*!'

And so she was: alert and confident, dark eyes bright and curious as she surveyed the world around her. They'd dressed her in a red jumpsuit with a matching squashy hat.

'Fola?' breathed Elizabeth, taking one tiny hand in both of her own.

Leila's smile seemed to hijack her whole body. 'No. She's Grace.'

'Hello, Grace.' Elizabeth pressed the little hand to her mouth. 'When did you get her?'

'We've been introduced over the last few days.' David stooped to kiss his baby's cheek. 'Mrs Bayley, the foster carer, gave us some much-needed lessons. Grace slept in the hotel room with us last night, and we set off from Suffolk with her after lunch.'

'It was terrifying!' Leila was lit from within. 'All that responsibility for another human being. We couldn't remember what temperature the car was supposed to be, or anything.'

'How old is she?'

'Almost five months.'

'Well, she's very alert,' said Angus, bending his knees so as to put his face close to the baby's, and grinning at her. 'She's taking everything in.'

'Could I hold her?' Kevin blurted out the words and immediately looked as though he wanted to bite off his own tongue. Leila hesitated and then slid the baby into the boy's arms. 'Support her head . . . that's right. Perfect, Kevin. Look! She wants to touch that gold ball on the Christmas tree. Clever girl.'

Vanessa pulled down a branch so that Grace could reach the bauble. She called over her shoulder, 'See, Mr Edmunds, I told you, didn't I? I expect you prayed for a baby, and you *got* one.'

'Yes. Well . . .' David's gaze flickered, amused, to Leila. 'Some of us merely sat and prayed. Others were rather more proactive.'

'And now you've brought her to church. I hope you're not going to dump her in here, like that poor little Samuel,' murmured Kevin, who seemed hypnotised by the life in his arms.

'Rest assured, Kevin,' laughed Leila. 'This baby is *never* going to be given away again.'

'The little suit's very smart.' Vanessa stroked the fleecy fabric. 'And a hat to match. She could be on a catwalk.'

'They were a present from my mother.' David pressed his toe against the altar steps, adding in an undertone, 'Along with a note, asking to be included in our child's life.'

'Gosh.' Elizabeth's eyebrows shot up.

'We phoned to thank her,' said Leila. 'Hilda came as close to grovelling as she can ever have done in her whole life. I think she's realised she could lose David. Begged us to visit her.'

'And will you?'

'Yes. Certainly. Grace needs all the family she can get, since she's lost her real one. *Mine* didn't wait to be invited—they're arriving on Boxing Day. Loads of 'em.'

'My father's away for Christmas,' remarked David blandly. 'Last-minute invitation. Golf tournament.'

'In Hong Kong,' added Leila with a twitch of her lips. She retrieved Grace from her fan club. The baby was gazing squiffily at the fairy lights, blowing bubbles, casually accepting her celebrity status.

Vanessa clutched at Kevin's arm. 'I'm going to ring the bells!' she announced. 'C'mon, Kev, Kimberley. This calls for a *real* peal!' And the three teenagers dashed into the vestry.

They were enthusiastic in their ringing, if not skilled. The joyous, discordant cacophony that exploded from the spire was enough to make long-dead bell ringers turn in their graves.

The wild applause floated on the clear, sparkling air; across the ruined play park, among the tower blocks. A pale child heard it, as he stood alone on a balcony. He pressed his face between the bars, listening.

An elderly man in the churchyard turned filmy eyes up to the old spire and then sank down onto a bench, patting the space beside him.

'Come sit here with me, love,' he mumbled peaceably, and turned up the collar of his shapeless coat. 'They're making a right old din this year.' He held a bundle of red roses, swathed in cellophane. 'I got your favourite.'

In the off-licence, Dora paused in the act of wrapping a bottle in brown paper and held up a forefinger. She walked to the shop door and leaned out into the street.

'They've got a team of monkeys swinging in the belltower tonight,' she said.

Her customer, the bank manager, glanced wretchedly at his watch.

'How very odd. They're *much* too early for Carols by Candlelight,' mused Marjorie Patterson, who was choosing nibbles. She patted her new blue rinse. 'I ought to look into it.'

'I shouldn't bother.' Dora wandered unhurriedly back to the counter. 'It's lovely to hear them, whoever they are. Such joy! After all, it's Christmas.'

Leila laughed aloud as the bells began to ring. To her, they were the beginning of everything.

Grace startled slightly at the sound, her eyes widening, arms thrown out. Then she yawned. It was a miniature yawn, and she lifted dimpled fists to her face. David pulled something soft and tatty out of his pocket, tucking it next to the red jumpsuit, and the baby's fingers closed tightly around the tangled bundle. It was a goofy-looking knitted lion.

Stepping close to the curate and his wife, Angus rested a hand on each of their shoulders.

'Well now,' he said calmly. 'You'd better take this miracle home.'

Chapter Thirty-nine

It was a luxurious journey. Shame I was in no mood to enjoy it. The stewardesses all had flashing Rudolph earings and tinsel in their hair, and they weren't grumpy old trolls like the ones in cattle class. They served us turkey and champagne, and we had seats that lay almost flat, and fluffy blankets, and enough leg room to kick a cat.

For the first time in my life, though, I didn't sleep on the flight. I tried to read a book but I never got beyond the first page. Mum was checking out. I hunched against the window, looking out at the sunset until one of the hosties bustled up and pulled down the shutter.

Then I gaped vacantly at the movies—all of them, even the cartoons. And when I closed my eyes Mum tiptoed into my room, smiling, a finger to her lips. She was hiding a puppy up her jumper. Just a tubby sausage with paws, really. We stroked the velvet ears, laughing softly together. And I loved her more than anyone in the world.

I had to change at Singapore, and spent two hours wandering restlessly among the glittering arcades of Changi Airport, watching shattered parents with crying toddlers, backpackers in frayed jeans, and flawless Singapore girls in long skirts. I felt like a ghost: unconnected, unreal, irrelevant.

She'd wait for me. I knew that. She wouldn't go without seeing me.

It was dawn as we crossed the Southern Alps. I could hear the cabin crew buzzing about in their little kitchen, making coffee and chatting above the rumble of our engines, and I pulled up the shutter to lean my face against the icy window.

New Zealand being just the right side of the International Date Line, I suppose I was one of the very first people in the world to see the sun come up on that Christmas morning. I was watching as it exploded into our darkness, pouring itself along the rim of the earth and making the scratched plastic of my window dance with rainbows.

We floated in slow motion above the crumpled mountains. Their peaks were made of shattered glass that glinted in the sunlight. I could almost see Mum standing alone on the snow in the frozen air, waving to me. She wasn't scared any more. She was free.

I didn't wave back, obviously. Well, all right, I did. Only very discreetly though, because they were bringing breakfast.

I fell into a weird kind of half doze as we crossed the Canterbury plains. I held her thin hand as she lay among the drips and tubes. I'm sorry, I told her. I'm sorry. I thought there was plenty of time. That's why I never came back, even though you gave me everything you had to give, even though you were my world. But I thought about you, every single day.

When I surfaced, the Pacific was glittering all the way to the horizon, and there wasn't a cloud in the sky. My ears had begun to pop, the seatbelt signs were on, and the crew were strapping themselves into their little seats at the front of the cabin.

We circled Christchurch, descending through the deep blue air in absolute silence. Even the engines seemed to have stopped. We were gliding down, and down, in a weightless trance.

Down, and down. In silence.

Abruptly, violently, I felt the wheels jar and grind onto New Zealand's soil, and we were cumbersome and heavy again.

I felt pretty cumbersome myself as I slumped in the queue for immigration. I'd been awake for nearly forty hours, and I needed a shower and a shave and a toothbrush. I didn't really care, though, because everything felt so unreal. I stood there behind the squalling babies and trendy backpackers, clutching my navy-blue New Zealand passport like a lost puppy. They were playing 'White Christmas' over the intercom.

A young woman in uniform came strolling up the line, stopping to speak to one or two of my fellow passengers, answering questions. She had springy red hair piled on top of her head, and freckles, and a smile that lit up the terminal. In fact, she was a model Kiwi girl. She halted beside me.

'Good morning, sir,' she remarked brightly, eyeing the passport in my hand. 'Merry Christmas. Returning resident? New Zealand passport holder?' It was odd to hear the accent again, with its flattened vowels. Matt would reckon she talked like me.

I had to think for a moment. 'Er . . . yes. I suppose I am.'

Briskly, she pointed further along the echoing hall. 'No need to queue, then. You can go straight through at number five.'

I must have looked as lost as I felt, because she touched my elbow to steer me across to the right booth, parking me gently behind the yellow line just as 'Silent Night' started up. She hovered briefly, casting an efficient eye over my crumpled clothes.

'Have you come off the Singapore flight? Your baggage is already in the hall.'

'Thank you,' I mumbled, trying to sound normal.

'You're welcome.' She gave me a small, professional nod and made to move away.

I looked at her. 'I never asked for any of this, you know.'

She didn't lose her poise. 'I know you didn't, sir,' she replied calmly. 'It's a very long flight, that one. But never mind, you've made it back in time for Christmas.'

And then she smiled, right into my mind.

'Welcome home,' she said.

I didn't cry. Obviously not.

Epilogue

Sunday morning Eucharist hadn't been so well attended since they filmed *Songs of Praise*. Full to the gunnels. The verger had to lay on extra service sheets.

The parish was throwing a christening party on the rector's lawn. They were lucky with the weather. The church spire shone gold-leafed against a flawless August sky. White thistledown seeds floated in their millions, gliding and swirling on the warm currents.

When their moment came, the parents and godparents gathered by the font. All five were at ease in each other's presence, as though they were very old friends. The choice of godparents drew raised eyebrows from the more conventional parishioners. Three men, all in their late thirties. Fairy godmothers, they called themselves, but it was hard to imagine a trio of less ethereal beings.

The Important Person who was to be christened had just learned to walk, and she was rather pleased with herself. She ignored the fuss at the font and trickled unsteadily up the aisle and back, in a minuscule red dress, collecting adoration all the way. She had two besotted grandmothers in the pews, vying for her attention. Often she lost her balance and sat down on a well-padded bottom, but someone would rush to pick her up again. Sometimes, tired of falling over, she crawled. A gold chain, christening present from one of the fairy godmothers, glowed on her cinnamon-brown skin.

When the rector swung her up high, kissed her and began to pour water over her forehead, she laughed. She knew him. He was her friend.

The choir surpassed themselves. The head chorister, Kevin—awkward in his robes—sang a glorious Welsh lullaby, hardly distracted by two girls in the row behind, who giggled and passed him lurid notes.

At eleven o'clock sharp the congregation burst out through the doors into a brilliant morning, while the organist luxuriated in the drama of his final chords. The rector stood in the porch, shaking hands. The catering committee hurried over to the rectory to fill giant teapots.

Children rampaged across the graveyard. A gang of her cousins—of various sizes and colours—played with the newly christened girl, jumping out from behind the stones and making her squeal. Adults stood around in the sunshine, chatting. Many began to make their way towards the rectory, hoping for tea or coffee or a glass of wine.

The curate and his wife each took one of their daughter's plump hands, swinging her high as they wandered along the path. 'One, two, three and *up* she goes!'

Anyone listening would hear the child's gurgles of delight, even after the three had disappeared through the rectory gate. Such a person would even be able to hear it from a graffiti-covered bench at the tangled end of the churchyard, half-hidden among the holly trees.

Within fifteen minutes, the place was almost deserted.

The rector was last to leave, locking the heavy main doors behind him. As he strolled towards the rectory he stopped in his tracks, as though an idea had occurred to him. He stood thinking for a long time, and then swung smartly on his heel and headed for the holly trees. He lowered himself onto the ramshackle bench with a sigh of relief, massaging his knees.

'Arthritis,' he said. 'Comes to us all.'

The powerfully built young man beside him seemed politely concerned. Although wearing a suit and tie, he had the look of someone who should be riding wild breakers on a surfboard. Very blond hair curled over his collar, his eyebrows almost joined, and his nose had seen some action.

'I'm sorry to hear that.'

Angus looked him over. 'You weren't in church, were you?'

The young man shrugged. 'I prefer to be outside,' he said.

'New to the parish?'

'Just passing through.'

'Just passing, eh?' Angus considered him. 'Where d'you call home?'

The stranger thought for a moment. 'Suffolk,' he said. 'But I'm going away next week. Visiting a friend in New Zealand. He's got a vineyard.'

'There's lunch on offer in my garden,' said Angus gently. 'Bubbly, and a band. You're very welcome.'

The young man murmured thanks, ruffling his wayward hair with both hands. Tendrils of light filtered through the leaves.

'We had a christening this morning,' said Angus. 'But I think you already knew that. It was in our online newsletter.'

The young man shifted. He seemed on the point of standing up. From over the rectory hedge came the sound of instruments being tuned and then a burst of song.

'What did they call her?' he asked, suddenly.

'Grace Serenity Fola,' replied Angus.

'Grace Serenity,' echoed the young man. 'Fola?'

'It means *honour*. And it couldn't be more appropriate, I assure you. The child is honoured. She is cherished.'

The stranger was silent.

'It's her first birthday today,' said Angus. 'I think you knew that too.'

The young man sat speechless, gazing at him with vivid blue-green eyes.

'You know . . .' Angus leaned back, luxuriously stretching his arms along the bench. He turned his creased face up to the old spire. 'I believe she's supremely lucky. Her parents want only the best for her.' He glanced sidelong at his companion. '*All* her parents.'

'Then she is lucky.'

The rector chuckled warmly, slapping his knees. 'Knows her own mind, I can tell you! Nobody crosses young Grace without good reason. We call her Your Grace.'

The young man smiled for the first time. It was as though a stray drift of sunlight had been caught and directed full onto his face. 'Her mother was like that.'

From the rectory garden came a cacophony of shouting followed by the clink of glasses. They were toasting the baby. The band struck up again: swaying notes, leisurely and syncopated; and suddenly a woman's voice hung languidly above them, pure and vibrant even through the distortions of the loudspeaker system. The crowd instantly hushed, as though she'd waved a magic wand.

'Ah,' said the rector. '"Summertime." This'll be worth listening to. Long, hot days in Catfish Row.'

The stranger seemed transfixed. 'She's good, isn't she?'

'She certainly is.'

'I've seen her on YouTube.'

'Oh, yes.' Angus inclined his head. 'Of course.'

Neither spoke again for some time. They listened quietly as the unseen singer conjured a mood of longing, of hope and love. The beautiful lullaby was nearing its end when the young man got to his feet, brushing thistledown from his knees.

'Thank you,' he said. 'I can go now.'

Angus stood too and held out a hand. 'Come and see us if you're ever passing through.'

'Thanks.' The young man took the proffered hand and held it for a moment. 'But I don't think I'll pass this way again.'

The song ended. Cheers and clapping swelled to greet its final notes, and over the loudspeaker echoed a woman's joyful laughter.

The young man stood listening, with a distant smile. Then he turned, and strode down the path towards the main road. He didn't look back.